LIGHT ANGEL

M.K. COLLINGS

The Caid Brand Publishing

Copyright © 2023 by M.K. Collings

Dagger Design Copyright © 2023 by M.K. Collings & Jason Miskell

All rights reserved.

No portion of this book (including graphics) may be reproduced in any form or by any electronic or mechanical means, including information storage and retrieval systems, without written permission from the author, except as permitted by U.S. copyright law. and for use of brief quotations in book reviews. Remember... Karma is a bitch.

The names, places, details such as incidents are all fictional and any resemblance is coincidental and were created from the author's messed up imagination. The location was randomly chosen based on the geographical location needed for the story. No part of this book or graphics were created by AI.

Cover/Title Page Graphics: M.K. Collings

Cover Typography: Pretty In Ink Creations

Editor: Hand in Hand Editing Services

ISBN: 979-8-9884883-1-6

Contents

AUTHOR'S NOTE

Runes are based on their ancient descriptions intertwined with an individual's interpretation & intuition received when casting. The interpretation in this book is a mix of my own and their original meanings.

Names of Runes are listed with the Chapter Header along with the meaning related to each chapter.

Warning: Not suitable for under 18 years of age. Strong Language, Adult Situations, Descriptive Violence, and a short mention of an Abusive Relationship.

Pronunciation Guide

- Ó Bradáin: oh brah-daw-in

- Anya *(Irish spelling: Áine)*: on-yah

- Aoife: E-fah

- Donnchadh: donn-uh-cuh

- Gudrun: goo d-roon

- Éabha: ay-va

- Ó Ceallaigh: o k-yal-lig

This story is dedicated to two of my Book Buddies, Mel and Bethany. Mel, if it wasn't for your heat exhaustion and complete boredom, I wouldn't have thrown out a wild and crazy story to entertain you.

Bethany, without your love for angsty books, this wouldn't have turned Paranormal, and honestly, I really don't think I would have written anything further. I would have just gone to bed like a normal human being and continued to escape into the worlds of many other authors' creations.

But instead, your late-night amusement over the craziness I spun off, turned into an obsessive addiction of writing this book.

Almost three years later...
Here it is!

Fate and Karma can be fascinating, yet scary.
The people placed in your path, the experiences you go through,
and the roads you journey on all bring you to where you are meant
to be and whom you are meant to be with.
Treat others with love and care, they were placed in your life for a
reason.
You were placed in theirs for the same.
Embrace them, learn from them, be kind to them.

-M.K. Collings-

Chapter One

OTHALA

(INHERITANCE)

"What if you get eaten on the way home?" James' eyebrows furrow.

"Then they'll get one hell of a bad case of indigestion from the amount of stress I'm under."

No thanks to the dragon lady.

"Are you sure you don't need a ride?" His deep southern drawl sneaks out, showing genuine concern.

"Yes, James, I'm sure. I'll be okay. You live in the complete opposite direction."

"You know I don't mind," he gruffs. His hand unconsciously rubs his salt-and-pepper goatee.

I know he's worried about me, but I refuse to take advantage of him. "Yes, but *I* mind. I've already held you up enough tonight."

If my boss hadn't woken me up early to rush into work for a 'small' assignment, I would've been wiser and realized what she *really* meant—two days' worth of research that needed to be completed in one. When she asks for miracles, it's my job to deliver. Being the only research investigator for Bordeaux Property Management, Inc., I can't say no. Not until I have a career backup planned, anyway.

Until then, I'll continue living the American Dream in this ordinary town. A life of being a slave to a job I don't enjoy, then retire—directly into a nursing home. Wasting away my days, staring at a TV screen, and wondering where I placed my dentures. The sadness of the thought hits me hard.

James gives me a playful wink. "All part of the job."

"Ha! That's for sure." I smile and turn to walk out of our office, with James following right behind me.

We're the only two required to come in on a Sunday. James' job as the security guard is to protect the company, but I swear he comes in mainly to make sure I'm safe. He has always placed our safety first. It isn't as though he needs this job–he could retire any day.

"Damn," I mutter under my breath as I open the door. It's a lot darker than I expected it to be. "You be careful heading home, and watch out for deer," I tell James once he locks up.

"Last call for that ride, Ms. Anya. It wouldn't take much for someone to pick up a little thing like you," he says with an expectant look.

The poor man thinks one day I'll stop being stubborn and finally accept help. Today's *not* that day. As tempting as it is to avoid walking home in the dark, I hate for people to go out of their way for me.

"I'm tougher than I look, old man," I joke.

To this 6' 3" retired Navy Command Master Chief, anyone would look small. I'm 5' 6" and, even though I'm on the slimmer side, I'm not as dainty as he perceives me to be.

James chuckles. "That you are, girl. That you are. See you in the morning." He gives me a nod before making his way to his car.

"Night!" I holler back at him.

Taking a deep breath, I start the one-mile hike to my house.

I want to get home, pronto. Not because I'm scared; my quaint little town is silent. Despite wrapping my jacket tighter around me, the chill in my bones doesn't dissipate. A shiver runs down my spine.

The only place still open is The Staggering Coyote, the local dive bar a couple of blocks back. Not even the soft music can be heard at this hour. As they do every Sunday, the rest of the local shops and businesses closed-up early. The only thing filling the streets is the dull glow of the street lamps. No cars, no people milling around, not even a stray cat prowling. The air is so still that the trees and flowers look frozen in time. This time of night, the dark encompasses everything light and creates a ghost town, leaving me the only living soul. The emptiness of the town is eerie.

My stomach growls as I pass Bitsy's Diner, wishing it didn't have a *Closed* sign hanging in the front door. With the delicious smell of greasy food still lingering in the air, I lick my lips, thinking about how a cheeseburger and a milkshake would help my hunger pangs right about now. Between my exhaustion and how late it already is, I can tell it's going to be yet another night of boring leftovers for me.

I make my way past a few more shops, slowing my pace when I come up to Jessie's Boutique. The perks of living in a small New York town like Shandaken are the simple and convenient shopping and services. With only one major road going in and out, the businesses are easily accessible on the main strip.

Past the stores, the sidewalk turns into a gravel parking lot.

I stop under the very last flickering lamp. The outside piping on the nearby building is the original from when it was built in the early 1900s, and, by the look of it, the hazy windows probably aren't much younger. Imagining being inside that empty place at this time of night gives me the creeps. Johnson's Steel Mill, the old steel factory, employs a large majority of the residents. Whoever doesn't work here drives a good twenty minutes or more to find work. Living in this town, it's definitely discouraging to be limited on available jobs. It's another reason why I'm stuck with my current job. That, along with a strange promise I made upon moving here.

I take out my phone and turn on my flashlight app. You would think they would at least want to brighten up the neighboring areas, with the amount of business this factory pulls in. Sadly, the town's streetlights stop here, and it's completely pitch-black down my road. Glancing up to the sky, I run my hand through my hair as I grumble in frustration. I often question what I did wrong in my life to get me on Karma's bad side. Luck won't even grant me a sliver of moonlight to illuminate my way home.

The stillness in the air suddenly changes with a gust of wind, sending a cold chill through me. I look up to the glimpses of sky between the tall, swaying trees and take in a breath of fresh air, preparing myself for this final trek. The usual calming music made by small creatures is even missing tonight, except for the occasional owl off in the distance. Moaning and creaking of the trees and rustling of the leaves replaces the absence of any other life.

My heart rate starts racing.

It's strange, as many times I've walked this path without a second thought, doing so in the dark is like I've been transported into the middle of a slasher movie.

What if there's something waiting for me?

I eye the dark path ahead with trepidation. It's putting me on edge, anxiety tightening every muscle in my body.

Knock it off, Anya. Stop thinking about the worst-case scenario.

I pick up my pace as I hightail it home.

A few more minutes pass, and I can finally make out my porch light through the trees.

I've always felt more at home in Shandaken than the place I grew up in. When my grandmother was alive, I would come visit all the time. Even though my parents and I lived a couple of hours away, I would beg them to bring me here. It was almost like a calling.

Just like it's calling me now. My sole focus is the porch lights in the distance; soon, I'll feel the warmth and comfort they bring.

The excitement in me fades when I hear something coming toward me from the forest, snapping my focus. I slow my steps and listen carefully.

My hands tremble, and my body shivers at the thought of what could be stalking me. In the dark, the cute and cuddly ones don't normally come out to play—evil causes everything else to run for cover.

I slowly crouch down. My hand slides into my knee-high boot to grab my only form of self-defense.

More movement comes toward me. The coldness I was feeling a minute ago is gone, leaving my body flushed with fear in its wake. I'm trying my best to calm my breathing, but it doesn't seem to be working; all I can think about is whether I'm going to turn into a midnight snack. Being out here in the dark is like playing Russian roulette—I'm not sure when it's my turn for the bullet.

Why did I think walking home wouldn't be a bad idea?

The stirring gets louder, and my heart pounds in my ears. I'm getting more nervous by the second. I can't see what I'm dealing with.

The sound bounces around me until I can narrow it down. It's coming from my left, so I back away slowly while watching the opening of the woods.

As soon as I feel it getting ready to attack, I draw my dagger—my Ó Bradáin family dagger. Mom said to never leave home without it; right now, I'm beyond thankful I always listen.

The creature leaps out of the woods, and I scream and jump back, holding my weapon in front of me. As I drop my phone on the asphalt, the flashlight faces up.

Shadows bounce around me, and where I expect to see a snarling beast looking at its next meal, blood dripping from its fangs, I see a...a *bunny.* A fluffy, brown and white little bunny.

This thing has more balls than I do. It's sitting there, twitching its tiny nose in the air, and looking at me. Meanwhile, I'm about to have a heart attack from Peter Cottontail.

I put my dagger back into my boot and try to catch my breath.

"You shouldn't be out here. You know it isn't safe," I say to the bunny as if it can understand me. "Did you nod at me?" I narrow my eyes, studying the fur ball.

Shaking my head, I bend over to pick up my phone, praying the drop didn't crack the screen. As I'm straightening back up to check out the damage, I hear movement in the direction the bunny came from. "I don't think we're alone, little guy," I whisper to my attacker as I stop, my eyes not moving from the entrance of the woods. This creature sounds bigger than the last.

Okay... Forget this.

"Sorry, buddy. You're on your own. But I suggest you run...and fast."

I turn towards my house as the bunny takes off. Maybe I could take a few survival tips from the little guy; he seems to have his life put together better than I do.

More stirring sounds come from behind me. I take a few steps as quietly as possible, before I break out into a run, hightailing it home while my eyes and flashlight continue to scan my surroundings. I pray nothing is following me.

I rush in, slamming the door shut behind me. Leaning back, I lay my head against the door and try to slow my rapid breathing. Sweat drips between my shoulder blades.

I take a deep breath and slowly exhale, calming the last of my trembling nerves. I don't want to guess what was going to jump out to greet me.

I remind myself that I'm safe now.

I push away from the door and head down the hallway to my bedroom. As I'm changing into my soft flannel pants and a tank top, my stomach growls for the second time tonight. I was hungry earlier when walking by Bitsy's, but the ball of nerves in my stomach made me lose my appetite. Another rumbling cuts through the silence of the room.

"Okay, okay. I'll eat something. Jeez!"

I forgo the leftovers and pull out a bag of popcorn instead, knowing full well that anything else would leave me with an upset stomach due to my nerves.

My mind keeps going back to the 'bunny incident.' I guess that's all the excitement I'll ever get in my life.

Grabbing the popcorn from the microwave, I plop myself in front of my laptop. With a click of a button, my stressful reality transforms into a world made just for me.

Being twenty-five years old and single, most would think I'd be exploring the world, partying every weekend, or trying my hand at dating. None of these sound the least bit intriguing. The thought of traveling alone holds no appeal and, let's be honest, the world lacks decent men.

Why settle for anything less than a gentleman?

We all know they went extinct years ago.

So, I stay home and fall in love with an unlimited supply of book boyfriends. It's safer that way, but some days...I wonder if I'll be single for the rest of my life. Who doesn't wish to have someone to hold them when having a rough day?

I had that once. He cared about me unconditionally, but there was something missing...or some*one*. I can't describe it. Anytime I think about what it could be, I'm met with a black wall.

Pushing aside my depressing thoughts, I start scrolling through my newsfeed until something catches my eye.

The Public Library made a 50th Anniversary post to celebrate the founders of Shandy Genealogy Society. A group of men and women from our tiny town had come together to track their lineage as far back as they could, all the while enjoying each other's company and drinking Shandy. They'd thought it funny and, amazingly enough, have continued the tradition for fifty years now.

I click on the post and pull up the picture; it doesn't take long to scan all the smiling faces for the very person I knew would be front and center.

My grandmother. She must have been in her twenties in this picture. Some say I look like a younger version of her, and I can see now that the resemblance is uncanny. We have the same brown-hazel eyes and chestnut hair, and we're both of a decent height and a smaller frame.

When her friends make comments on the similarities, I don't let grief overcome me; I hold my head up with pride for taking after such a strong and beautiful woman. A crazy one, but still.

A memory hits me, reminding me of one of the conditions I agreed to upon getting this place.

When she passed seven years ago, my grandmother entrusted her estate to me. I figured it would be left to my mom and dad, and based on their reaction at the time, they expected it to be theirs too.

When we met with the lawyer for the will reading, he explained the conditions.

"Ms. O'Clery," he'd said, "there are two conditions you must sign off on before I can hand you the keys and title to your grandmother's home. This first one I see quite commonly when the former owner wants to keep their property in the family. You need to agree you will live here and not sell. The items that are inside the house you are welcome to sell or donate, just not the property."

"That's not a problem. I love it here," I'd replied nervously, bouncing my leg up and down.

My mom had held my hand in encouragement.

"The next..." He'd cleared his throat. "The next request is a tad odd. Your grandmother said in these exact words, '*Anya, your responsibility is to protect the town and its people. They need you.*' Do you agree to both terms?"

I signed and became the new owner of my grandmother's home, in a charming little town tucked away in the Catskill Mountains.

As an 18-year-old freshly out of high school, it was pretty scary and exhilarating all at once. Being on my own, hours away from my parents, having to fully support myself was something I didn't think would happen so soon. But at the same time, being given the opportunity to prove to my parents that I could be independent and survive made me want to take on the challenge.

The memory of my grandmother's second condition has been coming to me more and more lately. I'm starting to think she meant for me to protect the people from my current employer. She wasn't a blind woman; she had to have figured out what was happening just as I have.

Chapter Two

Ehwaz

(Friendship)

I reach over to my nightstand in search of the source of the obnoxious shrill. I really need to change my phone's alarm. Keeping my eyes tightly sealed, I touch the screen with my thumb to shut off the god-forsaken noise. I'm met with silence—such a beautiful sound.

Ugh, I slept like shit.

And I blame Peter Cottontail for throwing off my groove.

The thought of coming out from under my warm comforter makes my stomach churn, but I sit up anyway and scrub my hands over my face. Grumbling, I drag my tired ass to my closet to pull on a new pair of jeans and blouse.

Dressed and ready to go for the day, I grab myself a mug and prepare my morning green tea with lemongrass. When I take the first sip, the warmth fills my chest, and the flavor soothes my nerves while it gives me the gradual wake-up boost I need without the large amounts of caffeine.

I have an hour to spare before I need to leave. I don't waste any time as I sit down with my tea and my latest addiction, *Unspoken Desires* by Gail Haris. A large part of me wants to call into work sick to finish it. Unfortunately, the repercussions aren't worth it. The last thing I need is to have my manager breathing down my neck.

Once my time is up, I take care of my mug and get my boots on. Grabbing my keys off the end table near the door, I start my hike to work. Even with the incident last night, I still choose to walk. Nothing can stop me from being outside on a beautiful day, especially in October. Being in the sun energizes me, like a cup of coffee would, and gets me through the day without the caffeine withdrawal.

Angling my face towards the sun, I take in the warmth, allowing it to flow from my head, down my chest and stomach, to spread to my limbs. As I soak in the sun's rays, I bask in the comfort it brings me.

A gentle breeze blows through the trees and onto my skin. It won't be long until we start to get snow dumped on us. Thankfully, it hasn't yet cooled off enough to be cold during the day. It's my favorite time of the year, with everything turning yellow, orange, purple, and red—the sight is breathtaking. Such a difference from last night.

My heart warms once I pass Johnson's Steel Mill and see the old brick-and-stone buildings lined up the street. Flowers adorn each doorstep with hanging vines and blossoms in a vast variety of colors—compliments of Heidi, our local flower shop owner. The flower shop is directly across from my office. In front of it, a Santa Rosa Plum tree grows. It has the most succulent fruit available for picking in the summertime. Multiple sugar maple trees, running down the side of the sidewalk between the buildings, bring life to the town.

The beauty of Shandaken pulls me in again, and I'm on auto-pilot because when I glance up, I've already arrived at my office building. This building is the least charming in town. Not even the pink, purple, and blue potted hydrangeas can cheer up the dull, lifeless brown brick building. You would think, being a property management company, they would care about their image. Not at all.

With my hand hovering over the door handle, I hesitate and stare into my reflection in the glass door. If I'm lucky, the day will go by quickly and painlessly. A sigh escapes me as I walk in.

James is standing behind his desk with his usual big smile. "Good morning, Anya. Do you ever leave this place?" he jokes, knowing he's here just as much as I am.

"Hey, James. I do…" Lowering my voice, I add, "But only on full moons, when I need to feast." I hold my finger to my lips. "Shh… Don't tell anyone, 'kay?" I give him a wink.

He chuckles as I walk past him and down the hallway to my cubicle.

As I reach my desk, I peek over the half-wall. It's no surprise to see Danielle here—early, as usual. I swear, she must have a cot in the back because she's always here before I start the day and stays after everyone leaves. And I thought *I* worked too much. What drives me crazy is how she is always chipper and wide awake. There are times I barely make it until lunch without yawning and my eyelids getting heavy.

With a big smile on my face, I lean my arms on the barrier between us.

"Hey, Sunshine! Looking good today," I tell Danielle.

"Good morning, Anya! Thanks. Picked up this top yesterday at Jessie's. Soo... Have you finished the book yet?" Danielle brushes her short brown hair out of her eyes that widen in anticipation.

"Ugh, no! I got stuck working all day yesterday. I was tempted to call in sick today; I was getting to a suspenseful part, and it's driving me *insane* not being able to finish. Want to be my lookout, so I can read instead of work?" Tilting my head, I bat my eyelashes and push out my bottom lip.

Danielle shakes her head, smirking. She knows that as much as I would love to read all day, my work ethic doesn't allow me to slack on my job.

"How far are you?" I ask her.

"Oh, I finished last night." She leans back in her chair, crosses her arms over her ample chest, and flashes me a smug smile. She knows it kills me when she finishes books before me.

"No, you didn't." I shake my head.

We started it two days ago—she couldn't have finished that quickly.

Her excitement breaks through. "I did, and it was amazing! Text me as soon as you're done—we have *lots* to discuss!"

The sounds of the front door opening and short footsteps coming our way interrupt my need to ask her a million follow-up questions. Her head peaks around the partition and her grin widens, causing me to glance over my shoulder.

Danielle jumps up from her seat. "*Heather!* How was your date-night with the fiancé?"

Heather strolls in, the sunlight from the windows casting a halo around her golden blonde hair; if it wasn't for the mischievous, satisfied grin on her flawless face, anyone would mistake her for an angel. We all know better than that–her halo likes to sport the occasional horns.

"Perfect, as usual, and always exciting. This lady at the restaurant was giving hell to the waitress, and I could see the tears in the poor girl's eyes. My vision started blacking out, my self-control was waning..."

I lean my elbow on the wall, cross my ankles, and prepare myself for entertainment. We've all been partners in crime since I met the two of them the first day on the job. Danielle immediately took me under her wing while Heather had me buckled over from laughing at her crazy, everyday stories. Having them in my life makes the job more enjoyable.

"Get this... Then the bitch intentionally tripped the waitress, causing her to fall and spill her tray filled with empty beer bottles. The waitress ended up cutting herself pretty badly. Instead of a look of remorse on that bitch's face, she was cackling like a hyena. *That* was my tipping point. I got up, calmly walked over to her with a smile on my face, and I punched her. K.O., baby!" Heather swipes her blonde hair back from her shoulder. "Oh, yeah. I still got it! The woman's friends ended up grabbing her and pulling her ass out of the place. They looked pretty embarrassed. Oooohh... And the manager said they won't press charges on me and comped us the meal. Apparently, they found out that night that the woman had been abusing the waitresses all week, and they were trying to figure out how to handle it. They agreed—she learned her lesson. Luck was on my side and I didn't get arrested. Overall, I think it was a great date! How about you, girls?"

Danielle's eyes meet mine, and we burst out laughing. It's never a dull moment in Heather's life. She has an amazing heart but is a Momma Bear to those in need, and she never backs down. She is definitely someone you want in your corner.

Danielle's laughter fades as she straightens. "Oh, shit. Is she looking?"

Our boss, Julie, is not only a horrible and vengeful manager—one that has no clue about this company or how to run our department—but she should be thankful we're self-sufficient since she's just a waste of space.

My two besties and I run this place single-handedly and train any new hires. Julie is just an acting messenger, delivering the owner's requests to us. We stopped counting the times we've caught her sitting in her office playing games on her computer. When the owner comes to visit, she makes sure she's constantly hovering over us, yelling and demanding the work gets done or the reports to be on her desk in an impossible timeframe. She has no idea what she's talking about. I have to remind myself this is a well-paying job, close to home, and I get to see my girls every day.

Heather shakes her head but slides to her desk, and Danielle sits back down. All of us act as if nothing happened while we get our daily work completed.

As soon as I think the coast is clear, I turn to Danielle and Heather. "Last night—"

"Ms. O'Clery, bring me the report on the Roberts property, now!" Julie yells in annoyance.

So much for being rid of her anytime soon.

Heather's eyes peer over the wall from Danielle's cubicle. "Didn't you put that on her desk last Monday?" she whispers.

Resting my head in my hands, I take a calming breath. Some days, I want to scream. Today is one of those days.

"Yup," I simply answer.

Heather pops up the rest of the way. "One point for me!" With a big smile, she disappears before getting caught.

Ha!

She's right—Mondays are hers. We all picked a day of the week. Every time Julie yells about a late report not turned in on the day we chose, we get a point. At the end of the month, the losers buy the winner dinner and drinks. It's a way of getting through Julie's temper tantrums and an excuse to make sure we have a monthly girls' night. Win-win. Days like today though, the game itself can't take the edge off.

I start my mantra... *I can get through this day. I will get through this day.*

I roll the tension from my shoulders right before I walk into Julie's office. She's sitting at her desk, playing solitaire. Stress must be getting to her since she is sporting quite a few new grey hairs on top of her head. I bite the inside of my cheek to hold back a smirk at the irony–she makes our lives hell and deserves more than the signs of aging.

The hard clicking of her fake nails pulls my attention to the mouse she is taking her frustration out on. She's choosing to ignore me; I can tell, even when her face doesn't change much. I'm not sure it could if she wanted it to–with as many botox injections as she gets, it's always a mix between a scowl and constipation. Too many times have I been tempted to ask Heather to make Julie some laxative brownies. I haven't, though; Heather wouldn't hesitate.

I turn my attention to the inbox tray where we place all the completed reports, and pick up the report in question. With a forced smile, I hand Julie the folder. "Here you go."

As I start to turn around, she glares at me and says with a cocky tone, "Was that so hard? To just hand it to me to begin with, so I didn't have to go searching for the work *you* should have had ready for me?"

My hands grip into fists, and heat floods my body as I look back at her. My mom always taught me to take calming breaths when my emotions felt out of control. My chest and diaphragm expand as they fill with air, before I blow out my breath.

"No, Ma'am. You are correct. I'm sorry. It won't happen again." I make my way back to my desk without throwing anything at her head.

There's a chocolate bar on my desk that I know is from Danielle. I hear the wheels of a chair rolling toward me.

Heather peeks around the corner. "Don't worry. I'll make you a voodoo doll of her tonight to make you feel better."

A different kind of warmth flows through me, and this one goes straight to the heart. I love these girls. "What would I ever do without you two?"

"I'm sure you would be on the 5th floor of the hospital, with a beautiful white jacket wrapped lovingly around you," Heather states as if it's a matter of fact.

"I'm sure one day *you* may bring her to that." I hear Danielle but don't see her. No doubt, she is plugging away on her keyboard.

A manila envelope comes sailing over the cubicle wall at me.

"Whoa, Danielle. Trying to kill me?"

Heather giggles. "I can see it now... 'Death by Papercut.' This could be made into a really intriguing movie."

Danielle's head comes up, suspiciously looking around. "That's the request you asked me about on the...ahem..."

"Huh?" I cock an eyebrow at her, confused.

"The request..." she repeats much slower.

It hits me. "Ohhh..." I rush to roll the envelope and fit it into my jacket sleeve that's hanging on the back of my chair. It's hidden from sight now.

Over the years, I've become suspicious of the owners. I have a feeling they're into some shady shit, and I'm pretty sure they are using their business to destroy families while acting as martyrs in disguise. They've been hurting people in this town more than helping them. It's been hard to collect what I need; the owners seem to be careful in covering their tracks, and I don't have enough evidence to go to the necessary officials yet.

But Danielle ran into a file on a few of the recent contracts turned into foreclosures. This envelope has to contain the copies.

I'm determined to help this town. It's what's right.

Maybe that's what my grandmother had meant.

Chapter Three

Laguz

(Introspection)

*W*alking in the woods, I follow the path ahead of me. The trees and shrubbery are so thick I have to push my way forward.

As the trail splits into a fork, I find my grandmother at the center, sitting on a large boulder. Her composure is unusual; her favorite grey wool cardigan is draped over her tight shoulders, and she has a forlorn expression replacing her usual sweet and cheerful smile. In her lap, her hands are tightly clasped over her black and green plaid skirt.

I wrap my arms around my body, dreading what she might say. This is a look I've never seen on her before.

"Hello, deary." She sighs, her body slightly slouched.

I can read the defeat in her eyes, even though she comes across as strong.

"Grandmother? What's going on?"

"I need you to listen to me." She hesitates before continuing, as if weighing her words.

"Remember where you come from, who you are, and who you are meant to become. There is danger ahead, and not much I can do to help."

I stay silent, unsure what to think or say.

"You must choose a path." Her voice is filled with sadness while her body remains stiff—her lips are drawn in a thin line from the tension. "Neither will be easy, and you will find loss in both. Taking the right direction, though, will open up a destiny filled with blessings. Do not let fear sway you. Choose not with your mind, but with your heart and soul."

Confusion overwhelms me, and my heart races. "What are you talking about? What danger? What path?"

She disappears before my eyes, and I'm left alone at the crossroad.

Giant trees block out the sunlight, creating dark shadows all around me. It's like I'm in a sinister fairytale, one where the trees are about to pull me into the depths of the forest, burying me deep in the ground, to be trapped forever.

I turn my attention to the right. There's a path filled with thorny vines, resembling barbed wire. Tree roots jut out of the ground, twisting up, only to sink back into the earth.

If I take this path, I'm bound to come out bloody and broken. I could become trapped with no way out.

My other option, on the left, doesn't look promising either. The path runs along a steep mountain. On one side, jagged rocks covered by slippery moss ascend up the face of the mountain, and, on the other side, is a cliff-like drop off descending into the black, empty earth. To take this path could mean death.

Turning around to go back the way I came, a wall of vines blocks my way.

I can no longer go back, and I'm trapped with only two options—neither weighing in my favor.

How will I make it out alive?

I wake up in a cold sweat on my couch. I have no idea what any of it means.

The dreams are happening nightly and becoming more and more intense. They scare the shit out of me. I've tried everything to wind down—reading, social media, TV, a bath... None of it stopped the hyperdrive my brain's been in, or chased off the vivid dreams I've been having of my grandmother's stern voice filled with warnings that have haunted me ever since Sunday night. It all seemed to start after my creepy walk home which is weird because I've never had any dreams like this before.

Ever.

It's affecting my ability to function.

Today, on my way to work, I tripped and caught myself on the glass window of the building. My heart skipped a beat, along with my step. In the window was a frightening, ghastly image of a woman.

Low and behold...it was *me*.

With my hair going in multiple directions, my complexion pale, and bags the size of quarters under my eyes, it was a startling sight.

I glanced around to see if anyone had been looking; thankfully, it was early enough that everyone was either at home or at Bitsy's for breakfast. I quickly tossed my hair up in a pony-tail and called it good. There was no hope for the face, and it didn't come as a surprise when Heather mentioned I looked like a ghost the moment I walked into the office.

I was so out of it, it took her calling my name multiple times before she caught my attention.

"Earth to Anya. You in there?" Heather startled me when she tapped on my head.

I swatted her hand away. "Hey! Knock it off."

"Where you at? Cause you definitely aren't here with us. And no offense, but you look like shit."

"Well, thanks for the flattery. I'm just tired." I didn't have to fake the yawn that followed.

Danielle popped up and caused me to jump. "Something's going on; you are never like this. You have two choices—tell us now, or we'll drag your ass out tonight to get you drunk enough to spill the truth." Her brows were furrowed in concern.

I groaned and rubbed my hands over my face. "Good luck with that. I'm sure I'll pass out without the help of alcohol."

Even through the exhaustion, I didn't miss the evil smirk that stretched over Heather's face. That couldn't be good. "Well, if you pass out without telling us what's wrong, we can have good ol' Kyle drive you home."

That snapped me out of it. There was no way in hell I wanted my ex-boyfriend anywhere near me. Especially while unconscious. "You wouldn't dare!"

She chuckled. "Haha, you're right. If I did, all my hard work would have gone down the drain."

What the hell was she talking about?

Better not to question Heather and her craziness.

I was too tired to fight those two off. If I couldn't trust Danielle and Heather, I couldn't trust anyone, so I told them about the dreams.

Heather's eyes blinked rapidly. "Wow, that's intense and extremely detailed. I can't even tell you what I dreamt about last night."

Danielle had come around our shared wall and placed her hand on my shoulder in comfort. "I think it's a sign you are spreading yourself too thin. When was the last time you actually took a day off?"

"Uhm... Never?"

"You are way overdue on taking some well-needed vacation days. You're working too much and, adding on the stress of your 'side project,' you need time away from here."

She was right. The closer I get to finding proof our employers are scamming and taking advantage of many people in need, the more stressed I'm becoming.

These dreams have to be related.

I toss my throw off my lap and lean forward, running my hands from my face to my hair in exhaustion. I can't deny I need a break. One day, that'll happen, but not until the evidence is strong enough. If I take a vacation now, who knows how many more families will be destroyed. Which reminds me—I haven't looked at the envelope Danielle gave me.

Even with it being a Friday night, I don't see sleep in the near future, so I pull myself up and walk over to pick up the packet and bring it back to the couch with me.

The contracts are exactly what I requested. Three in total, each one has the same information—Bordeaux Property Management agrees to take over mortgage payments to decrease late payments to the banks and prevent foreclosures.

At first glance, this is a blessing. Many live paycheck to paycheck and wouldn't hesitate to agree.

I keep studying the agreements. There is nothing here about consequences. No hidden requirements, holes, or exclusions. I read over the first contract twice; the other two are the same. What's weird is that the final page on each contract has slightly faded wording between the text. I can only catch a few words here and there. The copier must have been messed up.

I decide to call Danielle anyway, to be sure.

Danielle answers on the second ring. "Hey, what's up?"

"Hey, D, did the last page on the contracts you copied look like the paper was recycled, or was the copy machine acting up?"

"The copy machine was fine, and each page looked normal to me. What's going on?"

"Something's weird. The last page of each contract has the regular print over a lighter one. I want to see the originals. You think there is a way of making that happen?"

This is her department in the company, so if anyone has access, it'll be her. Anyone else pulling them would look suspicious, but Danielle handles all the contract filing. No one would think twice.

I hear her hum on her end. "Wait a second." There's a click of the phone being set down. A minute passes, and she returns. "You're in luck! I still have those with me. I brought home some work that still needs to be entered into the system."

"Seriously? This is perfect. Can I come over to check them out? I won't take long, I promise. I'll buy you lunch for the rest of the month." I heavily emphasize the begging in my voice while I pace my living room, hoping she says yes.

"No, Anya, you can't come over—"

"Oh, okay." Shit, I didn't even ask her if she was busy. "I'll let you go. I'm sorry if I interrupted anything."

"Wait a second. Why would you think I'm busy? I've got nothing to do." Danielle scoffs. "What I was *going* to say, before you so rudely cut in, was that you can't come over because you looked like death earlier, and I won't risk you driving in the dark while tired. I'm coming to you. Give me 15 minutes, and I'll be there."

I blow out a sigh of relief. "Danielle, you are amazing. Thank you!"

Danielle is on her way, and I may be able to get closer to figuring all of this out.

Jumping to my feet, a new wave of adrenaline courses through my veins like a double shot of espresso—I'm grabbing all my research to spread out on my table before Danielle arrives.

Chapter Four

Raido

(Journey Begins)

The day I overheard Mrs. Coltson talking to Jessie at the Boutique about the Turner Family was the day I opened this can of worms.

Listening to and digging into gossip isn't something I do, but this particular family had lost everything they owned to the bank. It's a little ironic that I had been the one who completed the evaluation on their property's net worth a few months prior. Preliminary work for the agreements with my company is pretty common and vital to help people prevent late mortgage payments. What I didn't expect was that, months after I submitted my findings, their address—along with a few others—came across Heather's desk as newly acquired foreclosure purchases from the local banks. She found it strange so many people were behind on payments; our small town isn't known for poverty.

That's when Danielle had sworn they were part of the mortgage assistance program. The pieces were all coming together. And now, we may have the proof needed to stop it all.

A knock has me jumping to my feet.

"Thanks so much for coming." I attack Danielle with a hug, whether she likes it or not.

"I wish I could tell you that you look better, but I'd be lying."

That's one thing I respect about my friends—they don't hold anything back.

"Yeah, yeah, hand over the goods." I close the door after pulling her inside and shift from one foot to the other, waiting, while she pulls a folder out of her bag.

"Here you go. Merry Christma—"

I snatch the folder, give her a kiss on the cheek, and hightail it over to my table, pulling out the first contract on my way.

I flip to the last page. It looks normal, yet the paper feels slightly different.

Thicker?

Everything appears to be the same. I hold up the paper and move it through my fingers; it feels normal to me. Light shines through the back of the paper, showing me the secret I've been missing.

"Gotcha!"

"What is it?" Danielle comes near me.

"This isn't the last page; it's stuck to another one."

I pull out the other two contracts, hold them to the light, and see the same print. With no hesitation, I run to my room to grab my dagger and bring it back to the table.

"Uh... What are you doing?"

I ignore her as I concentrate on sliding the tip of the blade to the corner of the paper.

"Anya, what the hell? Don't destroy that! I'm going to get in deep—"

The peeling and crinkling sound of paper stops her while I separate two thin pieces from each other.

"Is that carbon paper?" Her mouth drops open; she's seeing exactly what I am.

Hidden underneath the original, there is a new—and completely different—contract, with a matching signature line positioned in the exact location as the main page. From afar, you can't tell the signature isn't the original but a carbon print of the signed agreement from the client.

"Those sneaky bastards." I mumble, then turn to Danielle. "They're making these people think they're agreeing to the original contract and hiding the true conditions. This is how they're getting away with allowing the homes to go into foreclosure."

The details state that if the 10% interest is not paid within 90 days from the time of signing, Bordeaux Property Management is no longer required to make payments to the bank. These terms were hidden, and I'm sure no one is told about them.

The Bordeauxes are stopping the payments to the banks, causing these people to lose their homes. That's when the other part of our company purchases the properties to make money off of them.

Shit!

We're silent as we both collapse into our seats, understanding what we discovered. My hand goes to soothe the upset in my stomach; I'm going to be sick. Tears fall from Danielle's eyes. Swallowing the lump in my throat, I lay my hand on hers to provide her with a sliver of comfort I yearn to feel myself.

"I didn't know, Anya," she sobs, shaking her head in disbelief. "I've handled these on a daily basis and never once knew. I couldn't tell there was anything different, let alone *wrong* with these. How could I not know I was filing something that was destroying lives?"

"Neither of us knew. I've been the one helping research the properties to pick which will be the best investment. We need to call Heather and discuss how to handle this." I lay my head on her shoulder, trying to ease this dreadful sinking feeling.

Danielle doesn't respond, but I feel her head nodding in agreement, and I pick up my phone.

"I hope this is a call telling me you got laid and you'll be back on your A-Game Monday morning." Heather's immediate response has me sitting up and brings a chuckle out of us.

It was smart to call her—she's always our ray of sunshine on a cloudy day. Seeing Danielle's face soften lessens the knot in my stomach.

Rolling my eyes, I respond, "No, Heather, I have not and do not plan to anytime soon—as much as you have been hounding me over it. Now, we called for a reason. You have a second?" I know she'll drop everything if one of us needs her.

"You know I always have time for you." There's rustling, followed by a door closing. "Wait. We? I know you said you aren't getting laid, but... Does that mean you have male—"

"No, Danielle's here now, and we have something serious to discuss."

"I'm all ears." The anxious hope in her voice over the potential of me meeting a guy is replaced by seriousness.

Danielle and I fill her in with what we found.

"So, what's your take? Are you up for turning this into Shandaken's Police Department?" I ask Heather.

Heather's huff is brief before she gives into her seething rage. "Those lying, cheating, no-good fuckers! Oh, I want to strangle everyone involved. More than strangle... I want—"

"Let's stay on track here," Danielle reins her in.

Heather sighs loudly. "You're right. We need to think this out. The Bordeauxes have a lot of money; they can get bail easily, and our asses would be fired. They can't find out it's us."

Shit, she's right. This can be career suicide.

She continues, "We need to be smart about this. My suggestion is for everyone to get plenty of sleep this weekend and meet for dinner Monday after work. I want to go over everything. We have to make sure there is enough evidence to stop this shit."

"I agree. We all need to have a clear head before moving farther," Danielle adds.

Silence on Heather's end and an expectant look from Danielle tell me they are waiting on my agreement.

"You're both right. We can't do anything this weekend. We need to keep looking. As soon as more info arises, we will meet up." I sigh, placing my hand on my head to rub my temple. "Thank you, girls."

I really wanted this resolved tonight.

"Any time! Now, I better go. Grey's grumbling that I've abandoned him for too long. He's getting cold. Talk to you both Monday. Buh-bye!" The line disconnects.

Danielle snorts. "Do you think she left him waiting in bed?"

"Oh my God, I'm glad you said it 'cause that's immediately where my mind went."

We chuckle, letting the humor ease the tension.

We can do this.

I'll work on everything this weekend, finally get some sleep, then we can decide if we have what we need on Monday.

"I'm going to call it a night." Danielle stands and picks up her stuff to leave.

"Are you okay with leaving those contracts here for now? When are they due?"

She waves me off. "We have time. They give me a month to enter them into the system before I send them with a courier to the head office." Her body freezes. "You know... I never questioned why the originals were always requested to be sent to Mr. Bordeaux directly and not someone under him. That man never does anything himself. I should have seen the red flags." Her shoulders slouch in defeat.

"Hey, none of us figured this out in the years we've been working there. If you blame yourself, then blame me too. I'm as at fault as you are." I give her a half-ass smile.

"You're right, and if I go down, at least you and Heather will keep me company," she adds with a smirk.

"You got it! Thanks again for everything. Text me when you arrive home safely."

"Will do. Night." She pauses her hand on the doorknob before turning back to me. "And, Anya?"

"Yeah?"

"Do whatever you need to do to get some sleep; we need you back to yourself if we're going to figure this out." She knows it hasn't been for my lack of trying.

I nod my response.

Once I lock up behind her, my mind turns to our situation.

How much significance do my nightmares have in relation to all of this? Is this what my grandmother was warning me about? Can I sacrifice my career to help others and still somehow find a way to support myself?

Sinking down on my soft couch, I pull my laptop closer; I need to clear my mind.

And escaping into my book is the perfect fix.

After reading the same sentence multiple times, I finally call it quits. I can't turn my mind off. Anxiety floods my body, and I feel trapped. The air in my house becomes hot and stifling while my lungs can't seem to take in a full breath.

I take a sip of my now cold tea while I move a hand back to my neck, massaging away the tension that's building into a headache. It's not helping. Neither is putting my head between my knees.

I'm burning up and itchy all over, like my body is being bitten by a million fire ants. The ability to sit still is impossible.

I'm down to my last option to cool off, take a fresh breath, and sort things out.

I pick up my dagger, holding the cold Connemara Marble handle in my hand while studying the craftsmanship of the knife.

The coolness and energy from it usually provides a sense of calm. It was handed down to me over generations on my mother's side. It has a beautiful Celtic trinity knot and a triskelion—three spirals joined in the center, rotating outwards—on the hilt, which was made of light and dark green Connemara Marble. An emerald decorates the end; the gem still shines in its polished perfection. The crossguard—where the handle meets the blade—is silver, plated iron, shaped into leaves with triskelions on each side. Along the blade are ancient runic symbols that represent Light, Strength, and Protection.

Our family symbols—ones that have always fascinated me.

We are descendants of a strong line of Celtic female warriors. On my 18th birthday, I was told by my mother and grandmother that I *must* get these runes tattooed on me as a family tradition.

This included just the three of us flying to Ireland—dad stayed home, knowing this was a girls' trip. When we arrived, my mother and grandmother held a ritual with multiple colored candles within a large stone circle.

Mom and Grandmother told me each color had a different meaning and purpose—from ascension, all the way to protection. Whatever that meant. In the center of the circle, there were flat river rocks formed into the shape of the trinity knot.

My mom, grandmother, and I sat inside each of the three centers of the trinity knot symbol. The two of them chanted in Gaelic while my grandmother tattooed three runes on me by hand, using a natural dye from the woad plant with a few needles bound together. It was a painful and long process. And despite my barrage of questions, they kept telling me everything would be explained when the time was right. I ended up giving up on my inquisition when they both gave me deathly glares. Those two scared the shit out of me.

Even though they promised me answers eventually, a part of me was too curious to wait. I tried to research our family's lineage, but everything prior to the Ó Bradàins coming to America came to a dead end. The one interesting tidbit I found was that when they immigrated from Ireland, they settled here in Shandaken—which wasn't named that back then—and co-existed with the local Native American tribes.

Hundreds of years later, the Ó Bradàins' bloodline is the oldest in the area and, ironically, always has at least one living family member in town at any given time. I guess it's for sentimental reasons—always having someone here. The thought of me being able to continue the same unspoken tradition sends a warm, tingling comfort through my soul.

That, and the cherished memory of the last time we were all together. My grandmother passed away shortly after. The ritual, the runes, the house, and the dagger are all things that help me feel close to her.

Tonight, the dagger takes a bit of the edge off—but not enough. The urge to escape is still crushing me, and the need to leave becomes unbearable.

Forgoing my jacket, I pull on my boots and slip the blade inside before heading out the door. A walk may be the best thing to clear my mind.

There's a short path through the woods behind the house that takes me to a beautiful stream. This time the moonlight lights my way—a lot different than walking home in the dark the other night.

I need to make sure I make the right decisions because that's what it all comes down to. Choosing the right path, with the least amount of negative impact.

I leisurely walk down the trail, similar to the one in my dream. This one is tame however, with the occasional roots or rocks jutting out and acting as small speed bumps along the way. I pay attention to my surroundings for any wildlife. The overwhelming tightness in my chest from my upcoming decision outweighs the fear of another animal encounter, so I press on.

Walking down to the stream with the flowing natural spring water and listening to only Mother Nature always grounds me; it clears the hurricane of chaos inside my head. I arrive at my favorite large boulder—a reminder of all the times my grandmother brought me here when I was little.

She would tell me that any time I am having troubles, the spirits of the spring will take those troubles away and show me the right direction. She said the spirits hear my thoughts and can feel my aura, my energy. They will know exactly what I need.

As a child, I loved to think there was a magical world that my grandmother introduced me to. As an adult?

Yeah... I know better than to believe in those fantasies any more. Over time, with the assistance of my school teachers, I was able to rationalize that mystical creatures belong in books, not in the real world. They told me over and over that everything I *thought* I saw was just my imagination...until I believed it myself.

Eventually, I just smiled and nodded whenever my grandmother told an unrealistic story, no longer allowing myself to believe in the tales she spun but taking them for what they were—only tales.

I sigh in contentment as I watch the moonlight twinkle over the stream, reflecting off the water rushing steadily over the river rocks. Years ago, my imagination allowed me to think I saw little fairies skipping over the water while listening to my woes. I know better now, but this place still brings me comfort and makes me think of my grandmother.

Even though it's not real, I choose to believe they are listening tonight. Without speaking, I think only about the obstacles in my way, asking for guidance on the best path to take. Sitting on the boulder, I become mesmerized, watching the glistening of the lights on the water while the steady flow fills the silence, along with the chatter of the crickets and frogs.

Time slips by and, with it, the weight of my worries lifts off my shoulders and chest; I let my head fall back, and bask in the moonlight, finding peace wash over me as if I'm one of the river rocks being cleansed by the springs.

My lungs expand with a full breath, without the anxiety contracting like a Chinese finger trap. No longer is the invisible binding wrapped around me, squeezing harder and harder as I fight for air. My pulse is now also back to normal, telling me it's time to head back home. With the adrenaline coming down, the exhaustion follows, making me more than ready for bed.

When my feet hit the top step of my porch, I notice an old piece of parchment paper with a wax seal laying on my welcome mat in front of my door. The aged caramel paper is dense, not something people of this time would use, and I can't quite make out the symbol of the wax seal other than that it resembles the sun a bit.

I glance down the road but see no sign of taillights.

Strange.

Narrowing my eyes, I look from the paper to the road and back again, hoping some sign would suddenly materialize to tell me who dropped this off. It wasn't here when I left the house, and I don't think I was at the stream long.

Shrugging my shoulders, I make my way inside while breaking the seal and reading what's inside.

'DEAR ANYA O'CLERY,

I UNDERSTAND YOU ARE FACED WITH A DILEMMA AND YOU NEED ASSISTANCE. I WOULD LIKE TO INVITE YOU TO MEET WITH MYSELF AND OTHERS TO DISCUSS VALUABLE INFORMATION YOU MAY FIND HELPFUL.

PLEASE MEET US AT N41 58.487 W74 34.738 TOMORROW AT 8:00PM.

WE LOOK FORWARD TO WORKING WITH YOU.

SINCERELY,

MUTUAL FRIENDS OF THE TURNER FAMILY.'

How do they know I'm looking into the Bordeauxes? Only Heather, Danielle, and I know what we've discovered.

Is this a trap?

Shit.

I rub the back of my neck and read the letter again. It looks innocent enough.

Do I ignore it and find a way to bring down my boss alone, or do I accept the help?

Gah, if I pass this up, though...

Images flash in my mind of families being reunited with their homes—their torn lives being pieced back together. I bite down a smile to contain my excitement, all the while a lump sits in the pit of my stomach; my body is in a fight between elation and uncertainty, waging a war to see which will win. It's a rollercoaster ride; the fear comes from the risk, along with the thrill for what's about to happen.

An unexplainable pull tells me this is a risk I need to take.

What is the worst that can happen?

I guess there's only one way to find out.

Chapter Five

Inguz

(Shelter)

The deeper I go into the secluded mountains, the more my palms sweat on the steering wheel. My left leg bounces nervously as I follow my GPS to the coordinates on the invite. Discovering the ability to enter the latitude and longitude was a revelation in itself, but it didn't mean it wasn't a huge pain in my ass. It was twenty minutes of pure frustration.

I've been driving for what feels like forever, up and down asphalt roads that follow the curves of the creek through the mountains. The drive wouldn't be as bad had the sun not set an hour ago. It isn't only my nervousness over the upcoming meeting making me sweat, but my need to be on high alert for any wildlife that may decide to jump out in front of me.

How long would it take someone to find me if I ran off the road and was impaled by a tree? Okay, let's not think about the worst case scenario here.

It does make me quite thankful I went with the high-end LED headlights on my car. Seeing clearly instead of through the yellow haze of the manufacturer lights makes such a world of difference when deer come to play Chicken.

The GPS interrupts my concentration. "Your destination is on the right."

My heart pounds in my chest.

I'm here!

Is this anxiety or excitement?

Will I finally get the information I need to stop all of this? Or am I walking into a trap and sealing my fate of being unemployed?

Stop the doubt, Anya. You are here for a reason.

This *is* the right decision; I need to see this through.

With a raised eyebrow, I glance at the forest around me then back to the GPS.

Uh, what destination?

There's not a building or driveway in sight, only trees. Everywhere.

"Make a U-Turn at the next intersection," the navigator advises.

I zoom out on my screen. "What? You mean the intersection that's twenty minutes away?" Like an idiot, I didn't look at the meeting location prior, and I assured Danielle and Heather—who begged to come with me—that I'd be in a public place and completely safe. I *assumed* I would be in a public place. I only avoided bringing them by promising I'd keep in touch and report in ASAP.

Why couldn't we have met a town or two over instead of in the middle of the woods? These people clearly aren't risking any chances of someone overhearing or seeing us together.

Other than the Bordeauxes, there's no way of knowing who else is involved or who'll run their mouths off to them. Many want to have an in with the rich couple, thinking it will give them a leg up. If they're being this cautious, bringing someone might jeopardize getting what we need. I don't blame them for aiming for a secure and private location, but this is a little excessive. I may agree with their caution, yet it doesn't mean I'm comfortable with the situation.

"Screw it!" I turn my car around in the middle of the road. There's no one around.

"Where *is* this place? This has to be some kind of a joke," I mutter to myself, slowly creeping forward while my eyes bounce back and forth following the dot on the screen and searching for an opening.

That's when I find it.

Between tall trees and dense shrubbery hides a small entrance—a path covered with tall grass. It's rude not to flag it or even mow the damn path.

I squint at the opening, barely able to make out worn cobblestone under the grass and plants.

"This better be worth it," I grumble and turn down the uninhabited path.

My teeth press into my lips as I pray I don't get a flat trying to make my way through. My car has taken some rough gravel roads before, but this is a whole new level of off-roading. I'm not sure the shocks and struts won't need replacing after tonight.

An ache travels from my tense shoulders up to my temples.

Why am I doing this again? Is it worth it?

The memory of the Turner Family and many others who lost the only home they'd ever had flashes in my mind.

Yup, definitely worth the risk.

Regardless of the snail's pace I'm going, the uneven stones cause me to bounce around in my seat, which is not the best feeling; the jarring racks my body.

A screeching fills the silence of the night, causing me to brake immediately. The sound is as bad as nails on a chalkboard, and I cringe. Glancing in the direction of where it came from, I find the culprit.

There, against my front passenger door, a large thick branch scrapes the metal. Going into reverse isn't going to make it any better at this point; all I can do is continue forward and have faith I won't regret this later.

"Please don't scratch my baby," I plead. I'm really having doubts about this meeting being worth the hassle.

I make my way through and let out a sigh of relief when I see a clearing up ahead. Once I get closer to the opening, my jaw drops at the sight before me.

"Whoa."

The closer I get to the building, the clearer it becomes.

No way, is that…?

My headlights shine on the dark stone steps that lead to a set of old double doors. The wood is at least 8 feet high, with the tops rounded into an arch as the doors come together. Iron surrounds the frame, with no exposed hinges on this side. About 2 feet from the top, there's a thin plate of iron going across each door. At the center is an intricate design, similar to a sunray pattern—swirls start at the middle and go outwards in each direction. The same design is near the bottom, and there are old handles instead of doorknobs. Each door has an iron knocker.

As I study the building, I notice my leg has stopped bouncing; my nervousness has obviously been consumed by my fascination.

Pulling my eyes from the beautiful doors, I drag my gaze up. The place looks to be two, maybe three stories tall; it's a little hard to tell in the dark. I've seen things like this in pictures and in movies, but never have I visited something so...majestic and aged like this. I can only imagine how stunning it must be in the daylight.

The stone castle looks ancient. It must be hundreds of years old. *What the hell is it doing out here?*

I take in the view around the estate. It doesn't take me long to realize this place is well hidden. There are massive trees surrounding it, taller than the building itself. Many of them create a dome, shielding the castle from the outside world as though this unbelievable place doesn't want to be found.

Leaning forward in my seat, I remember why I'm here—to get more information. As much as I would love to find out more about the history of this place, what happened here, and who owns it, I need to focus. A hint of a smile nudges at the corner of my lips. If I'm lucky, I may be able to get these answers at the same time.

I continue to take in the castle and its dark surroundings as a knot forms in the pit of my unsettled stomach. Now that my initial enchantment with this place is gone, I realize the castle presents a perfect home for hauntings, demons, and anything else that would like to kill me. There is a good chance a serial killer lured me here with the letter, only to cut me up in pieces and scatter my body parts in the woods to be devoured by animals. It's the perfect place for a murder; I'm sure I'm not the only one who never knew it was out here.

"Snap out of it, Anya." I need to cut back on the paranormal books. This is the second time this week I've scared myself.

Shaking my head, I try to clear the disturbing thoughts. That's when I notice there are no other vehicles.

How exactly am I to get over my nerves when I'm the only one here? I swear the invite said 8:00pm.

I turn on my interior light, pick up the invite, and look at the time. Checking the clock on the dash, then my phone, I make sure I didn't mess it up.

Nope. I'm right on time.

Maybe they're running late?

After fifteen more minutes and no sign of anyone coming to join me for this secret meeting, I start to wonder if this is a joke.

How much do you wanna bet Heather put this all together?

My lips tighten and my muscles tense as irritation washes over me. If she did, I'm going to kill her.

Do I wait longer? Do I go home?

My shoulders slump, and my body sags in my seat. Defeat and disappointment flood my thoughts. There's nothing like having my hopes built up only to be crushed to smithereens. I guess it could have been worse; I could have become the first missing person from Shandaken.

With one last hopeful look in my rearview mirror for other headlights, I resign myself to the fact that no one else is coming. It's pointless to stay here any longer. Time to go home.

I turn off the interior light with a sigh and put my car in reverse.

Then I freeze.

My attention is suddenly drawn to a window on the top level of the building. A window that was dark a moment ago but now has candle light flickering and casting a soft, warm glow.

I lean farther in my seat and squint to see if I can make out anything else.

A shadow passes quickly in front of the light, scaring the hell out of me.

"Shit!"

I jump back against my seat and grab my chest.

Someone *is* here!

Do I go in? Maybe the mysterious writer of the note lives here?

I pick up my phone to call Heather. I need to see if she set this all up.

Of course, there isn't any signal here. Why would there be? I stare at my phone as though my will alone will change my situation.

I let out a frustrated sigh. There's only one thing I can do to find out what's going on here.

After mentally pulling myself together for a moment, I turn off my car, pocket my phone, and step outside. A chill travels through me as my feet hit the soft ground, and it's not because of the evening breeze. The pit in my stomach tenses, and I worry that this may not be a good idea after all.

Suck it up, Anya. I try to motivate myself to get this over with.

I place one foot in front of the other to make my way to the castle. Through the silence of the night, a crackling—along with the sound of something heavy being dragged across the ground from my right—stops me mid-stride. Followed shortly by a horrid, rancid stench. It reeks of dead, rotting animals.

I'm trying to stay silent, but I'm struggling—the stench makes me gag.

What the hell is that?

I am completely still, frozen in my spot, waiting to find out what direction the sound is coming from. It sounded close.

An unearthly growl comes from behind me as an ice-cold, putrid breath pulses at the back of my neck.

Oh, fuck!

Jumping away, I turn, fists in the air, ready to fight.

But...there's nothing there.

Shadows in the woods around me sway in the moonlight. The darkness has me questioning every movement, and I feel like I'm being watched.

An abrupt sense of dread washes over me. Sweat beads at my forehead and between my shoulder blades while my hands are cold and clammy.

This is *nothing* like the time I've encountered a cougar in the woods, watching my every move.

Yes, I knew I was in danger at the time, yet this is something entirely different and almost...evil.

I need to get away, and fast.

My head whips in the direction of my car, where the sound of soft crunching comes from. I'm being hunted; I can feel it. Still, I can't make out what's out there and my one shelter I had is no longer an option to keep me safe.

Without warning, vibration carries across the ground to me. Whatever this creature is, it's huge and coming at me fast.

"Fuck!"

I'm already running up the steps to the front doors as fast as I can, hoping and praying someone in there can help me. I push and pull on the handles hard, but they won't budge.

"Damn it!" My throat closes up as I cry out; tears stream down my face.

With one last hope of alerting someone I'm here, I start beating on the doors with my fists in terror.

The door shifts open a sliver. A hand shoots out and wraps around my forearm as I'm yanked in.

I lose my footing immediately, stumbling over the stone floor in complete darkness. I'm being pulled again, until I'm flush against a very large and very *hard*, muscular body.

The closed door is now behind us.

One of the hands is placed firmly over my mouth while the other is around my stomach, holding me close. The hands are large enough to easily close off the airway of my nose without moving from my mouth.

My muffled scream doesn't help in any way. It only causes my captor to secure me more tightly against his body.

A gruff, low tone warns, "Don't fucking scream again or you're dead."

The man's voice makes me shiver. I can't tell if it's from fear or excitement, which is...awkward. I don't even know why I would think the latter. Clearly, I'm overwhelmed with everything that's happened tonight.

Yup, it's fear... Definitely fear.

This is *not* the type of position I thought I would be in tonight. I expected a nice meeting with good people who—like me—want to help others who are being taken advantage of. Now, I'm being held hostage by a guy threatening to kill me *in here* while some type of animal probably wants to kill me *out there.*

I should have stayed home.

My mind reels, wondering what I can say next to help me out of this situation. My brain knows I should be scared, yet the longer I stand here, the more my heart feels like it's home. The only way to describe the feeling is as if I'd been out in the cold darkness for years, only to have stepped into a warm house with a well-lit fireplace, a creamy hot chocolate drink ready to consume, and a man wrapping me in his safe, secure embrace. In his arms, I know the darkness and cold will never get their claws wrapped around me again.

He threatened to kill you and that comforts you? What's wrong with you?

I've never experienced this before, and while my brain is yelling that this feeling doesn't make sense, everything else in my being is telling me this is where I need to be. Which confuses the shit out of me.

That alone should be throwing up red flags; talk about the ultimate internal battle.

The struggle I had with myself last night after receiving the invite was nothing compared to this new war going on. I know I should be afraid and cautious instead of jumping into the lion's den, saying, 'Here, kitty, kitty! I just want to snuggle.'

Pushing away my odd feelings, I weigh my chances of survival inside the castle with the kidnapper against the ones outside with the beast. The shadows that surround us thankfully aren't the moving kind. Point one for staying in here.

Scratching on the outside of the door startles me. A muffled squeak comes out of my mouth, and my heart pounds harder. The memory of a breath on my neck comes back to me, causing me to whimper. I was too close to being attacked by some kind of a large animal. I made my decision—there is no way in hell I want to see what's on the other side of that door. I'll take my chances with this guy.

Since we seem to be at a standstill, I reach back with my left hand to search for something—anything—that can help me, when I feel something long and hard...

"I'd be careful where you're grabbing if I were you," he whispers in a deep voice.

Another shiver runs up my spine, and I hear the asshole chuckle.

The mere sound of it sends heat running through my veins.

What is wrong with me?

My fingers have a mind of their own as they trace along the solid...

It's a...gun!

Why does this guy have a gun?

Well... I guess that makes sense. Any serial killer who knows what they're doing would have a weapon of some sort. A gun seems to be on par for his character up till now.

His hot breath is on my cheek, lips close to my ear.

I can't tell what it is about this guy—I haven't even seen his face—but my body reacts with a flush tingle. Awareness ripples over me, as if he were my long-lost lover.

Closing my eyes, I try to focus on his energy.

As a kid, my grandmother would have me block out everything around me and feel the aura from different people and objects, then describe them to her. She had a knack for spurring imaginary ideations in my mind. Most of the time, I saw colors and different patterns from one person to the next. As I got older, I tried to block it, thinking it was all my imagination like the fairies. As much as I tried, I would still occasionally feel pulls or see flashes of colors bouncing off someone, but I'd shake them off.

Being in the dark, my senses are heightened, and I don't have much of a choice *but* to feel out the energy around me. The need to see how I know him becomes my sole focus. It's not as though I have anything else I can do while I'm bound snuggly in his arms.

It's been forever since I've played around with reading auras.

His is overwhelming—dark blues into black, swirling all around me like wisps of smoke testing my energy, touching it hesitantly then retreating. When it touches mine, his blue turns cloudy then fades into a black wall like my aura is repelling his for some reason.

Is it because of my fear?

I'm not sure what else it could be but I can't shake this familiar feeling. *How the hell do I know him?*

I wrack my brain, unable to put the pieces together to figure out the familiarity of him.

Have I ever felt this comfortable with a guy before?

No.

The scratches on the door become louder, and our bodies shake from the creature trying to get in. I stiffen in fear, not realizing this guy was acting as a barricade. I sure as hell hope he's strong enough to hold the door closed from the animal outside.

My mind knows he is a stranger to me, but my heart feels we are connected somehow. Being in his arms comforts me more than the last guy I dated. I'm not sure what that says about me, let alone my ex, but let's blame it on the ex anyways. It's easier that way.

I try to ask him who he is but, of course, with my mouth behind his hand, all that comes out is a mumble.

"Shh!!" he whisper-shouts at me. "If I let you go, will you keep fucking quiet?"

Of course, I respond with my words.

His hiss of annoyance only proves he doesn't speak mumble.

Amateur. I understood myself perfectly.

I shake my head in irritation, which only causes his grip to tighten around me. The darkness around me dims further, and I get lightheaded.

Damn it!

It's getting harder to breathe. He apparently thought I was saying no. With a quick nod of my head, he finally lightens his hold.

I pull in a deep breath through my nose, making an unladylike snort in an attempt to fill my lungs.

Oh well, it's not like I'm trying to impress anyone. Especially this guy.

I focus on breathing in and out while I wait for him to fully release me. His grasp slightly lets up, then tightens again. He seems hesitant, fighting an internal battle over whether he should risk letting me go or not. I stay stock-still, not wanting to give him a reason to hold me longer.

After another minute or two, in the slowest of movements, he gradually lets me go. Which is lucky for him because I was two seconds away from using his balls as my own personal punching bag.

Ha! Just kidding... But badass wannabe me thought it would be cool. Heather would have been proud.

Coldness hits me like an ocean wave. Now that his arms are no longer wrapped around me, my whole body trembles as my teeth chatter. The shaking is more from fear over everything that has occurred up to this point rather than the temperature in the castle. I wrap my arms tightly around my body to try to soothe it.

I'm determined to keep my distance from the man who gave me warmth and security a moment ago. It can't be normal to seek comfort from a stranger, one who I'm not 100% sure has good intentions.

I watch the large outline of his body against the door, holding it shut.

I bite my lip.

Maybe I can help hold the door closed?

Without his nearness, the dark begins to creep in, grabbing me and pulling me under again—fear and anxiety taking hold.

No, it would be too easy to go back into the stranger's arms.

I shake my head, trying to stop the impulse to go to him.

What is wrong with me?

I need a clear head to think, and being up against him will *not* allow that to happen.

Every part of this night—including my emotional state—is fucked up.

A few minutes pass, and the noise outside stops.

The large wall of muscle cautiously steps away, and my eyes follow to see what he plans to do next. I'm not entirely sure I should trust his motives. Even with following my intuition, knowing he wouldn't harm me, I have to keep a level head about the possibility of being wrong.

He snaps his fingers and points in a direction a few feet away from him.

What the hell is he trying to say?

He huffs then whispers, "Get the bar."

I narrow my eyes, trying to see past the dark shadows of the floor until my eyes pass over something long and narrow in the corner. Picking up the iron bar, I hand it over to him. He must have tossed it aside when he pulled me in. His movements are silent, like the rest of him as he places the rod over the double doors. The bar secures the door now, and I release my breath, feeling a little safer. Instead of modern-day locks, the owner apparently felt a large iron bar was better to keep out a non-existent medieval army. Well... I *hope* they are non-existent. The way things are going tonight, I'm really not sure what the hell to think.

With the door secured, I walk around checking out the place. I may not be safe from this guy, but where exactly does he think I'll go? It's not like I'll be running out the back door into the jaws of some giant predator.

Wait... Is there a back door? If there is, I really hope it's barricaded too.

Not looking back, I make my way around, taking in the details of the room.

Everything is dark, with the slightest amount of moonlight coming through high windows—ones that are built to bring light in, not to look out. They are a very aged flat glass that is naturally frosted instead of modern-day clear glass. I remember learning about it during History class—in one of those rare moments I had actually paid attention. Then again, I perked up any time they talked about ancient infrastructures. Those *may* be my weakness.

The main entryway is a large room that has two hallways—or wings—leading out on either side. A few long wooden tables with benches are scattered around the room. My mind wanders to images of medieval times, where men covered in leather and animal furs are sitting around the hall. With a grand feast filling the tables, they eat their food with their hands and drink their mead from wooden or copper cups. Wenches move around the room efficiently, serving the broad, strapping, and *non-chivalrous* men. The room is overfilled with laughter, yelling, and manly grunts. Maybe a few brawls as well.

As my mind escapes from reality, my hands feel around for a light switch, only to come up empty. Breaking away from my daydreams, I continue to search the walls. I'm met with cold stone everywhere.

Is it too much to hope that someone would have wired this place with electricity in the last century? I let out a frustrated sigh.

A deep chuckle causes me to jump and reminds me I'm not alone. Completely lost in my own world and fantasy, I forgot this guy was still here and clearly watching my every move.

I can't tell what his intentions are.

Is this where he kills me?

No, he won't kill me—I would have picked up on negative energy.

He has to feel it too, right? But what if he's a very charismatic serial killer who plays tricks on women to gain their trust before he slaughters them?

My head tells me this is possible, but my gut and my intuition are rarely wrong. I hate this back-and-forth fight. I wish my intuition could answer all my other questions.

If he was in the attic, how the hell did he get down to the front door so fast? What happened to everyone else that was supposed to be here?

Agh!

All the questions are driving me insane. I need answers. I'm done waiting.

I take a minute to see if there are any more sounds outside.

There's nothing. I'm hoping that means the animal is gone.

Taking the risk and praying I won't be shot, I ask softly, "Who are you, and what are you planning on doing with that gun?"

He huffs. "My question is, who are *you*? And what are *you* doing here? If you were planning on meeting your rich, older boyfriend for a tryst, I'm sorry to tell you that won't be happening—*ever*."

What is he talking about? This guy must have just gotten out of the loony bin, or maybe he's on drugs. I know I didn't smell alcohol on his breath.

"Uhm... I was invited here for a meeting, and I have a feeling you weren't."

"Well, what gave you that idea, *sweetheart*?"

Is this guy dense?

"Oh...you know...the fact you have such a *shining* personality, for one," I fire back. "For another, the gun in your pocket. Based on the weight and coldness I felt, I'm quite confident it's real *and* fully loaded. That's not something someone brings with them to a friendly get-together."

Or at least, I sure as hell hope they wouldn't.

My trembling decreases as my temper heats up my body—starting with my flushed face. "Now, can we please cut to the chase, and you tell me who the *hell* you are and what the *fuck* is going on? Where is everyone?"

He's silent for what feels like forever. The only sound is our breathing. The scratching thankfully hasn't returned—regardless of us being loud.

Finally, the big man speaks. "The name's Hunter, and I'm a private investigator. Sometimes, my line of work requires me to carry a gun. I came here searching for your boyfriend."

In an unladylike way, my lips blow a raspberry as I release a breath.

Great news, everyone! This man is not here to kill me!

"Well, I just saved you *tons* of work since I don't have a boyfriend."

"Not anymore you don't."

Oh, this man is irritating and delusional.

"Not anymore?" I release an exhausted sigh. "Forget it; enough of this beating around the bush. My name is Anya. It means—"

"Radiance, named after a Sun Goddess," he interrupts.

I pause in shock. "How... How do you know that?"

He takes a couple of steps forward, and in the dark I can see his eyes narrow into slits like he's trying to study me. "Anya, is it really you?"

"Umm... no. It's the boogie man." I cock my hip and cross my arms. "Mister, I just *told* you who I am. No need to keep getting all weird on me."

"Just answer this one question." He tilts his head.

"Oohh-kay," I draw out and take a step back, unsure of what's going to come out of his mouth next.

"When you were younger, where did you sneak away to at night?"

Wait, what?

My hand shoots up. "First off, I never *once* snuck out of my house. And second, what does this have to do with *anything*?"

Maybe he won't notice if I begin to back away ever-so-slowly.

He shakes his head and runs a hand through his hair. "Never mind. Forget it."

"That's unlikely," I mumble. This night just keeps getting weirder and weirder. "So, anyways... I happen to have been invited to meet with some people to help me with some research I'm doing." I keep things vague since I don't know who this guy really is and if I can trust him. "And now I'm trapped here in a creepy castle, with some kind of animal outside that seems intent on attacking us, while arguing with a crazy man who thinks he is searching for a fictional boyfriend of mine."

"I found him."

"And now the crazy man is seeing imaginary people. *Just* great!" I throw up my hands and say, "Fuck it." Then I storm off.

No, I don't know where I'm going, but it has to be *way* better than being here with this guy right now. I get there has to be some reason we must know each other—despite this black wall I keep seeing when I try to place him. My mind is in a tug-of-war with this blind energy telling me I'm safe with him; at the same time, my brain keeps throwing up red flags that I may still be in danger.

The familiarity mixed with doubt didn't save him from me unleashing on him when he pissed me off. If I stay in the same room with him any longer, I'll end up strangling the ever-loving shit out of him. Walking away saves his life and keeps me out of prison. Win-win.

Taking my phone out of my back pocket, I turn on my flashlight to illuminate where I'm going.

The hairs on the back of my neck stand once I enter the hallway to the right of the main hall.

Cold air rushes at me as if blowing through an open window, taking hold and pulling me down the dark passage like a marionette to its master.

A tremble wracks through my body, and I'm beyond grateful I didn't wear the skirt Danielle and Heather were convinced would be perfect for the meeting.

You should look professional, and this skirt will do the trick.

Ha, I think not. Not only would I be freezing in the thin, flowy, black gauze skirt, but I'd feel way more vulnerable than I do now. There is absolutely nothing wrong with what I chose—a cute, blue floral, cold-shoulder blouse, leather jacket, dark jeans, and boots.

Shit, my dagger.

My stride falters briefly.

I completely forgot I had my dagger on me this whole time. *How flighty can I get?* There's no use having it to protect me when

I don't remember it in the first place. This should be a prime example that the warrior bloodline I apparently have got watered down quite a bit before it reached me.

I am *definitely* not a warrior. Just a naive girl who follows a strange invite that leads to being chased by a dangerous animal into the arms of a crazy man. And the way my night is going, I'm most likely being led to my death by giving in to this unexplainable draw.

"What the hell is going on?" I say under my breath. I needed the escape to avoid throttling Hunter, not go on a wild goose chase to soothe this weird agitation—a tension that is holding me hostage until I follow its rules, until I go to its desired destination.

I think, at this point, I'm the one who's gone crazy.

Maybe this whole thing is a dream, or maybe... I finally lost my mind after all. Seeing a counselor will be my top priority after I get through this. I sure as shit *hope* I get through this.

My body continues to be pulled farther down the long hall by invisible strings. I'm trapped inside the castle with no way of knowing when—or if—I'll be safe again. I only hope that wherever I'm being led will relieve this restlessness inside.

I pass closed doors on my right without peeking in. I estimate this to be the other side of the main room—the dining hall. On my left are a few tapestries hung on the wall. With as much dust and dirt as the hanging art is caked in, there's no telling what kind of designs they are. Add in the darkness, and there's no point in stopping to decipher them. Wouldn't matter if I wanted to, anyways—my legs take me wherever they plan to go. Maybe once I'm there, this anxious, urgent feeling will subside. I pass a few more doors and a set of stairs that lead up to the next floor until I come to a dead end. The only direction to go now is down the stairs to my right.

Into the dark abyss.

"Of course it would lead to a creepy basement," I mumble.

Why wouldn't it?

It couldn't have led me to a beautiful library, where I could spend the rest of my evening. Alone.

I hesitate, glancing down the dark, stone stairs. I take a step back, but the pressure wrapped around my body tightens, and with it comes a sensation of something crawling under my skin, making me twitchy. I groan.

I don't think I have a way around this.

Going into an eerie basement isn't usually a smart thing to do in a place like this, especially under strange circumstances like tonight, but what the hell. Might as well continue to go all-in at this point. Fighting this force is only making things worse.

As soon as I step down the first step, a hand grabs my shoulder and pulls me back.

"Shit!" Turning fast, I pull up my arms in defense mode, with my fists clenched and ready to strike.

Hunter drops his hand from my shoulder.

Damn, this guy is stealthy—I didn't even hear him follow me.

"Don't go down there," he demands in a deep yet quiet voice.

"Do you own this place? No? Okay, I don't really think you have the right to tell me where I can and cannot go." Stubbornness fuels me, and I start down the stairs.

This time, I hear him behind me. *I'm not even going to admit to myself that I feel safer with him following me.* I pick up my pace and go down faster. My foot slips on the stone step, and my hand shoots out to the wall to catch myself before I continue my pace to the bottom landing. It's colder down here, and a rotten smell hits me like a brick wall. I stumble back and bump into a hard chest.

Hunter reaches out to steady me. "I told you not to come down here." His hands are on both my shoulders.

"What *is* that smell?" I wave a hand in front of my face—it does nothing to make it better. Pushing more of the rancid stench into my face is making it worse. The lack of fresh, clean air causes a restriction in my airways. Coughs rattle my chest, making it even harder to catch my breath.

Hunter lets go of my shoulders and takes a firm hold of my arm. "Let's go." He's trying to drag me back up the stairs.

I snatch my arm out of his grasp and quickly take off down a hallway to my right. When it tees off, I briefly hesitate before I'm steered to the left. The scent keeps getting stronger. I have to be close to the source, and I can't say I'm excited to find out what it is.

I hear Hunter yelling for me, his voice echoing off the walls, sounding closer than he is. The hallway opens into a large room with a dark lump outside a large door, and I slow my pace. Cautiously, I walk closer while gagging from the scent, unable to stop the pull inside of me. Deep in my gut, I feel I need to be here—another confirmation that I should have my head checked after this.

I make my way over to the dark pile and step in a pool of liquid.

That doesn't make sense. We haven't had any rain recently for the water to seep into the basement.

I aim my flashlight down and stifle a scream.

There is blood everywhere, and I jump back, trying to get out of the dark, sticky puddle. I guide my light to the heap on the floor.

Is that... Is that an animal? That's a pretty big animal. Wait... Animals don't have hands.

Screaming, I stumble back.

Hunter is suddenly by my side, trying to pull me away.

"Wha... What happened? Did you...do this?" I stutter, looking around us like a crazed animal needing to escape. I'm sure my eyes are as wide as saucers as my gaze lands on him.

His features are mainly shadows since our lights are directed at our feet. I have yet to shine my light near his face to get a look at him. You know... In case he's a serial killer, maybe I can plead with him that I never saw his face, and he'll let me go.

I start to back up inch by inch, treating him like he's a predator ready to pounce at the slightest fast movement. I'm not confident he *won't* pounce. I whimper when he slowly creeps towards me.

"Calm down, Anya. I found him like this. He had to have been here for a few days based on the smell."

"Uh huh." I try to appease him. My brain is screaming at me that this is too much of a coincidence and isn't adding up, and my body remains on edge—Hunter could be the villain in this story.

My eyes shift from Hunter back to the body remains. A majority of the torso is ripped open, and most of the organs are missing. I'm glad I didn't eat before my supposed meeting, or I'm sure it would be coming back up right about now.

Despite my churning stomach, my shoulders drop; relief hits me, knowing he didn't kill this guy. A person couldn't have created this much damage and tear into someone like this.

Oh my God, is that his spine?

Bile rises in my throat, and I swallow to keep it down.

Hold it together, Anya.

There must be a reason why I'm here. My grandmother used to tell me that nothing is by chance. The sooner I find out, the sooner I can get out of here. I avert my eyes from the horror and try to see if I can make out who the person is. The claw marks slashed diagonally across the face make the features scarcely recognizable. I tilt my head to get a closer look. Something seems familiar about the person, but I can't place him.

"In case you can't tell by the mangled and mauled body, I found your boyfriend."

My vision turns red, and it isn't from all the blood. I take a few deep breaths—which proves to be hard with the stench—and ask calmly, "Why do you keep assuming he's my boyfriend?"

He laughs. The jerk actually laughs!

I back farther away from him since this dude is *clearly* unstable. Not the 'I'm going to chop you up' kind, but more along the lines of 'Hey, I'm still living in my delirious world where this bloody carcass is the man of your dreams.'

"You're telling me that he was here, and you showing up looking like a hot young side-piece for a 'meeting,'"—*Did he just air quote 'meeting?' Seriously?*—"that you weren't having an affair with him? I mean, I met his wife, and I can definitely see the appeal..." He looks me up and down. "But the guy could be old enough to be your father. You *that* desperate for money, sweetheart?" The energy pulsing off him is heated and pissed.

If I could see his face, I bet it would be beet red, with a vein popping out of his forehead. Why is *he* angry when I'm the one he's calling a whore?

If smoke could come out of my ears, now would be the time. "Wait one damn second! Don't you *dare* assume I'm someone's side-piece. I am *not*, nor will I *ever* have an affair with a married man, let alone one much older than me. I have a well-paying job, thank you very much. I don't need to sell myself for money, *asshole*." I'm fuming and want to wring his thick neck.

Only when I feel his hot, minty breath on my face do I realize that we have moved closer to one another during our yelling match. Our boots are touching, our faces mere inches apart, and both of us are breathing heavily.

I get a whiff of his cologne.

Damn it, why does he have to smell so good?

It's a little piece of heaven in this rotting pit of hell.

I shake my head to clear it.

Not now, Anya! Pull yourself together; there's a mauled body ten feet away from you, and this guy is crazy and infuriating.

I count to five, then I ask in a calmer voice, "If you knew he was down here, why are *you* still here and not on the phone with the cops?"

Hunter laughs again. "Oh, because it's so pleasant hanging around here that I didn't want to leave. Have you checked your cell service? Wait, there is none." His voice is heavily laced with sarcasm.

What a dick.

I get ready to respond when he cuts me off.

"Since you don't seem to have realized there's also some sort of animal outside that would happily prefer to make us its next meal, I can't quite leave the place, now, can I? I was trying to figure out if it would take off so I could get back to my bike to go get help. I heard your car pull up and had no idea how to warn you without being attacked myself. As soon as I heard you outside the door, I took my chances and pulled you in. You're welcome, by the way, you know... For saving your life."

Even in the dark, I can make out a shadow of a smirk and hear the cockiness in his tone.

"Ugh..." I grind out and narrow my eyes at him. This guy may not be crazy after all, but that doesn't mean I have to put up with his shit. "I wouldn't go as far as to say you saved my life, but sure. Thanks for opening the door." That's as far as I'll go. No sense in stroking this guy's ego.

"That's okay... Baby steps. The first step to acceptance is denial."

Glad someone finds humor in this situation.

I ignore his statement. "So, who is this guy anyways, and how'd you know to find him here?"

He's silent for a moment. I can feel his eyes studying me, as if he is weighing how much to tell me.

What's he hiding?

I wipe my sweaty palms on my pants as discreetly as I can. I don't want him thinking he is making me more nervous and unhinged than I already am.

He glances at the remains, then back to me. "His name is Grant Bordeaux."

Chapter Six

Jera

(Timing)

Air leaves my lungs, and blood drains from my head at the name.

Grant Bordeaux.

"His wife hired me," Hunter explains, "and told me that he got a tip about an abandoned castle in this area he wanted to check out. He was hoping to acquire it to sell. I'm sure he would have made a fortune off it. That was four days ago. I finally found the place this evening, and his car was parked around the back. That's where I parked my bike. I checked out the outside first, then made my way through the front doors which were left wide open."

I'm dizzy, and my arms—all the way down to my hands—tingle from the lack of blood flow.

"I went in, started checking out both wings, then decided to start at the lower level and work my way up. That's how I found him. I'm assuming some sick fuck locked up the animal in that small room." He points to the thick iron door. "He must have opened it and let it loose. Bordeaux happened to be the first meal in its path. Why are you looking at me like that?"

Hunter's voice sounds muffled in my head. I'm not sure what I look like, but I can't breathe, and the lightheadedness is getting worse. My vision is going in and out.

Hunter grabs me before I fall to the bloody ground. "Whoa. Let's go back upstairs," he says quietly, still holding me.

Everything is spinning as the walls are closing in. I need fresh air; I need out of here *now*.

We reach the top of the stairs, and I stop to catch my breath. Hunter doesn't give me the opportunity and continues to guide me towards the main room to sit me on one of the benches.

"Will you be okay if I leave you here and try to go find some water?"

I can't respond. My mind feels numb, my vision blurred, and I can't get my mouth moving. My heart's cadence is irregular. I'm not sure if this is what's considered shock, or maybe I'm having a heart attack. My eyes still seem to work as I watch a blurry Hunter head towards the hallway opposite from where we came. His eyes don't leave me until he rounds the corner.

It doesn't take long before he's back and offering me a wooden bowl with liquid inside.

"Here, drink. It's water. I found a kitchen with a water pump." Instead of handing me the bowl, he kneels in front of me and holds it up to my lips.

Silently, I take a big gulp and cough, inhaling some of the liquid. "Holy...shit!" I was not expecting mineral water. "Are you trying to kill me after all?"

Hunter shakes his head in disbelief. "Funny. Feeling better?" He's still kneeling in front of me.

I can't see his face clearly but enough that he seems genuinely concerned.

Who is this guy?

I clear my throat, trying to push the bitter minerals from it. "Umm...yeah... I guess? That stuff tastes like shit."

"Sorry, I left the sparkling water in my other jacket, princess. Now... You care to tell me what that was all about? Did you lie to me about him not being your boyfriend?"

Annnnnd the asshole is back.

The veil of red slides over my vision yet again, and I shove him back on his ass, causing the water to spill on the floor. I get up to pace the room, still shaky, but I don't care.

"After everything I just told you, you *still* think that this guy was my boyfriend? I received a letter with the GPS coordinates and time to arrive for the meeting with some people who were going to help my research. That's why I came out here. Someone clearly punked me. Or maybe there wasn't an animal attack, but a mass murderer is out there and he just lured me to my death?" Even though I know that isn't the case, my mind tells me to be careful. I eye him warily. "How do I know it isn't you?"

He's still sitting on the floor where I shoved him, his flashlight laying a couple of feet from him and shining in his direction, showing off his thick forearms resting on his knees. He's wearing a button-down plaid shirt, the sleeves rolled up, with faded jeans and dark brown work boots. I still haven't fully made out his face. However, I can make out a dark shadow of a closely trimmed beard and dark eyes.

"Are you a little slow? How exactly can it be me when something is outside trying to get in? I can't fake that. And who the hell meets strangers at an abandoned castle *alone?!*" His rising voice breaks me out of my inner war.

I hate that he's right. Right about him not being the murderer, and right about me taking a risk coming here alone. My mind was set on answers, not the risk.

How stupid can I be?

I take a few deep breaths. "Coming here alone is not one of my proudest moments." I clear my throat. "I'm sorry. Tonight has been a lot. Can we make a deal? I'll stop accusing you of murder if you can lay off the boyfriend idea. Agree?"

"I guess I can agree to that," he mutters like he doesn't quite believe my true reason for being here.

And really, who would believe me? It's not as though I can conjure up proof of my invite for my meeting since I left that in the car. Outside. With the animal. *Yup, he needs to take my word for it.*

"Thank you." I stare at him still sitting on the floor, studying me.

"Care to tell me what that was all about?" He repeats the question and waits patiently.

"That's my boss. Or was. He's the owner of the company I work for. I don't know him personally, but the fact he was killed and eaten by some animal is really hard to take in, okay?"

And now I'm wondering if Grant set me up. He could have found out we discovered what he was doing.

No, that's stupid, Hunter said he's been dead for a few days. I got the invite last night.

Shit, did someone set up his murder and try to frame me?

I lean forward with my elbows on my knees and rub my temples. None of this makes sense.

"What do we do now?" I ask softly. My head is pounding with all the possibilities and the frustration over not knowing what is happening.

He pauses before he gives his answer. "I don't think we have much of an option on what we *can* do. The only thing now is to wait until morning and hope that thing is gone."

I'm trying to think of how I can get us to my car and haul ass out of here.

"There must be another exit. Maybe a window we can look out of?" I suggest.

"The back door through the kitchen is barricaded, and this level doesn't have any windows. We may be able to see more from upstairs, but it's too dark and there are too many hiding spots."

"So, there is still a chance we have an alternative escape. Maybe if you distract it somehow, I can slip out the back and get to my car. Go find help." This could work.

"Whatever this thing is, it's smart. I've already tried to trick it. No luck."

"Maybe it's smarter than *you* but not smarter than me." Okay, that unintentionally came out a little cocky. "What I mean is, there are two of us now."

Hunter leans up against the wall and the shadow of his arms cross over his chest. "Have fun with that. Don't forget to lock the door on your way out."

Ugh.

"Just point me in the direction of the kitchen, *please.*"

He pushes off the wall and takes two steps forward, pointing down a hallway. "Turn right and go until you can't go anymore. You can't miss it. It's the room that looks like a kitchen."

"*Asshole*," I mumble.

He chuckles. "What was that sweetheart?"

"I said, thank you." And I take my leave from this infuriating man and make my way down the dark hall, turning on the flashlight of my phone along the way.

The single wood and iron supported door stands to the left of the large clay oven. A bar, like the one in the front, is over this door as well. I place my ear up against the cold wood and listen to what's beyond the barrier.

Silence.

Maybe I do have a chance.

Setting my phone light on the oven, I ever so gently lift the metal bar while bracing one hand against the door.

The lack of sound is reassuring, and I begin to pull the handle open. As soon as the door is cracked open, a rancid stench fills my nostrils.

What the hell died?

With a creak from the hinge, something long and black swipes by my head before a strong force behind me slams the door back closed.

My heart is flooding my eardrums, and I shove the iron rod back in its place.

Sounds of growling and scratching from the beast outside echo off the walls. I don't know what we're working with. Whatever the hell that was that almost tore my face off didn't look anything like a claw from a grizzly or cougar. But then again, it's dark, I'm scared, and it was too quick for me to make out. It's not uncommon for the occasional attack on a hiker by a wild animal. However, something like this is out of the norm.

Glancing up to the man who saved me *again*, I cringe. "Looks like we're staying the night after all."

"You planning on making this into a habit?" he growls out, not thrilled with my attempt to escape, or more likely from almost letting that thing in here with us.

"No. I can save my own self, thank you very much."

He huffs.

"Thank you, though. I hadn't even heard you come up, but I appreciate you being here." I'm trying my best to extend an olive branch here.

Hunter faces the door, double checking the security. "Ah, so the girl knows her manners?"

And the olive branch just went up in flames.

"Don't push it, buddy," I grind out.

This whole situation is ridiculous. I'm stranded with a stranger for the rest of the evening because some cruel idiot wanted to have some fun.

Why would anyone trap an animal in the dungeon of a castle?

No wonder it was pissed; depending on how long it was there, it could have been extremely hungry. Animal instincts kick in with hunger. Now that it's fed and outside, it probably won't take long to find other animals and plants to feed on and take off. At least that is what I'm hoping for. I'm chalking it up to fear with my close calls. Fear or exhaustion. Only way to find out if we are safe is to figure out what kind of animal it is.

"Since it seems like we'll be here awhile, I want to see the room that the animal was trapped in," I announce.

"Are you crazy? You about passed out last time you were down there, now you want to go back?" The tone of his voice is disbelief, with a hint of 'This chick is *loca.*'

He may be right.

"I want to see where it was trapped. We need to try to figure out how long it was in there and maybe see if there were any signs of what it could be."

I don't wait for Hunter to answer and make my way back to the dungeon.

When I arrive at Grant's body, I take a breath to prepare myself. Undoubtedly a stupid move because I start coughing from breathing in the rancid air. Carefully, I walk around Grant's body towards the door.

There are unique carvings of different symbols on the door that light up, glowing a pale green color the closer I get to them. Hmm... I didn't think there was any electrical wiring in this place. It appears I was wrong.

I step away and notice the symbols fade. I move my flashlight around the room looking for sensors, trying to find what triggers the ancient-like symbols. I can't find anything but cold, hard stone walls. Walking towards the door again, I watch as the symbols grow brighter. Bright enough that I don't need my flashlight anymore. I turn it off, pocketing my phone.

"What the fuck!?"

I turn and see Hunter standing in the entry of the room, a bewildered look on his face. "How the hell did you do that? Where'd you find a light switch? I searched and didn't see anything." He walks around the body to come next to me. His hands run along the walls, searching, studying the floor and ceiling just as I had a moment ago.

"What are you talking about? They just turned on. I've already looked around, but I couldn't find the sensors. I've no idea how it works. I'm sure it would work the same for you. You do it."

We retreat a few steps, and it becomes pitch black again. Hunter flicks on his flashlight.

"Okay, now walk back to the door the way we came. It should turn on." I give him a light shove in the shoulder in the direction of the iron door.

He walks over and... nothing.

Huh?

I begin to walk over, and the symbols start to glow again, brighter with each step.

What the fuck, indeed? What is this?

For the first time, I study the symbols burned into the door.

Wait, I know this symbol. It resembles an hourglass laying on its side.

I take my jacket off, pull up my right sleeve to my Light rune tattoo on my forearm. It's the same on the four corners of the door. *Why would this be here?*

I can't read the other runes, but I know my grandmother has some journals at home that will help. I pull my jacket back on.

Hunter stutters, "Ww...what... How...did you do this?"

"Apparently, if the light was off and now it's on and I was the only one around, I would say I did it."

Oh boy, if daggers could be shot from eyes, I would die a thousand deaths right about now. I don't think that's the answer he was looking for. Shit, *I* don't even know how to explain this.

"Why would you have that same symbol tattooed on you? Seems to be too much of a coincidence if you ask me. Who are you really?" He's looking at me with a mix of disbelief and suspicion.

Valid question. Why would runes that match my family's heritage be here, and why do they illuminate only when I come near? None of this makes sense. How do I come into play in all of this?

"Stop looking at me like that. I don't have a freaking clue, and I'm just as confused as you." Regardless of the strange events, something brought me here, and it's a puzzle I know I need to figure out. "Let me take some pictures of these symbols to decipher once we get out of here."

He stands his ground.

"Can you please move?"

Why is he still staring at me?

I grasp his arm and move him off to the side. He moves over in a huff and I know the only way I was able to manhandle him is because he let me. Heavens know he's much bigger and stronger than I am.

Pulling my phone out, I sigh with relief when I see it has 75% battery life. After taking multiple pictures, some with flash, some without, I look around for any other signs. As much as I want to focus on the significance, I need to clear my head and start looking at the clues, so I can figure out what they all mean. Especially, what they mean to me since I'm tied to this somehow.

The symbols are only on the outside. What's on the inside are scratch marks that look much bigger than ones made by a cougar or wolf—it could very well be a grizzly, though. It's difficult to determine the animal based on the marks gouged into the door; they aren't normal marks with five claws—these only have three.

A strong energy surrounds me the moment I step into the small prison cell that held the animal. My body trembles with a euphoric high. A vibration pulses through my veins, and I'm transported back to being a child visiting some of our relatives in Ireland.

While exploring the magical land, I came across a stone circle. The stones were four times the size of me, all perfectly spaced from one another. I felt as if I was in a bubble, with everything echoing around me. A large rowan tree stood at the center. Its trunk twisted and angled up to the sky. It was huge, with the reddest of berries mixed in with the thin leaves.

The tree called to me. Beckoning me to come to it like a moth to a flame. As soon as I was close enough, I reached my hand out and placed it on the winding wood trunk.

I gasped with the surge of power that washed over me. It charged me like a battery, filling me with a bright white light. At that moment, I heard whispers from the tree and saw fairies dancing, reaching to touch my han—

I'm taken aback when my body is shaken.

"Anya. *Anya!* Hey, where'd you go?" Hunter's hand, the source of the shaking, is on my shoulder. His dark eyebrows are pinched together in concern.

Looking around me, I try to figure out where I am. "What do you mean?"

I'm confused and disorientated. I see scratch marks on the door. *Oh!*

Realization hits, and I finally remember we're in the dark cell of the castle's dungeon.

What happened?

"Your eyes glazed over; I called your name multiple times, but you didn't respond. You weren't even reacting to my flashlight in your eyes. You were in some sort of trance, murmuring something in another language."

"What are you talking about? I'm fine. I had a memory." A vivid memory I had no recollection of until now. I wave my hand like it was nothing, even when I know it means something.

Why did this room trigger it? Why has this flooded back in now?

The only thing that felt the same was the energy, but why?

What does it mean?

I hate all the questions with not a single answer to shed some light on what is going on.

I rub my hand on my neck and ask with a shaky voice, "Instead of staring at me, do you think you can start looking around for clues? All I know is that it has three claws and is the size of a grizzly." I try to pull Hunter's attention to the room rather than on me.

Taking in the rest of the room—other than it being dirty—I see no sign of fur or excrements. If something was stuck in here for so long that it was hungry enough to do what it did to Grant, there would be *something* here.

I glance at Hunter. "Outside of the scratches, there's no other sign that anything was in here."

He shakes his head. "You're right. If something was trapped in here, it would be doing everything it could to get out."

"Why is none of this adding up?" I ask, hoping he has an answer.

His hand goes up to his hair, and he blows out an exhausted breath. "I don't know. Nothing makes sense."

Knowing we're at a standstill, I offer, "I think we need to see if any of the other rooms have anything useful for our night here. You up for exploring?"

"Lead the way, milady." Hunter does an exaggerated bow before he moves his hands in a gesture to go ahead of him.

"Don't get smart with me, buddy," I warn, forcing back a smile as I walk past him and out of the room. I hear his low chuckle behind me.

We both walk around the rest of the dungeon to see if there are any other rooms. All we find is a storage and open areas with chains on the walls. A little creepy if you ask me. We head upstairs and start scouring the other rooms to see if there's anything we can use. Maybe we'll get lucky and find a landline. We still haven't found any sign of electricity, other than from the runes on the door.

We continue our search, finding jarred foods that must have been there for who knows how long—not something I want to try. But when it comes to honey, I'm all over it. Especially when I find a large jar of it in the same room as the food. And next to the golden nectar, I find a large wooden crate filled with candles.

Jackpot!

"I found some candles!" I yell to Hunter, having no idea where he wandered off to.

"Grab them all."

I jump and gasp. The jerk snuck up on me *again*!

"Grab them yourself, asshole!" I storm out of the last room in the east wing and hear him snickering behind me, clearly amused. When I get to the main room, I turn and see he actually listened to me and is holding the container of candles. I walk up to him, without speaking, and grab a few to set them up.

"I sure hope you have a lighter," I say, looking up at him expectantly.

Why am I not surprised when he gives me another cocky smirk and pulls a lighter out of his pocket?

"Ah-ha, a smoker. Well, don't be lighting up around me. I can't stand the smell." I scrunch my nose in disgust. A part of me is relieved I found a flaw in him, but the other part of me is somehow disappointed.

"I don't smoke; I like to be prepared. Lucky for you I was. Saving the day yet again." He winks then starts to light the candles.

"Wow, such a hero complex you have." I start fanning my face. "Oh my, how would I *ever* get through life without you by my side? My hero!" I exaggerate a sigh before I can't contain my laughter any longer.

I don't expect his deep laugh to join me in my entertainment.

Our eyes connect, seeing each other for the first time in the candlelight. We stop; tension fills the air, causing my palms to sweat and my heartrate to quicken.

Dark mysterious eyes bore down on me with intensity, pulling my soul into the depth of his gaze. Hunter's chiseled jawline flexes under his perfectly trimmed, dark beard.

Why couldn't he be ugly? Why must Karma be so cruel?

The man who not only infuriates me also has to be the epitome of tall, dark, and handsome. This man is built like a linebacker.

While looking at him—all of him—in the light now, I realize there's something bothering me about him. He was already familiar when I was up against him, but seeing him without the veil of darkness between us, I have a sense that I really do know him from somewhere. I can't place it or put it into words.

"Do I know you from somewhere?" I can't help but ask.

He has to be feeling it too, with the amount of focus he has on me. "I thought maybe...but no. You don't." He seems despondent.

The energy is too intense and overwhelming; I have no choice but to shift my eyes away and shake off the silly notion that I know him. We would recognize it if we knew each other. He takes this time to set up more candles in our area.

Tilting my head I ask, "Where are you from?"

"Well, when a man and a woman have sex—"

I slap my hand over his mouth in a rush before yanking it back surprised by my impulsive actions.

"Oh my God, *never mind*."

He smirks. "Shandaken. I assume you know the place?"

"Huh." That must be it. "Maybe that's why you look familiar. I must have seen you in passing."

With no use trying to figure out Hunter or this connection, I force my mind to our current issue—being stuck here for the night. Candles won't provide much heat for us, we need to find more supplies that can hold us over until morning.

I risk a glance in his direction, skimming over his broad, thick chest before meeting his mysterious eyes again. "So far the dungeon and east wing on this level are done. How much did you check out before I got here?"

Hunter pauses, as though he is about to say something but decides against it and answers my question instead. "Not much, only the west wing. That's how I knew about the kitchen. The dungeon was the only place I went in the east; I stopped searching when I found Grant. The only sets of stairs are the ones we passed earlier, and I haven't gone upstairs yet."

"Except for upstairs in the attic, of course—you were there when I pulled in." I side-eye him and wonder why he left that part out.

Is he hiding something from me?

"What are you talking about? As of right now, I haven't gone anywhere you haven't." His brows furrow, causing a deep crease.

Being able to finally look him in the eyes helps me read him better. His eyes are a warm, milk chocolate brown—ones I am struggling not to get lost in. His posture is at attention; solid, muscular shoulders are pulled back, alert from my words. There are no signs of lying, like fidgeting, looking away, or masking his facial expressions. I study him for a couple more seconds before determining there is honesty in his response.

Since he's telling the truth...

"Oh, shit," I mutter to myself. My heart drops to the floor.

Hunter, of course, doesn't miss it. "What?" he draws out, clearly not ready to hear what I have to say next.

"We aren't alone." I'm kicking myself for not asking this sooner.

But how could I have known it wasn't him?

All this time we've been here, and there's someone or some*thing* else in the castle with us. I replay the image I saw while sitting in my car. I could have sworn it was a person.

Yes, it definitely was a person, or something that walks upright like one.

"What do you mean we aren't alone?" He straightens his back; seriousness washes over him, and his eyes dart around the room, assessing it for threats.

"When I pulled up, I was checking out the building. I didn't see any lights except a candle in what I thought was the attic. I saw a shadow cross in front of the light. After you grabbed me and pulled me in, I figured it was you. I thought you were pretty quick to come down that fast but didn't think twice about it. If it wasn't you... That means someone else is here."

Chapter Seven

OTHALA

(LEGACY)

My body shakes, the trembling wracking me with every shallow intake of air I breathe.

We aren't alone.

Hunter sees me shivering and pulls off his jacket. "Here." He goes to toss it over my shoulders, but I throw up my hand to stop him.

"I'm good, it isn't the cold."

I'm met with a blank stare.

"I'm fine, really. It's more me being nervous about what we're gonna find. I would rather stay here while you ensure our safety." I purse my lips. *Hmm...that's not a bad idea.* "You know what? On second thought, I think I *will* stay in the hall and wait for you."

"Yeah, that's not happening. There's no way I'm leaving you alone." He throws his jacket back on, and I get a slight hint of his cologne. The citrus and spice isn't a fragrance that would distract me, but the undertone of lavender and his natural pheromones causes havoc on my insides and warms me. The intoxicating scent briefly takes my mind off all the possibilities of who—or what—we will encounter next.

Looking up, I give him a sweet and endearing smile. "I have complete confidence that you can protect me better if I'm not with you. Now, go play hero and make sure no one is here with us." I wave my hand to shoo him off.

Take the bait...

"Nice try," Hunter says, amused by my attempt.

Shit. My shoulders slump in defeat. *Eh, it was worth a shot.*

"Think you can be quiet and stay behind me at all times?" He raises his left eyebrow offering me a questioning stare. "You'll be safer with me."

"If I say no, do I get to stay here?" I plead.

He sighs. "You've got nothing to worry about, Anya. I don't think there's anyone else in the castle, especially someone who's going to try to hurt us. But in the event there is, I'll do everything I can to protect you." His warm eyes are sincere in the glow of the candles.

I believe him, but I still don't want to go. "Well, I guess I only have to be able to run faster than you if something attacks, right? Lead the way." I exhale dramatically and hold my hand out for him to go first.

He forces a laugh. "You have such faith in me."

"Says the man I just met." I raise my eyebrow at him in a challenge.

"You're really becoming a pain in my ass."

My only response is a shrug. It's not like I disagree with him.

"Don't forget—I still have my gun."

I harrumph. With the current state Grant's in, I'm not sure how much good a gun would have done him if he'd had one.

"I hope your gun is big enough to get the job done if needed," I mumble.

"Oh, I *guarantee* it's big enough and *always* gets the job done." He winks and grabs my hand, pulling me behind him towards the hallway.

Well, lookie there, he does understand mumble after all.

Before we leave the hall, I pull out of his grasp to reach down and grab my dagger out of my boot—thankful that I actually remembered it this time.

Hunter's eyes widen, and he's slack jawed. His entire focus is on the dagger in my hand. "What the hell? You've had that thing on you this whole time?" His voice raises in disbelief. "Who walks around carrying a dagger in their boot?"

"As opposed to carrying one in a waistband? This is more discrete and comfortable."

"It's the fact that you're carrying a sharp weapon and acting like it's a normal thing for you."

I stare, waiting for him to continue. This *is* a normal thing for me.

His eyes go wide in realization. "You carry that around on a day-to-day basis? Are you kidding me? Who *are* you?"

"Seriously?" My hand goes to my hip. "This is coming from the guy with the gun? Don't go around judging—that seems to be all you've been doing tonight. This is a family heirloom I always carry around for protection."

He runs his hand through his hair while looking up at the ceiling, then takes a deep breath, and lowers his gaze back to me.

"Well, I appreciate you not pulling that on me earlier." He frowns, his voice tense as if the fact I had a hidden weapon bothers him.

I admit it probably makes me look suspicious. "I may have pulled it on you had I actually remembered it was there to begin with. Again,"—I hold up my hand—"no judging. I've never been in this type of situation before."

He tips his head to the side, studying me. Probably contemplating my sanity right now. Lord knows I'm contemplating it myself.

I shift on my feet, unsettled by his stare. Does he have to look at me with such intensity?

Forget this, I'm not backing down.

I channel my inner Heather and stand up straighter, maintaining eye contact. There is no way I'll cower under his gaze. I may be scared shitless, but I won't give him ammunition to think any less of me. He already thinks I'm a damsel in distress.

Hunter turns around with a flash of a smirk. "I just hope you use that for good more than evil."

I underestimated the size of this place. We spent the last thirty minutes checking out the rooms on the second floor. With each door we opened, I've been on edge and paranoid of discovering whomever is here with us. But every room was the same—only blank stone walls and floors. Undisturbed for years, judging by the layers of dust and dirt, and the stale musty air in them. We haven't found anything suspicious or useful, not a single shred of evidence that someone else has been here. Which unnerves me more.

"Hunter, look at this." I run my hand over an ancient wooden chest I found up against the wall in the current room we are checking out.

The chest has a couple chips in the corners but is in great condition overall. The top has a similar iron pattern as the doors—a sun in the middle of the top—but unlike the doors, one of the sun rays comes down over the front into a hinge where a lock would seal the chest. On the front, there's a carved dragon-like creature that winds around in a double knotted figure eight to come back and grasp its tail between its teeth. The intricate details amaze me with their ability to wind around the body without running into themselves.

"See if it has anything useful," Hunter says from his guard post by the door.

His large body has been tense during our search; not once has he let his guard down. I'm glad he is taking things seriously and believed me when I told him I saw someone.

Slipping my dagger into my boot, I kneel down and open the chest to find wool blankets and a rolled-up rug. I hold up the pile of blankets, shining my light on them to inspect further. I'm not sure what kind of pests have been living in these empty walls all these years. I'm not ready to spend the night itching and scratching myself because we become infested with fleas. When I discover the blankets are relatively clean, I look over to Hunter for confirmation.

"Those will come in handy tonight. Grab 'em," he says quietly.

I set them outside the door. We aren't done with our search, but I don't want to have to carry the blankets everywhere or leave them somewhere I'll forget. Hunter patiently waits for me to grab my dagger and give him a silent nod, letting him know I'm ready.

We finally arrive at the last door and, so far, we haven't found the staircase to the attic. This has to be the way to get up there. Hunter gets ready with his gun, and I'm on full alert with my dagger tight in my grasp.

We open the door, and my shoulders slump in defeat. Another empty room—

"Damn it! I know there's another level." A growl of frustration slips from my throat, and I lay my forehead on the cold stone wall.

Why can't I catch a break? I know I'm not imagining things.

"Let's head back down." Hunter turns.

A wisp of hair tickles my nose when a chilling draft blows in my face, sending goosebumps down my spine.

"Wait."

What the heck?

I lift my fingers and trace along the surface of the cracks until I feel the breeze again, as if the castle is exhaling a breath.

Trailing down the crevice, it continues down, one block below the next. I apply more pressure and with a creaking sound, the stones shift inwards. Depressing in farther, a whole section of stones gives way.

No way! There's a hidden doorway. *Why would someone hide the access to the attic?*

"Way to go, Sherlock," Hunter says, impressed.

I roll my eyes and focus on the narrow stone door—three feet by six feet will be a tight fit for Hunter. I'll make him fit, even if I need to shove him through.

I take a step towards the open door but a hand lands on my middle. I inhale a sharp breath. Surprising warmth radiates through me and before he pulls away—butterflies fill my stomach.

"Whoa, back up sweetheart. There's no way you are going in first. Let me check it out."

"Are you sure you'll fit?" I raise an eyebrow.

"It may be tight, but I always fit."

Heat floods my cheeks. *Keep your mind on the task, Anya.*

As Hunter holds his flashlight above his gun, it reminds me of a cop show when they enter a dark building in search of a suspect.

Does he have a background in law-enforcement?

My leg bounces. *This is the moment we get answers...or the slight chance we get killed.* A comforting heat radiates from the marble of the dagger when my grip tightens. It's like a surge of electricity—spreading through my body—until it fills every last inch.

The new sensation calms my nerves and sends a strong wave of confidence and power over me.

I'm ready.

Hunter ducks when he steps through.

His light bounces off the walls, illuminating the narrow, steep steps which lack railings. Hunter's ability to move with ease and control amazes me since his feet don't even fit on the step. Meanwhile, I'm hugging the cold wall to keep from tumbling down—landing directly on my knife.

A closed wooden door with an iron handle meets us at the top of the stairs. Peeking around Hunter, I see no locks, only the detail of Celtic trinity knots in each corner with an interwoven pattern connecting them.

The light under the door has me tightening my grasp on my dagger.

"Keep quiet and stay behind me at all times, got it?"

I glance up and am met with authority in Hunter's eyes. I nod and move my foot down a step, readying myself.

My body stiffens as he turns back and pushes the door open.

I release my breath. Despite the age of this castle, the door is remarkably quiet. A creaking door defeats the element of surprise.

Hunter moves into the room and silence fills the air. Moments later he returns to the doorway to motion me in.

My shoulders slump. I was hoping someone would be here to explain what's going on. That would have been too easy. Based on the way my night is going, easy has run and hidden, the chicken-shit that it is.

With our backs against the wall, we take in the room around us. A few large candles are sitting on an old wooden stand near the opposite wall. The room is bare and there's nothing here to help us. I can tell there hasn't been anyone here for a while—the floor is undisturbed. You can't fake covering up footprints with years and years of dust and dirt. It isn't possible. Even our boot prints are noticeable.

My head is reeling; I know what I saw, and none of this adds up. We walk around the room looking for anything that would give us any telltale signs as to who was here. Of course, my walking is more along the lines of pacing.

"Hunter, I swear I saw someone up here. How do you explain those?" I wave my hand towards the flickering candles and make eye contact with him.

My bottom lip throbs as I nibble it. His body isn't giving me any sign of how he feels about all of this. The added worry is making the tension headache that's been creeping up on me worse, and my toes are numb from this cold castle. I just want this night to be over.

Hunter has already turned off and pocketed his flashlight. He runs a hand through his hair while his eyes dart around the room with determination. "I don't know, Anya. I really don't. I'm not sure about anything right now," he grates out through his clenched jaw.

I continue to pace the room.

"Anya, stop!"

I freeze. Goosebumps spread over my skin, and my heart falls to the pit of my stomach.

"What? What is it?" Inch by inch, I move my eyes around me, expecting a snake or a large poisonous spider to be near me, ready to strike. "Hunter, *what is it?*" Becoming a little more courageous, I check out my surroundings, while I continue to keep everything from my neck down immobilized in case I am in danger.

Wouldn't that be the kicker—escaping a large wild animal to meet my fate with an insect or reptile.

Hunter's eyes are wide and focused on an area near my legs. I follow his gaze.

"Oh." The tension and the breath I was holding release.

Under the stand holding the candles, there's another light rune burned onto the stone. No one would've seen it if it didn't start glowing like the door in the dungeon. I kneel down on the floor, running my hand over the symbol.

What could be hot enough to burn a half inch into stone?

The glowing markings are warm to the touch—a drastic contrast to the cold, smooth stone around them. I apply more pressure. A stone pops out of the wall, causing me to fall backwards.

"Whoa." Similar to the attic staircase, the stone hides another secret to this place. I pull the stone out the rest of the way, and Hunter sidles up next to me with his flashlight and his gun holstered.

"What is up with you and these symbols?" he says in amazement.

My body relaxes even more. *Who knew I was wound up so tight? Okay, yes I knew. But who would blame me?*

I bring my attention back to the heavy stone in my hands. Like the iron door, there's no electricity powering this.

"I think I see something." Hunter pulls my attention to the opening.

"Really? Let me look." Without waiting for Hunter's response, I'm already reaching my hand into the crevice. A quick image of an Indiana Jones scene flashes in my head before I shake it.

"Just be careful," Hunter grumbles. He's as nervous as I am and it isn't even his hand he's sacrificing.

Moving my hand in slowly, I can make out a corner of something soft, yet stiff. Leather, maybe? I continue to trace around the object; it's thick with layers of thin, uneven material beneath the top cover. Some are cloth-like while others are stiffer, similar to parchment. On one side, there's a twine-like binding. *It's a book!* My heartbeat races, and it's no longer from fear but excitement. I pull it out and set it on the floor, then reach back in the hole.

Nothing.

The book has to be important to be hidden here—maybe it will give us some information about this place. I bring my attention back to the thick, leather-bound material laying on the floor before me.

"Wha—" My hand shoots to my mouth to stifle my gasp. The very aged and dusty cover contains *my* three runes across the top, branded into animal hide.

This once belonged to my ancestors, but why is it here?

Hunter attempts to grab it from my hands, and I jerk it back.

"*No.*" I yank it to my chest, protectively.

Shit. I sound like Gollum from *Lord of the Rings,* with how I'm reacting.

"I'm sorry. These markings represent my mother's side of the family."

When his mouth parts as though to speak, I hold up one of my hands.

"Before you ask... I don't know why or how it came to be here, but it *must* be something important." I hope my facial expression isn't portraying the complete and utter chaos I feel inside; I can't think straight outside of keeping the book safe.

"I wasn't going to ask. But you have to admit it's highly coincidental. You seem to be tied to this place for some reason."

"But why? I've never been here, let alone even knew this place existed." Heaviness fills my chest. *He can't think I have something to do with all of this, can he?*

"I don't know what to think anymore, but all logic has officially been thrown out the window." He sighs, looking resigned. "Let's look around to see if there are any other clues, then we can head back downstairs and check out your book."

"Okay, but I'm holding onto it," I add, pulling it closer to my chest with both arms while my right hand is still holding my dagger.

"Uh, Anya?" Hunter's eyes are big again.

Oh, what now?

"Yeah?" I raise my eyebrow and bite my lip, anticipating what he has to say won't be good.

"Did you know that your dagger glows like those symbols?" He points to my hand.

"What?" I look down, and he's right; it's indeed glowing.

Holy crap!

I move the dagger away from the book, and the light fades. I bring it back to the book, and it lights up again.

"It's never done this before; it's reacting to the book. I never knew it *could* do this. What does it mean?"

Hunter shakes his head. He's at a loss for words.

I sheath my blade and stand up from the cold, hard floor, surprised that my joints aren't creaking and in pain from the chill in my bones. Maybe the adrenaline has warmed me.

Still hugging the book to my chest, I continue to walk around the room.

I have to be sure we haven't missed anything, so I push on every surface—apart from the ceiling, of course, since Hunter is the only one who can reach it. He has no problem obliging and pushes on the stones above us. We don't find any additional symbols.

We come to the only conclusion we can—something, or some-one, drew me to this room. And it had to be to locate this book.

The steep steps are harder to descend. We go slowly so we don't fall, and I use one hand on the wall to steady me. We continue through the rest of the halls, stopping shortly for Hunter to pick up the pile of blankets, before we make our way to the stairs leading to the main level.

I continue to clutch the book; I don't want it to leave my side. Once we arrive back in the main room—where our candles are still burning and my jar of honey is sitting—my stomach rumbles, reminding me I never ate dinner.

Hunter laughs, "Either the animal is back, or you're hungry. I can't tell since they sound the same."

"Oh, shut it!" I give him a playful shove.

To think a couple hours ago I thought this man was going to kill me, and now look at us. It's like an old friendship. Something familiar tickles the back of my brain. *Strange.* I try to focus on what it is, but I'm met with a black wall. *Oh, well.*

"I don't know about you, but I'm going to try that honey. I'm starving, and I need to keep my blood sugar up." I lick my lips and hear a quiet groan.

I gape at Hunter staring at my lips. Thank goodness it's dark in here, or he'd be making fun of my blushing. Reaching for the honey, I try and fail miserably when I use one hand to open the lid. There has to be another way I can get this open.

"You weren't kidding when you said you weren't letting that thing go, were you? Here, let me help." He muscles the lid open for me.

Yeah, I'm pretty sure I still had no chance even if I was two-handed.

"Thank y—" The sweet aroma hits me, making me forget what I was saying. Unwilling to show my appreciation for Hunter's strength, I take the jar and hold it up to the light. There are no particles or mold; the thick amber color is clear and clean.

My lips go to the edge of the glass and sip the sweet nectar. A moan escapes me, and my eyes close in ecstasy. *Oh my god, this is amazing!* This almost makes this night worth it... Well, maybe not. Let's not go overboard.

I open my eyes and smile in appreciation. "Hunter, you need to try this!"

Heat radiates off him as he stares at the honey, wary of its contents.

"We're not sure how old that stuff is. I think I can wait it out." His stare darts from the jar to my lips.

"Newsflash... With proper storage, honey can last thousands of years due to the natural preservatives and helpful bacteria. This, my good sir, is still perfect but...your loss. More for me." I moan again as I take another drink.

Keeping my eyes on him, his intense gaze is focused on my lips.

"Sure you don't want a taste?" I wiggle my eyebrows at him.

His eyes get darker as he says, "You know I want a taste."

Whew, did it get warm in here?

I shove the jar at him and walk over to the pile of blankets to busy myself making two makeshift mattresses—a task which proves to be a challenge one-handed. I refuse to put the book down. It's the one thing I have control over tonight and I crave the comfort it brings me.

Hunter's laughter echoes off the walls behind me.

You know, I better space these out more—a good 200 feet apart should do the trick. His bed is now on one side of the large room and mine on the other. Perfectly appropriate distance for two responsible adults.

I turn around to catch Hunter sniffing the jar, his brows furrowed, and a frown pulls at his lips. He really is concerned about tasting it. He has to have worked up an appetite after all the excitement today.

"Stop being a baby and take a sip already. You act like such a badass, yet you're scared of a little honey?" I give a dramatic sigh. "There goes your macho hero complex. At least we found your kryptonite—old honey."

His eyes are set in irritation and annoyance. Laughter bubbles out of me before I can hold it back. Whether it's the sugar high or the fact that I'm enjoying his company, happiness flows through me for the first time this evening. He makes me smile. It's a sliver of light in this darkness.

I check the time. *Midnight already?* I guess it shouldn't surprise me with everything we've done tonight. The best part of our search was finding an old-fashioned latrine. More like a hole in the ground, with a wooden box built around it. But it's something. We knew it would have to do since going outside in the woods was *not* an option tonight.

I take care of my needs, have more honey, choke down some mineral water, and I'm ready to crash.

With an exhausted sigh, I plop my butt on the wooden bench, staring at the journal lit by candlelight. There are so many coincidences and I'm struggling to wrap my head around them all. This book may be what we need to figure out how my ancestors and I are tied to this property.

Staring at the lines of ink on the pages, I blink. Then blink again.

Okay, my eyes must be fatigued because the words on the pages are indecipherable.

"Hunter?" I look up from the journal to find him.

He lifts his eyes to mine. "Yeah?" Shaking out a blanket, he folds it back up and picks up the next one from the pile.

"Can you do me a favor and tell me what you see?" I hold out the journal to him.

"Are you sure?" His eyes drop to my boot where my dagger rests as he makes his way over to me. "Promise you won't cut me if I touch it?"

Rolling my eyes, I grumble. "Yes, unless you damage it. Then all agreements are off."

He eyes me warily before taking the journal into his hands and studying it. "Hmm..." Hunter flips a page, then another.

I bite my lip, then ask. "So, what does it say?"

"I'm sure it says a lot. What exactly, though, I haven't the slightest clue. It's not English."

So it's not just me. I'm farther away from figuring out the mysteries than I was before. I was hoping the journal would hold all the answers.

Why do I feel it's so important to know?

This wasn't the reason for me coming here. I was supposed to obtain information on the Bordeauxes and their shady dealings. Now, I'm in the middle of a complete and utter clusterfuck. Grant's mauled body is downstairs, I'm somehow connected to the castle, and I have more questions than answers.

That's not even talking about the animal trying to get in to eat us.

Hunter hands me back the journal with a shrug. "Well, it was worth a try."

This night should have turned out way differently, but I concede and stifle a yawn behind my hand.

He gives my shoulder a squeeze. "Hey, let's try to get some rest. Both doors are secured; nothing's coming in tonight. Get some sleep—we need to be alert in the morning. I plan to be up at sunrise to see if we can make it out to our vehicles." He blows out a couple candles, leaving two small ones burning in case we need to get up while it's still dark out.

"Okay. Night, Hunter. Thanks for helping me tonight."

"Not a problem. Night." He stands in front of me, waiting for me to make the first move.

Do I give him a hug? Pat him on the shoulder? I'm bad at being around guys. Oh, forget it.

I turn around, without acknowledging Hunter further, and walk to my makeshift bed. As soon as the book is secured under the blanket I plan to use as my pillow, I lay down with my back against the wall. The initial cold shocks me, causing me to suck in a gasp.

"You okay all the way over there?" Being the ass that he is, Hunter acts as though he is a mile away.

"Yup, all good!" I put a little space between the wall and my back—there is no reason to increase my chance of catching cold. Snuggling under my blanket, I realize it's not as warm as I thought it would be. The cold tries to seep into my bones again. Maybe being next to the wall wasn't such a bright idea after all. I sit up and look around.

"What's going on, Anya?" Hunter asks, startling me.

"Oh, nothing. Just looking to see if there is a fireplace in this room, but I guess not. Never mind. I'm all good. Sorry to bother you."

"We can move you into one of the rooms upstairs and start a fire if you want."

"I have no desire to be upstairs, especially after the attic inci-dent." I shiver, thinking of being up there by myself. It gives me the heebie jeebies.

"You know...you can come over here. Body heat is a great way to keep warm," Hunter says with a suggestive smirk in his voice. "I swear I won't touch you."

"Yes, because that is how body heat works...by not touching."

"Okay, smart-ass. You know I mean touching inappropriately."

I contemplate it for a bit but shake my head. "Yeah, no. I'm good, but thanks for the offer."

"Suit yourself." His dark shadow becomes level with the floor.

I follow suit by laying down, but instead of trying to close my eyes, I lay on my back and stare at the moonlight shining through the window slits. My mind can't stop thinking about tonight and all the events leading up to it. I start practicing deep breaths and continue to look at the ceiling for what feels like forever, until finally my eyes drift closed and my mind turns off from exhaustion.

Chapter Eight

KENAZ

(TORCH PASSED)

"Anya, darling... Anya," my grandmother's voice calls out.

"Not another dream. I just want to sleep. Why won't anyone let me sleep?" I whine. Cold, sore, and exhausted, I curl my body into a tighter ball and drift off again.

"Wake up, Anya."

Can I cry? I really want to cry. The voices in my head won't shut up.

"Anya!"

With my eyes wide, I bolt upright. My heart is pounding against my ribcage, hard and fast. I blink a few times to clear my vision because I swear I saw my grandmother hovering over me. Rubbing my eyes, I try to focus.

Nope, she's still there, looking the same as when I saw her last—seven years ago.

Well, maybe not completely the same; she's translucent, and her skin is younger and aglow. She's standing in front of me with her grey-streaked, chestnut hair flowing around her wool cardigan. Her plaid skirt skims the top of her levitating feet.

Out of all my dreams of her, this is the most intense and surreal.

What if I reach out and touch her?

The temptation is there, but I'm losing a battle with my heavy eyelids and slowing pulse. It wouldn't be the first time I dreamt I was so tired that I fell asleep.

My heartbeat has found its normal cadence, and I beg, "Grandmother, please let me sleep for once."

I drift down and fall back asleep.

"Anya Rowa O'Clery, get your arse up right now!"

Her demanding voice has me wide awake.

When Grandmother uses your full name, you don't question—you immediately obey. Even in a dream, I don't risk the consequences.

"Okay, okay. I'm up."

The moonlight shines into the room and onto my bed of blankets.

"Wait, what are you doing in the castle? You've always been in the woods in my dreams."

Has the stress of the night caused me to alter my repetitive dream?

"My light, you aren't dreaming. I don't have much time, but you must be quiet so you don't wake the lad. He may not take well to seeing me here." She nods her head to the dark lump across the room.

"What do you mean?" I strain my eyes. Hunter is on his mat—out cold.

How can he be here with my grandmother?

"Anya, don't be dense. We have talked about what happens to souls after they pass into the spirit world. We can come visit our loved ones occasionally, but only for a short time. The veil is easier to cross over this time of year."

A gasp slips out of my throat. "Grandmother? You're really here?"

"Yes, I am really here... but not for long."

Tightness closes over my lungs. "Grandmother, you have no idea how much I've missed you." The need to touch her, to feel her warmth again, is overwhelming.

As soon as I make contact, an ice-cold sensation runs through me. I jerk my shaky hand back as though I've been burned, rubbing away the lingering chill. I ask, "Why *are* you here?"

"I have led you here because *you* are the key to stopping the wendigo."

This doesn't make sense. What led me here was the mee—

"Wait, what?" My eyebrows raise as my mouth drops open. "*You* sent me the invitation?"

Grandmother chuckles. "Yes, my light. That was all my doing."

"Why would you bring me here? You could have come to visit me at home anytime. Why here?"

"Remember where you come from. This is the crossroads I've been telling you about. You need to make your decision. It will not be easy, but you need to choose the right path."

The dreams...they showed me both paths, and each was equally scary. I thought they were metaphors. I came here with the hope of choosing the right path, the one that would bring justice to those families.

I frown at that, and my temper rises with the memory of the night.

"Why would you give me false hope and drag me here? I could have been killed. Did you not see my dead boss downstairs?" At this point, I'm whisper-shouting and my body is trembling.

I take a deep breath and attempt to compose myself, but my breath catches. "You said a wendigo? Wasn't that the hideous Native American beast you told us horror stories about when I was little?" My hands are slick with sweat, along with a trickle of moisture forming between my shoulder blades.

"Keep your voice down," she scolds me. "Here, come with me."

She draws me to the opening of the dungeon.

I release a groan. I don't want to have to go back down there, *again*.

"Stop your grumbling, I haven't been gone long enough for you to forget your manners, lass."

Her condescending tone has me lowering my head.

"Sorry, Grandmother, I meant no disrespect."

She huffs. Her glow allows us to see our way as she takes me beyond the corpse, to the door.

I cringe when I step through the blood. This isn't something a person can become used to. At least, it's not something *I* could get used to.

"Do you see how the symbols shine when you are near? This is from the power in your blood. Now, touch the rune."

I'm in no hurry to find out what's going to happen next as I hover my hand over the door.

My grandmother notices my hesitation. "It's okay, go on."

Her calm composure, soft smile, and kind eyes reassure me.

I cautiously touch the tips of my fingers to the *light* rune. It feels warm like the one upstairs which reminds me...

"Did you lead me to the attic to find the book?"

She smiles.

A sigh of relief exits my lungs.

Oh, thank goodness it was her in the window.

It's still weird to think my deceased grandmother guided me to find the journal, but why? What's the purpose when I can't even read it? I have so many questions.

"Now, what do you feel? Close your eyes if you need to. Remember how I taught you to focus on the energy. See it in your mind," she coaches.

I push my thoughts back, for now. When I close my eyes, a yellowish-green color catches me off guard. I allow all my senses to become in-tune with the energy, opening up my third eye—as my grandmother always called it. Behind my closed lids, the visual of my body appears as though I'm watching with eyes wide open. The swirls of color wrap around my fingers, creep up my arm, and continue to spiral around my body.

"Yes! You see it, don't you? Tell me what you see." There is excitement in her voice.

"The colors are vibrant, and my body is consuming the warmth like my dagger did earlier. The longer I hold my hand here, the more it floods my body." I open my eyes and I'm greeted with my grandmother's wide smile.

"Yes, good, *good*!" She claps her hands together. "I have always called you 'my light' because you have a powerful light inside you. One that can fight *and* defeat darkness. Fear will dull your shine, you must be confident and strong. These symbols you see were to keep the darkness locked *inside* this room. It held for many centuries until *this* greedy man released it." Her face scrunches up as she glares at Grant's body.

My jaw drops. Disgust is *not* an emotion I've seen her portray before. My grandmother has never acted ill toward anyone, so this other side of her is new.

She continues, "Read the journal of our ancestors, it holds the secrets you need."

"I tried, I can't."

"My light, look again. You have the key inside you. *You* are the key. In daylight, you will have a clearer mind and you will see."

Why does that not bring me hope?

Rubbing a hand over my face, I ask, "Why *us*?"

"It is *our* duty as the remaining bloodline of the Ó Bradáin clan to keep the townspeople safe. This is why I needed you to move here to stand guard. I prayed that this evil would never be released, especially on your watch, but now that it has, you need to bind it back into this room or do what our ancestors before us failed to do—kill it. The runes you have on your body will protect you. Be careful, though; you can still be harmed. Learn to use the runes because they will strengthen your power."

If I wasn't already convinced this was real, I'd be blowing this off as a dream.

This is insane!

Come to think of it, the strange ritual and tattoos are now starting to make complete sense.

"Why didn't you teach me this when I was younger? You choose *now* to completely blindside me? How the hell am I going to handle this, especially alone? I don't know what to do." The walls are closing in on me, and I'm getting light-headed.

"I don't have much time left. Just know, everything I taught you when you were younger was my way of preparing you the best I could." She points to the ceiling. "You need the lad upstairs; he has been brought back into your life to help you on your journey. He grounds you, calms you, and he has power from his own Celtic bloodline that will help. Together you are stronger."

What?

I shake my head and pace. This is all too much for me to handle. I move away from the door and the runes begin to dim. I need to think and can't do it hovering over a dead, rotting corpse and a pool of blood. Once I'm far enough away, I pace.

Everything I was taught as a child—the old stories and tales—were imaginary. The Irish are known for their magical folklore, but how can any of this be real?

"Grandmother, there's a lot I don't remember from when I was younger, like those other symbols. I don't think I can do this. I don't know *how* to do this."

Overwhelming thoughts swirl around in my head, causing me to struggle to focus.

"It is ultimately your choice which path to take, but you *can* do this. Start with the journal, then use my books at home. You will find what you need."

My anxiety subsides a fraction, allowing me to realize a major detail.

"How do we leave the castle without being attacked?" I twist my hands in front of me, waiting for a response.

"The beast can't go out during daylight and only hunts when it is dark. But do *not* waste time, deary. Every second you waste, the chances of another person being killed will grow." She starts to fade.

"Wait! Don't leave me, I need you!" My heartbeat floods my ears, and my hands begin to tingle while the room spins.

"You know I must leave. I have to save up strength to come back when you need it most. Don't forget you are never alone—I am always with you. You must promise you will not leave the lad's side. It can mean death to one or both of you. I have faith that you will make the right decision on which path to take. I love you, my light. You are stronger than you know."

She's gone, and I'm met with pitch black.

Well, thanks there, Grams. That's a nice heads-up notice that you're taking your light with you.

I can't even see my hand directly in front of my face. I'm alone, in the dungeon, with a dead body. My rapid heart-rate is drowning out all other sounds around me, so I force myself to slow my pulse. Through the silence, I sense another entity with me. One that wasn't here before.

Fumbling around my back pocket, I pull out my phone, press the home screen, and turn on the light. As I turn around, I scream and drop my phone.

With the flashlight facedown.

And I'm enveloped in blackness again.

Arms reach out to grab me, and I scream again, my voice echoing off the walls.

"Hey, it's okay. It's just me. Calm down." A deep, warm voice surrounds me.

Oh, thank God, it's Hunter.

I'm bent over, with one hand on my chest while the other is resting my weight on my leg. I try to catch my breath, which isn't easy with the rancid, moist air down here.

"Fuck, Hunter! You have *got* to stop sneaking up on me." I would slap him in the chest but without light and with my luck, I would aim too high or too low.

"What the hell was that?" He sounds shocked.

What the hell was what? He couldn't have seen my grandmother. Right?

"What do you think that was? It was a scream—that's what happens when you scare the shit out of someone...*again*. I'm going back to bed," I huff.

The search for my phone is quick, but a dim illumination grabs my attention.

Hunter grasped my arm right when I was reaching down and now pulls me up against him.

How the heck did he even know where I was?

The heat radiating off his chest is doing weird things to my body, and it pisses me off further. I try to ignore the flutters and tingles coursing through my veins.

"Can I please at least grab my phone so we can continue this conversation with a little light?" My voice comes out a little breathless, despite my anger.

He reaches down, picks up my phone, and wipes it on his pants before handing it back to me.

"Do you care to explain now?" Hunter's voice is low but gruff.

"So, sometimes, when one person is startled, it causes a reflex from the fear and releases a loud and sometimes terrifying cry. Why does the body do it? No one may ever know. To scare away a predator maybe?" I shrug.

"I know what a scream is, smart-ass. I'm asking about what happened *prior* to the scream. Who were you talking to, or should I say...*what* were you talking to? It looked and sounded like an older lady. Yet, she wasn't all there. Where did she come from, and where the hell did she go? Is she the one sneaking around?" Hunter is out of breath and rubbing the back of his neck.

It's nice to not be alone and have someone else freaked out with me. The problem now is, how am I going to explain this to him so that he may believe me and not think *I'm* the crazy one? *He did hint that she wasn't normal.*

Well...with the events tonight, it may not be too hard to believe after all.

"Good news. I got us some answers about what is going on, *but...* I think we should go upstairs to discuss it."

He stands solid as a rock, not budging an inch.

"Please? I'll explain everything I know if we can just go back to the hall."

He sighs and turns around to head back upstairs.

I follow Hunter back into the main room; he doesn't give me a chance to walk fully in before he turns on me, anger pouring from his body.

"Do you know how scared I was to wake up and find you missing? I had *no* clue where you went. I searched the facilities and the kitchen, and when I was about to go upstairs—thinking maybe you caved and decided to sleep near a fireplace—I felt an insane need to check the dungeon. As relieved as I am that you are okay and didn't end up like your boss, it didn't prepare me for what I saw. Care to explain?" He arches one of his eyebrows at me and crosses his arms over his chest.

Mmm... I didn't realize how broad his chest was. His shoulder and arm muscles look like they want to bust out of his shirt. I lick my lips. Because they were dry, of course.

A deep clearing of a throat brings my eyes back to his.

Shit. Eyes up, Anya. Focus.

When our gazes meet, I realize the steam that was previously spewing from his ears is gone. His anger has dissipated, and it's replaced with amusement.

He cared about my safety. Maybe he's like this with everyone—due to his hero complex—but I can't resist the way it comforts me. His concern is sweet.

'Do you know how scared I was to wake up and find you missing?'

Recalling the hurt in his voice, I grimace and guilt settles in. "I'm sorry, Hunter. I didn't mean to worry you. I did *not* plan this, and I sure as shit didn't want to go back into the dungeon, but I had to."

"What do you mean you *had* to go? Did that woman drag you down there? Did she do that to Grant?"

My hand goes to my hip. "You know as much as I do that a person didn't attack Grant."

"A person is also not transparent." He sighs loudly. "But you're right—I'm not thinking straight anymore." Hunter runs one hand through his hair and turns his head up to the ceiling. "I'm not even sure I'm seeing straight anymore," he says quietly, as if it was only meant for his ears.

"What I'm about to tell you is going to make our whole situation sound a bit more crazy and...out of this world?" I wait for his confirmation to continue.

"I'm afraid to ask if anything else can get any more out of this world, Anya," he deadpans.

"Point taken. Anyway, Sunday night, I started having vivid dreams of my late-grandmother. She was trying to warn me and insisted that I remember where I come from." I run my hand through my hair. "None of it made sense. I thought it was all from too much stress at work. You know, the subconscious using my grandmother to bring me comfort and relief. But it was the complete opposite. Each night, the dreams became more and more real. I chalked it up to the lack of sleep and added stress; all of it made me exhausted." I take a deep breath to stop the lightheadedness that washes over me. It doesn't help. "Can we sit down, please?"

Hunter's eyes fill with concern. "Do you need some water?" He sits me down on a bench and kneels in front of me.

"I'm okay, but I need to sit for a moment."

He gets up and sits next to me, his leg close to mine. The nearness of him creates a calmness that washes over me in waves. The longer he is near, the more my body relaxes with the tide.

Do I tell him every detail?

What can it hurt?

The only risk is him calling me crazy and leaving me here first thing in the morning.

Alone.

To handle the situation with the wendigo. No big deal, right?

I sigh to myself. In the slight chance that my grandmother was right, and Hunter is here to help me, I can't afford to leave a single anything out.

I begin to tell him everything that happened.

"I thought I was dreaming of my grandmother again, just as I've been doing all week. Come to find out, it wasn't a dream..."

Hunter sits quietly, with a blank expression; I can't decipher what he's thinking. Now that I'm done telling him everything, including his part in this, I wait in trepidation for his reaction. I stare down at my hands twisted in my lap and try my best to hold back the tears filling my eyes.

Ironically, with everything we went through tonight, *this* is what makes me cry. A sniffle I've been trying my best to hold back sneaks out. My chin is tilted up by a warm, strong finger, and I am forced to look into Hunter's dark, chocolate eyes. The longer I stare into their warm depths, the harder it is to hang onto the ledge of my control.

"Anya."

One word.

It only takes one word. My name on his lips, in his deep yet gentle voice, breaks the dam. I start sobbing, the tears rolling down my face uncontrollably.

He wraps his arms around me and holds me in silence.

I'm cocooned inside the strong embrace of a man I just met—one who is now tied to my life—and somehow, it provides me with a sense of comfort while I let my emotions go.

It takes a bit, but I finally start to settle down. The waterworks stop, despite the continued leaking of my nose that I try to hold back by sniffling. There's nothing more attractive than snot running down a girl's face.

I could use a tissue right about now.

As if he heard my inner thoughts, Hunter's hand goes into his shirt pocket, and he pulls out a single tissue.

I laugh. I could hug this man right now.

"Always prepared, huh?" I hiccup and take the tissue, wiping my face. Then I blow my nose in an unladylike way.

So attractive, Anya. Let's see how many ways we can scare this guy off.

The guy who's supposed to help me protect our town, without getting myself killed?

Yup, that's the one.

Everyone has a line in the sand—once crossed, there's no going back.

I peek under my wet lashes and risk making eye contact.

"I'm so sorry. I promise I'm not crazy. Please, believe me. I'm not making this up. I really need you with me. Please don't leave me. I am not a desperate woman trying to keep a man with me—I need your help, and I can't do this alone. I am so, so—"

"Stop! Just stop, Anya."

I cease my rambling and gnaw on my bottom lip, unsure of how to prepare myself for what he's going to say.

His hand rubs the back of his neck. "I saw your grandmother too. I heard the end about keeping me around and why. If you're insane, then I must've jumped right on that crazy train with you. I am not going to leave you. As hard as it is to believe, with everything that's happened, I'm sticking this out with you until the end. You can trust me."

"What if she's wrong?" Dread fills my stomach.

"Your grandmother was right. And I do come from Celtic blood; my father would tell me stories growing up that were passed down from his father, and his before him. It's starting to make sense, but I need to wrap my head around it."

The fact he's taking this all so well, including seeing a ghost, is rather odd.

Narrowing my eyes, I say, "Wait, how can you believe me? Ghosts aren't supposed to be real."

"I'd like to say I've never had a supernatural encounter before, but I'd be lying. Just never up close and personal." He shrugs like it's nothing.

What else is this guy hiding?

"Who are you?" My eyes roam over the stranger.

"I told you who I am. Now it's time to try to get some sleep."

My jaw drops. "Are you kidding me? Sleep? Now? We have a lot to plan and go over." It doesn't matter that my legs are shaking from the weight of my body and my eyes are fighting the heavy weights hanging from my eyelids.

We need to prepare, not sleep.

"Anya, we need to keep our energy up, stay sharp, and figure out the next steps. Like your grandmother said, the good news is, we are free to go in the daylight. Let's get some rest, and tomorrow we'll discuss our next actions. Okay?"

Dark circles under his wide eyes tell me he's as tired as I am.

I nod, admitting we can't solve anything else tonight, but I can finally sleep knowing I'm not alone.

Chapter Nine

Nauthiz

(Distress)

"Shit." The sun blinds me and my body feels like it was hit by a semi-truck when I wake. It's apparent I had fallen off my bed sometime during the night, but I don't remember my floor being this cold. Even in the middle of winter.

What time is it? I continue to stretch out the kinks in my back while I allow time for my eyes to adjust to my room.

No, no, no, no!

Everything comes rushing back to me.

In hope I didn't see what I thought I saw, I sit up and rub my eyes. With a squint, I peek one eye open...*Fuuuck.*

My head meets my knees and I mumble to myself, "Okay, take some big, deep breaths and pull yourself together, Anya. You got through last night. You are a badass woman and nothing will stand in your way." I release a sigh and pick my head up—running my hand through my hair. "Oh, who am I kidding? I'm no Heather."

Hunter is nowhere in sight when I glance around the room. I pull my stiff and aching body up, wipe my sweaty palms on my jeans and walk to the front door. The one that is no longer secured with a bar.

Did he leave without me?

No, he told me last night he wouldn't leave me.

Or was he telling me that so he could sneak away? Why did I trust he would stay?

I really felt deep down that he was a hundred percent with me on this.

Now, how am I going to handle this by myself?

It's not as though Heather and Danielle would jump on the bandwagon to help me. They would be the first to send me to a doctor to get help.

And who would blame them? No one would believe me.

"Don't waste a minute of time…" a soft whisper is carried by a gust of wind that blows past me.

Goosebumps prickle at my skin.

Well then…I guess that's my sign that it's time to go.

I head back to my blankets to grab the journal and make my way towards the door. Taking a couple deep breaths, I pull my dagger out of my boot and brace myself for a fight. I know Grandmother said that the beast won't be out during daylight, but who knows if the rules of the game have changed.

I open the door, clutching the book close to me as I get ready to strike.

The bright sunlight should have been blinding, yet my eyes adjust much quicker than when I woke. I take in the view around me from the doorway. There's only the soft breeze blowing through the autumn leaves. No ominous dragging of limbs and crunching of leaves from last night, which removes a twenty-pound weight off my chest. The vibrant scene before me makes me feel like I've been transported into another world, a contrast to the recent hauntings that played out hours ago. Not even the small birds in the trees are bothered as they happily sing.

I slip my blade back in its rightful spot and grip the molding of the doorway, hesitant to go farther outside. My gaze passes over the blue of my car with my focus being on the opening of the woods. It's as calm as the rest of this place. Almost as if last night never happened, the horrors are now absent. I'm relieved to find normalcy and fresh air to clear my tight lungs.

What I don't find is Hunter waiting for me. A tear spills onto my cheek, and I wipe it away as I step out into the sunlight.

The sadness ebbs as I let the rays soak into my body, surrounding me in a warm embrace. I love how healing the sun is. It touches my head and I still, allowing the energy to swirl around me then through me, until it reaches my feet and draws into the earth.

Before last night, I used the sun to wake up; or give that little extra push I needed to get through the day, but it was never like this. This morning, my body is hypersensitive and feels like I'm storing the sun's energy inside every cell.

Wow, yesterday affected me a lot more than I thought.

When I pull myself from my solar shot of espresso, I make my way down the steps in the direction of my car, constantly glancing around to be sure I'm alone—with the exception of the birds. A few strides away from the stone steps, I turn to walk backwards. The last thing I need is for the creature to sneak up on me from the other side of the castle.

"Wow." A dreamy sigh escapes my throat and my pace slows to take in the stunning beauty before me.

I was right, this is a fairytale dream in the daylight. Hidden in a world of its own, a magnificent structure frozen in time. It would've been such an adventure to capture the historical secrets in this place—if not for the situation we—I mean *I* am in.

Even with the bright sun and my cleansing breaths to help my exhaustion, I still have a strong sense of emptiness. It's as though Hunter left and a piece of me went with him.

I need to come to terms sooner—rather than later—Hunter is gone from my life for good and I'm in this alone. Just like when I started my new life here in Shandaken, I'm thrown into a situation I'm not comfortable with, but I will rise up again and do my best to survive.

Oh, who am I kidding?

My shoulders droop and I rub the back of my neck while turning back in the direction of my ca—

"What. The. Actual. Fuck?"

Devastation hits me. I feel the need to scream—I would have if my self-preservation didn't kick in. Closing my mouth, I internally scream and clench my fists—nails digging into my palms. As hard as it is not to shout, I can't risk the chance the creature hears me. Regardless of it not being able to come out in daylight.

My car, my baby!

My beautiful, bright blue, metallic Dodge Charger is complete-ly, and *utterly*, destroyed.

I bought it as my reward for busting my ass at the office. Now there's nothing salvageable remaining.

Not taking any chances for the journal to end up like my poor car, I tuck it into the back of my waistband. Once it's secure, I lace my fingers together behind my head and survey the damage.

There are claw marks everywhere.

Hoof imprints and large dents are on the roof and trunk of the car, and evidence of three claws dragged their sharp daggers into the metal along the sides. The deep, jagged lines make the metal resemble tin foil—thin and easy to tear. The marks begin at the front and don't let up until they reach the back bumper.

Each window, including the windshield, is smashed in, the tires are flat and the rims have bite marks, as if they were used as a chew toy.

The hood took the worst of it. It's been peeled back like a tin can and the insides ripped out, similar to Grant's torso. The fumes of oil and gasoline permeate the air.

Well, I guess it could have been worse, the creature could have blown up the poor car.

On second thought, that may have made it worth it—if only it blew up the wendigo in the process.

Where is Karma when you need it?

"It's just a car, it's *just* a car, it's…just…a car," I chant. I will survive. Even if my insurance doesn't cover damage due to mythical creatures.

Okay, focus on the important task here.

Fuck Karma, I'll do it myself. I have people to save and a nasty wendigo to slay. Or more along the lines of capture, but who knows, maybe I'll get lucky.

Well shit, how am I getting home? Point one for Karma. Touché.

"Got any bright ideas, Grandmother?" I say, hoping she can hear me. My palms sweat and the knot in my stomach that was missing when I woke, is coming back with a vengeance.

I lean over, peering into the interior of my car. It looks like a pissed off, feral cat was trapped inside without any food.

The remains of the parchment invitation sit in my cup holder.

"Oh, thank goodness!" While avoiding the broken shards of glass, I reach in—snatching it up before folding and placing it in my pocket. It's a relief I won't need to stress over someone finding it. One issue down, another to go. Figuring out transportation.

I check my cell service. No bars.

Not a single one.

Of course not.

I walk around the remains of my car with my phone in the air trying to get one measly bar. Holding it up to the sky, I move towards the opening heading back to the road. Maybe I can get enough service to make a call. I'd rather not have to hike back to town if I can avoid it. The ride took me an hour and a half to get here, if I start walking now, it'll be past dark by the time I get home.

I glance back at my car and *will* it to put itself back together.

It's still the same pile of scraps.

I guess I have no other choice but *to walk.*

"I hope you weren't too attached to it."

"Shit!" My heart skips a beat and my pulse skyrockets.

Hunter's in stealth mode again, coming up from behind me.

Wait, he didn't leave me?

"Hunter?" My voice squeaks and tears fill my eyes. I turn around to face him.

With emotions high, I run fast and jump up, locking my arms around his neck, causing him to stumble from the unexpected force of my weight.

I don't care, I hold on for dear life.

"You didn't leave after all. Thank you!"

"Hey, it's okay. I told you I wouldn't leave you. But...do you think you can loosen your hold...just a tad?" His deep voice comes out strained.

"Oh..." I slip down his hard body; stepping back a couple feet. My hands clasp tightly to stop from reaching out for him. He's a lot taller than I remember from last night, with broader, linebacker shoulders.

Heat floods my face. "I'm sorry, I don't know what came over me. Well, I do, sorta. I was upset about my car and being stranded here alone, then the sight of you here caught me off guard, and I couldn't contain myself. I thought you left me and I would have had to walk home where I would become the beast's next meal. I...sorry...again..." Damn it, I was rambling.

Hunter tilts my head up with his finger and I'm met with a smile that warms me more than the sun ever could. "Hey, no complaints here."

A sigh escapes my throat. This is turning into a common thing with us.

We stare at each other, his brown eyes are kind and...still so familiar. His defined jawline has perfect trimmed dark hair that fails to hide the dimples in his cheeks. Those things are deadly.

Another spark of recollection washes over me but I can't place it. His eyes narrow like he sees it too.

I clear my throat awkwardly. "Soo...what do we do now?"

"We take my bike. Unless you want to go back and search Grant for his car keys."

Well, why didn't I think of that? I glance back towards the castle then cringe at the thought of digging through Grant's bloody pockets. Goosebumps cover my skin, making me shiver.

On second thought, I'm more than happy to take a ride on Hunter's bike.

"Are you saying that Mr. Hero doesn't know how to hot-wire a car?" I grin at him.

"Oh, I do, but I'm sure that will raise eyebrows with the police."

My smile falls. I am not ready to deal with law enforcement right now; I need to deal with the wendigo. "I'd rather not be involved when it comes to the police."

"What else would you suggest we do? Bury his body?" He cocks an eyebrow.

"Well, *you* may have a right to be here since you were hired to find him, but I don't. My deceased grandmother sent me the invitation, how do I explain *that* to the cops?" I run my hand through my hair and let out a harsh breath.

Tightness wraps around my chest. I've never needed blood pressure medication before, yet I see I may need it in the near future.

Hunter looks up at the sky with a hand rubbing his neck, then he stands straighter and aims a boyish grin at me.

One that screams trouble.

Run away Anya, you know what happened last time you fell for a guy's charm.

"Well, Honey Bear, we tell them you came to meet your boyfriend at the castle yester-"

What? Oh hell no!

"Are you seriously back to the boyfriend theory *again*? It hasn't even been 24 hours and you *still* can't get that out of your little brain, can you?"

Why is he smirking?

I cross my arms and narrow my eyes.

"If you let me *finish*, you wouldn't be flipping out. What I was saying, before you so rudely interrupted me, is that you came to surprise your boyfriend-" he holds up his index finger.

Clenching my jaw, I wait for him to continue.

"-at the castle yesterday. You missed me, because I've been out of town for a while."

I did what? My eyebrows crease.

"I was coming around the front, after checking out the back on my bike—hence the tracks—when you pulled up. Once you got out and greeted me, we saw the front door open, and searched the place. That's when we discovered your boss—my client's husband—downstairs. That'll explain the bloody footprints from us. We heard a growl outside when we came back up to call the cops, so we closed and locked the door to prevent us from being attacked as well. Which trapped us in the castle all night—the animal waiting just outside. It was gone by morning, probably onto its next hunt, and we went straight to the police station."

"Wait, you're telling me I'm dating you now?" For some reason, my brain has shoved the majority of his story to the back of my mind and I latch on to this detail.

"Yes," was his only answer.

"Wow. I mean, I move pretty fast. Only a day after finding my *boyfriend dead*, I already have a new man in my life? I didn't think I was a hussy, but here I am." I splay my hands out and compose a resting bitch face.

Hunter doesn't disappoint when he's rendered speechless.

I crack a smile then burst out laughing.

He catches onto me and palms his forehead, shaking his head.

It only makes me laugh harder and I have to hold my aching stomach.

"I couldn't resist. Sorry, not sorry." Holding up my hand, requesting a second to calm down, and my laughter dissipates into a chuckle.

"I'm not sure what part of that you find hilarious." His smile wavers.

"Oh, trust me, it was the dating you part. And how easy it is to tease you."

"Ouch!" His hand goes to his chest, rubbing an invisible pain. "Way to knock a man down, Anya."

"You have to admit, that was pretty presumptuous of you to assume I would be onboard with this. We met only yesterday. How long have you been concocting this elaborate story, pray tell?" I cross my arm and rest my chin on my hand—intrigued.

"I've been thinking about it since I woke up. You think you can survive claiming me as your man for a couple hours? I know it's a big sacrifice on your part, but it will solve our issue."

"Huge sacrifice."

He places his hands in his front pockets, his shoulders hike up. He almost looks...nervous?

Hmm...that's interesting.

"Stop pouting. Yes, I can. I just hope your acting skills are up to par, though." I crack a smile.

He turns away to glance back at the castle, and I hear him mumble something that sounded like, "Who needs to act?"

Did he say what I thought he said?

"What was that?"

He turns back around. "Are you ready to go?"

I guess we're ignoring that statement.

"Umm...sure? But Hunter?"

"Yeah?"

"In all seriousness, how will we be able to keep full access to the castle, while attempting to confine the wendigo? And who's to say they won't set up camp to try to hunt down an unknown animal?"

"They may monitor the crime scene, but it won't be closed off after they clean up and do an initial investigation. We need to report it soon so they can do everything, hopefully before nightfall. We both need to keep our stories straight. You think you can handle this?"

I bite the inside of my cheek, contemplating our story. It isn't all made up, only the facts twisted a bit. *Yeah, I can do this.*

"Yes, I can handle it."

Hunter's eyebrows raise and he clears his throat, breaking the brief silence that hangs between us. "Okay then, let me pull my bike around and we can head to the station and give our statements. After that, we can get cleaned up, eat breakfast, and discuss what our next moves are. The police might want us back here for a walk through and to show them to the body. You need to be prepared."

He stops, holds my arms, and places his face near mine. His eyes level with mine, and his warm minty breath is only a lick away.

If I lean forward, just a little bit...

"Anya, are you sure you're comfortable with this?"

"Comfortable with what?" My eyes linger on his lips.

"With our story." He tilts my chin up to bring my focus to his dark eyes—ones filled with humor.

"Completely." I nod.

"Good." He lets me go and backs away.

I release a frustrated sigh. It has nothing to do with talking to the police, but everything to do with this growing attraction to Hunter.

Hunter walks around the back of the building and a minute later, he comes into view; walking his bike straight towards me. He dangles a single helmet from his fingertips.

"What about you?"

A dimple pops in his cheek.

Damn, that's sexy.

"Aww...is my Honey Bear worried about me?"

Well, that moment of insanity didn't last long. I roll my eyes, place the helmet on my head, and climb on the bike—double checking to make sure the journal is secure in my waistband.

"Let's go, Big Guy."

With a chuckle, Hunter hops on.

The bike roars to life with a kick start. When he reaches back to wrap my hands around his torso, I'm pulled up against hard, unyielding, yet comforting muscles.

Hunter yells over the rumble of the bike, "Hold on tight!"

I hold on for my life, because it's the only way to get through this nightmare.

Chapter Ten

Ehwaz

(Trust)

We made it to the police station a lot quicker than it took for my drive to the castle. And let's just say, Hunter isn't keen on going slow. I had to hold on tight for fear of falling off, and I wonder if he did that on purpose.

Hunter backs into a parking space, dismounts, and lends me a hand. My usual stubborn self would have told him 'I got it', but we've been on the bike long enough for my legs to be sore and weak.

"You good?" He gives me a questioning gaze.

I drop my eyes to our joined hands. His hand is large in comparison to mine and I hold it a minute longer than needed.

No, I'm not good.

If I were good, the contact between us wouldn't come to an end.

Reluctantly, I pull my hand from his grasp and walk to the door—stopping when I remember the book in my waistband.

"Hunter, what about the journal? Don't you think it's a little suspicious that I am hiding something under my jacket? If I carry it, they may link the symbols to the castle. What if they confiscate it as evidence?" I bite the inside of my cheek.

"You're right. Will you be okay if we lock it in my saddle bag? They don't look busy, it shouldn't take long."

I hesitate, nervous to let it out of my sight, anyone can come and take the bike—easily.

Why am I so paranoid?

Maybe because with the luck I'm having, it's not out of the realm of possibilities?

I glance down the block where my office sits and an idea hits me.

Pulling my phone out, I'm greeted by eight missed text messages. Most of them are from Danielle, two from Heather, and the last from my mom. With zero missed calls, I know none were urgent.

"What are you doing?" Hunter asks.

"One second, I have an idea."

I scroll past my recent texts until I reach Danielle's.

Danielle: *Hey! How did last night go?*

Danielle: *Did you make it home? I know you had a long drive and might have had a late night.*

Danielle: *Can you please text me back to let me know you made it safely?*

Danielle: *Please message me, Heather said she hasn't heard from you either and she couldn't track your ass by GPS.*

Danielle: *Heather and I are freaking out, please please say something.*

Nausea hits me and it isn't from my empty stomach.

"What's wrong? Are you okay?" Hunter asks, his voice filled with concern.

"Yeah, I'm okay. Why?" My brows draw together when I meet his questioning stare.

He points to my hand rubbing my stomach.

Oh.

I move my hand and wave it between us.

"I'm fine. My friends have been really worried about my radio-silence last night. Sorry, give me one more minute." I hold up my index finger.

"Take your time." He sits on his bike with one arm leaning on the handlebars.

I smile. Any other guy would be rushing me.

Back to my idea.

Me: *Hey, you're right, it was a late night. The meeting never happened. My car had a little accident. I'm fine, I'm not hurt. I had to sleep at the place and hopped a ride back this morning with someone. I can't talk long, I have a lot of things to take care of today, but by chance are you at the office?*

Her typing bubble pops up and I release a sigh of relief.

Danielle: Thank heavens you're okay! We were getting scared. Yes, I came in to catch up on some work. Heather tagged along since her fiancé kicked her out. Apparently, she was baking like crazy from worrying over you. Every surface of their house is filled with cupcakes and pies. She even started putting them on the bathroom counter and in the shower.

Me: LOL, oh man, that can't be good. I am going to drop by really quick. Can I leave something very important with you guys for a short time?

Danielle: Sure, what is it?

Me: I'll talk to you more when I get there but I can't be long. See you soon?

Danielle: K.

"What's that smile about?" Hunter's smirk pops out that delicious dimple.

"I have a solution." My smile broadens.

"Care to share?" He hikes up an eyebrow.

"I'm going to my work," I say with finality.

He gets to his feet and all humor leaves his face.

"I don't think we have time for that. In all seriousness, Anya, you may want to take a leave of absence from work right now, until we figure out how to handle our little situation. We need to get the police out of the way first."

I shake my head. "No, no. Not to work-work. I'm leaving the journal with my friends who I *work with*. One of them would do some serious bodily harm protecting something important. I know I risk suspicion by hiding it, but I'm willing to take that chance."

"Alright, but we need to be quick."

Why is he assuming he is coming with me? Now is *not* the time to play protective hero.

"You don't have to come with me, I'll be right back. It's daylight—I'm safe."

In all honesty, I don't want my friends to see him. They're going to have enough questions for me as is, add this big guy to the mix, and the questions won't cease.

"You know your grandmother won't be happy if we separate."

Damn him, he brought her into this knowing it will make me cave. I narrow my eyes at him.

Does he have to be so smug about it though?

"*Fine,* but don't speak, not even if you are spoken to. I'll do all the talking. Got it?"

"Whatever you say, Honey Bear," he grins.

Why do I get the feeling he's not going to listen?

I roll my eyes. "I hope you know, this is a bad idea." I sigh. "Let's go."

We walk in and I give James a wave. His eyes go to Hunter, then back to me with an inquiring expression.

"Morning, Ms. Anya. I didn't know it was a work-day today," he says warily.

"For once, I'm not working. Just need to stop by to have a word with the girls, then I'll be out of your hair."

"You know you are never a bother. Let me know if you need anything. Anything at all." His eyes narrow at Hunter.

"Thanks, James." I loop my arm in Hunter's with a big smile—trying to ease James' fatherly instincts.

James gives me an understanding nod and goes back to his security monitors.

After we pass a few cubicles, I release Hunter and he gives me a little space.

Maybe I'll be lucky and they don't notice him?

When I approach, Heather and Danielle stand-up and their gazes fly to Hunter like he is a beautiful piece of art they can't tear their eyes off of, even if they tried.

Who was I kidding, there's no hiding this giant.

Their dropped jaws turn to huge knowing smiles and I mentally kick myself. I knew this wasn't going to be easy.

I wave my hands in front of their faces. "Hello, anyone home?"

Their heads rotate towards me, while their eyes are still glued on Hunter. I shake my head.

Going up on my tip-toes, I place my mouth next to Hunter's ear and whisper, "I told you it was a bad idea for you to come with."

He replies with his dangerous dimple.

"Agh." I step between Hunter and my friends. "Hey, I don't have much time. Care to help a girl out?"

Two sets of eyes snap out of their trance.

"Anya! What happened last night? Thank God you are okay. Do you have any idea what you put me through?" Heather pulls me in for a tight hug.

"I'm sorry, I would have texted you both if I had the chance." Guilt fills my chest.

"Well, we're happy you are okay. I wish you would have agreed to have me come with you." Danielle crosses her arms and frowns.

"So I could worry about both of you instead of just one? I think not. All for one and one for a—"

"We aren't the musketeers, Heather," Danielle interrupts.

Heather sticks out her bottom lip. "You're no fun."

Hunter clears his throat.

Right, stay on track.

"We have to go. But, I need to leave a family journal with you while we run an errand. You know how much my family heirlooms mean to me. Can you help?"

Danielle gives me a look that says 'don't ask dumb questions.'

"You know we will. What's going on, Anya?" Danielle replies.

"I'll explain more later. *Please* protect this with your lives." I unzip my jacket and start to hand it over. Heather grabs the journal and hugs it to her chest possessively.

This was a good idea.

Heather looks at Hunter and gives him a mischievous smile.

Maybe I spoke too soon.

"Hi, I'm Anya's best friend, Heather. And you must be the lovely gentleman that gave her a ride this morning...*and* last night." She wiggles her eyebrows and looks him up and down, licking her lips.

That's when I see the sparkle in her eyes.

Uh oh. The transition comes in fast like a storm squall.

In a split second, Dr. Jekyll disappears and Mr. Hyde emerges. Her face shifts from the flirty little light-haired pixie, to a serious, take no prisoners alive banshee. "But if you hurt our girl, I will make sure you will regret it for the rest of your short-ass life. Every time you look in the mirr—"

Danielle gives Heather a shove and glares at her. "Knock it off!"

This little blonde may be small, but she packs a powerful punch.

I wonder how the wendigo would fare with her...ugh, forget it. I can't risk my friends getting hurt, or worse.

Danielle turns to Hunter. "Don't mind her, she has a malfunctioning filter *and* is a little protective. She *knows* Anya had car trouble and needed a lift. She *also* knows that Anya can take care of herself, *right* Heather?"

Heather holds the book tighter to her chest and rolls her eyes.

"I'm Danielle, Anya's other best friend. The sane and level-headed one."

Heather snorts which causes me to smirk.

"Heather?" Danielle scolds.

"Ugh, fine." Heather releases an exaggerated sigh and mumbles like a kid in trouble, "Sorry. I get a *little* carried away. But you *are* a stranger. I'm sure you understand my reaction?" She then flashes Hunter a sweet smile and bats her eyelashes.

I turn to Hunter and catch his silent nod to Heather.

He surprises me with his ability to follow my directions by not talking. I guess the nice thing to do would be to introduce him.

"This is Hunter, he is..." My brows furrow.

Should I say my friend? "He is..."

"Her boyfriend," Hunter's deep voice finishes.

The girls gasp and my eyes snap up at him, he flashes a devilish smirk and winks.

The ass!

Danielle's lips purse.

Shit. This isn't good. She knows something is fishy, since I haven't had a man in my life since last summer.

"Her boyfriend, huh? How exactly did you two meet?" Her inquisitive mind doesn't miss a beat.

"He kidnapped me."

"I was her knight in shining armor."

We answer at the same time.

"Well...it sounds like a match made in heaven." Heather laughs.

"Ladies, it's a pleasure to meet you both, but Anya and I have somewhere important to be. If you will allow, we will return in about an hour to retrieve the journal."

Danielle's intensity softens and Heather is acting as if Christmas came early.

"You have *a lot* to tell us, and soon." Danielle adds.

"I will. Please don't let anyone else see or touch the book, it's very important to us. I mean…me." I pause, hoping they didn't hear my trip up.

"You can trust us. You remember the time I…"

"Heather," I interrupted her before she could get going. "I can't keep track of how many *times* you've had your crazy moments, but we really gotta go. I'll text when we are on the way back."

"Okay. You kids, go have fun, and feel free to go a second round. Hunter, Anya likes to cuddle afterwards. No need to rush back here so soon." Heather's eyes gleam.

I'm going to kill her.

My face heats as Heather pulls me in for a big hug, whispering in my ear, "Give him a chance, I can feel he's nothing like that asshat, Kyle."

Yet, Kyle was great in the beginning too. I'm not sure I can go through that again. I don't respond, only hug her back for a moment then release her.

"Goodbye you two," I tell them, grabbing Hunter by the arm to leave.

As soon as we turn around and take a couple steps, I hear 'goodbye' in a sweet unison, followed by the two giggling like childish highschoolers.

And I thought battling a mythical creature was bad; now I have to put up with those two.

At least they aren't mad at me. That's one positive out of all of this.

Chapter Eleven

Isa

(IDENTITY)

Talking to the police wasn't as bad as I expected. The moment the word of someone's death spilled from our mouths, they split us into different rooms and ran us through a series of detailed questions. It surprised me they hadn't even asked our names before they brought us back.

I stuck to our script and they accepted the information without suspicion. In this situation, I'm not sure how foul play could even be considered, but I wasn't going to take the chance. I didn't dare risk veering from our story.

The door opens and my heart flutters when Hunter walks in with a smile meant only for me. It's no act when tears flood my eyes.

He walks over to me, kissing me on my temple and whispers, "How you doing?"

I don't respond because I don't know *how to* respond. But there are people watching us, so I reply, "I'm okay."

Lines crease his forehead before he shakes it off and sits in the chair next to me—placing his arm across the back of my chair.

I can't help feeling on edge. Not because of what happened last night, but because Hunter had the 'supportive boyfriend' act down pat and I didn't know how to handle it.

He's held my hand, wrapped his arm around my shoulders, and when we walked in the station, he kept touching the small of my back.

None of it is real, but with my growing attraction to him, it's hard to separate real from fiction. I only hope I was giving off the vibe of a concerned and scared girlfriend—one who recently found a dead body—instead of the suspect in a murder case.

The officer on the other side of the table slides a small notepad between us. "If you can please write down the address to the location of the body. We need to get a crew to the scene soon."

My eyes go wide and my palms sweat. I plead with Hunter with my eyes for help. I can't pull my letter out of my pocket without raising suspicion and my GPS is in my destroyed car.

Hunter moves his hand off my chair and grabs the notepad—jotting down the coordinates by memory. I let out a breath and relax into my seat.

Damn, he's good.

"Thank you both. We understand you've been through a scary and traumatic experience but Detective Shane Macaby will need you there to run through the events again."

I put my head in my hands and Hunter provides soothing circles on my back.

"I'm sorry, ma'am, I promise you'll be safe. There will be enough officers to protect you if the animal returns, and you won't be forced to see the body again."

I groan.

Hunter speaks up, "Sir, as you can see, my girlfriend is quite exhausted and neither of us have eaten since lunch yesterday. Is it okay to clean up and get some food before coming out?"

My head shoots up fast. *Wait, that's a possibility?*

"That is no problem at all. We will be out there cleaning up and checking out the scene for a while." The officer stands. "We will see you in a bit."

Hunter pushes open the door and ushers me out of the police station. I brush by his chest to make my way back into the sunlight. The warm rays wrap their loving arms around me and I take a deep, cleansing breath.

"How are you doing? And be honest with me." Hunter comes up from behind me and places his hand on my hip.

Heat spreads through my body, and butterflies are doing a Cirque du Soleil act in my stomach. It doesn't make sense, there's no one else around—only the two of us.

"What did you ask?" I rub the back of my neck.

"I want to know what you're really feeling." He's subtle in his movement to pull me closer.

"I'm happy that part's over." I tilt my head to the side. "How come you weren't nervous in there?"

"This ain't my first rodeo, sweetheart."

I place my hand on his chest. "Hold up, you've dealt with situations like this before?"

"No. Not *this* type of situation, but dead bodies? Yes." He rubs his hand over his face, stopping when he gets to his short beard.

"Is that normal in your line of business?"

"It occasionally comes with the territory. My goal is to find them before it becomes a possibility." An emptiness fills his eyes.

Heaviness weighs on my heart.

"Do you work with a partner? So you aren't dealing with it alone?"

"It's usually just me. Come on, we need to go get your journal back."

I take that as my cue to stop while I'm ahead with the twenty questions.

Hunter slides his hand to my back and it remains there on our short, silent trip to the office. We give a quick 'hello' to James at the desk and work our way back to the girls. This time, they don't hear us enter. Heather has a hold of the journal and is discussing the next culinary creation she wants to try and Danielle is inputting data.

"Hey," I tell them.

"Ooh you're back! That was fast." She narrows her eyes. "Why don't you have an afterglow? Hunter, why doesn't she have an afterglow? You know how to put it in, don't you? It's not that hard. Oh, wait... Was that the problem? You weren't that hard?"

"Oh my God, *Heather*!" Forget my face being the only thing red, my whole body is flushed right now.

Hunter is behind me wheezing and having coughing spasms.

Danielle's head is on her desk—her shoulders are shaking.

I raise my eyes to the ceiling and count to ten. When I am more collected, I stare down the green-eyed blonde in front of me. The one with the innocent smile on her face.

"Hand over the book. Your duties are over." I hold my hand out.

"Was it the afterglow comment? It was *hard* to tell." She sucks in her lips to contain her laughter.

A snicker escapes my throat. "Book, please."

"*Okay*, okay." She hands it over.

"Thank you for helping. Thank you both." I say in a serious tone.

Danielle lifts her head, tears stream down her face before she wipes them away.

"Anytime," she offers. "How about a girls' night to discuss the ...meeting?" Her eyes flip to Hunter and back to me.

"Raincheck? I have a...family emergency that came up," I cringe. Both of their faces drop.

"I hope everything is alright." Heather worries her bottom lip.

"Me too. I'll keep you posted." I give them both hugs.

"Take care of our girl, Hunter." Danielle says.

"Always," Hunter replies and pulls me to his side.

Why does he have to do and say things that make my mind turn to mush?

We wave to James on our way out and walk back to Hunter's bike.

"Do you want to stop at your place or mine first?" he asks.

"Yours. You can pick up anything you need and then we can head to my house. If you don't mind staying at my place? I have a lot of resources that can help us." My palms sweat, which is crazy. It's not like we're going to do anything other than eat, research, and sleep.

"Sounds perfect." He flashes a cocky smirk.

Hunter's place has the bare minimum; a couch, TV, and kitchen appliances. Without checking out his bathroom and bedroom, which I'm sure are the same, I find it all lacks any personal touches and doesn't even feel lived in.

While he's in his bedroom packing, I stroll around, checking everything out. I spot a few familiar books under his TV, a sign he has good taste, which is a plus. The fact his home is void of any signs of family is a little depressing, though.

Is he really that alone?

I want to get to know Hunter, particularly since we'll be spending a lot of time together; but his sparse belongings don't help me get to know the *real* him.

Who is he? What are his likes and dislikes?

It's apparent his dislikes are 'things.' But I can't decide if he is just neat or if he recently moved in.

I stand in the center of Hunter's small kitchen and yell, "What kind of person doesn't have a kitchen table?" I guess with only two stools at the island, it's all a single man would need.

Huh… I didn't even ask him if he was single. It's best to keep my distance and avoid the drama of a jealous girlfriend along with the inevitable broken heart. With my luck, I'd get both.

I'd be shocked if a man like him were single.

I've been in a few different relationships and none of them ended well. I'm not sure I want to risk him turning into someone completely different or leaving me like I had to leave someone else, heartbroken and crushed. I'm better off alone.

I purse my lips while I continue to check his cabinets for signs of habitation, or hints of who he is. Despite my reluctance to start anything romantic with him, I still want to get to know him.

"No point in wasting money for things I never use. I'm not home much." His voice comes out of nowhere.

"Ouch!" I cry, rubbing the back of my head. He caught me with my head under the sink. "Why do you have to always sneak up on me? We need to get you a bell," I scoff.

Hunter chuckles. "You done snooping?" He leans against the counter with his signature smirk.

"I'm not snooping; I was looking for a glass for water."

Why couldn't I have come up with something better?

"*Sure,* you are." He shakes his head and says, "I think I got everything I need. You ready?"

My gaze shifts to the two bags up against the wall. This guy packs heavy. Not sure what toiletries Hunter needs, but it seems a little excessive—if you ask me.

The list of questions in my mind grows longer by the minute.

"You wanna tell me how exactly you'll be fitting both of those bags on your bike?" I imagine trying to juggle them on my lap while preventing my ass from falling off the bike.

I don't see it ending well.

"We're taking my truck. Do you really think I drive everywhere on my bike? You have such little faith in me."

I harrumph. *Says the man stuck on the idea I was dating a much older, married man.*

Hunter's eyes narrow to slits.

My eyes widen. *I didn't say that out loud, did I?*

"Are you ready to go, or do you still have more snooping to do?"

My hand lands on my hip. "Ugh! I told you I wasn't snooping."

He snorts. "Then I take it we can leave?"

"Let's go, Big Guy."

Hunter holds out his hand. "Lead the way, Honey Bear."

I raise my dull, throbbing head, square my shoulders, and march myself out the front door...to wait.

He walks past me with a smirk. "Come on, it's around the back."

As soon as his truck comes into view my mouth drops. It's huge! I'm going to need a damn ladder to get in this thing.

"Need a hand?" The smart-ass asks.

"You can wipe that smug smirk off your face. I'm a big girl, I know how to climb into a truck."

"Feel free to take your time." His voice comes out rough.

I glare back at him; his focus is on my ass. Finally grabbing the black 'oh shit' handle that matches the sleek, black exterior, I pull myself up and sit with a huff.

Hunter shuts the door behind me.

After he tosses his bags in the back—one of them clanking like metal—he pulls himself into his seat with ease.

Show off.

"Trying to compensate for something with this monster?" I ask in amusement.

He turns to me and winks. "I'll let you be the judge of that."

Heat floods my face. *Damn it!* I need some space from Hunter, and soon. The longer I'm with him, the more confused I become.

"Just drive," I demand.

Hunter chuckles and starts the truck to make our way to my house.

Our drive is silent—besides my occasional directions. My mind's stuck on going over our past conversations in my head; the familiarity of him, my strong attraction, and his ability to flip a switch on my emotions without lifting a finger. No other man has had this power before.

We pull into my driveway and I don't wait for Hunter to turn off the truck before I leap out. I need my space and a distraction to get my thoughts in order.

I let myself in my house—leaving the door open—and peel off my leather jacket. I drop off the journal at my kitchen table on my way into the library. I know exactly where my grandmother's book of runes is, even though I've never had much reason to read it until now.

After locating the book, I lower my head with my hands on the desk and allow myself a few deep breaths to collect myself.

You can do this, don't get attached. Treat him as a co-worker because that's all he is. It's an agreement to partner temporarily, to achieve a mutual goal. After all of this, he will be back to traveling for work. Once he is out of your life, you can go back to living your boring life, just like before—with your heart fully intact.

Giving myself another minute, I make my way back to the table with a new wall built up. One that protects my fragile heart.

Hunter has already dropped his bags by the door and is strolling around—eyes scanning my living area. His large body makes my house feel small in comparison.

"Are you *snooping*, Hunter?" I ask, acting appalled.

"You betcha." He winks and continues checking out the place.

Why am I not surprised?

Trying to pull my attention from his thick, broad shoulders; I make myself comfortable at the table and flick through my pictures of the dungeon door.

It's strange to be studying it in a well-lit room. We had been engulfed in so much darkness last night, the change is refreshing.

Hunter hovers over me and I freeze; I take a risk and glance up—wrong move. His brown eyes bore into me, as if he is staring directly into my soul. I shiver and goosebumps spread over my skin.

He needs to go away...*now.*

"Ba—bathroom is on the left." I clear my throat and make sure I'm done with my bumbling words before continuing, "towels are in the cabinet under the sink and there's an extra toothbrush in the drawer. Help yourself." I point down the hall.

"Don't you want to clean up first?"

"I want to check out these symbols. I'll wash up after you. Go on."

"Are you sure?" He hesitates to leave my side.

"If I wasn't sure, I wouldn't be telling you to go. Now go. You stink."

He doesn't, but the sooner he's out of my hair, the quicker I can focus on these runes.

Hunter shrugs then turns to grab one of his bags. I admire his backside as he strides with confidence towards the bathroom.

Deep in concentration, I sense I'm being watched. It's no surprise to find Hunter leaning against the wall—arms crossed over his chest—watching me. His black t-shirt stretches across his chest and tucks into a pair of dark jeans—a black belt adorns his hips. Since I'm already staring, I follow the jeans down over his thick thighs to the flare partially covering his dark brown work boots. I want to look away but like a hunting dog that has located its prey, I'm frozen and can't tear my eyes from him.

I reach my hand up and catch myself about to check for drool.

How many times can I embarrass myself in front of this man?

It's still frustrating how Hunter can pull so many emotions out of me. Ones I didn't know I even had. Between the flustered, hormonal teen buried within me, to the hot-tempered woman I've become, the man has some skill. There's no doubt he knows it and I think he enjoys every minute of driving me insane. I wonder if he has the same effect on other women. *What am I saying? Of course he does.*

A jealous heat burns through my chest.

"How's the research coming along?" He asks in a low voice, breaking me out of my trance.

"The what?" I shouldn't be surprised my perusal of him was blatantly obvious.

He nods to the table.

"Oh, the research." I release the breath I was holding and swallow hard. "I think I made good headway with deciphering the other symbols. Check this out." I shake off my attraction—yet again—and push the runic book between us.

He comes to sit next to me and scooches his chair close.

A little too close if you ask me. Stay strong, Anya.

I point to the beginning of my grandmother's book, "I've always known my family's bloodline originated from Ireland. They adopted the use of runic symbols after the Vikings came. Hundreds of people were slaughtered, but many in our clan escaped with the help of a Viking witch, also known as a seeress. Once my family's clan was safe, she stayed with them and they worked together to help establish a new home. This is the reason there are a mix of Viking and Celtic symbols on the door and in these books. It's not common, but it's what they used for communication, along with their belief that it could protect them."

"So, you're telling me, your family put them there?" Hunter leans on his elbow and he pulls his attention from the book in front of us, to me.

"That, I'm not sure. It sounds like it, but none of her words mention the castle, this book only focuses on the runes and their uses. But that's not the most interesting thing I've found." My leg bounces.

"Go on..." he encourages.

"This says, 'the Viking witch was unlike many witches, she was pure and good'—which I figured since she was willing to help—well, she recognized a similar light power in my ancestors that she *too* possessed. The kind my grandmother told me about."

"It's not unknown for people to have gifts."

I bark out a laugh. "You *still* believe my grandmother?"

"Well, yeah."

I give him a blank stare.

"Was that it?" He asks, coaxing me to talk.

"Umm...no. Sorry, there's more. The witch helped my ancestors enhance their gift, which were said to be passed down from generation to generation on the women's side. With her assistance, their gift allowed them to thrive and help other neighboring clans. They made crops flourish, healed minor ailments, anything from people to livestock, as well as ward off, *or in this instance, bind* evil. It's said that, the power of light is the strongest energy in existence."

"I guess we have to figure out how to tap into your gift," Hunter states as a matter-of-fact.

"Ha! Well, I can tell you now, I don't have a lick of this 'light power' my grandmother talked about. I can't heal ailments or grow crops. I'm afraid we're royally screwed." I slouch in my seat.

Hunter nudges me with his shoulder. "Hey, cheer up. We'll find a way to handle the wendigo. And keep in mind, your grandmother saw the gift in you, right?"

I stare at the hands in my lap.

"Yes. But she's also dead, so...there's that." I shrug, and tightness wraps around my chest.

A warm hand wraps around my fidgeting ones.

"Hey, we *will* get through this, I promise." Hunter's determination has me glancing up at him.

"How can you promise something like that?" My brows furrow.

"Because we have each other. And I feel it in here," he taps his chest, "that we will succeed. It won't be easy, but I know we got this."

The stern expression on his face tells me he believes it. Even when I know we're still screwed, I like the fantasy world he lives in, and the best thing I can do is believe him too.

"Okay." I say under my breath.

"What was that?"

"I said, okay. I believe you." My voice is louder and more confident.

"Good." He nods and smiles. "Now, tell me what you found in the journal." He squeezes my hands before letting go.

"So far, I've only gone into researching the runes around the wendigo's prison. I haven't cracked open the journal yet. Are you up to hearing more about them?"

"Absolutely," he exclaims, turning in his chair and placing one hand on the back of mine.

I grab my phone, with last night's pictures on it, and point to the symbol in the center of the door that looks like a thorn on a stem—or a flag, "This is a rune called Thurisaz, it means danger; a warning to others but it's also an enchantment weapon to weaken and bind. The use of this with any others heightens the success of them."

"So, it's an important one we will definitely be needing. Got it." He leans in closer to look at the picture on my phone.

His short-trimmed beard is inches from my face.

Is it soft or scruffy? Would it leave scratch marks on my—

I need to focus on anything else but his beard. I take a deep breath and kick myself for doing so when his clean scent of citrus, spice, and a hint of lavender fills my nose—making me lose my battle to keep the rebellious butterflies in my stomach at bay.

I clear my throat.

"Now, look at this one. It looks like three spirals. This is one of the *oldest* ancient Irish symbols. It has a few names like Triskele, Triskelion, or Triple Spiral. With the many names also comes many meanings which vary with cultures and individual beliefs. To some, it represents the Father, Son, and Holy Spirit. Others, it is the Past, Present, and Future. It really is used as a universal symbol.

Its power is based on what your intentions are. For this,"—I point to the symbols on the door—"It gives movement to the other symbols to keep the energy flow constant. This way, the symbols do not lose energy and they continue to work with no interruption."

"Wouldn't you think one would be enough?" Hunter asks.

"You would think so, but there are four Triskeles surrounding the Thurisaz like a compass to draw energy in from the north, south, east and west." I look at Hunter to make sure he is still with me.

He nods, encouraging me to continue.

I point to the next symbols that represent an hourglass laying on its side. "Of course, these you've seen glow when I'm near. This is the Dagaz—the 'light rune.' They are located in all four corners of the door to box off the entry—ensuring what's behind the door, cannot pass the light barrier."

"These runes help make sense of how that door could hold a beast like that. Your grandmother said it didn't like light, what better to use than a symbol that creates light. What about this one? It looks familiar. I've seen it before."

"That's the tri-spirals which are another ancient Celtic symbol, called The Spiral of Life, or, the 'life force.' The spiral goes around three times. Each single spiral represents the Sun—again—used in this instance for the light energy. These are placed between the Triskele and Dagaz. The runic coordination is how they kept the beast trapped for who knows how long."

"And hopefully the journal will tell us more about that," Hunter says.

"Exactly! The good news is, we know the placements of all the symbols, and they are still burned into the door." My palms start to sweat so I wipe them on my jeans.

"What's the bad news?" One of his eyebrows hike up.

"The bad news is...we have no idea how to activate the symbols again." I blow out a harsh breath.

Hunter rubs the back of his neck. "You're right, that is bad."

"My thought was, if we can figure out how to trap it, get it back *into* the room, we may get lucky and figure out how we can destroy it once and for all so this never happens again."

"Also, you wouldn't have to worry about activating the symbols if you don't have power," Hunter adds.

"You got it. What do you think?" I know my idea is out of left field; I pray we have a chance though.

"Umm...first off, how long was I in the shower for?" He tries to hide a smirk and fails.

"Not long, why?" I sit up straighter in my chair.

"Well, based on everything you figured out, I'm thinking I must have been in there for what...two hours?" Hunter looks impressed.

I laugh and say, "Yeah, you're worse than a woman getting ready, you took *forever*." I roll my eyes dramatically which earns me a poke in my side—causing me to squeak. "Hey!" I narrow my gaze at him as he rolls his eyes this time.

"Whatever, it couldn't have been more than twenty minutes. But seriously, Anya, how did you get this all done so fast?"

"The history of my family has been ingrained into my head for years, except the magical component—that's new." I stare down at the tattoo on my arm, tracing it with my fingertip. "As for the symbols? Didn't take much. I knew I recognized them, I just needed to cross reference them in my grandmother's book to confirm their meanings, then...put it all together."

His smile is filled with pride. "You did an amazing job. *You* are amazing."

I'm not sure about that. Regardless, it makes my heart leap out of my chest and want to jump him. The traitor.

"Umm...thanks?"

"Don't doubt yourself."

We stare at each other for a few moments until Hunter breaks the silence.

"Alright, you go get your shower and I'll see what I can scrounge up in your kitchen for food rations. I'm starving and I know my Honey Bear is going to start growling if she doesn't tame the beast with nourishment soon." Hunter stands, pulls out my chair, and takes my hand to help me up.

When I stand, we are chest to chest. Heat spreads through my whole body.

"Okay, thanks. Be right back." I say breathlessly, and I take off quickly down the hallway into my room for fresh clothes, then into the bathroom.

A little time away from him will do me good. But when I enter the bathroom, all I smell is Hunter.

Sigh.

So much for getting away from him; however, a girl can certainly get used to this.

The perks of Hunter showering first is not waiting for the water to warm up. I strip down and step under the hot spray. With one hand on the cool tile wall, and the other on the glass door, I let glorious water ease the tension from my neck and shoulders. My body is *not* built for sleeping on a stone floor.

Knowing we don't have much time to kill, I push myself up and grab my shampoo. Squirting it into my palm, I rub my hands together and massage my scalp.

Mmm... It's exactly what I need—

The bathroom door flies open and I scream.

"*I fucking knew it!*" The thundering voice fills the small room and I attempt to cover myself.

My heart thumps hard against my chest under my hand and I try to catch my breath. Who knew I'd ever regret cleaning the shower with anti-steam products.

Never again.

"Hunter! What the *hell* are you doing?"

"I knew it! I, uh..." His eyes widen as if he is surprised I'm in my birthday suit, soap in my hair, standing with only a piece of glass between us.

The heat coming off me no longer has anything to do with the hot water, and everything to do with a mix of embarrassment and...*is that arousal?*

"Uh, do you mind?" I raise my eyebrows at him, hoping he'll turn around at least.

Is that a picture frame in his hand?

He clears his throat and his face and neck turn beet red. "Shit, sorry. I didn't mean...I'll just...eh...I'll go now. We can talk after." He turns abruptly and high-tails it out of the bathroom, shutting the door behind him.

"Well, thanks for that!" I call after him.

What the heck was that all about? What was so important that he had to barge in on me naked?

So much for enjoying my relaxing shower now that Hunter's not only invaded my bathroom but my thoughts too. I finish up in record time while grumbling. He had an uninterrupted moment, but could I?

Oh noooooo.

Now that I'm dressed in clean clothes, I glance at the mirror and purse my lips. My wet brown hair lays on my shoulders and I'm not quite sure what to do with it.

The time on my phone makes my decision for me when I realize we need to get back to the castle soon. Instead of blow drying it, I put it up in a French braid. Practical and out of my way. I also forgo any makeup; Hunter has already seen me at my worst, why put more energy into getting ready? With my boots now on and my dagger in its rightful place, I give myself one final look in the mirror.

Eh, I'm decent enough. Now to figure out what made Hunter lose his mind.

"Care to explain yourself?" I say as I walk down my hallway into the kitchen and dining room area.

When I see two club sandwiches, a side of chips, and glasses of water sitting at the table, I smile before I tamp it down. I should be annoyed from my interruption, not turn to mush because a man made me lunch. But I give him props...he was serious about finding us food, and my heart beats a little faster knowing he put the work in for a decent meal. The only thing missing is the man in question. I turn around and find Hunter in my living room quietly studying a portrait. It has the same frame as the one he was holding when he barreled into the bathroom.

With a closer look, I see it's the one from when I was fifteen with my parents.

My smile drops and a knot forms in the pit of my stomach. It's not because of the picture, or the fact that he is looking at it. It's the look on his face.

He is frozen in shock.

"Hunter?" I say hesitantly, taking a couple steps towards him.

Hunter looks up. "Oh, hey." His eyes shift to the image then back to me.

"Are you okay? You look like you saw a ghost. Wait... Grandmother didn't come back, did she? Is that why you barged in? You saw her and lost it?" I start to look around the room. Oh man, if she came back when I was gone, I'm going to be pissed. "Did she come back? What did she say?"

"You." His mouth falls open and his eyes...I can't even describe, but I've seen deer caught in headlights look more relaxed.

"Me? What about me? What did she say, Hunter? Please tell me." Confusion clouds my mind and I'm becoming more worried as each moment passes. Whatever came over him before is now replaced with shock.

He shakes his head.

"No, she didn't come back. It's...it's you, Anya. I can't believe it's really YOU! After all these years, I finally found you again. I wondered. I saw a resemblance but then I thought it was my mind playing tricks on me. Showing me what I wanted to see. I felt it was Karma being cruel to me for my past." The shallow rise and fall in his chest slows and his pale face cracks into a grin, then into a beaming smile.

I may be re-evaluating his sanity after all.

"What do you mean, 'all these years?' We just met last night."

"No. We didn't," he says in amazement.

"Care to fill me in? I'm a *little* lost right now."

Hunter walks over to me, he grabs my face in his hands and turns it from side to side studying me, then looks me straight in the eyes.

"Umm...Hunter?"

He mumbles, "I should have known with those hazel eyes, it was you. The rest of you has changed, even your hair." He grabs a loose strand of my hair and rubs it between his fingers. "It used to be much lighter and straggly."

My eyes are bugging out of my head. I have no fucking clue what he's talking about.

Clearing his voice he says, "Bear with me a minute, okay?"

"Uh, o-kay?"

"Think back ten years ago, you were fifteen years old and you were best friends with the boy next door until he had to move away. That is the *last* time you saw each other." There's a hint of desperation in his voice.

My eyebrows crease and I purse my lips. "I never had any boys as friends growing up. Actually, I never really had many friends until later on in my teenage years." When I try to think back to a boy, a friend when I was younger, I only see a black wall.

That's weird.

"Think harder. How can you not remember, Anya?" Hurt forms in his light-brown eyes.

I close my eyes not only to avoid watching the pain in his, but to push through the strange wall, attempting to break it down—to remember.

The feeling of déjà vu is there but that's the extent of it.

I shake my head. "I'm sorry. I really think you have me confused with someone else."

"No." He holds up the picture and points to the younger version of me. "This is the girl I knew. This is the best friend I had to leave behind."

My eyebrows scrunch, I wish with everything in me that I knew what he was talking about. Yes, he's familiar, but I would have remembered a friend. A best friend even.

"You're mistaken, I'm not—"

Hunter's lips press hard into mine. As if he's trying to transfer his memories.

On instinct, my mouth welcomes him and tingles run from my lips down my body like a vortex lifting a thick fog. Confusion bounces around my head at the same time heat begins to spark in my abdomen. Then I see a crack.

What the hell?

As much as I don't want Hunter's warm, soft lips to leave mine, I push away from him as the sliver in the wall of my mind begins to fracture.

"Shit. I'm sorry." Hunter's strained voice sounds so far away.

But I can't answer. Not when fragments inside me are breaking away and I'm lost inside my consciousness.

It's a struggle, but I raise my hand up to stop him. To silence him while I sort out whatever this is.

Closing my eyes, I shove harder into the barricade of light and it teeters back and forth.

"Anya."

I can sense him nearing me and I take another step back away from him. I need space. I'm so close to whatever is happening. I just know it.

One more push. The wall splinters in every direction and I watch as the barrier shatters into a million pieces.

Gasp!

Memories flood me like a levee broke and I'm drowning. Heaviness fills my chest and my legs go out from underneath me.

I open my eyes when my body doesn't make an impact with the floor.

"I got you, Anya. I've *always* got you." Unshed tears flood Hunter's eyes.

Realization of Hunter's identity dawns on me. My face drops and a cold chill runs down my spine.

No fucking way! It can't be. But...how?

None of this makes sense. And I didn't remember a goddamn thing until his lips touched mine. It's like he's woken me. He broke down the wall that had him hidden from me for the past ten years.

But why?

My mind may have forgotten, but clearly, my heart didn't. It's been telling me all along who he is. These strange pulls, the feeling as though part of my soul left with him when I thought he was gone this morning.

My soul recognized him before I could.

Why would my subconscious block him? Was it from the pain of him leaving me? Was it a matter of survival?

I squint my eyes trying to see the younger version of him. The boy I knew was scrawny with unkempt brown hair and the warmest milk-chocolate, brown eyes. I see the resemblance, it's him...all grown up and drop dead gorgeous.

I whisper, "Hunter McAllister?" When I put it all together, I realize my jaw is hanging on the floor so I close my mouth and swallow. *Let's add not only a Christmas card for Fate, but a freaking Christmas present too.*

"This is why you asked me about sneaking out of my house when I was younger when we were back at the castle."

He nods.

Because that's exactly what we did, and often.

"I need to sit down."

Hunter helps me over to the couch and I plop down ungracefully. I lean over my knees and rest my head in my hands.

I didn't have many friends when I was younger. I was pretty much an outcast. That was, until I was ten and I met our new neighbors. This little brown haired, brown eyed boy was all smiles and he didn't think twice about being my friend. We clicked immediately and were inseparable for the next five years. Our parents couldn't keep us apart, and many nights we would sneak out to meet up. We'd lay in the grass and stare at the stars discussing our plans for the future, like one day we'd get a house together, where we could eat tons of junk food and not have parents telling us when to go to bed. Hunter would tell me how bad he wanted to be a police officer to save lives, and I told him I needed to be a librarian. I dreamt of being surrounded by books all day, every day.

We talked about everything and anything. One night, we'd made a promise that we would always be best friends and be there for each other, no matter what. We agreed nothing could separate us.

Then my worst nightmare happened. The moment my life stopped was the day I found out Hunter was moving away. I didn't know where and his parents wouldn't tell him. We both cried and clung to each other as our parents pulled us apart. My tears continued for months.

My dad talked about sending me to a counselor, but my mom said she wanted to give me time to grieve. She started coming into my room every night before bed, and instead of just tucking me in like she always did, she would lay her hand on my back and sit in silence.

It was strange. I'd felt a sense of warmth from her hands, and next thing I knew, I was in a peaceful sleep. I didn't know how she did it, but it now makes sense she was using her powers to heal my soul and build the wall to forget. Each day got easier and easier as the pain and memories faded, but there was still a feeling deep down that some part of me was missing.

I sit up and rub my face. My chest feels like I have a stack of bricks sitting on it. The pain of losing him, then knowing I forgot about him—not by choice—crushes me.

Hunter rubs my back and warmth radiates from his hand and lessens the load on my chest. I turn and can't believe I'm staring at my best friend, my other half from ten freaking years ago.

I chuckle to myself. My grandmother told me he was brought back into my life. It was odd, for sure, but I didn't think twice about it. She knew all along.

Hunter reaches up to wipe tears from my face I didn't know were there. A variety of emotions course through me—the sadness of losing him years ago, the confusion of how he came back into my life, the calmness he gives me by being near, then the happiness of having him back.

When I finally wrap my head around Hunter coming back to me, I tackle him, causing him to fall onto the back of the couch.

Hunter laughs as he holds me tight. A moment later, he sits up and repositions me to sit across his lap with my legs to the side and my head laying on his chest.

My arms are still locked around his neck. I never want to lose him again. I can't get over him being back in my life after all this time. More tears roll down my cheeks.

"I missed the fuck out of you, Anya. Every fucking day of my life." His chest rumbles with his deep yet quiet voice.

I pull away to look at his face. "Hunter, I can't believe it's really *you*. Every time I looked at you, something familiar stirred, but I couldn't place it. I knew that now was *not* the time to try and figure it out, since we have so much crap we're dealing with. But boy, have you grown! You aren't the scrawny little kid you used to be." I squeeze his bicep. "You have big, manly muscles and all!"

He starts laughing, "Well you filled out pretty well yourself." He gives me that knowing wink.

How could I have ever forgotten about those dimples?

I know I have my best friend back, but the feelings I'm having for him are far beyond friendly. Breaking eye contact, I stare down at my lap and see his strong legs under mine.

"Oh shit, I'm sorry. This was inappropriate of me." I realize I'm sitting on this grown man's lap being very intimate with him—I unwrap my arms from his neck. Add in the kiss... "I should have probably asked if you have a girlfriend before I tossed myself at you. I mean... I'm not trying to make a move on you... I don't want to overstep our boundaries either." I need to shut up. I try to pull away.

Hunter's arms are wrapped around my back holding me to him. He shifts and drapes his left arm over my legs while his other arm is still holding my back.

"Do you hear me complaining?"

My face heats.

"I wouldn't have pulled you into my lap if I had a girlfriend. Like I said earlier, I'm not home much. Work keeps me too busy to think of anything else. Plus, I've never found someone I wanted to start a relationship with. I don't see a point in being with someone if I can't see a future with them." A flash of yearning crosses his face before it disappears.

Hmm... Must have been my imagination.

"Wow, those have been my thoughts exactly. I don't get how others can casually date for the heck of it," I tell him.

"I would ask you the same question about a boyfriend, *but...* I'm pretty sure if I even *hint* that you have one, you may cut my balls off and feed them to the wendigo." He smirks and I burst out laughing.

I pat my leg. "Come here boy, Momma brought you a snack if you go in the cage like a good boy. Hmm..." I tap my chin.

Hunter grabs my hand and holds it to his chest—peering down at my boot with narrowed eyes.

Ha! He's worried about my dagger.

I give a devilish grin.

I'm still laughing when I say, "Hunter, I just got you back. I wouldn't want to hurt you on the *first* day you came back into my life. I mean...that would make me an asshole." I briefly pause, then say, "I can wait another day or two."

He shakes his head. "Second day, Anya. Today is the second day we've been together."

I narrow my eyes at him. "Nope, doesn't count. I didn't like you much when we met and I had no clue who you were either. At first, I thought you kidnapped me, and you were going to murder me before the night was over. I didn't even want to look at your face. If I could prove to you that I couldn't recognize you in a line-up, I may have had a chance at survival."

"You thought I would kill you?" His mouth drops and his eyes go wide.

"You tell me. Your first words to me were, 'Don't you fucking dare scream or you're dead.' That wasn't much of a friendly welcome, now was it?" I cock an eyebrow at him.

Hunter put his head in his hand as his elbow rests on my thigh, "Shit, you're right. I can see how you'd think that. I hope you know now, I meant you'd be dead because of the animal. I was trying to keep us safe."

"No shit, Sherlock! Yes, I figured that out when you *didn't* kill me last night. Then I started to realize you weren't *as* crazy as I initially thought."

"*As crazy*? Are you still hinting at me being crazy?" He gives me a side eye.

"Well yeah...the jury is still out." I stick out my tongue at him.

He rewards me with a poke.

"Hey, knock that off." I playfully slap him on his chest.

He pulls me closer until our foreheads touch.

"I'm sorry for assuming you were Grant's mistress. I got one look at you and instantly thought you were meeting him out there to be together, alone. For some reason, I had this strong sense of jealousy, and, if he wasn't already dead, I would've wanted to kill him. I can't say I've ever had that feeling before. I want to say... I'm sorry."

He was jealous? But we were complete strangers.

Did his soul recognize me as well?

I smile and wrap my arms around his neck and lay my head on his shoulder. My lips are close to his neck—which smells delicious.

"I forgive you. I just can't get over everything. The strangeness of this whole situation to begin with, then add in us and our history? We're hours away from our hometown and both end up in the same place anyways. It just doesn't make sense."

"Can I ask you something?" His voice is barely audible.

I lift my head to look him in the eyes. Worry washes over me when his smile falters a moment.

Shit, is this where he apologizes for kissing me and tells me it was all a mistake?

Maybe if I can play it off as no big deal, then he'll drop it. It'll probably be best to just brush it off and forget it anyway. I'm sure it was an innocent way to help me remember. Which is weird because we never kissed as kids.

Ugh, I need to stop overanalyzing it. It was a kiss between friends. Harmless. Means nothing.

I force a smile to encourage him. Hoping my thoughts weren't transparent on my face. "You can ask me anything."

"Why...how... *Shit*, I don't know how to say this." He rubs his hand over his face.

"What's going on?" I try to move off his lap again, but he holds me tight.

"How come you didn't recognize me or remember me? Even when I tried to jog your memory, you were clueless."

The big, strong, confident man is gone and he's replaced with the little boy from years ago.

My heart drops into my stomach.

How can I explain this to him in a way that would make sense?

"My mom." I take a deep breath. "The last thing I remember before, was her helping me sleep. I clearly didn't know what she was doing to me at the time, but in her effort to help calm my broken heart, she apparently put a wall up between my memories of you and the cognitive part of my brain. Every time I tried to figure out how I knew you, I was met by a block. I know it sounds crazy, and at first I didn't know how it happened, but then it started coming back to me."

Hunter lets out a relieved sigh and rests his head on my shoulder.

I reach my hands up and hold him, rubbing my hand over the stubble of his hair.

"I hate that I didn't recognize you, especially when you said your name. It was too much of a coincidence and...I don't know. There have been quite a few times in the past where I would see a girl and think she was you, only to be disappointed. I begged my parents to come back, even for one summer but they always refused."

Why would they refu—

"I'm so thankful I have you. I'm *not* happy about how it came about, but like I said before, we'll get through this. I promise," Hunter reassures me. Pulling me closer and holding on to me as if I'll slip away.

I let my question slide...for now.

"That's a pretty big promise to make, Hunter. You better keep it."

Hunter chuckles, then, with a sigh, he pats my thigh. "As much as I would love to just sit here like this the rest of the day, we need food. Let's go eat then head back to the castle to meet with the police. We need to get that over with and hope they can get out of there before dark. We can talk on the way over to figure out a plan for tonight."

Chapter Twelve

SOWILO

(ENLIGHTENMENT)

"If I walked nonstop, it would've taken me a little over a day to make it to town." I tell Hunter on our way to the castle. We had been trying to brainstorm different ideas on how to keep the wendigo from heading towards our town.

"Wait, you were going to walk home? With the wendigo on the loose?" Hunter pulls his eyes from the road and focuses on me. His knuckles turn white as he grips the steering wheel.

"Eyes on the road." I use my finger to push his face forward. "Clearly, you came and saved me *yet again* from having to do that. Don't get upset over things that never happened."

"You're right." He forces out a breath and the color rushes back to his knuckles when he eases his hold. "How fast can the wendigo go?"

"If my grandmother was right, it can only travel during the night. I would think if it's moving at normal speed, it could reach the town in"—I tap my chin—"two days? But, if I remember the tales correctly, it's fast—except when it is cold or hungry.

Hunter rubs a hand over his short beard, bringing my focus to the spot where the line of bristles stop.

I lick my lips, imagining my tongue trailing along the edge of where his jaw ends and his neck begins.

"Luck may be on our side between the cold front moving in tonight and the lack of food in this area, both should slow it down," he replies, bringing my focus back to our discussion.

"Plus they have to eat a lot *and* often. Since they prefer humans over animals, its diet will be very limited." Heaviness lifts from my chest and I take in a breath of fresh air.

"As long as it doesn't come back while everyone is still there. Let's hope they can wrap up the scene before dark." His voice is strained.

And...there goes the ability to breathe—again.

We don't even know where the wendigo went or who's at risk. The responsibility of keeping others safe is one-hundred percent on my shoulders. The Chinese finger trap grabs hold of my chest and tightens around my burning lungs.

"Hey, we will figure it out. Relax." Hunter pries my tight fingers from the center console between us and holds them.

I huff. *He* was the one stressing a minute ago, and now he's trying to comfort *me*? It's not fair to him. Pulling my hand away, I reach into my bag for a water and the journal.

Before we left my house, I decided to be better prepared this time and filled a bag with a few waters, snacks, my notebook, and the journal. I refuse to live off mineral water and a hundred plus year old jar of honey. Hunter had the same idea and loaded his heavy bag in the back.

After a few swallows, the liquid cools my overheated insides, and I go to place the bottle back in the bag when Hunter narrows his eyes at me.

"You want some?" I hold out the water to him.

He shakes his head and shifts his body, placing his right arm on top of the steering wheel and leans towards the door.

And clearly, I've now upset him.

I shrug and close up the bag. My fingers go to the thick parchment of the leather-bound book in my lap. The only way to save everyone is to figure out how my ancestors trapped the wendigo to begin with.

"Hey, Hunter?"

"Hmm?" He keeps his eyes straight.

"Why do you think the wendigo waited and didn't attack me right away like it did Grant? Was it playing with me or do you think it has anything to do with the light energy my grandmother was talking about?" Angling my body towards him, I lean my back against the door.

He taps a couple fingers on the wheel in thought. "I think it has to do with your energy or maybe your runes. The wendigo is cautious around you, which will give us an advantage. If it hadn't hesitated, you wouldn't have had the time to react, let alone run to the door. We may need that same hesitation next time we cross its path but, we can't rely on it," he gruffs out.

He's right. Whatever prevented it from attacking me right away won't save us. I need to figure out how to create the energy my ancestors used on the wendigo if we have any chance of survival.

"How many runes do you have, exactly? I just saw the one." Hunter's deep voice startles me out of my thoughts.

"Three. The Dagaz, which you saw on my forearm for 'light,' on my left shoulder blade is the Algiz for 'protection,' and Eihwaz for 'spiritual strength.' That one's on my lower back, near my left hip."

"Yeah, I don't have the slightest idea what the others look like. I only saw the little horizontal hourglass on your arm." Hunter glances at me.

Alright, I give him the benefit of the doubt.

"The Algiz is like a solid line, a tree trunk with two limbs branching out near the top. Some think it looks like an old pitch-fork."

"Sexy." He wiggles an eyebrow at me.

"Oh, shut up." I slap his shoulder. "They weren't *my* choices."

"Hey, they may have been what saved your life. Now, *that's* sexy," he drawls.

"You worry me sometimes, you know that?" I cock an eyebrow at him.

He shrugs.

"But you're right, it may have saved me." A shiver rolls down my spine. It's the thought that three simple drawings on my skin could have made the difference between life and death that creeps me out.

I fill him in on the Irish ritual my grandmother and mom performed on me when I turned eighteen. Everything from the trip to Ireland, the stone circle and chanting, all the way to the tattoos done the old-fashioned way. If it wasn't for Hunter knowing me as a kid, I'd be worried he thought my whole family were escapees from an insane asylum.

I mean, who has their family tattoo them and hand them an old dagger on their coming-of-age birthday?

"Wow, and how did you feel about it all?" he asks.

"The whole time, it gave me a sense of high but I thought it was from all the emotions my mom and grandmother were emanating, like empathy. I learned all too quickly that questioning them got me nowhere. I sure as shit didn't know it was going to be something to help me come into a magical power years later."

"You've gotta admit, it sounds pretty damn cool."

I shrug. It does, a little.

"How about the other sign, the... 'I was' one?" He smirks.

"It's Eihwaz. Yew-waz." I pronounce it slow for him.

"Yes, I. Was." His dimple pops, a clear sign he's screwing with me.

"Ugh." I swing my body around to face the front—away from the smart-ass—and close my eyelids.

A squeeze to my thigh pulls a sharp inhale from me and I shoot a glare at Hunter.

Brick by brick, he's breaking through my walls. Every minute I'm with him, my feelings grow stronger—despite how much I fight.

"I'm screwing with you. Yes, what's the Eihwaz look like?" His strong grip lingers.

Warmth radiates from his palm and a tingling sensation crawls up my leg to places it shouldn't be going.

"You're going to drive me crazy, you know that?" I push his hand away.

"That's my plan." His mouth tilts up and he winks.

"*Anyways*," ignoring his charm the best I can, "The only way I can think to explain this one...is a letter 'Z.' Invert it then tilt it on the bottom corner."

"Like the Harry Potter symbol?" His voice is laced with sarcasm.

I narrow my eyes.

He puts a hand up in defense. "Okay, okay, it's not a lightning bolt then."

Wait, my tattoos are also on my dagger. This could have been a hell of a lot easier to show him the damn thing. As I pull my dagger from my boot...

"Whoa! I was teasing you, Anya, no need to get violent. Just playing around, like when we were kids." He eyes my dagger. "You can put that away now."

A Cheshire cat grin spreads across my face.

"I'm teasing you, *Hunter*, no need to be *scared*." I mock him and laugh. "In all seriousness, though, I'm trying to show you the symbols. Here, look." I lightly touch the tip of the blade, holding the dagger out for him to view.

"Ah, okay. I'd still rather see it on *you* than on something that can gut me." His side-eye ping pongs from the dagger to me and back as I put it away.

"Har-har. Can we get back on topic now?" It's a long drive but not long enough to figure out this light energy before we arrive at the castle.

As he tilts his head toward me, there's a twinkle in Hunter's eyes. "Right, what's next on the agenda?"

"Figuring out how the hell I'm going to tap into this power I'm supposed to have. I don't have the slightest clue where to begin." I bite my lip.

"Maybe I can help. Like you, I have a little Celtic background but mine is on my Dad's Scottish side. They were what most people call apothecaries. They used herbs for many different reasons, not only for medicinal purposes. Our family can create protections and enhance someone's emotions and natural energies in their body. I *may* be able to concoct a tincture or tea to help get you past your mind and become more attuned with your emotions and spiritual side."

"When the hell did you learn about herbs?" My eyebrows raise to my hairline—or so it feels. He never talked about this when we were younger, yet it makes more sense why we were brought back together. Our families had a lot of similarities with gifts handed down from Celtic clans—his from Scotland, mine from Ireland. This gives me hope that we will make a perfect team.

"Growing up, I watched my dad mess around with herbs. It was natural and didn't seem strange to me. We never hung out with our parents so I doubt you ever saw him."

"That's true." I think back to us escaping our houses to meet. We didn't care one bit about what they were doing. I wouldn't have paid attention if I saw his dad messing with herbs. But what I still couldn't wrap my head around was why he never tried to reach out to me. "Can I ask, why did your parents refuse to let us know where you were moving, or allow us to keep in contact?" I'm not mad, I'm more hurt that his parents apparently didn't like me.

Hunter clenches his jaw and tightens his grip on the steering wheel. "My father moved us around a lot. After we left that day, we couldn't stay in the same place for more than six months at a time. He blamed it on his job. He was always switching jobs and with it, he had to switch phones. I wouldn't have had a number to give you. Any time I asked to borrow his phone or write to you, he told me I couldn't yet and to give it some time. I had no idea why I needed to give it time. I was miserable and needed to hear your voice."

My heart skips a beat. Knowing he missed me just as bad as I missed him, I melt. I wasn't alone, but I don't get why he couldn't find another way to contact me.

"What about a house phone? Did they hate me that much?"

"They definitely didn't hate you, Anya. Mom told me that house phones cost too much money so, during moves, I tried calling you from the hotel phones. Every time I went to dial, the line was dead. I figured we were too poor to get a room with a working phone. I didn't find out until much later that they were disconnecting the phone so I couldn't reach out." He grinds his teeth. "Years later, I found out the real reason we had to move." He pauses.

I wipe my sweaty palms on my jeans and leave them there, trying to avoid ruining the journal still in my lap.

"Dad said people were after me."

I straighten in my seat.

"What? What do you mean, 'after you?' Did you get arrested for something?" I lean forward.

"No, I wish that *were* the case." He takes a deep breath and rubs the back of his neck. "Like you, I have some *unique* traits passed down through my blood. Much stronger than what my dad possessed."

"O-kaayy..." That doesn't sound too bad.

"There was a certain group of people after us...well actually, after *me*. We thought we were safe since we successfully stayed hidden for five long years. The only reason they found us then must've been because they'd found someone with better tracking skills and our location was compromised. After we left you when I was fifteen, we continued to run successfully for years. Until one day they finally caught up with us and ran my parents off the road."

I gasp.

"They thought I was with them and they had every intention of kidnapping me. Once they trapped my parents and realized I wasn't in the car, they"—he cleared his throat—"tortured both of them. Their only goal was to find me. My mom and dad died trying to protect me. I am pretty sure even if I was with them, they would have still killed my parents."

Tears stream down my face.

How could this happen?

There shouldn't be that type of evil in the world. My heart aches for Hunter and what he lost that day. I can't imagine how it would feel losing not one, but both your parents. Especially because someone wanted you for their own selfish reasons.

I reach over and place my hand on Hunter's fisted one, not sure if I'm trying to comfort him or me—it doesn't matter.

"How old were you?" I ask softly.

"Just graduated high school. I didn't know what to do with my life and without my family... I felt lost..." His voice drops off and he swallows hard.

My eyes catch the bob of his Adam's apple and bile rises into my throat.

Tightening his grip on the wheel again, he continues "I was alone in the world and had nothing better to do, other than continue doing what my parents fought so hard to do—avoid being captured by those assholes." Rage radiates off him in waves.

As much as his energy and words cause my own fury to build up inside, I rub my thumb softly over the back of his hand to relax him. "What did you do?"

"My first thought was to find you. I had no choice but to bury that need because I wouldn't be able to live with myself if I brought the same fate onto you as I did my parents; so I enlisted in the Marines. I figured, my dad had already trained me as a tracker, and along with my natural talent—or gifts as you would call them—it wasn't hard to find my place in the military. It didn't take long to become valuable. I could locate enemies that our government had been incapable of tracking." His fist relaxes under my hand. "It's the main reason why I was wanted by the wrong people."

Was the kiss his way of tracking my memories down? Was he the one who pulled them to the surface? A burning sensation enters my stomach. But does that mean he kissed others to do the same?

Do I ask him?

Nah, not right now. Or maybe never.

"It must have been a relief to be able to make such a positive impact serving our country and being safe from that group, huh?"

Hunter's hollow laugh fills the truck cabin. "You would think. I was on tour overseas. Something that group *didn't* know was that I have the ability to disappear without a trace so no one can find me. I wish that was the case for my parents." He says the last part under his breath. "Even with the assistance of tracking dogs or heat sensors, no one could locate me unless I wanted them to. I was an ocean away from them so I never felt the need to hide."

"How is that possible?"

"It started with my gifts and specific herbs my dad taught me. Then the military added to those skills by training me how to use nature, like rocks with natural lead in them, to disappear and how to cover my tracks. I thought I'd be able to breathe and not have to look over my shoulder twenty-four-seven. I was wrong. So very wrong."

A knot forms in my stomach. "What happened?"

"My enlistment was public record and the group used it to track me down."

My hand flies to my mouth as my heart drops.

Slowly I drop my hand and grip my chest. "Oh my God, they found you!?"

"One day, they located where I was stationed. I'm not sure if they had a tracker of their own or a spy in the military watching me. When they couldn't find me immediately, they captured a few of the marines assigned to my Company—my men." Hunter looks at me—guilt hardens his face. "Just to lure me out. By that point, I'd guaranteed I was untraceable, but I couldn't leave my men to suffer at their hands while I escaped."

I squeeze his hand in reassurance that I am ready to hear what came next.

"I snuck into their complex late at night and took out each and every one of them. I'm not proud of what I had to do. My brothers never deserved to go through what they did because of me, especially the ones we had to bring home in body bags. But I finally ended it, I ended *them.*" He lays his head back against the headrest, his exhaustion is evident while he steers us around the mountain curves.

I grind my teeth. "Did you know who this group was?"

"I called them *Ghost*, because many don't believe they exist, but only those who have the ability to see, know they do. They were some powerful people and were responsible for a lot of kidnappings. I know they mainly took children since they're easier to manipulate. I was one of the lucky ones who was able to escape their grasp, even when they kept pursuing me, regardless of age."

Children? What the fuck is wrong with these people?

"What happened to everyone else?"

He shrugs. "I've tried to ignore that part of the organization after I eliminated them, but to this day, it still keeps me up late at night. I have software set up to monitor the dark web if anyone like them pops up again."

The thought of an evil like that in the world is beyond scary. "Thank you for sharing that with me."

Hunter fidgets in his seat. "Yeah, well...you deserve to know."

It's strange to see him uncomfortable.

"I appreciate it—more than you know. I can't imagine what you went through, and it's unfortunate when the loss of others or unfortunate situations lead us to who we are meant to be. I really wish you never had to deal with it to begin with."

"It was a shitty hand to be dealt, for sure, but you're right. I'm a different person because of it. And I'm here with you now." He gives me a weak smile.

"Well, if it makes you feel better, I can certify that you've got that stealth mode *perfected*. Add in your tracking gift? I can see why becoming a private investigator would be the perfect job for you."

"You're right about the PI job, it *is* perfect for me." His voice brightens, and I can see him trying to shake off his memories.

I start to smile, but stop when I think about his parents and military family. "Do you...blame yourself for their deaths?" I tighten my hold, hoping the answer is no. I don't want that guilt weighing on him from something he couldn't control.

He clears his throat. "At first, when my parents were killed, I felt it was all my fault. But the military helped me grow up a lot, and I quickly learned that what happens in the hands of others is out of your control. There's so much evil in the world; you can fight your hardest to stop them, but the blood on their hands is on *theirs* alone, not yours. So, the answer is...no, I don't blame myself anymore." He pauses. "The situation will be the same with the wendigo, Anya."

He flips over his hand and laces our fingers together. "Please know that we will do *everything* in our power to stop it. But if there are more casualties, I need you to realize that we did what we could to prevent them. I'm in this with you one-hundred percent. I want to give you fair warning that this may not be easy, and there are *no* guarantees that no one else will get hurt. Can you promise me that you won't take on the blame for any negative outcomes?"

Fuuucck...I never thought of the emotional trauma this may cause me in the end. I know a lot's riding on how I handle it all.

Can I really live with myself? Even if something happens to someone I know?

Hunter's words about the blood being on the hands of evil, not ours, fills my mind.

I nod and give a heavy sigh. "I can't make any promises, but I'll try my best. At least I'm not alone in this. I'm glad I have you."

Everything he's gone through to become the man he turned into amazes me. Giving him a smirk, I say, "You certainly do have that hero complex down, don't ya?"

That gets his lips to curl at the sides and I can almost see that sweet, vulnerable boy from years ago peeking out. I study his strong jaw under the dark stubble. He's changed a lot.

Why couldn't things be different?

There's been too much time lost between us; the need for answers overwhelms me.

"Why didn't you look for me after you got out of the military?" Knowing what I know now, it would have been easy for him to locate me after it was safe.

As if he was afraid to let go, his grip tightens around my hand.

"I wanted to. Too many times to count I'd been tempted to track you down, but I was scared you wouldn't know who I was, or worse, you would be mad at me for leaving. Unable to forgive me."

"You were a child. How could I *not* forgive you?" I argue.

"I refused to risk it. To have you in front of me, but want nothing to do with me? It would be like losing you twice," his voice chokes up. "The decision was hard, but I took the coward's way out and left you alone."

"You really didn't know I lived here?" Keeping the hurt out of my voice proved to be impossible.

"No, no clue. If I'd known, do you know how much I would've driven myself crazy on the 'what ifs?' Shit...back in the castle, I thought the coincidence was some cruel joke of fate. Punishment for my past."

I digest his words. "I'm not sure what I would've done if my mom hadn't hidden you from my memories. And to be honest, if you'd have come to me, I'd have thought you were a crazy stalker." I chuckle. "Not like our situation was much different, but I came to trust you, and it helped soften the blow of all this"—I wave my other hand between us—"weirdness. I'm beyond grateful that I have you back."

He nods, "Me too, Anya." He caresses the crook of my thumb with his. "Me too."

In another world, maybe there could be something between us—more than our rekindled friendship. But in this world, once this is over, he leaves. Going back to traveling for his job. He's used to moving around. I can't hold him back. Even if there were something else between us, I couldn't risk him living with the regret.

My focus needs to be on our current issue. To give me a bit of space, I slip my hand out of Hunter's and finger the leather cover of the journal.

"How long do we have until we arrive?" I ask.

From the side of my eye, Hunter gives me a curious gaze then brings his focus back on the road.

"About forty-five minutes. You thinking about trying again with the journal?"

I nod and trace the Dagaz 'light' rune on the cover. "Grandmother said daylight will help me. Do you think she meant some of the pages are in English? I only flipped through the first couple pages. Or maybe it's like disappearing ink that becomes visible in UV light."

He chuckles. "Well, we won't know until you try."

Spreading my fingers over the book, I take a few deep breaths. Relaxing my mind and body to prepare for...what? Disappointment?

It's hard to relax when my stomach is performing acrobats.

Am I placing too much faith that words on a page will make everything go away? I NEED this to have answers.

I close my eyes, and, like a sailor called by a siren on the sea, the book calls to me. Energy filled with warmth pulses from the journal and radiates into my palms, then rushes into my chest. I open my eyes and light shines between my fingertips. Bright, beautiful white and yellow light emanating from the book. My heartbeat quickens.

Are they coming from the runes like the door and stone?

Trying not to distract Hunter, I lift my hand, angling it away from him, and my heart drops, catching in my stomach.

The light isn't coming from the runes burned on the cover of the leather binding, it isn't even coming from the book at all. It shines from the center of my palm, as though I'm holding an illuminating orb. I stare into the orb and images begin to appear. Like a moth to a flame, I'm pulled in. My surroundings disappear as I'm engulfed.

Like a miniature movie projector playing, I make out thick woods with trees cleared from a large area and stacked in piles near the edge of the forest. Men with axes are removing branches from the trunks of the maple and birch trees, adding the limbs to a roaring bonfire.

Based on their thick slacks tucked into leather-soled boots, tunics tapered at their waists by leather straps, and wool tossed around their shoulders, this happened many centuries ago.

A huge area has been dug out and prepared for an infrastructure. Torch flames flicker, bouncing off the walls of the fifteen-foot-deep section—illuminating the ground and partially bricked floor that the afternoon sun doesn't touch. More men are digging with hand-crafted tools and a mound of siliciclastic stones—a mixture of clay, limestone, and quartz solidified together—sit in a corner of the crater.

Dirt stairs align two sides to allow an in and out for the workers.

The men work efficiently with pointed poles and axes to break up the dirt and shovel it into buckets. Younger men take the heavy loads up to the woods, returning with empty pails.

My attention is drawn to a man in the corner. He leans on his shovel-like tool and gapes at the ground. Bubbling out is a thick, black liquid.

Tar?

Oil?

The man backs away, the liquid no longer pooling over the dirt but beginning to solidify. More and more of the ooze comes up from the earth and shapes itself into the body of an animal.

The body is covered in the black, tar-like substance with thick coarse hair developing underneath. The man backs up slowly while the animal continues to grow. The substance drips off its protruding rib, hip, and shoulder bones. A low growl rumbles like an impending thunderstorm, echoing off the empty walls.

The man doesn't break eye contact as he backpedals, bumping into others as he goes. His strange behavior pulls the attention towards him instead of the growing creature in the corner.

The animal becomes larger by the minute, and its features become more prominent. Horns branch out from a head that's a mix between a buck and a bear. Red, glowing eyes peek from beneath the melting ooze. A lizard-like tongue sneaks past snapping jaws filled with razor sharp teeth ready to feast. Its long, hunched torso is still missing patches of flesh, but it doesn't seem to be gaining anymore either.

The growling intensifies as the hideous beast starts to get up. That's when the other men realize what's happening. Screams fill the air and they push each other out of the way to escape the deep pit. Men fall over one another, some getting trampled in the process.

Behind them, the beast stands upright on its strong, hooved back legs. The two front ones drag three extended claws on the ground.

Once it's fully erect at about nine feet tall, it leaps onto the closest man and tears into his throat, leaving the cervical spine visible. The man's blood seeps into the dark dirt. When the monster picks him up, the man's neck folds in half, his head dangling from the remaining tendons. His eyes are blank and lifeless.

He had no chance, no *hope* of surviving.

Horrified, I can't tear my gaze away from the scene unfolding before me.

The creature continues to feast on the flesh, tearing at the limbs and abdomen. Its demon eyes glance up from the current appetizer to see one last man still in the pit, tripping as he scrambles his way up a set of stairs.

With the speed of a lion, the beast pounces on the man, slicing his back open with its dagger claws. Blood-curdling screams turn to drowning gurgles as his body is dragged away from the last step and the animal devours its second course.

Two older women appear at the edge, a thin veil of light surrounds the shorter one and even with the monster below, her narrow eyes and set jaw say she is more determined than scared. The taller one in the dark robe stands back, her mouth moves but I can't make out anything.

The creature makes its way over to her slowly. Compared to the men, it hesitates with her.

The smaller woman kneels next to the drop off in a corner, her palms facing out. She closes her eyes and raises her head to the illuminated moon. A vibrant energy emanates from her palms and spreads to her fingertips. The radiance heats up like a meteor hitting the earth's atmosphere. Just as the burning brightens as the gasses heat up, so do her hands. A wave of warmth emanating from her hits me in the face. It surprisingly doesn't hurt like a radioactive flare, but comforts like a warm fireplace.

The few who remain near the dig site shield their eyes from the magical sun she creates.

Drawing in a deep breath, she slams her hands to the ground. A blinding, white light shoots out across the ground and over the opening. It creates a force field, trapping the creature in the pit. It scratches the walls in a frenzy to escape and lets out an inhuman cry. As it rears back to leap through the light field—I jerk back; my heart beating out of my chest.

I'm back in the truck and it's pulled haphazardly on the side of the road. *Did we get in an accident?*

Panicking and confused, I look to Hunter to make sure he is okay.

Despite the pair of sunglasses he put on at some point, he's staring at me with his eyebrows raised high on his forehead and his lips parted.

"What happened?" My voice trembles.

Did we hit something? I touch my head for any injuries and my hand not only comes away clean, but I don't feel any pain. "Hunter? What's wrong?" The shaking in my voice becomes more prominent.

"What's wrong?! You're asking *me* what's wrong? What the hell *was* that, Anya?" He's out of breath, as if he sprinted a mile.

"What the hell was what?" I ask, anxiety courses through my veins, making my skin crawl.

"Your palm became its very own flashlight. I tried to keep driving and leave you alone. The more you did"—he silently waves his hand around like a crazy man—"whatever the fuck you were do-ing, it became a little hard to ignore. The light blazed even brighter. I called your name over and over, but you didn't respond." He rubs a hand through his hair. "Fuck! I was *yelling* your name and still nothing. That shit was heating up the truck and I did *not* want to risk burning myself by touching you. You had a miniature sun in your hand. I couldn't see a fucking thing. What *was* that? What happened?" His body turns towards me and his chest heaves.

My jaw hangs open. "I... I don't know. First, I was feeling the energy of the book, then light started coming from it. Only it wasn't from the book at all—it was from *me*. I tried not to distract you, but there were images inside the orb. I couldn't tear my eyes away. But I saw it, I saw it all." My leg bounces uncontrollably.

"Hang on." Hunter pulls the truck further off the road into a safer area and parks it before turning to me again. "You saw what exactly?" His spine goes straight.

"The beginning," my heart rate quickens. "How the wendigo was found and who released it..." I explain to Hunter how it all played out.

When I finished, he was staring out the windshield, deep in thought.

"Wow." He rests his forearms on the steering wheel. "I, uh... I guess you didn't need to worry about not reading the journal; it seems you found your own way of reading it." He makes a half-hearted chuckle. "You said you saw the old woman place a light field above the wendigo, trapping him in. That was when the woman's hands were the brightest, at the end, right?"

I nod. "Yes, it was almost blinding."

"Well, sweetheart, from what I saw on my side, I think you tapped into that same exact energy. What I saw was *extraordinary*—and retinal burning. That energy didn't come from the journal, it just showed you what you already have inside." He reaches out to grab my hand but pulls back quickly.

"I'm pretty sure you're safe to touch me now." I reach over to him.

He nods. "This is good, this is all *very* good. How do you feel? Tired? Hungry? Do you feel any different?" He flips my hand over in his, spreading my fingers out as he studies them.

"I actually feel more alert and have a burst of energy. Physically, I'm great."

That energy is seriously inside me?

If someone told me this years ago, I could have saved a crapload on my electricity bills.

"And emotionally?" he coaxes, running his callused finger over my palm.

"I'm pretty freaked out." But the tingles he creates in my hand lessens the overwhelming feelings.

A little.

I can't get over the vision...hundreds of years ago those men unearthed the wendigo while building—what I'm pretty sure was—the castle. The woman has to be my ancestor, but why was she there to begin with? And how did she know what to do? She saved so many lives that night, it could have been much worse than the two men.

I shiver.

Their screams and all the blood. If the energy wasn't coursing through my veins right now on a leftover high, I'm pretty sure I would be puking from what I saw.

Two demon eyes flash behind my vision, sending a hard ball to the pit of my stomach. The ginormous creature from Hell, with black ooze dripping off the patches of fur and protruding bones, is something even a nightmare can't conjure up. We are in over our heads when it comes to the wendigo.

"We don't stand a chance against the wendigo."

He narrows his eyes. "What do you mean?"

"I mean, if you had one look at the thing, you'd be driving us out of the state. *Shit*, you'd probably leave the country and still not feel it was far enough away." I shift in my seat uncomfortably. My body's temperature rises as anxiety trickles its way through my nerves.

Hunter grabs the back of his neck, massaging the corded muscles. "I guess it's a good thing I haven't seen it because I'm not ready to back down."

"But what if *I'm* ready to back down?"

His gaze holds me captive. "Are you?"

I sigh and lean back in my seat. "No," I grumble.

"Good. I knew you weren't one to give up easily."

And boy, do I wish I were.

Let's hope that stubbornness isn't what gets us both killed.

Chapter Thirteen

PERTHO

(MYSTERY)

"Do you think you can replicate the same energy?" Hunter's voice interrupts my thoughts of our possible demise from a mythical creature.

"I don't know. That was the first time something like that ever happened. I'm not sure how to do it again." I wish we had more time to practice, but I'm not going to try until I'm out of this truck and the officers at the castle are gone. If I can do this again, I'm not sure how to control it, and the last thing I need is casualties from my experimenting.

Sitting in Hunter's truck on the side of the curvy road is not the place to be playing with magic. Or whatever *this* is.

"What do we do now?" I bite the inside of my cheek.

"How about you *open* the journal this time, maybe with less *feeling* and more reading?" He suggests with a nervous smile.

I laugh. "Are you calling me an emotionally unstable woman?"

He coughs and tries to backpedal, "Whoa, now. Those are your words. Not mine. That's *not* what I meant, you are completely stable, what I was trying t—"

"I was joking, settle down." I hold my stomach as I chuckle. "Sometimes, you are just too easy."

He shakes his head and snickers. "Only when it comes to you." He points to the journal in my lap. "Hopefully the thing will have something legible or maybe pictures."

"Ha." *Can we be so lucky?* "And maybe it has a table, graphs, and checklist too on how to defeat something twice my size?" I glare at him, hoping I conveyed my sarcasm clearly. "Sorry, Hunter, I highly doubt it. Last time I checked, it was all foreign." A thought hits me and the ball in my belly decreases in size. "But...if there are runes on the outside, maybe there are some that are recognizable inside."

"One way to find out," he suggests and reluctantly releases my hand, putting the truck into drive and pulling back onto the empty road. Maybe it's a good thing that we haven't seen another soul since we've been driving. Less chance of gapers.

Given the thickness of the parchment bound together by leather ties, I estimate it to contain around seventy-five to a hundred pages.

I'm fingering the pages when Hunter asks, "You nervous?"

I gulp. "You can say that." I try to push in the few loose pieces of parchment, not wanting to lose any.

His gentle eyes meet mine. "It'll work out."

"How can you be so sure?" I'm wound up tighter than a two-dollar watch. My leg shakes and my chest heaves.

"If you don't have faith, you have nothing. Without it, you will never survive. What's the worst that you'd find?"

"Oh, maybe it'll have absolutely zero answers for us and we're back to square one. Or that it *has* the answers but in an ancient language that no one can translate." I raise my eyebrow and purse my lips.

He sets his hand over my twitching one laying on the book. A wave of sedation spreads from his hands into mine, the tension eases, and I relax my body into the seat. I don't know how he does it but I'm thankful for his ability to ground me.

"And if that happens, we will still figure something out."

I groan and he rubs his thumb across my knuckles before returning his hand to the wheel. My eyes are zoned in on my hand where I can still feel Hunter's touch lingering and I shake my head.

Knock it off, Anya, get your priorities straight.

I pull back the cover of the journal as Hunter pulls back onto the road.

It's now or never.

One parchment page after another flips through my fingers and I continue to have no recognition of the characters before me. The author felt the need to keep their experience a secret. What they should have done was list the instructions on the side of the door in the dungeon as a 'how-to.'

Tension in my shoulders kinks and with each turn of a page, the knots wrap tighter, causing pain in the back of my eyes and forehead.

Why is nothing going right for me?

"Well, the worst-case scenario has officially happened." I rub the center of my brow to alleviate some discomfort.

"What?" Hunter glances to me.

"Not a fucking thing that will help us. If the answers are here, I don't know because, *oh yeah,* I can't flipping understand any of it!"

His mouth pinches. "Are you sure you looked at all the pages? You were skimming through pretty fast. Maybe you missed something. A key to decode it, maybe?"

"Oh yes, sorry, I forgot my decoder ring in my cereal box this morning." The blood in my veins begins to boil. "None of it is in English. I think it's Ancient Gaelic but since I can't read it, I can't say. All of this freaking book is written in an old foreign language. No pictures, no runes, nothing that can help. So yeah, Hunter, we've got nothing."

His hand runs over his beard. "Maybe—"

I raise my hand and cut him off. "*No.* Whatever you are going to say next, no. Unless you want to give it a try. I've looked it over and it's not something I can decipher. But have at it." I hold out the journal to him. If he thinks he has a chance, he can go for it but if not, we're fucked.

He releases an exasperated breath and pushes the book back to me. His hand returns to the steering wheel, his knuckles white from the pressure. "We'll find another way," he mumbles to himself more than to me.

Will we though? Can we turn back around to find that alternative path to take instead of this failing one?

Aggravation buzzes through my system like an electric current set on high frequency. Wishing on a make-believe star, I open up the book to humor myself. The pages again sit there and mock me, causing the current to build up.

Argh! I need a release, but I'm stuck in this stupid truck with no answers.

"Goddammit!" I slam the journal shut in frustration and—

Gasp!

My surroundings disappear, along with Hunter. I'm falling into a tunnel of yellow light and images flash by me while I continue my descent.

Shit, shit, shit...

I throw my hands and feet out to somehow stop the fast falling but there's nothing I can grab onto beyond the light.

Suddenly, everything goes black and my feet are on hard ground. Blinking, I try to focus. I hear words. At first they aren't in English but as I continue to blink and shake my head through the blackness, the words become clearer and I can understand them. People start forming from the darkness. I cough from the smoke-filled air and try to make out why I'm hearing cries from men, women, and children.

Did Hunter and I get into an accident? Are there others involved?

"Hunter? Hunter!" I yell.

I can't hear him. *Why can't I at least feel him?*

"Hunter!" I scream his name, but it's drowned out by the other cries.

Damn it. Another vision.

I stumble and look down at what I tripped over. I reach my hand up to stifle a cry. A woman's bloody and dirty body lays at my feet, her eyes wide open and lifeless. An ax is impaled between her shoulder and neck. The earth around her sucks up the blood pouring out of her as though her essence is its life source.

What the hell is going on? This is nothing *like the last one.*

I take in my surroundings. Off in the distance are the recent remains of an old, stone church. The stone is stained black, and smoke is still coming from the remnants. Near the church, men with metal studded helmets are carrying axes, swords, and spears. From afar, only the lower half of their faces are showing, along with their dark eyes hidden behind metal brow ridges—the metal acting as a shield for their eyes.

Bone chilling cries come from the direction of the armored men as bodies fall quickly at their hands.

What the fuck, I need to get out of here. Wherever here is.

I search for an escape. To my left are woods, to my right, boats line the shore with more men filling the decks.

Why is there water and boats?

There are no lakes around where we were driving.

What happened when I slammed the book shut?

Replaying it in my mind, I run through every small detail. I was pissed I couldn't read the words in the journal. Then I laid my hand on the front of the book and pushed it closed.

Hard.

All while wishing I could understand some part of the text. Any part.

I bump into a man as he scrambles to pick up his belongings.

"I'm so sorry." I say, but he doesn't respond. And come to think of it, he never budged when I ran into him.

"Sir, can you help me, *please*?"

He ignores me and keeps working. I tap him on the shoulder and still nothing.

"Does anyone hear me?" I scream at the top of my lungs. Taking in the frantic faces around me, not a single person flinches or looks in my direction.

I move around the woman's body on the ground and start walking. I need to find answers, or a way out of here.

How can a vision feel so *real*?

A little girl hides under a fallen cart.

I move closer and lean down to her as she trembles. "Hey, don't be scared. I can help you." *But can I?* "Do you know where your parents are?"

She looks past me as though I'm not there.

I reach in slowly and try to pull her, but I can't. She doesn't budge. She is like an image in stone before me, just like the man.

I glance around and tremble.

I can't help these people.

I can't do anything.

Everyone around me is dealing with this horrible reality, but it's like I'm in this alternate universe where I'm unable to alter a single detail. I need to find a way out. A glow catches my eye. I drift towards it and see a woman, the same woman from my first vision—my ancestor. She's kneeling over a man who has a deep cut across his chest. Her hands illuminate before she places them over his wounds. She whispers words I can't hear and the man's pain eases. His cuts are still there but not as deep.

Just like a flashlight, she turns off her power and pulls out a cloth and some clumpy green paste from the side pouch she's wearing. As she's dressing his wounds, he thanks her.

"Please, I wish I could do more. I can only lessen the severity, but your body still needs to heal the rest of the way."

The man stills the woman's hand, "Aoife, this is more than anyone can do. You are a blessing."

She nods her head and finishes wrapping him before helping him get up.

"Hurry, we don't have time, the dark foreigners are getting close," she tells him.

Once the man is steady, the woman named Aoife walks briskly over to a woman struggling to grab things with a toddler on her hip.

I follow her.

This strange way the journal's showing me events this time is so realistic. I'm no longer watching, I'm here *with* them.

"Here." Aoife picks up a bag and makes quick work of packing up as many supplies as possible then hands them to the woman.

"Oh, thank you! Gods be with you," the woman says before rushing off.

Aoife continues to make her way around the broken and beaten, she moves farther away from the 'dark foreigners' as they called them and closer towards the woods. She abruptly stops and stands taller, pulling her shoulders back. One of her hands goes behind her back and creates a 'light' orb in her tight grip.

I step around her to see what has her on edge.

A woman with a long, dark robe with runes sewn into it stands tall, staring at Aoife with parted lips.

I suck in a breath.

Is she the *Viking witch? The same seeress my grandmother would tell me about who helped our family escape Ireland?*

My heartrate picks up speed as I watch the two in a stare down. They don't take their eyes off each other while tension fills the air.

The seeress moves first, holding one hand up as if she is trying to portray a sign of peace. Aoife must not feel threatened because she puts out her ball of light.

"Please, I come to help, not harm."

"That's not what the men you came with are doing." Aoife tilts her chin to the ruins and horror they've created.

"Yes, but I came to this land only by means of escaping them myself. I don't condone their actions and have been trying to free myself from them. We can help one another." The faintest sign of uncertainty flashes in the seeress' eyes.

"And why do you feel I can help you when my people are the ones under attack by your savages?"

"Because, you are like me. You are born of magic."

Aoife gasps. "What do you want?"

"I know the route my people plan to take so I know the paths to avoid them. I can help your clan in exchange for safe passage, food, and shelter." She glances over Aoife's shoulder to the men and back to Aoife. "Please, we don't have much time."

I try to read the honesty behind her eyes and even though I know what happens later, I'm curious if that was the seeress' initial intent.

Aoife nods her head in agreement. "Follow me."

It's hard, but I keep up with the women as they make their way through the woods to a cave. The men standing guard outside let them both through with a nod from Aoife. They, of course, give me no notice. Only showing curiosity with upturned eyebrows towards the stranger.

Dim light illuminates the inside of the cave and the women approach two men I recognize from the vision. They were there the night the wendigo was freed. One is around seventy, with white hair and beard. His body is slim and frail. The other may be in his early fifties with blondish-red hair. He appears a lot healthier with his tall, thick build.

"Chieftain Donnchadh, Chieftain Ó Bradáin," She bows. "I come with news. This woman is offering her help in exchange for safety from the same people we are running from." She looks to the seeress and back to the men. "I trust her. She will not lead us astray."

The men converse in whispers, sparing glances at the two women often.

I can't hold back biting the inside of my cheek and twisting my hands. Even when I know their decision.

"What is your name, woman?" They narrow their eyes at the seeress.

"Gudrun. I am a seeress like your gifted woman here," she gestures towards Aoife, "I have skills to help you. My gods told me that you would allow me to help and not take advantage of me as my people have."

"What do you know?"

"My people plan to take over this land. They have already destroyed the resources where we came from and they will exhaust the resources here as well. They will kill all who oppose them, enslave your people who do not fight them, and take your women as their own. We must leave and go far away. They have good trackers. The best route to take, to avoid detection, is over water."

"Ó Bradáin, I know of a place, but it will take us long to arrive," the older man says to the other.

"To the new land?" he grunted.

The other man nods and turns his attention to Aoife. "What are your suggestions?"

"I have felt for a while now that we need to leave our home and create a new one. This journey to the new land is what will save our people. How fast can we prepare?"

Once more, the Chieftains huddle together, nodding and whispering. The women stand patiently.

"We leave by nightfall; the dark foreigners are too close for it to be delayed further."

Chapter Fourteen

Mannaz

(Past Knowledge)

Sitting against the cave wall with my arms curled around my bent knees, I'm stuck in Ireland's past—however many hundreds of years ago that is. Whether this is the result of an accident or I've been transported into the words of the journal, I don't know.

I'm praying it's the latter, and not just for my sake but Hunter's too. I'm worried about what he's going through. Last we talked, it was an argument that *I* had started. He didn't have any more answers than I did and I lashed out in fear.

What if he's hurt and bleeding out while I'm trapped—unable to save him?

I shiver against the damp stone walls, trying—and failing—not to break down. People are coming and going while Aoife and Gudrun talk about their powers and the upcoming trip. Gudrun has skills of herbs, spells, and guidance from her gods. Aoife has the power of light, minor healing, helping crops, and creating fire, but she doesn't get into too much detail, which irritates me further. She also doesn't discuss how she creates the magic to begin with.

I tried many times to leave the cave, but I can't go outside the vicinity of Aoife. I hit a black veil that hurts like hell. When I first attempted to walk through it, it was like slamming into a wall. I rub the knot on my forehead and wince.

I wish there's a fast forward on whatever this is. I'm wasting too much time—time I don't have—and all I want to do is get back to Hunter.

"It's time," the red-headed Chieftain announces. Everyone grabs their final supplies and leaves the cave. I get up and follow them out. We walk through the forests for a while until it opens to an inlet with a large boat.

Gudrun halts Aoife with a hand. "How did you prepare this in such a short time?" Her hand points to the ship.

"The Chieftains have talked of leaving for a long time but struggled to make the final decision to go. They built this many seasons ago. Come." Aoife walks up to the ship, placing her hand on the wooden exterior and lights burst as wisps of smoke swirl around her palms. She lifts her hand and a protection rune—Algiz—appears, burned into the wood.

Gudrun traces her hand over the scorched marking. "How do you know of this symbol?"

"It's been passed down in my family. Why?" Her brows furrow.

Gudrun shakes her head. "It's an old language, one I didn't know was established in your land. It...caught me by surprise." She places her hand over the symbol, chanting a few words under her breath and when she steps away, it glows. "We will have a safe journey. You and I have a blessed future ahead."

Everything surrounding me fades, my heart rate increases, and I begin to sweat.

Please tell me I'm returning to Hunter.

My body free falls into the yellow abyss. The pounding in my ears from my hammering heartbeat intensifies as I drop until the light goes black.

"Hunter?"

I'm met with silence.

My vision clears quicker than before and I'm in the woods.

"Are you sure this is it?" Chieftain Donnchadh asks Aoife and Gudrun.

Shit, will I ever escape this place?

"Yes, I consulted with the spirits, both ours *and* Gudrun's gods. This is the site we need to build on." Aoife assures him.

He turns to the man beside him. "Send the men to locate supplies and clear out the area. We need to prepare to dig."

The darkness takes over before the light drops me again. One could only wish this were the moment I go back.

I'm dropped back to the site. This time, I've returned to what the journal showed me in the orb.

"Something is off. Do you feel it, my friend?" Aoife asks Gudrun.

Gudrun sits near the fire, casting her purple stones with runes etched into each one. Laying her hand over them she says, "Danger is here. One we can contain, but there will be death."

Screaming and an unearthly growl startle me and both of the women. They jump up and run to the pit—I go with them. They're scared but the determination they show reveals their courage underneath it all.

My hands fly to my mouth as I watch everything from the initial vision play out before me. I know what happens but watching gruesome images play out like a movie is very different from experiencing them in person. The pain, fear, and metallic scent of blood carries on the wind, circulating around me. Bile rises in my throat and my shoulders rise in defense. I'm not completely sure that my own safety isn't being threatened right now.

I have no clue how I'm here or what it all means, but I won't take the chance I die here before I get the chance to defeat the wendigo in my own time.

With my nerves on edge, I spend the restless night by Aoife's side as she traps the beast and ensures it remains contained.

I rub the exhaustion from my face as the golden sun rises and with it, the beast is imprisoned in a dark corner. It remains motionless. Aoife uses her energy to create a box-like force field six inches above and around the beast, restricting its movement. The wendigo stirs with the increase of light and releases an inhuman scream every time it comes in contact with its prison. It takes a while before it finally stops fighting and remains still in the translucent, glowing cage.

"Why were we not warned of this? Why have we been guided here only to be slaughtered? We could have stayed in Ireland if we wanted that." Exhaustion fills Aoife's eyes as she sits near the smoldering remains of the fire.

"Keep faith, Aoife, we would have found disease and famine if we went elsewhere. We were meant to release this darkness before someone else could. My gods and goddesses knew we would be able to contain it and prevent further demise." Gudrun calmly states.

Aoife's face drops. "They told you this? They *knew*?"

Gudrun's hands raise in defense. "They did not tell me until I spoke to them late last night. They knew if they warned us, our fear would overpower our faith and destroy everyone instead of the few who were sadly sacrificed."

Aoife runs her hand over her face. "What if we just leave and travel farther away? There is no one else here. By the time it recovers, we will be long gone."

The seeress shakes her head. "It has our scent now. Once they latch onto a scent, there is nothing that will stop them from searching the person out and consuming them."

Turning to her new friend, Aoife asks, "What do you suggest we do to 'contain it' as you say?" She searches her face for guidance.

Gudrun closes her eyes, raising her face to the sun. Aoife is way more patient than I am while silence sits between them.

"We need a rock, a special one that my people used to contain monsters. With your power and my knowledge, we can trap it and prevent any more destruction," Gudrun advises.

"And how do you know we can find this rock?" Aoife paces the ground.

Gudrun gestures to the fire pit. "Do you mind?"

With a flick of a wrist, a small orb is tossed onto the glowing embers and flames engulf the remaining kindling.

Gudrun sits and gazes into the center of the inferno, murmuring foreign words while her eyes glaze over.

Sitting on a log, I rest my chin on my hands and watch the flickering flames. I'm not sure how long we have to wait but I know she's using the fire to speak with her gods. I've heard about some cultures doing it, I just don't know how long it takes.

My eyes become heavy and I start to dri—

"Iron ore. There are mines nearby. I will show the men where to find it." Gudrun's voice has my heart racing and my body shooting up straight.

"But we have that in our weapons and some with our building supplies we brought."

"Not enough, we need much more. Round up your men and as many carts as they can find. Prepare your blacksmith to create a large enough forge not only to build our home but also a thick door to hold the beast."

Aoife nods and I'm being pulled up by an invisible force to stay close. Instead of fighting it, I walk faster to keep up with her. We arrive at the Chieftains' tent where she provides them with an update.

"We need to leave here now. Pack everyone up, we leave by sundown," Chieftain Donnchadh announces.

Aoife stands taller. "If we leave, we will only be hunted. There is no escape. The only thing we can do is trap it to prevent any more deaths."

"Are you sure about this?" Chieftain Ó Bradáin asks.

"Yes, we are absolutely sure," she nods.

After hushed discussions, they agree. They order immediate action to acquire the supplies.

When Aoife returns to the fire, Gudrun was creating an herbal concoction to calm the nerves of the men. As she serves it, she explains to them the steps needed to start building both the walls and the floor of the pit—leaving an open area in the center for the wendigo's prison. The woman emits such confidence and power. Many cultures frown upon women having any kind of power, but they have a lot of respect from everyone here.

The clan immediately gets to work and Aoife puts together a sack of food and leather pouches with mineral water for Gudrun. It doesn't take long before she and a group of men with carts leave in search of the iron.

While we wait for the iron, I sit next to Aoife and watch men bring stones from the mountains and stack them in a pile for another group to hand down into the pit for others to build the base of the dungeon. They have a great system but the anxiety coursing through my veins makes me twitchy. I wish they had a fast forward. I can't handle this trapped feeling.

The air here is thick with fear, sweat, and smoke. And there is no walking away from it.

No escape.

I place my hands on the back of my neck and look up through the trees and into the glittering sky. I need to find out if Hunter is okay. I need information and to return from this time travel or unconscious state I'm in.

A haze falls over my sight, it's a little different than the other times I moved forward in time.

My vision comes into focus and night has fallen at the pit. I blow out a frustrated breath. Aoife places a new barrier around the beast to ensure it is secured. The moment she finishes is the moment I'm falling into the light.

Coming into these events is similar to how one would write important events into a journal.

Is that it? Am I in the journal?

If that's the case, then Hunter may be in the truck still—safe. My pulse quickens at the possibility, and I don't fight the transition anymore. There's no reason to when I have absolutely no control over it. And the sooner I allow this to play out, the sooner I can get back to Hunter.

I'm not sure how many days have passed when everything comes back into focus. Gudrun and the men have returned and the blacksmith is already working tirelessly to create an iron door. I've heard about iron being a substance that the supernatural cannot pass through, and some use it to fight the paranormal, like my favorite show, *Supernatural*. I guess their fiction is based on some facts after all.

Gudrun and Aoife watch the blacksmith finish the last of the door. Gudrun turns and speaks. "We will use runes and spells to enchant the stones and door. The metal will work as a generator, keeping the energy constantly flowing."

"So you are saying I will not need to energize it each night?" Aoife raises an eyebrow.

"That depends on the runes we use and if we can make it self-sustaining."

"I have some ideas that can help," Aoife adds.

Okay, this is good. They used the iron material of the door along with the runes to strengthen and allow the energy flow to remain steady—without ever needing to be charged again. It would act as a nuclear, or self-energized, battery. It makes sense as to why they placed the runes the way they did. I mean, I had a good idea already when I was looking them up, but I have butterflies in my stomach from the excitement. We are getting closer to answers.

Doesn't quite make sense that they never thought anyone would stumble upon the door and release the evil inside, yet here I am—the lucky girl who gets to deal with it.

When the men have the floor and walls bricked in—except the center where they will place the creature and the corner where it currently resides—the two women instruct them to take a break while they ready the next steps.

Aoife and Gudrun make their way down to the pit where a pile of stones waits for them. I, thankfully, was able to stay at the top instead of by their side. If something goes wrong, I don't want to be the first stop on the wendigo's *all-you-can-eat buffet*.

They direct the men to spread the stone out instead of stacking them. Once they are individually laid out, Aoife burns runes into them while Gudrun chants—what I assume are spells—over each one.

When they're satisfied, they advise the Donnchadh Chieftain it is ready.

His large, deep Irish brogue bellows his orders to the workers, advising them to brick in the flooring where the prison will stand and leave the opening for the door of its enclosure.

The men hesitate but with additional reassurance, they make their way down to the pit while I follow Aoife and Gudrun back to camp to continue preparation.

"What are those?" Aoife motions to the dried leaves and flowers in small jars that Gudrun removes from her pouch.

"These will be what we need to help slow this monster down. To immobilize it while we move it to the new area. Angelica, Basil, Betel Nut, Cloves, Ague Root, Hemlock, Peat Moss, and Althea Root."

Shit, shit, shit... What if Hunter and I can't get those herbs? What if they aren't able to be found or even purchased in New York?

Okay, remember Angelica, Basil, Betel Nut, Cloves, Ague Root, Hemlock, Peat Moss, and Althea Root.

Angelica, Basil, Beetle Juice? No. Betel Nut. Fuck, I better not forget these. Cloves, Ague Root, Hemlock, Peat Moss, and Althea Root.

That's only if this is a vision and not my unconscious state of mind.

Gudrun places the herb mixtures into tied cloth bags then begins mixing more to place in a copper cup. She adds water from a pot on the fire and hands it to Aoife.

Aoife cradles the cup, peering into it curiously. "What is this?"

"This will help your light continue to burn bright without faltering. It will keep your energy up."

Aoife narrows her eyes at her.

"Baby, come back to me," a disembodied voice echoes into the wind. "Please, Anya."

"*Hunter?* Can you hear me?" I search around frantically to see beyond this veil that has me trapped, hoping and praying I find a rip. A tear that either allows me to go back to Hunter, or bring him to me so I'm not alone.

Hunter's voice is absent, gone as quickly as it came.

Gudrun chuckles, unaffected by what just occurred. "It is only Lemon Balm, Rosemary, Rhodiola, St. John's Wort, and Siberian Ginseng. All plants found on your home land. It is safe. I wouldn't want to poison you before I needed your help to trap the darkness, would I? Deep down, you know you can always trust me."

Aoife sighs. "Yes, yes. You are right. My apologies, my friend." She tips the cup back and downs the concoction.

Hunter and I have a lot to discuss and I pray his knowledge with herbs will help figure out the seeress' recipes.

The familiar fog comes in quick, and goes away just as fast. When the cloud lifts, red demon eyes pierce mine with intensity.

"Oh shit!" I back-up and gasp when I make hard contact with a solid object. Aoife stands tall, locked in a stare-down with the wendigo.

It was staring at her, not me.

I release a shaky breath but my spine remains erect and on guard.

Gudrun approaches the beast with her cloth pouches. As she gets closer, the wendigo begins to stagger—screaming each time it stumbles into the light field. The herbs in the satchels act as a sedative.

"It's time. Quick!" Gudrun demands.

Aoife shakes out her hands and aims them at the creature. A bright glow shoots from her palms and connects with the existing barrier. Once she makes contact and strengthens the illuminated prison, she takes a deep breath.

"Okay, I'm ready." She glances at Gudrun and receives a confirming nod.

Inch by inch, the terrifying beast is pushed forward. Every time it makes contact with the light, it screams in pain while parts of its body burn. The horns, hair, and many patches of flesh are singed from the damage. As Aoife drags it across the laid stone, Gudrun stays close with her herbs.

Despite the cool air, sweat pours off my face and back. I wipe my damp hands on my pants and keep Aoife between me and the wendigo at all times.

The edge of the force field hits the charged stones but Aoife strains and screeching fills the air. The muscles in her biceps bulge as she fights to move the creature even farther.

Is it...afraid?

I step around her. The animal's hooves are pushing against the stone in front of it while its long arms are burning as it pulls its body back where they came from. Black ooze melts off its body and a thick rancid smoke billows in the air.

I gag. I'm not sure what is worse, this, or seeing Grant's body when I was with Hunter.

Hunter.

Damn, I miss him so much. It's been days since I was driving along in the truck with him.

Did I simply vanish? Am I lighting up the inside of the truck with a sun again?

I release my grasp on the what-ifs and pull my attention back to the struggling wendigo. It wants nothing to do with the power-charged stones. This is both good and bad. Good because it proves the stones work—if I can replicate what Aoife did. And bad because it presents a problem. How strong is Aoife and how strong will I need to be to do the same thing?

I worry my bottom lip.

"Take a break. I'll be right back." Gudrun sets the satchels of herbs around the wendigo.

"*What?* I can't let the darkness go or we are doomed." Panic fills Aoife's eyes. "Where are you going? Do not leave me!" Her voice raises. Her hair is plastered by sweat to the sides of her face and her skin is pale.

Is Gudrun abandoning her?

Our eyes follow Gudrun as she bolts up the steps, leaving us alone with the beast.

"Fuck." I take a few cautious steps back—unsure how long Aoife can hold it. Without the herbs placed around the wendigo, there would be no way she would keep it at bay.

My gaze ping pongs from the wendigo to the dirt stairs, praying reinforcement comes fast. I release a gasp when the familiar flowing gown and leather boots descend the stairs. It felt like forever but she did return. Gudrun holds up her skirt and sprints back with another satchel.

Aoife sighs in relief and her arms begin to quiver from the stress. "I hope that will help."

Gudrun nods. "Angelica and Basil. They will help. Now push." She stands behind the wendigo and chants under her breath which I'm sure is in her Germanic native tongue. All I know is, I don't understand one bit of it.

The wendigo's long claws are sliding across the stone and it keeps losing its balance, tumbling. If this were a movie, I would find it almost comical. But the fact that this hideous beast can break through at any minute and kill us all has my nerve endings in defense mode.

A bone-chilling howl breaks from the creature and has us all gasping. They got it into the prison. Aoife decreases the size of her light field to fit right inside of the stones and Gudrun places her herbal sachets around it to continue to keep it weak and bound into place.

The women stay while the men are called back to finish installing the iron door. Aoife refuses to release her hold until it is complete.

When the door is bolted in place, she cautiously lets go but is ready to react if needed.

There is no noise, no banging, and no screams.

Looking to Gudrun, Aoife gestures at the locked door, and I move closer to see exactly how this next step is done.

I can't forget a thing.

Aoife lays her hand over each individual rune and ancient Celtic symbol until they illuminate a bright green. Gudrun holds her hands out and chants to what I assume were her gods to ask for assistance, which tells me Hunter and I are screwed. Unless he is a witch, it's up to me to do this.

The women step back and survey the work. I stand next to them with my hands on my hips and my cheek between my teeth. I glance at the two and know that they are overdue for some much-needed peace and rest after working nonstop for the past two days.

"Come, my friend. You need tea and rest." Gudrun takes Aoife by the shoulders and turns her.

If this were real, I would think Gudrun could read my mind.

Aoife stops with furrowed brows. "What if..." she begins.

"My gods say it is safe. We are safe and will continue to be. You are stronger than anyone I have ever encountered. We *are* safe."

We walk away and, as I look back, the glow on the door fades, just as it did with me. It is definitely tied to our blood. Aoife is provided more herbal tea and, in the middle of sipping it, she looks up at me—which is impossible. Behind me, the men continue to work around the prison. She must be watching them.

Yet, why does it feel like she is looking at me directly? Creepy.

"The light calls to you. It needs *you* as much as you need it," she speaks like she's talking to me. I shift in my seat, it's only us sitting here. Gudrun is silent by the fire, oblivious to what Aoife is saying. "Embrace your bloodline, embrace your destiny. And remember, light conquers all."

My skin tingles from my head to my toes and goosebumps pepper my skin in its wake.

How could she be speaking to me? These are just words in a journal, right? Did she know I'd be here?

Bright yellow floods my vision and I'm engulfed in light again.

Falling to who knows where.

I continue to drop as the light turns to darkness around me. Each time I fall, it's a new scene from the past.

How long will I be trapped here? Does the wendigo break free? Do I now get to sit and watch the long process of the castle being built?

All I can do is pray for Hunter to catch me and wake me from this nightmare.

Chapter Fifteen

NAUTHIZ

(NECESSITY)

In the dark, the hard ground bites into my back while my head rests on something soft, yet firm. My upper body is wrapped in thick fabric, which confuses me. One of my hands rests on the journal laying against my stomach while the other flexes in the blades of grass tickling my palm.

This is all new. In the visions, I wasn't able to feel textures before.

"Anya, come back to me," a muffled male voice cracks.

My mind attempts to concentrate on where I am but I'm disoriented. Which is...*odd*.

Wait...someone said my name.

Who would be talking directly to me? No one has been able to see me, let alone hear me.

The darkness opens up to daylight and I blink my eyes a few times to clear the remaining haze. The sun's warm rays welcome me as my body basks in its glow. It's bright, but I begin to make out a blurry face leaning over me. I jump when a firm hand grips my face and I shoot straight-up—almost colliding with the other person. The material that was around my shoulders falls, sending a chill through me at the same time my heart pounds out of my chest.

"*Fuck*, baby."

Strong arms pull me across the ground and hold me tight. This isn't normal. It's rather nice—but not normal. Nothing adds up from when I walked away from the iron door until now. Maybe I'm hallucinating. It's the only logical explanation. With having no sleep in days, my mind is playing tricks on me.

A familiar pineapple, lavender, and lemon scent fills my nostrils and seeps into my bones.

Mmm...Hunter.

"Hunter?" I shove away from him and my eyes meet his tear-filled ones. "Hunter, you're here!" I cry out, grasping his face and throwing my arms around his neck. I ignore the thump of the journal dropping to the ground. My hands slide to Hunter's hair. It feels so real. *He* feels so real.

I'm finally back!

"Of course I'm here, where else would I be?" His damp eyes narrow.

I sit on my heels in front of him and grab one of his hands between both of mine; allowing my fingers to trace over his calluses and scars. This really isn't a hallucination or dream. It's not part of the vision at all.

But why are we outside on the side of the road? Did I actually cause an accident this time?

I run my eyes from his head to his toes looking for injury. He's shaken up, bad.

My body feels normal. Even the bump I got testing my boundaries with Aoife is gone. I glance to the truck and find it still running with the passenger door wide open.

What the hell happened?!

"Holy fuck, Anya." He brings my focus back to him as he runs a hand through his hair, stopping when he gets to the back of his neck where he squeezes.

"Do I want to ask what happened this time?" I shift to relieve the increasing discomfort on my knees.

"You have to stop doing that shit or you're gonna give me a heart attack," he gruffs out, the vein in his forehead is prominent and his face is flush.

"But... I didn't do anything." Except travel back in time. Which I'm *not* quite sure how to explain *that*.

"You...first you were...then you weren't... Hell, how the fuck would you explain what just happened?"

"Obviously I wasn't coherent to see your side of things. Did I...disappear?" I cringe after I say the ridiculous words out loud. But I need to know.

Is this a new power? Can *I time travel?*

"No, you didn't disappear." Hunter scrunches his face and shakes his head. "Why would you think that? Come on, Anya, that's not even possible."

I snort. If he only knew what *could* be possible. Like the fact that some part of my consciousness was transported back in time—via an ancient journal.

Hunter releases his neck and brings his large hand up to cup my face. His rough thumb caresses my cheekbone, sending shivers down my spine. "I thought... I lost you," his voice breaks.

The emotion I read in his eyes confuses me. They're intense and filled with...*Oh God, is that love?*

No, I'm not thinking clearly. I shake my head and place my hand over his—holding onto his warmth as long as I can. "As you can see, I never left." I give him a half-hearted smirk. "Right?" I add with slight uncertainty.

"Physically? No. But you were unconscious after a blinding light exploded between your hand and the journal."

"How long?" It's been days since I saw him last but maybe it was only hours here.

He glances at his watch. "Twenty minutes, maybe? I didn't exactly time it. I didn't know what to do. You were lit up like a Christmas tree so I wrapped my jacket around you—unsure if I'd be burned—and pulled you out of the truck. I wasn't sure if you would spontaneously combust at any moment. I felt you'd be safer out here." Darkness fills his eyes and he moves his hand to my chin. His thumb is close to my bottom lip.

I look down at his jacket, remembering the weight on my shoulders when I came back. Warmth engulfs my heart over his worry and actions to keep me safe. It's hard to imagine everything that played out for Hunter.

"Care to tell me what was so important as to scare the living shit out of me?" His voice raises.

My head snaps back. Well, *that* wasn't where I thought this conversation was going, but okay. The problem is, I don't know where to start. He said I was gone for twenty minutes, but that isn't nearly the amount of time I was living through the...*memories?*

When I don't answer, he drops his hand and turns to stares at the road beyond his truck. His jaw clenches, taking my silence as refusal.

"I need...just...give me a minute. Please," I stutter out.

Hunter takes a deep breath then nods, satisfied with my answer.

Closing my eyes, I bring myself back to the beginning. The opened journal in my lap filled with indecipherable text. My inability to decipher it. I was upset and while wishing with every-thing in me to find the knowledge in the pages—I fell into the light until I *was* in the pages.

There really is no other logic around what happened to me and if I needed to start anywhere, I guess that's the place to do it.

Sucking in air, I struggle to release it because once I do, I'm forced to explain the *Twilight Zone* I was in.

I stare into the trees, preparing myself, only to realize my mistake as the forest closes around us like a horror movie. I attempt to slow my heart rate and blink away the tunnel vision.

Here goes nothing.

"I fell into the journal." I blow out warm air, causing the flyways of my hair to tickle my face. I wipe them away.

Well, that wasn't so hard. I pick up the book that haphazardly fell to the ground in my excitement over seeing Hunter. There's no damage from the drop. *Thank God.*

"You what?"

With the journal clutched in my hands, I cautiously turn to face Hunter, whose eyebrows are high on his forehead above wide, brown eyes.

And...there goes my street cred.

"I know it sounds weird. But somehow, when I–"

"Had your temper tantrum?" He smirks.

Ass.

"When I was *frustrated*..." I bore my eyes into his, challenging him to interrupt again. His lip twitches but he remains silent. "...and felt defeated, I wished for once things could be easier for us. I wanted so badly to be able to read the journal that I was pulled into it. Similar to when I watched the unearthing of the wendigo. This time...this time was a lot different though."

The hint of amusement falls from Hunter's face.

"No shit, it was different. For one, you didn't ignite a miniature sun in my truck but even *that* I can handle again. What I can't handle is for half your body to light up and you lose complete consciousness. I couldn't even check your vitals, the heat you were expelling I'm pretty sure would've burned me. I'm surprised you didn't melt my jacket."

"Was I lit up the whole time?"

He nods. "Right until you came to." His eyes drop to the journal. "Can you...umm...put that thing away before we both somehow get pulled in?"

I gasp. I didn't even think of that.

My hands have a tight hold of the journal sitting in my lap. "Oh. Yeah, that's probably a good idea."

With my luck, we would be right back there living it all over again.

There is so much I don't know about this power and right now, I need to find out as much as I can. "Was every part of me hot to the touch or only the areas that were glowing?" I ask while bending down to store the book in my bag.

"Well, I can't say I tried to touch *every* part of you..."

Heat fills my cheeks.

"But yes. Even when it was only your torso and arms that were lit up, there was a lot of heat coming off the rest of you. I didn't want to risk it."

"I mean, I get that being unresponsive is worrisome and I'm not trying to downplay what happened, but I was still breathing. I'm not sure why you feel I almost gave you a heart attack."

"We don't know what your power can or *will* do. Let alone if any part of it can hurt you." He runs a hand over his face. "Anya, I don't know what the hell I'd do if I lost you again. Please promise me you won't do shit like that anymore."

"Like I can control that." I try not to roll my eyes—and fail miserably.

"You know what I mean. If anything feels weird, if you are up set...I want you comfortable talking it out with me instead of—"

"Instead of what?" I interrupt. "Thinking? I don't get how I can control this." My pulse quickens with my temper and I throw my hands up. "How the hell do I prevent anything from happening going forward?"

"Argh." Hunter throws his head back to the sky and closes his eyes. He is quiet for a bit. "I'm sorry. I don't think I'm making sense." He opens his eyes and tilts his head towards me—exhaustion in his eyes. "All I'm trying to say is...let's talk it out. Whatever it is. You see a ball of light? Before jumping into it, tell me what you see. You get pissed, you talk to me."

I hold up my hand. "I'm all for having someone being supportive, but that sounds a tad like you are trying to *control* me. Control something even *I* don't have the ability to handle myself." I bite the inside of my cheek and weigh my next words. "I get that you care. I really do. But I also need to think things out on my own. I've been on my own for so long, it's second nature to figure it out myself. And I'm not a fan of you trying to control what I do or when I do it."

"I'm not trying to control you." His face flushes and a vein on his forehead pulses.

"I know you aren't trying to, but I had some bad experiences with a man trying to control me. This sounds a lot like it." I stare down at my hands twisted in my lap.

Hunter grabs my chin and brings my head eye level with his. "I don't know what this other asshole did to you, but I will *never* try to control you. Ever. Do you hear me?"

Blinking away the moisture forming in the corners of my eyes, I nod.

"It doesn't bother me if you try different things. I'd just rather be a little more prepared. You know, maybe pull off the road and be ready for...anything? I'm here as your equal. Your partner. Not your boss, not your puppet master. I am only asking that you try to give me a little heads up and tell me a bit about what's going on in that head of yours. I can't help you if you don't let me."

My eyes bounce between both of his. His milk-chocolate eyes convey the truth. He isn't like Kyle. He isn't trying to manipulate every aspect of my life.

I pull Hunter's hand from my chin and grasp it in mine.

How can we go from everything being great, to at each other's throats, then back again as quickly as we do? The emotions between us are always so close to the surface. It's a struggle to hold back my feelings with him and he's the same.

What does that mean?

Hunter squeezes my hand. "Let's get back in the truck."

"Oh, thank heavens, I think my legs fell asleep."

He helps lift me and I hand him his un-melted jacket. Then I slowly pick up the journal. Once I'm hoisted back in my seat, Hunter closes the door and jogs around to his side.

"Alright, I want you to tell me what happened when you were pulled into the journal." He cringes once he says it.

A smile slips from my lips. *Now* look who sounds ridiculous.

"When I said this time was different, it wasn't just with me going unconscious. I fell through a tunnel of light, until I landed in Ireland during the original Viking invasion."

"Oh, shit." Hunter's eyes go wide.

"You can say that again. It was scary. I had no idea if it was another vision or if I really *did* time travel. I called for you and you were nowhere to be found. I was there for days, Hunter."

"Whoa, how could you have been there for days? You were only out for about twenty minutes."

"Yes, in the land of Oz, time was slow and it took days. Days of worrying. So, think about that next time you want to yell at me, okay?" I narrow my gaze at him.

"Yes, dear. Will you forgive me?" He winks at me.

I chuckle. This man has a way of making me smile when I need it.

Shaking my head, I continue. "Anyways...everything felt so *real*. The smells, the thick air, the fear coming off of everyone... I was experiencing it all. Well, all but being able to interact with others. They couldn't see me and when I tried to touch them, they were solid, immovable statues. It's hard to explain." The visions coming back to me send a chill down my spine.

Hunter runs his thumb over my knuckles in an attempt to relax me. He must sense how this whole event had me stressed and still does.

"And you didn't realize you were in the memories of the journal? Were you in someone else's head? Experiencing it as if *you* were the person?" His attention hasn't wavered from me this whole time.

I can tell he listens, not because he wants something in return, but because he actually cares. The way his eyebrows crease in the middle when he's concerned for me, especially when my anxiety takes control, he knows. He senses it and seeks to comfort me, to sooth the beast that tries to swallow me whole.

How could I have ever compared him to Kyle?

I let out a breath. "The experience was that of a great grand-mother of mine, Aoife. And no, I didn't *become* her. But she very much made an appearance and stayed there the whole time. I was bound to her with no way to escape. The Viking witch—or seeress—Gudrun was there to help her but everything followed Aoife's point of view."

"So, you were trapped and had to go wherever she went?"

"Yup. I tried to see if I could find my way out but that only ended up with me slamming my head into a black veil that was as hard as a concrete wall." My hand goes to the spot on my forehead, thankful the knot didn't cross back over with me.

Hunter's hand comes up to the spot on my forehead I was rubbing. "Good thing you didn't get beaten up in your time travel or we would have some splainin' to do with the cops."

I laugh at his very poor imitation of *Ricky Ricardo*. I'm not sure I would have survived this far if not for Hunter.

Shifting in my seat to face him directly, I cross one leg under the other to get more comfortable.

"That was one thing I was really concerned about. I had to get up close and personal with the wendigo and I have to say, I wasn't sure how things worked there or if I could be killed. It wasn't like I could run away."

His shoulders pull back. "You're telling me you were close to that *thing* with no way of getting away?"

I nibble on the inside of my cheek. I nod.

"What the hell, Anya. Why didn't they make a run for it? Escape while they could?"

There's growing anger in the undertones of his words causing my stomach to tighten.

"They knew it'd hunt them down. There was no escaping it. Trapping it was their only option."

Hunter rubs a hand over his beard then reaches up to the back of his neck again. His hand tightening around the corded muscles showing me how bothered he is right now.

"How exactly *did* they trap it?"

"They decided to build the room *around* it instead. It makes sense, but—"

"We won't have the same advantage." He finishes my sentence in a gruff tone.

"Exactly. With that being the best method, along with not having Gudrun's help, the cards are stacked against us. I have no idea who in the world can fill in for the seeress."

"I think you forgot the little part of *me* being here to help? Why do you think I'm incapable?" His lips are pressed in a hard line and his eyes convey hurt.

My heart drops into my stomach. *He's right.* I need to place more faith in him and his ability to be my partner.

"I'm sorry… I didn't mean it like that. I know you aren't a Viking witch…are you?" I narrow my eyes. "Is there something you aren't telling me?" I nudge him and offer him half a smile.

"Well, I can do magical things with my fingers." He wiggles his digits in my direction. "Would you care for a demonstration?" His eyes twinkle in mischief.

Heat flushes my cheeks.

"I trust your word. You can keep your magical fingers to yourself."

But now all I can think about is his fingers trailing up my thigh, close to my core. I'd open my legs wider…

"Let me know if you change your mind."

"Huh?" My face grows hotter realizing what I was doing. I clear my throat. "Yes, but…how are we going to trap it and drag it back to the dungeon?"

Stay. On. Track.

Hunter hums. "You're right, it's going to be trickier for us to trap it than it was for them. We'll figure it out though. As you keep forgetting, you're not alone and I'm glad you aren't. I wish we didn't have to do this to begin with. I'd rather spend time with you doing something else, you know…less dangerous?" His eyes wiggle suggestively.

Trying to ignore him, I respond. "Me too." I wonder what we'd be doing if our situation wasn't sucking all the time and energy from us. Sitting around and chatting? We aren't kids anymore who run around outside and explore.

"I want to hear more, but we are really behind on meeting with Detective Shane. Do you feel comfortable continuing to talk about this on our way?"

A lump forms in my stomach with the reminder of more fun coming our way.

"Sure. It's better we get that out of the way sooner than later."

Hunter squeezes my hand before starting the truck again. "We got this. What do you think I can help you with? Other than being your big, sexy bodyguard."

I buckle up, laughing at Hunter's comment. "Haha…you wish, Big Guy. But one thing you *may* be able to help with is to replace Gudrun in your knowledge of herbs. Precisely, how good are you with them?" My eyebrows crease.

He flashes a confident smile. "*Real* good. I have a full background of local and foreign herbs. Plus, along with my gift, I can make any mixture, tea, or tincture to the exact measurement."

I sit up straighter. "You can make anything we need without a recipe?"

"Yup." He says with a cocky smirk.

"How? How can *anyone* even do that?" My mouth drops open. He can't do that, no one can. That's a process of trial and error, unless you learned the recipes before but without seeing them? *Ever?*

"How can you create a small sun in the palm of your hand?"

And that damn dimple pops out. Ugh!

Huffing out a breath, "Touché." I slouch back in my seat. "What if the herb you need isn't possible to find?"

He shifts and leans towards me. "Well, that's a little trickier, but I do know a lot of alternatives we can use in a pinch because herbs are plants. They were once living, and with all living things, they have their own energy and frequency that emanate from them. Some of them share similar chemical makeup and can be used to fool the body or another body of energy into thinking it's the same."

Okay, this guy is really good at this. I breathe in a deep breath of fresh air without feeling like I'm trapped.

"Why do you ask?"

"They used sachets of herbs as well as tea to help them." I list off the herbs from memory then bite my lip.

"Hmm...it makes sense to use those. A couple of those will be tough to find, but if we head back into town after meeting with the police, I know a place. As for the others, lucky you..." He wiggles his eyebrows. "I actually have them on hand. I like to carry a variety in case the need arises."

"What kind of needs do you expect to arise on a daily basis?"

"You have no idea." A dry chuckle escapes his throat. "But I think we'll be okay with the herbs, leave that part up to me."

My muscles unknot themselves. The challenge ahead of us isn't *as* scary. We may be able to do this after all.

Right?

We turn down the grass-covered stone path.

"You ready?" Hunter asks.

I take in his warm, brown eyes and nod my head.

Yes, I'm okay. *We* are going to be okay. I have my best friend—my rock—with me and we *will* get through this. Together.

Hunter flashes the officer his ID and we are waved through.

I try to ignore the occasional scraping of the tree limbs on the truck, but like a fork dragged on a plate, it makes my teeth hurt. The opening clears, and my breath hitches when I see it.

Chapter Sixteen

Jera

(Patience)

The shredded and mangled remains of my once beautiful, blue car sit waiting for me.

Mocking me.

How could I have forgotten about my poor baby?

A whimper escapes my throat and I turn away. It hurts too much to see the loss of what I worked so hard for. I still hold out hope the insurance will cover the damage, well...more like the replacement since the best collision repairman in the world couldn't bring my car back to life.

Hunter gives my hand a reassuring squeeze before he steers the truck next to the police cars and parks.

We get out and Hunter rounds the front of his vehicle with a confident stride and a sympathetic smile. He pulls me into a hug once he reaches me.

I wrap my arms around his muscular back and rest my cheek on the shirt that peeks out from under his jacket. Taking in a whiff of his delicious scent, I hum with contentment.

"I'm sorry, Anya, about your car and you having to deal with all of this again. Are you going to be okay if the police ask you more questions?"

I shake my head to reply, which causes my face to burrow farther into the soft cotton.

"I don't have an issue answering more questions. I'm more nervous about what happens *after* they leave." I lean back and meet his warm gaze.

The sun brightens his chocolate eyes, adding a touch of warm honey to them, accentuating the mix of auburn and brindle in the scruff of his beard. I must tread carefully. Like a mouse to cheese, my heart is struggling to resist the temptation, the delectable pull that I know will be delicious...until it's gone and I'm left empty.

Then be crushed when he leaves for his next job.

Alright, time to get over myself.

I reluctantly pull out of his arms. "Come on Big Guy, let's get this over with." I grab his hand and lead him to the front steps of the castle before stopping. "Can you stay with me though?" I say under my breath.

In my head, I mean during the questioning.

In my heart, I mean forever.

What? Where did that come from? My eyes go wide.

I slip my hand out of his. The faster this is over, the faster I can go back to my boring and unassuming life.

Hunter leans down with his lips next to my ear. "I'm never letting you go."

The deep rumble sends chills down my spine and my heart skips a beat.

Down girl. He just means until this is all over. Right?

He stands straighter and places a hand on my lower back. "Let's go meet with the detective, Honey Bear."

An unladylike snort comes out of me. My mind rushes back to when I'd asked him if he wanted a taste of honey and heat rushes over me.

Ugh! I shake my head. Now is *not* the time to be getting worked up.

Head in the game, Anya.

Detective Shane stumbles out of the doors with his hands on his hips and inhales a deep breath as we make our way up the steps.

He looks a little pale and my only guess is he saw the gruesome scene in the dungeon.

Hunter either doesn't see the state the detective is in, or chooses to ignore it when he thrusts his hand out.

"Shane, sorry we took a while, we're here to answer any follow up questions you may have."

Clearing his throat, he shakes Hunter's hand and gives him a curt nod, "Hunter, Ms. O'Clery,"—being that they know each other, they are on a first name basis, yet *I* still get the formalities—"thanks for coming all the way out here. You weren't exaggerating about the state of Ms. O'Clery's car. I didn't realize how bad the situation was until I saw it for myself." He glances towards the open door then back to Hunter. "The coroner ruled the time of death to be about four to five days ago. And it's definitely due to an animal attack. I sure hope that thing is far away from here."

"Us, too." Hunter chimes in.

"I have a few officers combing through the woods right now trying to spot any signs of it. If it can do something like that to a man, it needs to be put down immediately."

My body tenses at the detective's words and Hunter notices. He rubs small circles over my back.

The detective's mouth is creased in a thin line as he glances at me then back to Hunter. "You two are *damn* lucky not to have been killed by it yourselves. We're thinking it's a bear based on the size of the claw marks. I've never seen anything like it before. Someone must have trapped it in there and Mr. Bordeaux was the unlucky bastard to find it." He frowns, "Pardon my language, Miss."

I give him a dismissive wave. I've spoken worse—but he doesn't need to know that.

He continues, "Do you have any idea *why* Mr. Bordeaux was out here to begin with? I had my men look into this place and there's no record of it anywhere. No way of tracking down an owner."

I see the shift in Hunter's posture before he turns on *PI mode*. "When Mrs. Bordeaux called me Wednesday night, she'd been worried Mr. Bordeaux had not contacted her and didn't return home Tuesday evening."

"Why didn't she call the police?" Detective Shane cocks an eyebrow.

"She was worried he may have been sneaking around on her and needed someone to keep things hush-hush. You know how it is, man, once you guys are involved, the town's gossipers are not far behind creating elaborate stories and spreading rumors."

The detective blows out a breath and runs a hand through his hair. "You aren't joking."

My palms get sweaty and I hold my hand up. "Wait, what's to prevent those same gossipers from coming out here and endangering themselves? Plus, if the place really is abandoned, it's not safe."

"In this situation, we will be keeping the location confidential. You two are the only civilians who know, as long as you keep it quiet, we can hopefully prevent anyone from knowing about this place for a few more days." Detective Shane waits for me to nod in acceptance before continuing with questioning Hunter. "Why didn't Mrs. Bordeaux just go look for him herself?"

"She claimed she was too busy with her job to go herself, so she hired me. She thought, if he was with someone else, she would rather have photographic evidence before confronting him. I was just coming back into town Thursday afternoon and met with her to get more information about the last place he was going, what his schedule looked like, and if he had done something like this before. Apparently, this was the first."

Detective Shane hummed. "What made her suspicious of an affair?"

"She stated he was exhibiting strange behavior—"

The detective interrupts, "What kind of strange behavior?"

Hunter chuckles. "Get this, extreme happiness and excitement over something that he was keeping to himself—becoming very secretive. Mrs. Bordeaux said she'd never seen him like that before."

I fail to contain my snort.

Coughing to try to cover my reaction up, I say, "Excuse me, sorry."

It says so much about a person when his wife has never seen him excited or happy before.

Detective Shane attempts to tamp down his own smirk. "Well, based on the state of his body, we can rule out foul play from the wife *or* a mistress. When did you begin your search for him?"

"Thursday evening. I started doing some research with the recent property he had acquired. I made a plan on where to start looking Friday morning. When he wasn't at the other places, I met with Mrs. Bordeaux to make sure I wasn't missing anything regarding his schedule and daily activities. I requested the login information to his computer to see what he'd been doing the days leading up to his disappearance." Hunter scratches his scruffy cheek and quirks an eyebrow. "For a 'concerned wife', she became defensive and aggressive quickly. She refused to let me go anywhere near his office—let alone his computer. Even when I assured her everything would be completely confidential, she became more agitated and told me to use my 'own damn resources' to do my job since that's what she's paying me for."

Detective Shane rubs his chin. "That behavior isn't common for someone in her position. Even one suspecting her husband of cheating. Did you get the vibe she may have been embarrassed she didn't have access to his stuff? That he kept the records hidden from her?"

"No, I don't think that's the case. She seemed to be hiding something. But that wasn't my job to figure out. My job was to find her husband and I did." Hunter pulls me closer to his side.

Looky there, sounds as though the Missus was paranoid Hunter may find out about their shady business scam. Confirms she *is* involved.

The detective pulls me out of my thoughts. "What happened after she refused to provide you access?"

"Oh, she kicked me out of her house. I started by visiting his usual coffee and lunch spots but came up empty. He was last spotted Tuesday morning, so I went home and continued to look into his recently acquired properties."

"Is that how you found out about this place?" asked the detective.

Was Hunter exaggerating earlier about having impeccable tracking abilities?

Something I'll be questioning him later about. Right now, I watch the men talk and feel the strong need for a bowl of popcorn and a soda. It's like I'm watching a crime show—live.

"That would have been Saturday morning when I got a hold of his CFO, Derek Metch. He told me some hikers came across an abandoned castle in the mountains, and based on the appearance, they assumed it wasn't owned. They figured they may get a finder's fee by notifying Mr. Bordeaux. It's not a secret the property management company rewards people for finding uninhabitable structures but most still have owners. Mr. Metch stated there were no records of property ownership because the location wasn't even reported."

The detective glances to the castle and the overgrown plants and trees surrounding it. "It's no surprise. This place looks as though it's been abandoned for several years."

Hunter chuckles. "You're right about that. It was like hitting a gold mine. It's no surprise Mr. Bordeaux insisted on checking it out himself before anyone else submitted an Abandoned Property Claim Form on it. He wanted to evaluate the state it was in, estimate repair costs, before they met on Monday to discuss it further. Mr. Metch didn't think twice about touching base with his boss prior to their arrangement. He's the one who provided me with the coordinates. Chances were, Mr. Bordeaux's car broke down and he was stranded."

"Why was Ms. O'Clery out here with you?" Detective Shane narrows his eyes at me and I resist wringing my sweating hands.

"As you know, I returned to town recently and haven't seen Anya for a while. By the sound of it, the place was big. I figured I could kill two birds with one stone. See my girl and get a second pair of eyes to help me search. If I knew we would find anything but a stranded and starving Mr. Bordeaux, I'd have called you to help. Never her." He brings me to his front wrapping his arms around my stomach in a possessive hold.

My hackles rise and pulse races at him referring to me as his girlfriend. But I can't help but relax into him in this new hold.

With a satisfied smile, Detective Shane says, "Thank you for the details. By the way, we had an officer break the news to Mrs. Bordeaux. I would *strongly* advise you to follow up with her this afternoon to wrap things up on your end. From what the officer stated over the radio, she didn't take the news too well."

Hunter nodded. "I can understand her being upset. Anyone finding out their spouse has died would be traumatized."

"Oh no. It didn't sound as though it was due to the loss of her husband. She became enraged when my officer refused to give her the location of the castle. If I were you, I would close out your case and cut your ties with that woman as quick as you can."

I study the detective's face in the event he's jesting.

Shit. He's not.

Hunter runs his hand over his face and groans. "Thanks Shane, I appreciate that piece of information. I'll make sure I take care of that today."

The detective pats Hunter on the shoulder on his way back to meet with the paramedics.

Why would Margaret Bordeaux want to come out here? Does she want to see where he died?

Oh no! Oh no, no, no.

I bite the inside of my cheek to control my facial expressions from displaying my internal breakdown.

What I've heard about Margaret is that she's as ruthless and greedy as Grant was. She will stop at *nothing* to get more money even when the woman has everything she ever wanted.

Fuck.

That officer's refusal won't prevent her from coming out here. We need everyone to leave now.

"Patience." Hunter's breath heats the side of my face.

I clench my jaw, hating that he's right. We need to speed this along to handle the wendigo and *now* Mrs. Bordeaux. I get we can't do anything right now but it doesn't mean it's not driving me insane.

Turning around while pulling out of Hunter's embrace, I watch the coroner and EMTs load up Grant's body in the ambulance. The trauma clean-up crew carry out two large black trash bags and pack them into their van, taking off their coveralls. It wasn't normal protocol but after we advised them of the bloodbath, they wanted to prevent attracting the animal back and potentially hurting someone else who happens upon the castle.

"Why aren't they putting up crime scene tape?" I keep my eyes on the crews packing up and making their way back to town.

"They have everything they need. No need to save the scene for further investigation."

"Hmm..."

An officer strolls up to us. "Detective Macaby said you are both free to go. We're wrapping up and heading out." Squeaking and chains clinking pull our attention to the small entrance. "I take it that was *your* doing?" He nods to the tow truck with Grant's car making its way back to the main road.

Hunter flashes his phone. "Yes, sir. The detective gave me the clearance earlier to arrange the pick-up. I feel bad enough for Mrs. Bordeaux, this is one less thing she needs to worry about. I also called a second tow truck with a flatbed for Anya's car. We're just waiting for it to arrive."

Well that's news to me.

It keeps Margaret from coming out to the castle. Lord knows she would want to supervise anyone going near her husband's precious vehicle.

"I don't advise being out here alone." The officer's brows furrow and he purses his lips.

"They should be here soon and we'll be out in no time. We promise, we will remain aware of our surroundings. Thank you for your concern, but if you'd rather stay with us—"

"No, no, that won't be needed," he interrupts and glances around nervously, finding he's the last officer on the scene. "Try not to take too long, okay? And be careful."

"Yes, sir." Hunter nods his head.

"Thank you," I add.

The officer quickens his step to his car, kicking up dirt as he peels-out.

I giggle.

"What?" Hunter cocks an eyebrow.

"You." I suck in my lips, smirking.

He points to himself, "Me?"

"Yes, you," I poke his hard chest with my finger. "You scared that poor officer away."

"Would you rather he stay here with us and help?"

"No."

"Okay then, I found a way to get rid of him and acted on it. Saving you, yet again. You're welcome." He flashes a dimple.

"Aww..." I pat his cheek. "There's that cocky hero complex. I knew it was hiding in there, somewhere."

He catches my wrist and brings my hand to his chest. "Now that we've admitted I'm your hero once again, what do we deal with first?"

I straighten and pull my hand out of his warm grip. "Let's start with your gift."

"Huh?"

"I mean no offense, but for someone who claims he can track down anyone *and anything*, it doesn't sound like you've had much luck the past few days. Does it, you know...take you time to warm up the tracking ability?"

The laugh that bursts out of him startles me.

"*Now* you're questioning my performance?"

"Well...I didn't mean..." My face heats.

He reaches out and grabs my arm, "Anya, it's okay."

The knots in my stomach loosen up.

"I don't use my gifts unless I suspect someone's in danger. I work hourly, so why cut the time down to an unhuman rate to solve the issue quicker? That raises suspicion when I find the person or item without doing the research behind it. I need to keep a realistic expectation for my clients, and I can't cheat my way either. I can't grow as a private investigator if I take the easy way out. We become better people when we are faced with challenges and learn from them. It leads us to where we are meant to be."

"How can you tell the difference between someone who's in danger and someone who's not?"

"I have an intuitive trait I tap into, but this time it was different. Between my exhaustion from finishing up from my prior job and not feeling an immediate threat to Grant because he was already dead, I didn't feel rushed. It certainly didn't help that Mrs. Bordeaux caught me off guard. It seemed like a simple jealous woman wanting to catch her cheating spouse in the act." He pulls on the back of his neck. "I had a weird feeling about this case. Something felt...off. But again, I chalked it up to my exhaustion."

"Do you think the whole wendigo situation was what felt wrong?"

"And me finding a half-eaten body? Yeah, I think so. Who knew my life would change the day I took that job." A sweet smile tilts up at the corners of his lips.

"Just think, if you hadn't taken the job, I would be stuck with some other random dude attempting to help me."

"He'd be a dead man in no time." He deadpans.

"Are you overestimating your skillful abilities again?"

"Not overestimating, only stating a fact. There wouldn't be anyone else that would have survived if in my shoes. They would have stood frozen in shock instead of reacting as quickly as I did."

Another reason why I'm beyond thankful he's helping me.

"That's true. I'm not sure who would survive an encounter with the wendigo. Speaking of... How are we going to handle the situation with Margaret Bordeaux?"

"Situation? There isn't much of a situation. After we figure out our next steps, we'll stop by her house for me to close the case."

"I don't think it's going to be that easy, Hunter. She's as stubborn and money hungry as Grant is—or was. Now that she knows about this place, she'll stop at nothing to come here and try to take it for herself." My breathing becomes shallow as my chest tightens. "You know I work for them. But it goes beyond that. I've been collecting evidence for the past few years on the illegal and unethical ways the Bordeauxes go about acquiring properties to sell. I'm sure that's exactly why she refused to allow you access into Grant's office and computer. They have information they don't want anyone else to see."

Hunter's face drops. "Fuck, you're right. We need to keep her far away from here." He places both of his hands on the back of his head and stares up at the sky, sucking in a large breath of air. "Okay," he releases a harsh sigh and begins pacing. "We need to track down the wendigo during the day to find the direction it went. But first..." He moves to his truck, pulling out a small pouch and tosses it to me. "Put this in your pocket."

I snatch it out of the air and catch a whiff of thyme, mint, rosemary, and something else I can't place.

My hands massage what feels like herbs inside. "What's this for?"

"It'll keep the wendigo from tracking *you*." He crosses his arms, ready for a fight.

It's weird how he knows me so well.

"Wouldn't that be a good thing? Use me as bait to find it faster?" Saying that in my mind sounded way better than the actual idea of it. I tap my foot to cover up the trembles in my body.

"No, that would be a death sentence. The wendigo had the chance to get your scent outside the castle and again at the kitchen door. From the looks of your car, there's no doubt it's after *you*." He cocks an eyebrow. "You didn't see it destroy my bike, did you?"

Shit. "No." His motorcycle was left alone while my car was torn to shreds. It was searching for me. Destroying anything that had my scent on it.

"That's because it's after you and won't stop until it succeeds. I refuse to risk it coming after you," his voice comes out stern.

"I'll be fine." I shakily wave him off.

"Anya." His voice lowers. "Humor me." It wasn't so much a request but a demand.

And boy does the vibration of his voice replace the fluttering anxiety inside the pit of my stomach, turning it into a warm pile of mush.

I shove the satchel of herbs into my jacket pocket and grumble. "Fine."

He nods, pleased. "Thank you."

But I won't hesitate to ditch this thing if I need to and do it my way.

"Mmhmm. And what do we do when we find it?"

"You contain it."

"You have such confidence in me," I deadpan.

"Because I believe you have what it takes. And you should believe in yourself, too."

I cock an eyebrow. "That's easier said than done. Okay, so let's say I contain it. Then what?"

"How long do you think it would stay trapped?"

"Twenty-four hours. Well, based on what Aoife did with her magic." Which I sure as hell hope I can replicate, somehow.

"Okay, say it gives us a day, we then head back into town to speak to Margaret. I know this is the last thing you want to do, but we need to persuade her to stay away since the *animal* is still on the loose in the area," he pauses, "Let's get some supplies for our hike. We need to find the wendigo soon and you need to start tapping into your 'light' energy."

Grabbing my bag filled with supplies from Hunter's truck, I watch him drag his bulky duffle bag out and place it on his front seat. I choke when I get a glimpse at what he considers necessary supplies.

Holy Shit! This man has a whole armory in that thing. The weapons range from knives and a few machetes to guns of all sizes... No wonder it was bulky.

"Umm... Hunter? Do you really think we'll need all of that right now?"

He shakes his head. "Nah, I already have my gun on me. I need to grab my knife and strap, a rifle, and some herbs. The rest of this is for back-up, like if we get stuck here overnight again. I just brought a couple extra things from my collection to give us a helping hand if we need it."

My mouth is hanging open and my eyes feel like they are bulging out of my head. "A *couple* extra things from your collection? How much more do you actually have?"

He taps his chin, "Well...after last night? Clearly not enough. You want to carry anything on you?" he says, offering the open bag of weaponry.

I peek in G.I. Joe's goodie bag, tempted, but I shake my head. "No, thanks though. I'll be good with my dagger. But tonight I may take you up on the offer if I can't figure out how to recreate the magic."

He looks at me curiously, "Are you scared of guns?"

"What? No? What would give you that idea?"

"Many people are. It's okay. Have you ever held or shot one before?"

My right eyebrow shoots up as I grip my hip and stick it out. *Does he really think that I'm such an inexperienced girl that I haven't handled a weapon before? Pfft.*

"Yes, Hunter." I roll my eyes. "I actually have *two* guns at home. I don't bring them outside of my house nor do I walk around acting like it's normal to have a bag full of them in my car. My guns are for home defense and sport. Heather and I do a lot of target practice in the woods. I *guarantee*, I can handle myself with one. *Thank you very much.*" I mumble the last part under my breath.

His smirk spreads into a full smile—dimples and all—and oh my God, it makes me feel weak in the knees.

This guy is killing me.

The look on his face is one of awe. "That's my girl."

And in that moment I know, without a doubt, I'm already falling for him.

Chapter Seventeen

ISA

(FOCUS)

While I was getting our supplies from the truck, Hunter located a set of tracks that are—without a doubt—the wendigo's. At a glance, the hoof prints suggest a moose—a rarity in this area—and the claw marks resemble someone dragged sticks along the ground.

The moment Hunter points them out at the entrance of the woods behind the castle, the image of being face-to-face with the wendigo comes flooding back.

Am I ready to go head-on with the real thing?

My grandmother warned me about making the right decision when I'm at a crossroads.

Are we on the right path or am I leading us to our death?

Standing here isn't the answer, neither is choosing the safe road and risking more lives.

To hell with it.

I push myself forward.

"Hold up a sec." Hunter places his warm hand over my forearm—stopping me.

"What?" I try to ignore the tingles from his touch.

His expression unsettles me. Except for the wind blowing through the trees, we are met with silence.

Does he sense something I don't?

"Do you...feel comfortable trying to replicate the light?"

My face scrunches up as I meet Hunter's brown eyes studying mine.

"Huh?" Here I was expecting him to hold me back from the beast we're hunting, but he wants me to play with my power—*now?*

"I think you should practice your...umm..." He scratches his cheek. "Magic? You know, before we enter the woods."

"It's fine, I'll practice along the way." Waving him off, I say, "It's daytime still, the wendigo will be hiding."

"As confident as you may be, I would rather be in an open space your first time..."

My cheeks flush.

My first time...

Mentally, I give myself a facepalm. He doesn't mean *that* first time.

"...in case that light burns a little too hot."

The man is not *helping things.*

"I think it'd be best to prevent any forest fires from your solar flares—if we can avoid it." The undertone of sarcasm snaps me out of my carnal thoughts.

Ones that are way too inappropriate for the moment.

I glare at him instead. He thinks he's *so* funny.

I tap my chin. "Good thinking. What are your thoughts on me aiming at *you* instead of the woods?" I cock an eyebrow and a small smirk slips past my lips. "You can catch, right? I think *that* would be much safer, don't you?" Turning on puppy-dog eyes, I bat my lashes at him.

Hunter's hands come up. "Hey now, let's not go overboard."

"You're right, I still have to create the light first. And *then* we can play catch." Rubbing my hands together I say, "*Now,* we need to get to work."

His stunned expression gives away his nervousness and I smile—knowing I was the cause. It's about time someone knocks this cocky man down a few notches.

Gotta keep him on his toes.

The forest ahead of me remains calm. A few more minutes shouldn't make much of a difference. Plus, if I can't tap into my power before we come across the creature, things could get dangerous.

I pull my bag off my shoulder and move away from Hunter—for his safety. Oxygen fills my lungs as I suck in the cool, crisp air and I release my fear, my anxiety, my...frustration. In my mind, I see the light orb in my hand. I open my eyes and...nothing.

"Fuck." That didn't work.

"Performance anxiety?" The teasing in Hunter's deep voice behind me has my vision going red.

Narrowing my eyes, I turn around to face him. Heat courses through me. "Would you like to try this? Would you like to tell me exactly *how* to summon a power in *your* hands?"

"Umm... sure?"

As my irritation rises, so does the heat.

"Sure? Well...have at it." My fingers bite into my palms as I ball my fists. "Please, oh wise one, pray tell. How do I create a ball of sun?"

Hunter backs up and slowly raises his hands. "I'll tell you…only if you promise not to hurt me."

I stick my hip out. "Why the hell would you think I'd hurt you?"

His eyes bounce back and forth from my sides. "Look. Down." The command in his voice has me doing what he says.

"Holy Shit!" My eyes go huge right before my heart sinks.

Both of my hands have a white and yellow light emanating from them. The heat wasn't from my anger but from the energy.

But now it's gone.

"What happened? You had it, why'd you stop?" Hunter asks, no longer creeping away from me.

"I didn't do *anything*. I looked down and it just went away." Turning my hands over, they look normal and cool to the touch.

"Try again." He demands.

With a glare, I say, "That's easier said than done." I close my eyes to tap back into the light again.

Hunter's energy is behind me now. I remain focused and attempt to ignore his presence.

"What were you feeling when your hands were glowing?" He whispers into my ear, his hot breath tickling the hairs on my neck.

"A-anger. Frustration."

I hate how he can turn my brain into a ball of mush.

"And what do you feel now?" The back of Hunter's fingers trail down the sleeve of my leather jacket. So softly that it's like a feather is touching my skin through the fabric.

"Definitely not anger." My breath comes out as shallow pants.

He runs his hands down to the back of mine and holds them in front of me.

"What did your hands feel like?"

"Heat." *The way my whole body is feeling right now.*

He releases my hands and takes a step back. "Imagine that same heat and watch as your hands light up."

I know exactly what he's doing. He's trying to distract me from being stuck in my head and helping me to manifest the power. I concentrate on my right hand and it begins to warm. Focusing everything on it, I imagine an orb of light.

"That's it, baby, keep going."

A surge of warmth flashes over my body from his words and a dull illumination appears in my palm.

I'm doing it!

With my attention focused on the power coursing through my veins, I guide it to my hand and concentrate on the charge it creates. The flicker of light engulfs my palm and glows brighter with each breath I take.

"This is...awesome." My mouth parts in awe.

"I knew you could do it." Hunter's voice is farther away. "Try to see if you can manipulate it."

He's about ten feet away from me and my new flame. It's attached to my palm, but I need to figure out how to release it to use it as a force field or weapon. I can't simply walk over to the wendigo and say *hold still while I figure this out.*

Cupping my fingers around the energy, I take the power from my hand and turn it into a ball. A lightness fills my chest with each passing moment. My control, along with my confidence, grows while I juggle the glowing sphere back and forth.

This is unbelievable!

I bring my attention to Hunter who is still a good distance away, staring at me in amazement.

With an evil grin, I yell, "Here, catch!"

"Fuck, no!" Flinching, he moves his knee to block his crotch and holds his hands out to attempt to protect himself. "Don't you dare, Anya. You don't know what that will do to me."

Tremors of laughter have me almost dropping the energy ball. "I may be flighty at times, but I'm not *stupid.*"

A nervous chuckle escapes his throat. "Okay, good. I'm too handsome to die."

"A couple scars on that pretty face would give you some character though." I purse my lips like I'm really thinking about it.

Hunter's face drops. "You wouldn't."

"You're right, I wouldn't." I hold my hand out to give him a better view. "Check it out, though." Giddiness replaces my enjoyment from torturing Hunter.

Hunter side-eyes me but comes over anyway. "I had no doubt you could do it." His eyes lower to the light. "It really *is* amazing. All that energy and power coming from inside you. It's *mesmerizing*." He shakes his head as if he's trying to break out of a trance. "*Please* be careful."

"I'll try, but I don't know how to control this yet." I roll the sphere around in my hands. With the amount of heat coming off it, I realize I'm immune to burns.

"You'll be great. Just trust in yourself." He begins to back away and I stop myself from reaching out to him.

Would it burn Hunter? Would I burn him?

"Hunter?"

"Yeah?"

"Thank you."

The softness of my voice carries in the wind and I figure he doesn't hear me but he shakes his head. "Thank you for what? You did this all on your own."

"No, I mean thank you for supporting me."—I release a breath—"I couldn't have done it without you. I'm not sure if anyone would even believe any of this. Well...except maybe my mom." *Shit.* I never once thought to contact her. She is the only living person who may have some guidance for us. But if I call her, would she come rushing to help?

Could I live with myself if she was hurt because of me?

No, I can't risk it.

"I'll always be here for you. If I hadn't moved, I would have never left your side." His voice becomes quieter the farther he moves away. But I don't miss the warm look of love as he gives me a final glance.

Love for a friend or...something more?

As much as I want to wish one or both were there, they would be short lived. He would honor his words to never leave my side, until he reports for the next job and moves, going from one place to the next, again and again. Breaking my heart a little more each time.

That's if we make it out alive when this is all said and done.

I hide my frown in a weak smile.

Hunter continues to walk away backwards. "You haven't changed from when we were younger. Anya, you are as stunning and talented as before."

My pitiful smile turns into a real one and I have to bite my lip to contain it. His words send a burst of energy through me and the ball grows brighter.

He pulls out a few bags and a small copper bowl from his messenger bag. "While you work on playing with your new toy, I'm going to start mixing some herbs together for tracking."

He kneels on the ground and measures out different herbs. His hands hover over the bowl and he's concentrating hard, muttering under his breath words I can't make out. His focus is directly on the contents inside the bowl.

"Get to work, Anya," he stops to chide me.

My breath catches.

How the hell does he know I'm watching him?

My lips blow a raspberry and I march farther away from Hunter.

In my palm the light has grown so large, it overflows beyond my fingertips. One would think the larger it became, the heavier it would be yet the weight is nonexistent. It's like I'm holding a balloon filled with hot air.

In the beginning, I struggled trying to create this power, but it was when I stopped and allowed my energy to flow freely that it came naturally.

With the globe in my right hand, I hold out my left.

Could I create the energy in my non-dominant hand?

Once I put the thought in my head, the energy surges through my fingertips and another ball appears.

YES! Bouncing up and down on the balls of my feet, I hold back the squeal I'm dying to release.

The excitement has me wishing I could call Danielle and Heather to tell them about it. Maybe one day I can share it with them. My happiness sizzles a bit.

Would they even believe me? The thought tightens around my chest in a vice, but I do my best to ignore it to focus on what's important right now.

It's time to play.

In one hand, I toss a ball into the air and catch it. It feels warm, comforting, and completely weightless. Placing my hands together, I combine the two balls into one then make it grow.

Once it is about two feet around, I kneel down and lower it to the ground. Sitting back on my heels, I watch to see what happens.

Absolutely nothing.

It stays solid and constant—no burning of the grass, no fire starting. I stand up and walk away while watching the light. It doesn't fade or change in any way.

This is good, this is very *good.*

Ten feet away seems like a smart distance so I stop. Hunter is still working with his herbs and thankfully he's far enough away to be relatively safe.

The next test is if I can use my mind to alter the state of the energy. I imagine it growing in my mind and laugh. I increased the size by another foot.

Look, Mom, no hands!

I bounce back and forth on my feet feeling like I'm a boxer ready for a fight. The adrenaline that's buzzing through my body is acting as a double shot of espresso.

Pulling out four corners of the giant sphere, I form it into a box.

Another success.

I close my eyes and visualize the box. Once it's in my mind, I double the size.

It's exactly how I saw it in my mind when I open them again. I don't need my hands or my eyes to control it.

I raise my hands in the air.

"Yes!" I shout, then wince and steal a glance at Hunter.

Whew, he's still absorbed in his task.

My shoulders drop. It's a little disappointing to admit I wish he saw the crazy, awesome force field I created.

Oh well, what do you expect of men. Simple minded and focused on only the task at hand.

This is going better than I ever imagined.

There are many more tests that still need to be done. Like how bright I can get the energy. Can it burn things? And can I create and move the light without my hands? I don't even know if this power has any long-distance limitations. I'd rather not be up close and personal with the wendigo.

I decrease the light until it shrinks and diminishes into nothing.

A tightness, I didn't notice in my stomach, releases. I have control over my power; I just have to find my limitations so we know what we're working with. The problem is, we may not have much time to figure it out.

Hunter stands from his kneeling position over the first set of tracks. He brushes off the dirt on his pants when I make my way over to him. "Hey, how's it going? You feeling okay?" Hunter's eyes are brighter than usual.

"Yeah... I'm good." I glance at him, unsure what he's thinking. "Great, actually. For something I thought would take me weeks to figure out, it's invigorating to know the possibilities of what I can do."

"Damn, Anya..." He shakes his head. "I checked on you a couple times and you've *really* gotten the hang of controlling your power. Do you think you're ready to start tracking?"

Heat floods my face and I bite my lip. "Do you think we can take a little more time or do we need to head out now?"

Please say we have time...

Hunter looks at his watch and then the sun, running a hand over his beard. "We can spare twenty minutes but that's pushing it. I would rather leave now, but we can't risk you not knowing your barriers."

"If we need to leave, we can leave. I should be okay." My stomach forms a knot the size of an apple.

I'll have to be okay.

"I'm not a big fan of *should*. I'm all set on my end, so take a little more time to see what else you can do. I'll let you know when we have to go. Sound good?"

The heaviness releases from my shoulders and stomach and I nod, "Thank you. Hopefully it won't take long."

The area behind the castle isn't large. The openings above me between the trees are spotty this time of year, and, if I'm not careful, the drying timber risks the fast spread of fire.

Hmm... I need a target.

I scan the area until I spot a boulder not too far away that should work perfectly. It's both large *and* heavy. This may be the closest in size comparison to the wendigo that I'll get. In weight? I'm pretty sure the boulder is heavier, which will definitely test my strength.

I attempt and fail to use only my mind to create the light.

Barrier one, my hands are a vital component in creating my power. It's not ideal, but I don't have much of a choice in changing it.

With my right hand raised, I shoot a beam of light to the rock. *Damn it!*

I missed the boulder and trapped a poor, innocent bird on a tree branch just beyond it. Running up to it, I see it isn't hurt but stuck inside a small orb, flapping its wings and bumping into the sides.

It's more of a force field like my ancestor used, but this proves it's harmful only to evil entities.

This makes me feel a lot less pressure in accidentally hurting someone.

The problem I have now is releasing this little guy instead of whittling it down to nothing. I rub the back of my neck.

Think Anya, think. Okay, it came from my hand, can I absorb it too?

Just as I allowed the current to flow from my body to the stone—technically the bird—I should be able to pull it back in. Keeping my attention on the orb, I channel the same energy that is part of me and draw it back in.

"Ah-ha!" It absorbs into my hand and charges my body as if I plugged into a power outlet. And my feathered friend flies away as fast as he can. "Sorry!" I yell after him.

Well...that was interesting for sure.

I aim lower this time and throw my power at the boulder. *Gotcha.*

The light encloses the rock in its entirety.

Now's the fun part—trying to move it. I don't want to waste more time since we need to leave, so I'm crossing my fingers that this works.

To start, I use my mind to push the boulder away from me. It creeps slowly along the grass and weeds. It's not moving how I want it to, so I bring both hands up and push.

The boulder shoots like a rocket a good fifty feet. *Oh crap...* A little too much force.

"Holy shit!" I hear Hunter say under his breath.

I ignore him, knowing our time is short. I pull the rock back to me—slowly, then stop.

Why not test how far my range is?

With a flick of a wrist, I push it out at a steady pace and continue until it begins to crawl to a stop. There's nothing else I can do to get it to move any more, but I can still bring it back to me. I leave the boulder where it stops and turn to Hunter, who's standing off to the side, watching from a distance.

"How far do you think that is?" I suck at measuring distance but I can remember the comparison if push comes to shove. *No pun intended.*

Hunter glances from the boulder to me and back. "I would say a hundred and fifty feet. Why'd you stop?"

I shake my head. "I didn't, my powers only reach that far. I want to try something else. Are we okay on time?"

"Do what you need." He crosses his arms as he watches me—making his biceps bulge in the black t-shirt.

To think, he once was a scrawny kid. He must have eaten quite a bit of Wheaties to build up that bulk. I shake my head and get back to work with my new audience.

If it were anyone else, my anxiety would be elevated to the max.

I turn and bring the boulder about twenty feet from me. When I reduce the size of the force field and connect with the rock, there is a resistance pushing back. With a little more force, the rock starts to crack.

Good thing I didn't try this with the bird, the field crushes whatever is inside.

I weaken the light until it's transparent and push it against the stone which allows it to pass through with no damage. A smile crosses my face with everything I'm learning in such a short time.

Placing the force field back over the boulder, I turn up the heat and make it burn brighter and brighter to see how far I can take it and the effect it has.

With the power contained, I've eliminated any risk of setting fires or hurting anyone. Except maybe blinding Hunter. The poor guy has his back turned from the sun I've created. I don't blame him, the light is beyond bright. The rock is no longer visible. Yet somehow, the light doesn't hurt me. I push a little more despite the heat feeling like the sun's rays on a hot summer day. I keep going, harder.

"Anya, tone it down!" Hunter yells.

Immediately, I dissipate the light until it's gone. And with it, the large boulder. The only thing that remains is a circle of charred land with a red and black puddle of steaming liquid on the ground.

I did that. What the fuck?

This is both fascinating and scary all at once.

"Umm...did *that* just happen?"

Hunter walks up behind me, "Yeah, that really *did* happen. I'm struggling to wrap my head around it too. I know what I saw was real but it's..." He clears his throat. "Do you think you can do that to the wendigo? That may kill him. Eliminate him once and for all."

Shrugging I say, "I guess it's worth a try. If anything, we know I can trap it." I look at the melted liquid and squint, "Does that look like lava to you?"

We walk over to the area and my hand flies to my mouth with a gasp.

"Shit. That *is* lava, Anya. You melted the stone into magma. I have no doubt you can trap and kill the creature. You. Are. *Extraordinary.*"

An awkward smile tilts up my lips. I'm glad someone has the confidence I'm lacking. I need to believe in his words, believe in my power, and get past the fear.

"I think I'm as ready as I'll ever be. Let's get started."

"Aww...is my Honey Bear blushing?"

"Shove it, Hunter, and get to work."

Yes, I damn well am blushing but he doesn't have to get all cocky about it.

We move to the first set of wendigo tracks and Hunter kneels down, pulling out the mixture of herbs and sprinkles it on top of the footprints. In an instant, it ignites with tiny green flames, lighting a path heading into the woods.

My jaw drops. "Well then...here you thought *my* gifts were weird. You're just as full of surprises yourself, aren't you?" I hold out my hand, offering to help him stand. Knowing damn well he doesn't need it, we are partners in this, and I need him to know I'll help him even when he can do it on his own.

Hunter packs away his supplies then takes my offering and pulls himself to stand next to me. What I don't expect is the hug he pulls me into.

"Oh, just you wait, Honey Bear. I'm *full* of surprises." His voice lowers. "Remember, I can do magical things with my fingers." I look up at him and he winks, a dimple popping out.

That has me rolling my eyes while still getting hot and bothered. "Yes, but you didn't say you needed performance enhancements to make that magic. Pity. What a disappointment." I harrumph.

Hunter leans back from our hug with his mouth parted and his eyes wide.

"Anyways, I take it we follow the breadcrumbs?" I smile and gaze up into his eyes.

He clears his throat and his fingers flex against my back. "I don't need breadcrumbs to find my way. *Umph!*"

After I give him a smack on his chest, I rest my hand in the center. "That's not what I was talking about and you know it."

Hunter chuckles. "Okay, okay. You are correct, we follow the flames directly to the wendigo."

"Easy enough."

His playfulness disappears and he furrows his brows. He leans down and places his mouth up against my ear, "Hey, whatever we encounter, whatever happens, I *will* put my life on the line to protect you. I hope you know that and trust me. I promise you that I will do *everything* in my power to keep you safe."

"I appreciate that but as you saw, I can keep myself safe too," I reply softly.

He stands straight and wraps one arm tighter around me—tilting my chin up. "I know you can. You always could handle yourself. Now more than ever. You have your power, but it would make me feel better if you had your dagger ready too."

I nod.

"Can you conjure the light in both hands, or only one?"

"Both. If I hold my dagger in my dominant hand, I can use my left for my magic. It won't be a problem." Anticipating the danger we are about to walk into, I hold onto him tighter. This could be the last time. "I do trust you...that has never been an issue—not counting when I thought you were a serial killer. But now that I realized who you are? I trust you with my life, but I, too, will do everything that I can to protect you. We are in this together."

Hunter leans down and I have no idea what he is about to do. My body stiffens and I freeze until his lips make contact with my forehead. I relax into his arms, allowing my weight to lean on him. His warm lips linger before he takes a deep breath and releases me.

I don't want to leave his embrace but lives are at stake.

Am I sure this is the right path?

Chapter Eighteen

Fehu

(Discovery)

The sun drops farther down in the sky and sends my nerves screaming like a tight wire about to snap. In a few hours, we won't have much light left to protect us. One would think with how long we've been following a set of tracks, we would get somewhere. Yet, I have no idea how close we are to finding the wendigo. All I know is, in the past fifteen minutes the green flames have become bigger and brighter.

Hunter stops and turns to me, "We're getting closer." He rubs a hand over his beard. "I really wish we had hot water. It would be helpful to have you drink some herbal tea for an energy boost."

"I'm okay, I don't need anything."

"You say that, but from what I could see, the energy comes directly from you. A person only has so much in them before they drop from exhaustion. I'm worried you'll burn out too quickly especially with the energy you've already expended testing your powers." He places his hands on top of his head. "Shit, I wish I was better prepared."

"You seem pretty...upset over this." I don't get it. I narrow my eyes. He has nothing to be worried about, I'll be *fine*.

He drops his hands and meets my eyes. "Yeah, you can say that. I don't know what the consequences are of you using your magic—if there are any. But I don't want to risk you running out of energy and passing out at the feet of that monster."

He has a point. I pace the small area until a thought hits me.

"You have your lighter right? Why not heat up a bowl of water?"

"It'll take too long. Not to mention we're running out of daylight."

I stare at my feet. If I didn't take a while testing my power, he wouldn't be wound up with worry.

Hunter grabs my hand. "Are you feeling okay? You sure you're ready for whatever comes next?"

Hmm... I have the water, he has a bowl, and we just need a source of heat.

"I'm fine," I assure him.

"Oh, that's promising coming from a woman." He grumbles.

"Hey now, I *am* telling you the truth. I'm not tired, but...if you don't mind me trying something? Give me two minutes, tops."

"Do what you need. We can stop here and take a break to pull ourselves together and prepare, anyways. What do you have in mind?"

I wiggle my fingers and smile. "Let's test out my magical fingers."

A deep laugh comes from his chest and he gestures with his hand to go ahead.

I hold out my hand. "Bowl, please."

He narrows his eyes, slowly pulls the copper bowl from his bag and hands it to me.

I grab a bottle of water and rinse out the bowl.

No need to risk poisoning myself in my first attempt to make hot tea by hand.

With the bowl placed on the ground, I pour some water into it and hand the bottle to Hunter. He eyes it before taking a drink himself.

I rub my hands together and pop my knuckles getting them ready. It isn't needed to create the energy. It's my way of getting my mind ready to control the light to a certain temperature. I don't want it too weak and definitely don't want to melt the metal bowl either.

Hovering my hand over the bowl of water, I release a small amount of light. Just enough to make sure it's only touching the water. I increase the intensity while watching the liquid beneath my hand. Once steam rises and it begins to bubble, I shut down my power. With my palm still over the bowl, I can tell it's quite warm. I dip my finger in to give it a true test and a smile crosses my face. It's the perfect temperature.

Carefully, I pick up the warm bowl, confirming it won't burn, and hold it in front of him. "You ready with those herbs?" I struggle to hold back the joy this little experiment provided me.

I made hot water all by myself.

Now, that may sound childish if I said it to anyone. I mean, it isn't rocket science to boil water but to do it with only your hand?

Boo-Yeah! Ladies and Gentlemen, this girl's got talent.

"Damn, why didn't I think of that?"

I shrug. "Probably because your hands can't heat things up."

"Really?"

The heat from his stare has me melting and I gulp. Holding the cup closer to him I manage to say the word, "Herbs."

Chuckling, Hunter grabs a few bags of herbs, adding a pinch of each into the water. When I am pulling the cup back, he grasps my wrist, almost making the liquid slosh over the sides. He holds his hand over it for a minute quietly. "Okay, it's ready," he says. All humor has left his face. "You can drink it *with* the leaves. But if you don't want to, sip it carefully to avoid them. Either way, this will help you recharge."

I sniff the concoction and scrunch my nose. "Are you sure this is safe?"

He smirks. "Sorry, Honey Bear, I don't have your precious, sweet nectar to doctor it up for you."

I give him a playful shove and cock my eyebrow. "Lucky for you, I don't add sweeteners to my tea." With a last bit of hesitation, I give in and take a sip.

Hmm...this isn't bad.

Without delay, I chug the concoction down. The hot liquid coats my throat and warms my insides.

Handing Hunter the bowl to store in his messenger bag, I say, "You know how to make a good cup of tea. I may keep you around after all."

His eyes darken. "You better. Even if you try to get rid of me, I'm not going anywhere. You're stuck with me."

This sends another type of warmth coursing through my body. There are so many questions I'm scared to ask.

Like how *stuck? Like stuck in bed together? Or stuck together like family that has no choice but to be there?*

But if I can get through this, I'll be brave enough to get through discussing what is really going on between us.

Right?

His low voice breaks me out of my thoughts. "You ready?"

Releasing the breath I was unaware of holding, I reply, "Yup, let's get going."

We pick up the pace to get to the wendigo quickly. A surge of anxiety hits me out of nowhere. I'm flooded with unease and my skin crawls with a million spiders underneath. I want to run—to escape.

We have to be getting close. There's no other explanation.

I grasp Hunter's arm and slow our pace. Something is wrong. Ahead, on our path is a dark lump on the ground.

Is that the wendigo? No, it can't be.

It has to be a rock, a fallen tree, or an animal. But deep inside, I know that whatever it is, it isn't good.

Hunter pulls his gun from his holster with one hand while the other holds me back.

"Stay." His low demand rumbles from his chest.

Oh hell no, I'm not staying behind while he goes and plays the hero, again.

"No offense, Captain America, but I think Iron Man has more control in this situation than you. Let me take the lead and you can hang back until the coast is clear."

"It's cute that you think of yourself as Iron Man but...no."

I ignore him and make my way around.

Gasp!

Hunter pulls me back to his chest and is holding me—close. My back pressed against his front.

My body is aware of *every* rigid muscle rippling from his chest down his torso.

He leans down and touches his lips against my ear. "I will *not* risk losing you. No matter what." He loosens his grip a bit, but I'm hyper aware of every bit of contact between our bodies.

"I'm not your damsel in distress who needs saving. I thought we were partners."

I'd rather he stay behind, but if he's going to put up a fight, it's better with him at my side instead of on his own. It would be impossible to live with myself if something happened to him.

He rests his forehead against the back of my head. His breaths tickle as they blow across my hair. "I'm sorry. You're right, we'll go together. But *please* be careful and stay next to me. Never ahead of me. Do you understand?"

I can do that.

"Yes, but that goes the same for you. Got it?"

He grumbles, "Yes. Partners all the way." He gives me one last squeeze and inhales a breath against my hair before releasing me.

We slowly make our way to the mysterious lump. As we get closer, the body of a seven-foot bear—or what's left of one—begins to form. My hand flies to my mouth at the grotesque scene.

The wendigo has feasted.

I drop my hand. "This isn't good."

The closer we come to the body, the more my stomach sinks. It's not only a large bear but a bear cub too. A baby.

I choke down the acid rising in my throat.

"I assume you're talking about the recent recharging the wendigo had with this meal..." He gestures towards the two bears. "...and not the fact we have huge ass bears roaming the woods?" His voice elevates at the end.

"Definitely the part about the wendigo. But when *did* we get bears this big in the Catskill Mountains?"

"Fuck if I know. This is news to me." Hunter scratches his head. "Where there is one cub, there are more. And if there are more of them, the wendigo is going to keep getting stronger."

"Damn, it's just like Grant." Hunter crouches next to the giant carcass while I stand over it, surveying the damage, trying not to look at the baby.

The wendigo tore into the bear's chest and torso, devouring the heart like it did with Grant Bordeaux. The puncture wounds in its neck span the width of it and multiple claw marks slash across the animal's face and body.

Hunter reaches into his bag, pulls out a small vial, and uncorks it. Tipping it back, he downs it then shakes his head—cringing as he places the empty vial back into his bag.

I suspect whatever he drank wasn't as good as my tea.

Hunter places his hand on the undamaged back of the bear and closes his eyes.

"What are you doing?"

"Shh…"

Did he just shush me?

I narrow my eyes at him but it's hard to be mad when I'm way too curious.

Hunter shakes his head.

"What is it?"

"It was definitely the wendigo. The large bear put up a fight but it didn't last long. Thankfully, he was killed before he was eaten. The baby was a small snack after."

"Wait…what?" My mouth drops open and I stare down blankly at Hunter.

What is he talking about? Did he…

Hunter ignores my question and continues, "I got a good look at what we are dealing with. Anya, the wendigo is *huge* and hideous. This is something straight out of a horror movie. Are you *sure* you know what we are walking in on?" Worry creases his brow.

I hold up my hand. "Whoa, whoa, whoa. Wait just a minute. What the hell did you do?"

He stands up and rubs the back of his neck as if he's nervous I would judge him.

He's worried about that now? *Not in the moment he was doing his…voodoo-thing?*

"Every once in a while, I use a tincture and focus on the negative energy left behind to see someone's last images. They're quick flashes from the eyes of who—or in this case what—I'm touching."

"If you could do that, why didn't you use that skill on Grant?"

Why is he holding back his gift? What else is he hiding from me?

"Situations like that don't usually happen so there hasn't been a need to carry the tincture with me."

"But you felt 'wendigo hunting' *was* one of those times to bring it?" I cock an eyebrow.

"I wasn't sure what to expect, that's why I brought a lot of supplies. But back to you realizing what we are up against. Are you sure you are ready for this?"

"I know what we're dealing with. Don't forget, I saw it...when I visited the past." Taking a deep breath, I continue, "I know what it looks like, how it moves, but I also know how it can be contained in an energy field. I can do this," I insist. "*We* can do this. Plus, we really don't have a choice one way or another, do we?"

Hunter's mouth flattens. "I know we don't have a choice. I just don't want you to be surprised. When people get scared, their fight or flight instincts kick in. And at times they can go into shock. I need you fully prepared to act fast."

"I'm prepared for what comes next. Don't you trust me?"

He grasps my hands. "It's not that I don't trust you. It's more that I'm scared shitless that something will happen to you."

Butterflies swarm my stomach with a few making my heart pitter patter. My mouth tilts up in a smirk. "Oh, the only thing that will happen is I'll kick its ass."

He pulls me in for a hug. "You drive me crazy, you know that?"

Taking advantage of my cheek resting against his thick pecs, I smile, then reluctantly let go. "Yup. Now, are you ready to go?"

He rolls his shoulders, like he's trying to pump himself up to get ready for a fight then says, "Alright, let's do this."

We follow the path until we reach a wide stream. It wouldn't take much to cross to the other side, but what's worrisome is watching the iridescent flames dimly flicker over the water and dilute as they are carried downstream.

"The wendigo didn't cross, did it?"

Hunter shakes his head. "Nope, it's following the water, heading..." He glances up at the sun and when his eyes meet mine, my stomach drops to the dirt ground.

I know exactly what he's about to say.

"It's headed down the mountain." He grimaces. "This stream runs directly into town."

Shit.

"Do you think...could it have picked up my scent from town?"

"Is that possible? Are their senses that strong?"

"Gudrun said there's no escaping once it latches onto someone's aroma. What if it tracks where I've been, or who I've been with?" A bear trap snaps and bites into my chest. With each breath, the clamp tightens its hold.

Heather and Danielle.

I can't live with myself if it hurts them. Forcing air in and out of my lungs is a struggle so I pull out my dagger to try to calm myself.

Hunter's hand gently rubs circles on my back. Between his comfort and the cooling energy from my dagger, the confinement that holds my ability to breathe hostage loosens.

"Shh...it's okay. Everything will be okay. We'll find it."

"How can you be so sure? We lost the tracks," I snap, anger replacing the panic.

Hunter points to my dagger. "You mind putting that thing away before you stab me?"

Slipping my dagger back into my boot, I say, "I'm not going to stab you."

"Could have fooled me with how tight you were gripping it." He reaches down and grasps my hand, placing it over his heart.

"Because we're in this together. We make a great team, and we *will* succeed."

"Or die trying," I mutter.

"That too, but you won't be alone. We're in this together." His heart thumps in a steady, relaxed cadence. "Do you feel that?"

Puzzled, I ask, "Your heartbeat?"

"As long as this is beating, I'll be by your side fighting to keep you safe."

"But what keeps everyone else safe?"

He smirks. "That's easy. *You.* You have the power. You have the drive. And heaven knows you have the stubborn determination."

The glint in his eye has me shaking my head.

"Yeah, yeah." Now that my nerves have settled and my pulse becomes in sync somehow with Hunter's heartbeat—which I'm sure was part of his plan—I drop my hand and reach for my dagger.

Hunter throws his hands up. "Hey now, I was complimenting you, not insulting you."

I place a hand on my hip and stare him down.

"I'm getting ready in case we run into the giant man-eating beast. I don't think it'll wait for me to draw my blade." I take a few deep breaths and warmth simultaneously flows down my arm to the weapon. Glancing down, I find my blade glowing—pulsating with power.

"I think you made that knife far more deadly than it was. I'm feeling a little under prepared now." Hunter shifts back and forth on his feet.

That makes me smirk until I think about what his weapons are made of. My smile drops.

Damn, he's right.

Based on what Aoife and Gudrun said, iron is a weapon against the wendigo. Hunter's large knife and gun may not do anything.

"You can have my dagger." I flip it in my hand and offer the handle to Hunter.

"And what good will that do me? I don't have your power to charge it, now do I?"

A gust of wind blows, sending a chill down my spine.

"Enchant them..." my grandmother's disembodied voice whispers.

Well, that was odd.

"Did you hear that?"

Hunter jumps into a combat stance and scans the area. "What? Did you hear it?"

"No, not the wendigo." I wave him off. "Sorry to worry you. I heard my grandmother's voice. You didn't hear her?"

He shakes his head at me and relaxes his stance. "I didn't hear a thing." He rubs a hand through his hair. "Shit, don't scare me like that."

I cringe. "I'm sorry. That wasn't my intent. There was a gust of wind—"

"I felt that," he interrupted.

"That's when I heard her voice. In the wind. I think she means for me to use my light power to enchant your weapons. And I think I know how."

After my dagger is back in my boot, I hold out my palm to Hunter. "Do you mind?"

He unsheathes his knife and hands it to me.

I find a dry rock and sit, laying the knife in my lap.

Alright, what's the best way to do this?

While it rests in my lap, I light up both palms then lay them across the knife and imagine the *protection*, *strength*, and *light* runes being burned into the blade—just enough to mark it but not enough to melt the blade itself. I create a *light* field around the blade then release it, observing my work. The markings now resemble those on my dagger.

I stand, holding the blade out for Hunter's inspection.

He takes a step back and eyes the metal warily. "Are you sure that won't burn me?"

"Nope."

Is it bad that I can't hold back my grin?

It's hard when a scared rabbit looks more at ease than Hunter is right now.

Then again, Peter Cottontail from the other night probably has more balls than both of us put together.

There's no way to explain it, but I know deep down that it's safe for him. My grandmother wouldn't have told me to enchant his weapons if it would harm him.

He crosses his arms in a defiant stance. "Yet, you want me to touch it anyways?"

"Yup."

"You're not helping my confidence here with your nonchalant answers, Anya."

Does he think making his voice deeper will make a difference?

The only difference it makes is the increase of blood flow in my southern regions. I'm hoping one day I may become immune to it.

"Annyyyaaa..." Hunter drags my name out like I'm in trouble.

Which I probably am.

"It's safe. You can touch any part of this and it won't hurt you. Well, except if you cut yourself, it *is* still sharp."

He runs a hand over his face and groans.

"Your mom taught you to not run with knives, *right*?" I suck in my lips and bite down, trying my hardest not to burst.

"Yes *smart-ass*, I can handle myself around a knife. I'm more worried about the possibility of burning my hand or clothes. I saw what you did to that boulder."

"Do you trust me?"

His brown eyes bore into mine and he says, "With my life."

The butterflies are let loose in my stomach again, and I swallow hard to tamp them down. "Well, okay then. Touch the knife. I promise, no burning of you or your clothes. *We can burn your clothes off later.*" My eyes bulge out of my head, and I slap my hand over my mouth.

Oh shit!

In a dream world, I would have said that in my head. But my life has turned into one nightmare after another. Of course I said that last part out loud.

Fuck me. And not in the literal sense.

Hunter's sweet, gentle smile grows into a full-on devilish grin. "Promise?"

My jaw almost drops but I catch it behind my hand.

Is he serious or is he messing around with me? He's gotta be teasing.

"Uh...I was kidding, you know, trying to make light of things?" My voice raises awkwardly.

Please ignore any of what just happened, please?

Laughter bubbles up from Hunter's chest. "Well, I'm not. But that's something we can talk about later." His voice comes out velvety and smooth.

How much practice has he had in the years he's been away?

"You better not make me regret this," he grumbles and hesitantly reaches for the hilt of the knife. His shoulders drop when he makes contact and his hand remains unscathed. His thick callused hand wraps around it, fully grasping it.

"It's amazing," he says in awe.

"I'm glad you approve. Since there's no return policy on my craft."

"I definitely approve. I think we're ready now."

Hunter turns to start walking downstream, but I grab his arm to stop him.

"Wait."

"What is it?" He sheaths his knife and moves closer.

"Can I try something with your gun? If this works, it may prevent you from getting up close and personal with the beast."

Hunter pulls out his gun and switches the safety on.

"Is that a... *Holy shit!* That's a Desert Eagle." I've heard of it, but to actually hold this solid black, fifty caliber beauty?

Wait a minute.

"You didn't have this back at the castle, did you?"

"No."

"I thought so. What I felt was a lot lighter and shorter."

"Ouch. You know how to strike a man down, don't you?" He pretends to rub over his heart. "Haven't you ever heard, it's not about the size, but how you use it?"

"Is that why you had to replace the smaller one with this large one? Are you not confident in your shooting?" I cock an eyebrow at him.

"Oh, Honey Bear, my shooting never misses its target."

"Mmhmm... Now you may want to back away a bit so I can get to work." Making myself comfortable on the ground, I stare him down.

When he doesn't move I shoo him away.

"One of these days..." he mumbles as he walks away.

Isn't the saying 'curiosity killed the cat'? Nevermind.

I'm not ready for him to finish that sentence. This little banter between us has been a nice reprieve from the stress of the situation, but we need to get back to work.

"Hold up." I eject the magazine and empty the round in the chamber then hand both to Hunter. It's best if they aren't close when I'm doing this, and it would suck if I accidentally fired a bullet in the process of burning runes onto his gun.

With the muzzle turned away from both of us and the safety on—for safety measures—I place both hands on the gun like I did with the knife.

Once I'm done, air whooshes out of my lungs and my shoulders drop.

It worked.

Something about this layer of protection isn't sitting right with me though. The gun itself helps protect Hunter, but I don't think anything he shoots out will be as effective. I mean, it will help, but I need it to make a bigger impact.

While rubbing the back of my neck a thought hits me.

"Can I have one of those?"

He walks over and I exchange the gun for the ammo.

"I hope you know what you're doing," Hunter warns.

I don't. But no use worrying both of us over it, so I give him a smile.

Placing the tip of the bullet away from us, I create a small marble of energy between my index finger and thumb.

It needs to be strong enough to charge the bullet. The challenge is not to heat it to the point it'll degrade the gunpowder or primer inside or, heaven forbid, build pressure to discharge.

I carefully place the small orb over the bullet and wait. Nothing happens, except now, the ammo is glowing—still cool to the touch but houses enough power to injure the wendigo.

I hold out my hand. "The rest please."

"These aren't going to explode on me once I fire them, will they?"

"Isn't that the point of a bullet? It uses pressure to force out—"

"Annyyaaa..." he scolds me.

Probably not the best time to be a smart-ass. "You are completely safe."

Hunter passes the magazine to me then I unload it and repeat the process until each one is charged and clean before loading them back in.

"Gun, please."

He grumbles something under his breath I don't catch and lays the heavy metal in my palms.

I load the magazine along with a round in the chamber then lay my hands over it to feel the energy. White wisps of electricity reach out from the loaded gun to make contact with me. The peace that washes over me is all the confirmation I needed.

"All set." My voice is as confident as I feel, which right now is pretty damn strong.

Hunter helps me to my feet and eyes the weapon. "Not bad. This is really coming naturally for you now, isn't it?"

Hmm... he's right.

"Yeah, it really is. I'm not second guessing myself, and I know what needs to be done. Grandmother just had to give me that extra push, but the more I use the light energy, the more comfortable I get and it becomes second nature."

"I'm happy for you, Anya." His eyes show the truth of how proud he really is of me and tingles rush over my body. "You ready now?" He squeezes the hand he is still holding.

I nod.

Wendigo hunting season is officially open.

Chapter Nineteen

Hagalaz

(Fear)

"It's time to turn back." Hunter pulls me to a stop two hours later.

My mouth drops. "But—"

"I know. You feel responsible, but we still have tomorrow. It can't travel during the day, right?"

"Right, but it already has a lead on us." We've been walking for a couple hours now and there's been no sign of tracks. It's as though the wendigo vanished.

"Maybe, or maybe not. We don't know that yet."

"Why? Because it stayed in the stream the whole time? Can't you say some magic spell and have the tracks reappear on top of the water or alongside it?"

He sighs. "It doesn't work that way."

"*Ugh*. Of course it doesn't." I run a hand over my face and when I open my eyes, Hunter is staring at me. "Nothing against you and your skills. It's the fact that we're giving up that doesn't settle with me."

"We aren't giving up. We're taking a break and resuming tomorrow. That's all."

I'm tired and my legs are sore, but I can't stop until we finish this. It doesn't help that I'm getting peeved with Hunter acting nonchalant. "How the hell can you stand there and act like this is a 9-5 job that we can quit and our duties will be waiting for us when we return? It doesn't work that way."

Hunter runs a hand through his hair and paces. "What do you expect me to do? My job is to keep *you* safe, and getting you out of these woods before dark is my way of doing that. We aren't giving up. We are taking a break. We're getting rest so we have our energy back for when we *do* run into the wendigo."

My hand rubs my neck. "Why does giving up and taking a break feel like the same thing?"

He stops pacing and comes to stand in front of me, lifting my face to his. "Because you feel responsible for the lives of others. Losing control over the situation is something you hate." He takes a deep breath. "It'll be okay."

It's so easy to say that but it's not okay. My anger gets the best of me and I push him away. "See? You keep *saying* that, but you can't be so sure. Your gifts don't include being a psychic. No one can be sure."

"Why can't you trust me, Anya?" His brown eyes dip in the corners.

"This has nothing to do with trust and everything to do with the not knowing what that monster will do. *Who* will it kill next?" Channeling energy into my blade, I allow the cool marble to glow and flow back into my veins—calming the boiling in my blood.

"What if I screwed up and took the wrong path?" I say under my breath to myself.

"We're following the right path. I can guarantee you it didn't leave the water."

"No. Not *that* path. The path *I'm* on. The path I was supposed to choose. The one my grandmother warned me about. If I choose the wrong one, we all die." My shoulders drop in defeat.

"You need to have faith."

"Sorry," I harrumph. "But Faith is being a two-timing bastard. I had faith before, only to have it laugh in my face for being so naive. The only way I'll feel things will be okay is if we keep going."

"And who's going to save the world if you're dead?" Hunter's temper rises. "*Huh?* Who?" The echo of his voice ricochets off the trees.

And there he goes making sense, which pisses me off more because I want nothing more than to keep hunting.

"Fine." Without waiting for him, I march my way back the direction we came. He thankfully gives me the space I need and keeps his distance...probably because he knows he's getting his way.

Between the small openings in the treetops, I can barely make out the setting sun. Glancing around the woods, I realize just how late it has gotten and a cool breeze peppers my skin. If I wasn't on high alert, I'd enjoy the walk. The mossy damp scent fills the air while the trickling stream runs over the rocks, creating a soothing serenade.

"Anya."

The water isn't soothing enough to have me forget I'm not thrilled with Hunter right now.

"Anya, you need to stop. *Now.*" Hunter whisper-shouts now, more urgently.

Rolling my eyes, I turn and see his hand hovering over his gun and my body freezes.

Twigs not too far away snap and leaves crunch under someone—or something's—feet. The air is still fresh, no stench of rotten flesh, which is a plus, but how close would the wendigo have to be to smell it?

Ever so slowly, I rotate on my heels until I lock eyes on the source of Hunter's worry. Eyes like a crystal blue sky stare back at me.

It's the most majestic creature I've ever laid eyes on. The silver-grey wolf stands tall and proud. Until it looks to Hunter. A low growl vibrates from it as it arches its back, hackles up and ears pinned back.

Hunter draws his gun, but I hold up my hand to stop him. My eyes meet the wolf's and a soft light shines in them. It stops growling and its posture shifts to a non-threatening stance.

It isn't so sure about Hunter, but with me, it's more curious than anything else.

An invisible force pulls me like a magnet towards it as it saunters towards me.

Hunter sucks in a breath behind me. "Anya, what the hell are you doing?" His low voice demands. "Get back. I have a good shot."

I hold a hand up behind me and speak calmly, "Wait. It won't hurt me."

"It's a wolf, Anya. It sure as *hell* won't hesitate to hurt you."

"Please," I beg. "I can't explain how I know it won't, but I do. Please trust me and whatever you do, *don't* make any sudden movements and do *not* shoot it."

There's no response, but I have faith he'll listen to me. I lower the hand I was holding Hunter off with and hold it out—slowly making my way to the beautiful beast. I'm careful and pay attention to his body language to make sure I didn't make the biggest mistake of my life.

The last mistake of my life.

Wouldn't that *be the kicker. Going through everything I just did only to get eaten by a wolf? HA! That'd be my luck.*

I maintain full eye contact. For some reason, deep down, I know the animal won't hurt me, just as I know it understands I won't hurt it. I can't describe it, call it intuition. There is no fear, only a weird sense of tranquility.

I stop and allow the wolf to come to me, stopping a couple feet away. It surprises me by shoving its forehead directly into my palm. I gasp when I absorb the strong male vibrations coming off it. *His*, to be exact.

Similar to when I read Hunter's energy, the animal is searching mine for confirmation.

I slowly release a bit of my light and an internal message that I'm no threat to him or his pack.

He pushes past my hand and nuzzles his head into my chest.

What is happening right now?

My mind is completely blown and I attempt to settle my heart rate from the excitement. Here I am, in the middle of the woods cuddling with a wild, grey wolf, who is not known to be social with anything but its pack.

I allow my hand to glide along his coarse fur. A mixture of thick strands on the top cover the soft fluff underneath.

Closing my eyes, I allow my aura to reach out to his, to see what I can pick up. It doesn't take long until his emotions hit me like a tidal wave, smacking me hard and pulling me under.

He's scared of the evil that came into his home and the animals it's killed. I respond with a comforting warmth, to not only calm him but to let him know we are here to help.

I have never connected with an animal as I am now with this amazing creature.

Yes, I've run into a wolf in the woods behind my house before, but, at that time, I was scared and pretty sure I'd be attacked if I didn't leave immediately.

I respected that I was in their territory and was able to get away safely, but *this* experience is very different. There is no threat. Only...a strange connection.

This has to be my power evolving. It's providing a bond with the light in other spirits that allows communication and understanding.

The wolf lifts his muzzle, staring directly into my eyes then bows his head.

I place my forehead on his. There's a mutual respect and loyalty that passes through us. Like a sixth sense, I know that he will keep watch over us and help protect us. And he knows that I'm here to help get rid of the creature threatening his home and his pack.

I can't explain why this makes me feel better but it does.

The waves of emotions become overpowering. There is yet another in my corner during this battle. Knowing I have more help makes me even more determined to keep the wendigo from hurting anyone else.

Grudgingly, we disconnect. The empathy that overwhelms me for this wolf and the rest of the animals hits me hard. They are fearful and helpless against something they have no control over and no fighting chance with.

The wolf gives me a final look then starts to walk away.

I stand there, stunned and speechless. Once he's farther out of view, I turn to face Hunter. He's holding his gun loosely pointing towards the ground with a look of shock.

When I am standing directly in front of Hunter, I pat him on the chest and say, "It's okay, Big Guy, you can put your gun away now. No one is hurt and we now have a guardian for the rest of our trip." A sweet smile spreads across my face. My prior irritation with him is pushed aside when I stifle a laugh at his dumbfounded look.

He holsters his gun and clears his throat. "Is that new or have you always been able to do that?"

"Definitely new."

"Okay. Because I don't remember you communicating with animals before. In fact, I remember quite well you running and screaming for your life when the neighbor's tabby cat was chasing you. If I can recall, it was because you never tied your shoes. They always dragged on the ground. I'm pretty sure it only wanted to play, while you thought it was trying to kill you."

I give him the stink eye. "For *your* information, that cat *was* evil and attacked everyone. I *was* running for my life. That was the devil incarnate."

"That cat was sweet as pie, but I'll drop that subject...for now. Only because I need to know more about what the fuck just happened." He smirks.

I try to put it into words. "I don't know how, but I somehow connected with the wolf. He showed me that the animals are unable to rest due to the wendigo. He knows now that we are here to get rid of it and in no way wish to harm the animals or their homes. He'll make sure other predators keep their distance from us."

Hunter runs a hand over his beard. "I'm not sure how you did all that, but, at this point, I think if anything else weird happens going forward, it shouldn't surprise me. I'm beginning to think I may need a lot of therapy when this is all said and done."

Ha! It's not just me.

"You aren't alone, Big Guy. *You aren't alone.*"

The rest of our trip back was uneventful, I'm still disturbed that we're leaving the wendigo to have free rein in the forest. But I'm not angry at Hunter any more. I get why he feels we need to call it, despite not agreeing with him.

We hear a crunching noise here and there, but when I check, our new friend was there making sure we were safe. It felt like a warm blanket was wrapped around me, protecting me from the cold, hard outside.

When we arrive at the edge of the woods, I send a small pulse of light to the wolf thanking it and promising we will be back tomorrow.

Walking past the hardened lava, we make our way to Hunter's truck. My car remains in the same place. Since it isn't doing any harm, that is something we can tackle another day, but I do want to get all of my stuff. Making my way over, I snap a few pictures for the insurance claim, then reach into the smashed window—very carefully—and grab my stuff out of the glove compartment. Thankfully, with the car being new, I haven't given it the *lived in* attention yet.

Heading back to the truck, Hunter is already packed up and holding the passenger door open for me. We don't speak and I welcome the silence to allow my brain time to process the past few hours.

I climb up the steps of the vehicle and buckle up as Hunter makes his way around the front to the driver's side. Once he is situated in his seat, he flashes me a smile, then puts the truck into drive. I lay my head back and look out the window at the castle.

It is quiet and empty yet again.

Hunter takes the roads a little faster than he did on the way to the castle, I don't blame him for wanting to get away as quickly as he can. The trees fly by and with them, so does my last bit of hope. He's right though. Who knows how much longer it would take us to finally find the wendigo. Plus the darkness wouldn't help. It's time to concede and jump to the next move in this challenging game of chess.

Let's hope I don't lose any pieces because my side of the board is rather sparse right about now.

"What's next on our agenda tonight?" I break our silence.

"Well... I was thinking of feeding the Honey Bear first before she starts growling." The humor leaves his voice, "And then we need to stop over at Margaret Bordeaux's place to close out the case. I don't *plan* on being long, but, with her, you can't predict what she'll throw at you. A shoe, a brick, a knife..."

"Ha, I'm not sure if I should laugh or be scared of how true that statement may be."

He chuckles. "After that, I hope to stop at my place to stock up on more provisions then drop by a shop to see if they have one of the herbs from your list I don't have. I can also refill the supplies I used today. I want to have everything on hand."

Smart guy, prepare for the worst and pray we never need to use it.

"Sounds good to me. Do you think we should go to the shop for the herbs first before Margaret's though? I don't want to risk them closing before we can get there."

"You know, that's not a bad idea." Hunter rubs a hand over his beard. "Mind us stopping there before we get food?"

"That's fine with me. I don't think I can eat until we get this all wrapped up anyways. Can we plan on ending our night with food?" Maybe by then I'll actually have an appetite. Or at least nibble on something without feeling like I need to puke from my stomach churning. The wendigo is doing a number on my nerves.

He smirks, "I like that, as long as you can make it that long without chewing my arm off."

My jaw drops. "What?!"

"I'm just saying, I wouldn't put it past you. You did just *connect* with a wolf. I don't know if any of its instincts rubbed off on you."

"I must have heard wrong, did you just compare me to a hungry, wild animal?"

Going back over his words in my head again I confirm he did indeed refer to me as an animal.

Jerk!

"Your words, not mine." He sucks in his lips, holding back his laugh.

With my arms across my chest, I glare at him. "Wanna call me a dog again? I don't mind roasting chestnuts over an open fire, you know."

I hold out the hand that is closest to him and manifest a small flickering flame between my fingers. I cock an eyebrow and tilt my head, waiting expectantly for his answer.

He starts coughing and clears his throat. "Uh... no, not at all! I was messing with you about getting too hungry. I was *not* calling you a dog—or any animal for that matter." One of his hands goes up in defense, "It was a joke. I'm sorry. Can you please put that out? I like my chestnuts just the way they are...*uncooked*."

I extinguished the flame and the laughter I was holding bubbles over.

Hunter frowns as he studies me and my now empty hand. I see it the moment he realizes I'm messing with him and he joins in on the humor.

"I've got my hands full with you, don't I?" Warmth fills his milk-chocolate eyes.

You have no idea.

Chapter Twenty

Dagaz

(Revelation)

Relief shouldn't be what I'm feeling right now, but it's hard to stop it. It's a tough job trying to save the world from a mythical creature. Taking a moment or two won't kill me.

Hmm...probably not the best choice of words, but I guess I need this break, so I'm going to try my best to take advantage of our time away from the endless nightmare.

Hunter did make things easier for me by distracting me with his stories and jokes.

We pull up to a small brick building with a neon 'Open' sign in the window.

There's no name on the building. It's weird I've never seen this place before. But...there's a slight chance I never paid attention to it.

"This shouldn't take long."

I stare out the windshield. "How long has this been here?"

My stomach tightens with the unknown of what I'm walking into with this hole-in-the-wall shop. It doesn't help we're the only ones around—it's more than a little creepy.

"It's been around for quite some time. I discovered it when I moved here a few years ago. It's the best place to get the herbs I need. You'll like the owners."

A few years? Wait, how could we have never once crossed paths?

"We live in the same town and the first time we met was at an abandoned castle—in the middle of nowhere?"

My grandmother's words pop in my head...*he has been brought back into your life to help you on your journey.*

Who, or should I say what, orchestrated all of this?

"It's not surprising. I never get out much when I'm home. All my time is spent doing laundry or resupplying before I leave again."

"Hmm..." I can't respond with anything else because a lump forms in my throat as if I swallowed a golf ball.

That's right, when this is all said and done, he'll be gone again.

If we make it out alive and succeed in capturing the beast, where would that leave us?

Or maybe the more important question is, how long do I have left with him?

It doesn't matter, I need to tamp down these rogue feelings bubbling up to the surface. I doubt he feels the same. All I know is, allowing myself to fall for him even more is a recipe for heartbreak.

Okay, Anya, what better way to shift your mindset but to think of him another way—a...platonic way.

I think the only way to make him less attractive is to think of him like a festering boil. The more he pushes and prods me, the closer it gets to exploding.

Eww... I think I threw up in my mouth a bit. Maybe that is a little extreme. But if I repeat that ten times, I'm sure I'll get over this fantasy quickly.

Nope, not working. What else can I think of? Hmm... Well, an explosion keeps coming to mind. Is that how our love would be?

Oh, who am I kidding?

I'm sure it would fizzle out and free fall to the ground just as fast and hard as it started. Laying broken and battered in the dirt where there would be no way of salvaging what's left.

I shake my head, trying to bring myself back to the present—which is in Hunter's truck.

"Well, let's get this over with," the harshness in my voice has me cringing.

I leap out of the truck and my eyes land on the nearby woods. A sense I'm being watched hits me, and an icy chill runs through my body. Shaking it off, I high-tail it to the front door, grabbing the handle—

"Hey!" I exclaim as I'm spun around to face Hunter.

His large hands hold both of my arms, preventing me from escaping.

"What just happened there?" Hunter's lips are drawn into a tight line.

"What do you mean?" I slow my words for this next part. "We got out of the truck and we're on our way into this creepy-ass store." I force a sweet smile, but I know he can see right through it.

"No. We were having a nice conversation, and you shut down on me." He lifts my chin with that damn callused finger. "What's going on in that head of yours?" The crease in his brow ages him a few years.

Not that he doesn't age well, because I'm not sure anything can ruin his ridiculously handsome mug.

I grit my teeth. All the more reason to back off.

"Nothing, I'm ready to relax for the night."

Does he deserve a reason for my sudden flip? Yes.

But I can't say, *Hey Hunter, I just got you back only to lose you again due to your job. Why don't you give up your career to stay here with me? As a...friend?*

Because I'm too much of a chicken-shit to say that, let alone confess I have this building attraction to him. Which isn't entirely true. I already know it's not his looks that have me falling.

It's everything about him.

Hunter's eyes dart around my face and I shuffle my feet. I can tell he's reading me like he's always done. He's always had the knack of knowing when something is wrong or when I'm worried. It's both annoying and endearing.

"I'll get you home safe and you can rest. But that isn't *really* what's bothering you, is it?" He cocks an eyebrow.

That's another thing I adore about him—his constant need to protect me.

"I guess your silence is your answer as to why you have your panties in a bunch?"

"I'm telling you, everything is *fine*. Can we go now?" It takes everything inside me not only to keep my temper at bay but also my emotions. My brain and my heart aren't agreeing one bit at the moment.

There's a line in the sand. My head tells me I need to run away and my heart wants to jump him—all while smearing the line and preventing the brain from getting in the way ever again.

"There you go with that infamous code word 'fine' which really means *I'm pissed, but I refuse to tell you because you should already know*." He pauses. "Am I getting warmer?" His voice lowers. A mix between irritation and teasing.

And for some reason, it kicks my racing heart up a few notches, the same as it did the moment he first pulled me in and held me against him.

Why can't I be immune to his witty banter and that deep, sexy voice?

It's no wonder why I can't avoid the pull towards him—physically, emotionally, and spiritually. He's always been the other half of my soul. The missing piece that mine has been searching for since the moment his parents drove away with him.

My rock.

Hunter narrows his eyes at me, probably still reading me.

The question I need to figure out is, how do I distance myself without losing him completely?

I can't imagine going through that pain if my heart and soul were torn to pieces—again.

Why can't I fix this as easily as it is to manifest a miniature sun in my palm?

I turn towards the entrance of the shop.

"Our conversation isn't over." Hunter growls in my ear, teasing the tiny hairs on my neck, before he releases me.

I'm sure it isn't.

I sigh in defeat and open the glass door.

The bell over the door chimes as we walk in, and I'm suddenly hit with a thick wall of smoke. Sage to be exact.

My lungs heave in an attempt to expel the fumes that permeate every bit of my airway.

Well, if they were concerned about keeping out negative energy, I don't think they have anything to worry about. There's no doubt evil won't get past that sage plume.

Holy water would have been a little more welcoming and refreshing but beggars can't be choosers.

Once we pass the doorway, the air is clear. I turn to find where the smoke is coming from but there doesn't seem to be a source. From the top of the door to the floor, it hovers motionless.

Weird.

Hunter pushes me forward, and I decide to leave the smoke mystery alone for now and scout out the store. It's not scary once I'm inside and the corner of my lips tilt up.

It's a New Age shop. The shelves contain different herbs, resins, tinctures, and crystals.

Again, how did I never know about this place?

Beyond the wall of sage, there is a subtle scent of lavender and ylang ylang. The atmosphere feels...perfect and balanced.

The lighting is absent of those annoying fluorescents. Down the aisles, hanging from the rafters, are brass, orb-shaped, antique light fixtures with illumination encased inside.

I close my eyes and focus on the energy around me. So many beautiful colors surround me and flow freely throughout the store. It is relaxing and almost soothing.

A soft chime of singing bowls play in the background. The sound and frequency evens out the upheaval that I was battling before I entered. I'm still wound up, but this is like a shot of tequila—minus the burn.

Hunter wanders off to who-knows-where, so I take my time down the aisles. I have no doubt he will find me once he's ready.

Like a kid in a candy store, I explore the treasures and wish for every last item to be mine. I could spend hours here. I pass a section with runes and oracle cards that makes me slow my pace before continuing.

A wall filled with books catches my eye and my adrenaline picks up as excitement bursts through me. I make my way there—rather quickly.

"Whoa, these are amazing." I am in complete awe.

Many of the books look to be hundreds of years old. Gliding my hand across the leather spines, I read the titles, browsing to see if any pop out at me.

I stop when my hand lands on one about mythical creatures.

I wonder...

The age of the book—and I'm sure the price tag too—has me opening it cautiously. I place my finger at the edge of the pages and open to a random spot.

Gasp!

A cold sensation runs through my veins while a rush of goosebumps pepper my skin, spreading fast until every part of me is affected.

I'm shivering in its wake.

I check to see if anyone is watching me and huff out a breath. I'm alone in the back of the store.

What are the chances I'd open this book and land directly on the wendigo?

Skimming through the text, it briefly talks about the main locations where the Native Americans shared stories of the creature. It's no surprise they were in this area, farther up North into Canada, as well as Minnesota. It's scary to imagine there being more than the one out there.

This means we aren't the only ones who have experienced this—not counting my ancestors.

Nothing could have prepared me for the information I read next.

My head swims and the shop spins around me while my vision darkens. I slide my body down the wall next to the bookshelf until I'm on the floor with my knees to my chest. With the book set aside, I place my head on my forearms. The air around me disappears and I'm gasping for any bit of oxygen I can salvage.

"Are you okay, dear?" The sweet voice of a woman startles me.

Bringing my gaze up, a few feet away from me stands an elderly woman with a grey bun on top of her head and a few misshapen stones strung around her neck.

She's maybe seventy years old? A tiny little thing wearing a worried frown on her face.

This must be one of the owners.

"Can I get you something?" she offers. "Water maybe? I know it can get stuffy back here."

With every breath I take, it's like I'm breathing through a straw as I suck in just enough air to prevent myself from passing out. My nerves want to jump out of my skin at the same time my body screams to run.

"Thank...you," I manage to say while taking in air between words. "Long...day...if I can...have a moment...please."

The room disappears while my tunnel vision focuses on the woman. Her brown blouse and long, dark burgundy skirt sway as she comes near.

I haven't had a panic attack in years.

Why now?

Okay, remember to focus on the main five senses; feel, hear, see, smell and if possible, taste.

Unless I lick the book, taste isn't possible.

Keep calm, Anya, you still have the other senses to work through.

See.

Okay, I see this lady. Her feet are covered in natural animal hide with blue and red stitching. What are they called? Oh, moccasins.

The tightness around my throat and weight on my chest loosens a fraction.

Keep going, it's working.

Feel.

Shit! I can't feel anything! My fingertips have gone numb.

Tears flood my eyes, threatening to spill over.

Don't lose it, just move on.

"Oh dear," the woman's voice interrupts my panic, "let me get you some water. You can stay there for as long as you like. I keep telling Harold that we need to put some chairs and a fan back here, anyways. Maybe this will finally convince him. I'll be right back." She winks then quickly sashays away.

Who's Harold? And why can't I calm down?

An invisible fist tightens around my throat. I need to keep going. Hear.

With the woman gone, I only hear buzzing.

Closing my eyes, I place my head between my bent knees. Since my focal point ran away like I'm a crazed animal, I need to focus on something else.

Soft chimes and ringing breaks through the consistent vibrating in my ears.

Singing bowls.

I allow the harmony to take me away from this place.

The sun is shining, bouncing off the sparkling black sand beach. A cool breeze gently caresses my skin. But instead of the fresh sea air, there's incense and essential oils. I allow the wisps of herbs and flowers to fill my lungs and relax me with each and every breath.

Breathe in the relaxing essence.

Breathe out fears and helplessness.

And repeat.

The swelling in my chest and throat slowly recedes and my airway begins to open.

"Anya?"

I groan. Hunter seeing me weak is about as embarrassing as someone hearing me pass gas. You know everyone does it, but you still would rather die than do it in front of them.

Hunter kneels down next to me. "Anya, what happened? Are you okay?"

Then again, this is *much* worse.

"I'm fine." My words release in an exhausted breath.

"Is this an effect from using your energy earlier? We need to get you food." He places his hand on my arm and I shake it off.

"I said, I'm *fine*." The raising of my voice has me flinching.

Shit, I'm losing it.

My eyes bore holes into the floor beneath my knees as I refuse to meet his gaze. Part of me wants to push him far, far away. The other part wants him to wrap me in his arms and tell me this is all a dream.

It's not his fault I'm quickly losing control of everything.

My life, my job, the safety of the people in this town, and soon ...the other half of my heart and soul. It's all swirling down into a deep, dark abyss with no chance of recovering it.

Forever lost.

And who's to blame?

Me.

I'm in way over my head and I'm likely to leave a trail of destruction in my wake. If I can't toughen up and figure out how to handle this, I won't be getting through the next few days alive.

And maybe that's just it, I chose the wrong path and this is my end. The end of my book with no happily ever after, no exciting epilogue, forget a sequel, *The End.*

Even if it is, I don't need to bring anyone else down with me. The last thing I need is Hunter to sacrifice himself to be a hero.

My hero.

Fuck that. I'll find a way.

There has to be a way to save everyone, even if it means risking every part of me in the process.

An agitated sigh has me pulling my head up.

Hunter's jaw clenches while his eyebrows turn down in a frown.

Is he concerned or angry?

"Let's put aside whatever issue you have with me right now," he growls.

And...angry it is.

"And tell me why you're sitting on the floor as white as a ghost...and crying."

My hand swipes under my eyes and the wetness covering my fingertips tells me the tears broke through the dam without me knowing.

Instead of the risk of pissing him off farther with my words, I gently slide the book across the floor to him—page open to my finding.

Hunter's eyes narrow at the words on the page, and I resist the temptation to bury my head in my knees again.

"Okay...this is all interesting stuff, but I don't see what's making you upset." His face scrunches up, which deepens the lines in his forehead.

My finger lands on the section that pretty much knocked me on my ass.

"*Fuck,*" he says under his breath. His eyes bounce from the book to me and back.

The moment I drop my head is the moment the woman returns.

"Here you go." I look up as she comes down to my level with a sweet smile while she offers me a glass of water. "Harold finally accepts that a chair or two would be a good idea back here. It took long enough for the ol' coot to listen." She lightly chuckles and stands back up. "How are you feeling?"

Her gentle tone has me checking my temper before I speak. I can't fault this woman who is only trying to help this destructive tornado called Anya.

"Thank you." I nod, unsure how to answer her question and take a large gulp of water.

Huh. Something is...off.

The water tastes like water, but it doesn't *feel* like water, which makes zero sense.

I study the glass and cock an eyebrow at the woman in front of me.

Her saccharine smile transforms into a forced one. One filled with guilt. Dark pink floods her cheeks and she wrings her hands in front of her.

"I'm so sorry I didn't ask for your permission."

"What?"

What did she do? Did she poison me?

"No one ever notices when I add healing properties to their drink." Her teeth bite into her lip. "I meant no harm."

"What did you add?" Hunter demands.

"I think it's okay, Hunter," I reassure him. I mean, I'm not at the brink of passing out or have pain coursing through my body. I'm actually the complete opposite. I feel...good.

"It's a tincture to help calm and bring her aura back to that beautiful rainbow of colors she walked in with. I have never seen an aura like hers. It is absolutely magnificent!"

What the hell do I say to that?

"Umm...thanks?"

"And don't you worry, the tincture won't inhibit any of your abilities. You don't have to worry about it dimming your light."

My jaw drops faster than a racehorse let out of a gate.

She knows.

I close my mouth and shoot daggers at Hunter.

He throws up his hands in defense, "Don't look at me like that, I didn't say anything."

"Mmhmm..."

"I probably should've given you a heads up. Greta has gifts of her own, and there's not a single person that can hide their power from her." He rubs a hand through his hair. "Myself included. We can trust her and Harold. They are nothing but good, caring people." He turns to apologize to Greta, "Sorry I got defensive."

"That's understandable, Hunter. I can tell she means a lot to you," Greta replies as she continues to twist her hands with a sheepish look on her face. She silently pleads for forgiveness for spiking my drink.

I release a sigh and flash her a warm smile. "Thank you, it was odd and definitely not normal. It scared me for a moment because nothing has seemed to be going right for me recently. Being poisoned would have been the kicker to top off my night."

Now that I know the drink is safe, I down the rest of it, and a cooling vibration rushes through my body. It's as though it's bringing balance to the scales of my soul—chilling the heat coursing through my veins, calming the storm electrifying my nerves, and clearing the fog in my mind to allow clarity.

The fog filling my brain has retreated and, with it, my stress and fears. I make my way up, standing with strength I didn't have before.

"I have no idea how you knew I needed that, but thank you. It was extremely helpful."

Hunter stands and asks, "Do you mind if we purchase some of that tincture? We may need it again soon."

Greta's smile spreads wider when she looks at Hunter, but it's me who she addresses, "It will be *my pleasure,* but this one's on me. Neither of you will pay me a dime." She shakes her head and crosses her arms the same way my grandmother used to when she refused to back down. It's better to give up while I'm ahead.

She tilts her head. "Do you mind sharing what put you in a tizzy from that book?" She nods to the book Hunter is still holding.

Who is *this woman? Do I tell her?*

"It's okay, go ahead," Hunter confirms while he hands the book to me. Again, the man knows me too well.

I hold the pages out to Greta. "Ironically, I found this book and opened right to this page. We're dealing with a wendigo."

With a quick glance, her face pales. "Oh, no," she touches her fingertips to her lips. "I was worried it might escape." Her mouth thins. "My dear, nothing comes by chance. It is all in our cards with what our future holds, what paths we are led down..." She smirks at Hunter. "And who comes into our lives, like our true soulmates brought back to us."

My mouth drops for the second time tonight.

"*Everything* happens for a reason." She gives me a knowing look.

Puzzled, I shift my eyes from the old woman to the giant next to me.

What did you tell her, Hunter?

He shrugs, giving me an 'I don't know what she is talking about' look.

I roll my eyes and shift my gaze back to Greta. "How do you know about the wendigo? And how did you know about it escaping?"

She taps the graphic in the book and says, "Now this beast..." She mutters under her breath what sounded like *oh my heavens*. "This same beast plagued this land close to a thousand years ago here in the mountains." She shakes her head. "So many more lives could've been lost. Thank the gods for the Irish Light Angel who was able to trap it and prevented more death and destruction to the land and its people." Greta swallows hard. "It will use its freedom to leave a path of destruction and terror in its wake. The horrors will be unimaginable. May the gods watch over us all."

Chapter Twenty-One

THURISAZ

(CONFLICT)

I narrow my eyes after hearing her solemn declaration. "How do you know all of this?"

Greta's blank expression isn't what has my stomach in knots, it's the fear hiding behind her pale, green eyes that doesn't bode well.

"My ancestor helped the Light Angel capture the wendigo. Together, they used their gifts to trap and hide it for hundreds of years—until now." She wrings her hands. "I was worried this would happen one day, but I prayed it wouldn't be in *my* lifetime."

Her ancestor?

I shoot up my hand. "Wait, your ancestor was the *Viking witch*?"

A knowing smile spreads across Greta's lips. "We always called her a seeress, which was *much* more respected, you know...since 'witch' was believed to be associated with the devil." She shakes her head. "Can you imagine? I wouldn't even *be* here if someone used that word in relation to my family. The churches would have killed every last bit of my bloodline." A slight smirk peaks out of the corner of her mouth. "*Everything happens for a reason.*" The last part she says in a sing-song melody.

I cringe as images of women burned at the stake, drowned, and hanged flash through my mind.

Greta waves a hand. "As you can tell, I'm a *little* passionate about my family history."

"Wait... If you're related to the seeress, then you can help us!" Maybe fate is finally taking pity on me. "We need you to come with us and help trap the wendigo again."

She grasps her chest. "Good heavens, no. I don't have the powers and training my ancestor possessed. You have more knowledge when it comes to that stuff than I do."

My shoulders deflate. Guess I really am on my own.

"Anyways, what I was going to say before I got carried away..." Her hands clap in front of her and her eyes widen. "I am *so* elated we have another Light Angel here to help us! I can't imagine the terror the wendigo would spread across the land without you here to trap it again."

Say what?!

"I'm no Light Angel."

"The Irish Light Angel was your ancestor. A grandmother of sorts." Greta frowns. "Didn't you know that?"

"Well, yes. I figured that was who you were talking about. I read Aoife's journal. But a Light Angel? *Me*? Plus, you don't even know me."

And why angel? Why can't they use a different nickname? It makes it sounds like I should be sprouting wings out of my back at any time.

I discreetly shift my hand under my jacket and relax when my back feels normal.

"My dear, there is no mistaking you. You look just like your grandmother and your energy is very unique. You can't lie about the power you harness. It's the same as your ancestor. You *are* the most powerful descendant of the Light Angel."

She was right when she said nothing was a coincidence. Something brought us to this shop—to this woman who knows about Aoife, Gudrun, *and* the wendigo. It's no surprise she'd know about my grandmother, they lived in the same town and she was a big part of this town. I'm still not sure about the whole *angel* thing, but she may know more that can help us.

Everything happens for a reason.

My shoulders drop and I release the air I didn't realize I was holding in my chest.

Maybe I *am* on the right path.

"I'm sorry. You have to admit, it's a lot to take in."

Hunter's hand makes contact with the small of my back, rubbing circles and causing me to relax into him.

Just for a minute.

He whispers in my ear, "Ask her about the book."

My body stiffens. I was relaxed and enjoying the little bit of cuddle time with Hunter and he goes and ruins it by reminding me we have a problem. I'm not ready to dive into this finding but know I have no choice.

I clear my throat and stand up straighter, pointing to the book she still has in her hands; my finger lands on the section that has me the most concerned. "Do you know anything about this? The journal didn't say a thing about it."

Is it too late to pray, asking for Greta to say what's in there isn't true? Anything to ease some of my fears?

"Ah, the possession of a human. Some stories say possession by a wendigo was a state of mind that caused cannibalism and extreme greed in people. That was certainly a cop-out for what it really was."

Ugh, so much for wishful thinking.

"Wait, couldn't they tell they weren't...human?"

Greta's lips tighten. "I'm not sure if it changes the physical appearance. All I've read was they have the look of a crazed person. But believing a real-life monster walked the earth let alone possessed someone?" She shakes her head. "It's human nature to avoid the truth when it doesn't make sense, and further, when it brings fear."

"Same as demon possession. There are a lot of stories, but it's hard to believe they are real. It's frightening to believe it." I shift my weight, uncomfortable where this conversation is going.

"Exactly! The wendigo only eats humans but, as a last resort, it will feast on animals. If it finds that its current form is not allowing access to enough food, it *will* possess a human...but not just any human."

My breath catches. "Please don't tell me this person needs to have some kind of power."

Her hand comes to my arm. "Oh dear, no! It's the complete opposite. They can only inhabit souls filled with greed and with very little compassion. This is why it's not common, it is very rare to find someone in this state, but it *has* happened."

The trembling through my body subsides. Hunter and I have one less threat against us. But it's still one more threat against the town.

Greta continues, "Possession is also the *only* way that a wendigo can be killed once and for all. It is immune to death in its original form."

I choke. "What?!" I grab the book and flip through the text. "This says nothing about that."

"I've done my own research over the years and many texts mention it. Only one describes it in detail. To kill it, it would need to be stabbed in the heart with a special blade from a *magical* land." Her head lowers and she stares at the ground. Disappointment radiates off her. "I am sorry. Your only hope is to trap it again. You will need to teach your children and their children about your abilities. They can keep guarding the prison inside that castle."

Hunter's hand stills on my back.

"Fuck," I say under my breath. Our chances of killing this thing went from a slim chance down to none.

"I wish I could have better news for you, but not only would it need to possess someone, you would need to locate a rare, fabled blade that will kill it. It's not possible." She places her hand over mine.

A rare, fabled blade... What if...no.

I shake my head. Luck isn't on my side, the odds that my dagger could be the very same one she's talking about, are like finding a needle in a football field sized haystack.

Well, there's only one way to find out.

At a non-threatening speed, I reach down and pull my family heirloom out of my boot.

No need to scare the poor woman by having a stranger pull a knife on her in her own shop.

Greta's eyes widen and her jaw drops as I position the Connemara marble handle and steel blade between my hands. Out of the corner of my eyes, Hunter grins with pride until the wind is knocked out of him when Greta shoves the book into his stomach and holds out her hands for my blade.

"May I?" A smile stretches across her face and she wiggles her fingers.

The moment I hand over my dagger she gasps, "Oh, my heavens!"

I know it's beautiful, but I don't quite think it's *that* amazing.

"It looks brand new, but it is *thousands* of years old. This is it," she says under her breath.

My brows furrow. "This is what?"

"This is the blade, my dear. The very one I was telling you about." A tear slips from the corner of her eye. "Oh, it's such a relief."

"So," I wave my hand to the weapon. "*This* is it? This can kill the wendigo?"

She nods. "The wendigo as well as many other evil entities. It brings protection and comfort when you are afraid. It's tied to your bloodline, you know, helping you strengthen your power."

Apparently, the odds are finally in my favor, but it doesn't mean we have an end game.

"But if this is the *true* blade, we still have the barrier of needing a possession, don't we?" The room dims and my breathing labors.

I can't kill someone. A bug? Sure. A person? Ugh. I can't subject someone to having a monster from Hell enter their body so I can murder them both.

Tremors surge through my body, but a warm breath against my ear and a strong hand on my back has me relaxing into a hard chest.

"It's okay. We'll get through this." The rumble of Hunter's deep voice soothes me and I take the moment to sync my heartbeat and breathing to his before I take two steps away.

My detachment has Hunter recoiling like I've hit him.

I can't keep allowing him to help me. I can't get used to this...us. Because one day—soon—he will no longer be there for me.

"Tell me child, has this been passed down through the women in your family?" Greta's voice pulls me out of my thoughts.

My mouth opens and shuts like a fish out of water—unable to put together words. This woman knows more about me and my family than I do. It shouldn't surprise me she knows about this too.

"Yes, it's been in her family for a long time," Hunter chimes in, saving me yet again.

She bounces on her feet. "This is magnificent! My ancestor documented only once that your ancestor had a dagger, but there were no specific details about it. She didn't know it was of any importance." Greta sighs. "You have a chance now to finally destroy this darkness, once and for all."

Like a pinball, my brain is paddled between Greta, Hunter, and my consciousness in a losing match.

I do have to agree, knowing we may have a chance at defeating the wendigo is a tad exciting. A small seed of hope begins to blossom in my chest that we aren't alone in this battle.

Now, if I could just get past the idea of killing someone... Ugh!

Greta hands the blade back to me with tears in her eyes. "My dear angel, I am blessed that you were brought here. Thank you for sharing with me your journey as well as your family relic."

With a deep swallow, I find my voice, "Thank you, Greta. I'm sorry I've come in here acting like a loon. I can't tell you how grateful I am for you, for your tincture, and your vast knowledge."

She waves me off. "Oh, it's nothing." Her composure becomes serious. "But if you need anything, anything at all, please come see us. We will do *everything* in our power to help you. I know you have what it takes to defeat this evil." She points her chin in Hunter's direction. "And keep this one close to you; you need each other."

Hunter places the book back on the shelf while I sheath my weapon, then the three of us walk back to the front of the store.

Greta pulls me in for a fierce hug—which reminds me of my grandmother's.

She whispers in my ear, "May your journey be blessed with helping hands and luck on your side. I have faith in you. Don't forget, it's okay to allow the light to consume you, Light Angel."

I cringe at the name, but hug her back tightly.

"Thank you so much."

Hunter grabs his bag at the counter and we head outside to his truck. He hasn't touched me again, knowing I need my space. When we get into the truck he turns to me. "We need to get food."

I really don't want food right now. "Can we please get Margaret out of the way first?"

He gives a resigning sigh. "Yeah, sure. You mind staying in the truck while I handle her?"

Oh, thank goodness! "You won't see me jumping at the chance to be near that woman. I have no shame in hiding in this truck." Margaret is the last person I need to deal with right now. Add the fact that one of her employees is currently hanging out with her hired PI won't help either.

The drive to the Bordeaux Mansion was a quiet one. It's clear that Margaret and Grant try to keep unwanted guests away with not one but *two* sets of gates barricading their home.

Once we are buzzed into the last entrance and parked, Hunter grabs a manila envelope from behind his seat.

"I have no clue how long this will take," concern laces his tone.

I hold up my cell phone. "All good here. I have some catching up to do anyway."

My eyes follow him as he makes his way to the front door. In no time, an elderly gentleman with silver hair answers the door and ushers Hunter in.

Damn, they even have a freaking butler. Do they consider themselves royalty?

Margaret is a woman who never has to want for anything in her life. And she knows it too. She has no issue rubbing it in everyone else's face. We're all below her, peons who aren't worth her time.

Yup, definitely a royalty complex.

With Hunter now inside, I open my text messages and go back to the oldest ones. Scrolling through, there are ones from Heather when I wasn't responding last night, then Danielle saying she and Heather are waiting impatiently for a thorough explanation about my boyfriend.

Ha, that will be an interesting conversation. Next.

Clicking on my missed calls, my mom's name pops up with a voicemail. Dread and worry hit me hard in the gut. She rarely calls because she knows I'm usually busy and it's never urgent.

With some hesitation, I hit the play button then lift the device to my ear, praying this isn't more bad news.

"Hey, Anya, I know you are busy after everything happened at the castle last night. I'm trying not to worry too much, but I feel like I failed as a mother because I haven't prepared you for this. Shit," she says under her breath. "I didn't want to believe any of it growing up myself. None of us, other than Aoife, has had to deal with this before. I thought it was a ghost story. You know, one that a parent tells to keep you in line?"

My jaw drops.

How the hell does she know about this?

Just as if she heard my question, she says, "Your grandmother decided after all this time that she'd make an appearance to tell me what's going on. So nice of her, right? A little late if you ask me," she quips. "Anyways... I was about to run out the door to come help my baby girl, but she told me I'd only make things worse, and it could risk your life. I hate when I have to admit that the old bag is right." She whispers into the phone, "Don't tell her I said that." A sigh comes out. "Never mind, she's probably listening."

I chuckle. She always thought grandmother was a little touched in the head. They loved each other but bickered often.

Rubbing the back of my neck, I imagine my mom here with me. That feeling of having a caring parent by your side in troubling times is comforting, but I'm relieved she isn't in danger.

"It's not like I have much power left to do any good anyways. I was never strong to begin with, but I passed down most of it to you." I can hear her smile through the phone. "But I hear that little Hunter came back to help. It also sounds like he isn't so little anymore." She chuckles and I know exactly what she's hinting at.

"I knew one day he would be back in your life. There wasn't much that could have kept you two apart forever." With a clearing of her throat, she continues, "I...uh...assume you have your memories back by now? I'm so sorry, sweetie. I hope you aren't mad at me for blocking them."

My teeth grind, but I take a deep breath to let go of my anger.

"Please don't be upset. It was the only thing I could do to give you a shred of peace after Hunter's family moved away."

My dad's voice comes on in the background, "Is that Anya? Is she okay? Can I talk to her?" Concern laces his voice.

"No honey, it's her voicemail. Mother said—"

The voicemail cuts off there.

Wait, Dad knows about all of this? How much about this, about us, does he really know? What did Grandmother say?

Staring at my phone, a second voicemail waits for me.

"Ugh, why is there a limit on messages? We live in a digital age now," her voice is incredulous and she releases a frustrated grunt. "I'll try to stop rambling. I'm sure you are busy." Her voice softens, "I'm so sorry for everything you are going through. Please know that if anyone can deal with this, it's you. You are *so* much more powerful than your grandmother or me. Plus, you aren't alone. I'll be sending prayers for you and Hunter. Text me to let me know you are okay. I'll let you go now. I love you. Bye."

I start to pull my phone down but I hear her add, "Oh, and don't forget to kick ass and shine on!" She makes a kissing sound then finally disconnects.

Despite all the different emotions from that one message, the smile on my face is inevitable. I love that woman. I just don't understand why she sounds like this is all normal. My brows crease. There's been *a lot* that she's refrained from telling me.

Not knowing when Hunter will be out, I keep things short for now, fully expecting to give her the third degree later.

> **Me:** *Hi Mom, sorry for the delay. I'm okay. I think it's expected that I'm a tad overwhelmed, yet you're right, I have Hunter (for now). Once this is all settled, you and I need to have a chat that is long overdue. The blocking of my memories...as much as it sucks, was needed.*

My thumbs hesitate over the keyboard.

Do I bring up my dad right now and my million questions? Does he know about everything?

Better safe than sorry. I finish my message before hitting send.

> **Me:** *I may be outside of cell service but call and leave a message if it is an emergency, and I'll get back to you when I can. I love you so much, give Dad a hug for me, and I'll update you when I can. Going to take it easy tonight. We are safe.*

There. That addresses most of her concerns. And she doesn't need to know the creature is still at large.

It would have been nice if my mom had been able to give me a heads up into the chaos that was dumped into my lap. Who knew, after a few short days, my life would become something out of a paranormal fiction book. I just hope this book has a happily ever after.

Hunter is still inside, so I switch gears and think about what to do with work.

What are the chances Julie will believe I have a family emergency that requires indefinite time off? Would a week suffice?

A groan escapes my throat as I rub a hand down my face. I can't afford to lose my job, and moving out of town to get a new job is out of the question. Now I know that my purpose in life is to protect this town. It won't pay the bills, though.

I wish I had a couple more days to sort things out before I had to report back to work. But surprise, surprise, luck isn't on my side—again.

My eyes go to the gold-plated door handles of the Bordeaux mansion and my leg begins to bounce. It's a good sign I haven't heard any screams from someone being murdered, right? Unless the Bordeauxes have soundproof walls...

I blow a strand of hair out of my face and rub my hands together. "Alright, I'll give Hunter fifteen more minutes, then I'm going in with *hands blazing*." *Wait, that doesn't sound right. That sounds more like a burning rash on my hands.* "Okay, I'll go in there with *guns* blazing—and never try to personalize an idiom again. He better get out here soon."

With my elbow on the door's armrest, I lay my forehead in my hand. Ugh. Talking to myself from boredom is at least a better option than trying to fight for my life. I still think I need to question my sanity after this is all said and done.

Onto more distractions to pass the time, I open up the group chat with Heather and Danielle.

> **Me:** *Hey, sorry about the craziness. I'll see you both at work in the morning. I need to see if there is any way of taking the rest of the week off for this family issue. When this is all over, I'll update you both. Sorry.*

Not skipping a beat, three dots on the bottom of the screen pop up.

> **Heather:** *You're alive! I was getting ready to stalk your ass down and see what bitch I needed to throat punch. You know, there would be no hesitation. If it was Julie, I would have even given an extra punch to the cooter because we all know she deserves it.*

I raise my brow and release a chuckle. She never ceases to shock me.

> **Danielle:** *(facepalm) Heather, sometimes I feel you may need anger management.*

> **Heather:** *Who needs anger management? I can manage my anger just fine. Punching someone is stress relieving. You should try it sometime D, it's like yoga, soo...relaxing.*

> **Danielle:** *ANYWAYS...so glad you are okay, Anya.*

Whatever is going on with you and your family, it's...weird, but we love you anyways.

Heather: *You take care of yourself, even if that means having your man take care of you (wink). We will be here when you are ready. Can't wait to see you tomorrow!*

Danielle: *Have a good night, talk tomorrow.*

Me: *Night Ladies. And please do me a favor, stay in tonight. Stay home and lock the doors.*

Heather: *Well if that isn't mysterious and serial killer-y. It's like telling a kid keep their hands to themselves in a shop full of breakables. If I wasn't baking, I may not listen. But lucky for you, I'm in for the night.*

Danielle: *Okay...I'm not planning on going anywhere either but Heather's right, that sounds creepy.*

Heather: *I never said creepy. Your words, not mine. It sounds like fun.*

Me: *(facepalm) I'll explain more later. Please be safe. Night.*

Shutting off the screen of my phone, I sit back in my seat and smile. Even when my heart breaks from Hunter leaving, I may have a chance to get through it with my great support system. It's inevitable that it *will* be broken, but maybe I can control how much it shatters.

That's assuming my heart isn't devoured by the wendigo. Or one of them isn't killed.

My stomach drops.

No, I have to think positive. We'll find and capture the wendigo, keeping everyone safe.

The air from my chest comes out in a burst as I shake off the *what ifs* and bring my attention back to the missing man.

What's the worst that could happen? Margaret hits Hunter over the head with a silver candlestick, knocking him unconscious then dragging his lifeless body to the backyard?

No. She can't do that by herself; she couldn't even reach his head, let alone drag his huge body around. But the butler could... And someone else might be in there with them.

I look around for other vehicles but don't see any.

I throw my head back against the headrest. I need to stop jumping to the worst possible thing. Exhaustion, boredom, and my active imagination are driving me crazy.

I check the time.

Screw it, it's go time.

Without hesitation, I unbuckle and grab the door handle—ready to do whatever I need to do to save my man.

Frozen in my seat, I clear my throat awkwardly.

My man? Come-on, Anya. You were thinking about keeping your distance and now *you are quick to jump back into this fantasy where he is yours?*

I groan.

Why is this so hard?

Friends. I can be a good friend. And good friends save their buddies in need.

Rescue the hero, take two.

I open the truck door—

"Don't you EVER tell me what I can and cannot do! That place is MINE, do you hear me?"

A mouse must be in the truck because I swear that tiny squeak didn't come from me. I crouch down in my seat to prevent myself from being seen.

Margaret is standing outside the front door while Hunter faces her. Based on his stiff profile and clenched hands at his sides, he's just as angry.

She's screaming in Hunter's face. Well, more at his chest with her five-foot stature. She shoves a finger at him but he doesn't budge. Which I think pisses her off more.

My body tightens and a strong need to protect Hunter from her venom washes over me. But... Hunter is a big boy and my presence will only make things worse.

Her ear-piercing shrill echoes through the air, "I will continue what my husband died trying to do, and you can't stop me. All you are is a jealous low life who wants nothing else but to steal what is rightfully *mine* and that castle *is* MINE! You try to stop me, and I will ruin your career along with the lives of *everyone* you care about. Take your money and leave me the hell alone!" She throws her hands up in the air as though she is trying to scare off a bear.

Hunter walks around the front of the truck, I can practically see steam coming out of his ears. His hands are at his sides gripped in fists. Like it's the weight of a feather, he effortlessly yanks the door open then slams it shut and punches the dash.

I flinch. I have never seen him this mad before.

When we were kids, he'd been angry and punched a kid for making fun of me in school, but I have never seen him like *this*.

Hunter is quiet and doesn't acknowledge me as he places the truck into drive and we make our way to his house.

Afraid to poke the bear, I leave him to stew in his anger.

Chapter Twenty-Two

WUNJO

(CONTENTMENT)

The smoke from Hunter's ears is still billowing out by the time we pull into his drive. The amount of concentration he has on the road makes me think the gears in his brain are on overdrive. I have a pretty good idea of what is going on inside his head from Margaret's words. I'm still curious to find out what parts I'm missing and what we need to do about it.

"Be right back," Hunter growls out. He keeps the truck running and hops out, grabbing his bag before letting himself into his house.

If I hadn't sat witness to the Margaret's lovely send off, I may have taken his cold shoulder and pissy attitude personally. Which I may deserve. But it's a clear sign he needs to be alone right now. He doesn't need me asking questions, and I have no problem allowing him space to process and cool off. He'll tell me when he's ready.

My eyes shift to the night sky. The stars are brighter than ever but staring through the window doesn't do them justice. I'm sure I have a few minutes before he returns, so I hop out of the truck. Hunter's view of the sky is clearer than what I usually see from my wooded home. There is no mistake that the twinkling fairies in the sky are saying hello to me, and only to me. A chilling breeze has me wrapping my jacket tighter around me, wishing for a tad bit of warmth on this October night.

My light!

I'm sure one of these days I'll get used to these new powers. I warm my palms, watching them to make sure they heat up without drawing any attention to myself by having flashlights for hands.

Heat fills my hands and a giggle trickles out of my mouth.

I've always wanted one of those heated jackets for the wintertime, but now I've saved myself a hundred bucks by making my own.

Who knew I would never need a space heater or a million blankets ever again?

This is pretty wicked.

A day and a half ago, I was living a boring and unassuming life and now look at me. If I make it past tomorrow, I can guaran-damn-tee that I will no longer take anything for granted.

The moon's illumination pulls my attention back to the velvet sky, and I lay down on the thick, crinkling grass. Another breeze travels around me sending a slight chill, but my hands keep it tolerable. I focus on the crisp wind. It's refreshing as I take in each cool breath. The woodsy musk from the fallen leaves brings me back to the moments that were blocked from my mind.

It's hard to come to terms with the fact a large part of my childhood was hidden away from me. I get that it brought me pain, but my heart aches because I couldn't relive the memories of Hunter and I sneaking out at night to stargaze. Those were some of our best times.

The most peaceful times of my life.

We always looked for signs of an existence beyond our world. Of course, Hunter said it was aliens and if we kept staring, they may come and kidnap us. He thought it would scare me, but it only made me giggle and shove him away. I believed the stars were the souls that were whole from finding their other half. They reunited and their sparkling essence would travel into the galaxy to shine down and watch over us all. The thought would bring me such peace in knowing maybe one day, that would be me.

My eyes drift close, and I allow the moon's energy to absorb into every part of my being. Entering the top of my head, circling down throughout my body and out my feet, into the earth below. My mom always told me the sun's reflection bounces off the moon down onto the earth. The strong gravitational pull that affects tides also impacts the human body and some are more sensitive than others. My body has always reacted positively to the power of a full moon, so basking in it tonight feels heavenly.

Another gust of wind rushes over me, and the heat from my hands is no longer taking the edge off. Greta's words come back to me about letting the light consume me. The only parts of my body I've been able to conjure my power are my hands.

What if I try to allow it to flow through my entire body?

Channeling the energy from inside my chest and stomach, I create soft waves and allow them to ebb and flow gently down my arms into my hands. But instead of balling up all the light in my palms, I allow a steady stream to move through my extremities, across my chest and up to my head.

Warmth floods through the top half of me and a gentle, revitalizing tingle prickles over my skin. I take the same waves of energy and give them freedom to course through my hips, legs, and feet.

It's as though I've jumped into a natural hot spring, the relaxing heat lapping back and forth. A smile escapes my lips when I know, without a doubt, this is what Greta was referencing. I've allowed my power to fully consume me.

And it's amazing.

Light shines through my eyelids as sun rays would on a bright, sunny day, so I open them.

Oh shit. Shit, shit, shit!

My whole body is glowing. Like a tsunami, I quickly pull back the tide until it's absorbed back to my core.

I spring up, looking around to make sure I didn't cause a scene and release a breath when I see it's just me, the trees, and the northern winds.

Resting my arms on my knees, I look down at the browning grass and slow my heartbeat. That could have been bad. Very bad.

A sense of being watched has me shooting my head up and turning around to meet Hunter's wide eyes. His bag is resting on his broad shoulder and he stares at me, unmoving.

"You didn't happen to see that, did you?" I cringe.

If it wasn't for his shocked composure, I would pretend it never happened.

"Yup." He purses his lips and gives a slow nod.

I worry my lip before I say, "I'm sorry, I was taking Greta's advice about letting it consume me, but I didn't think it would be this bright. I...I didn't know *what* to expect."

He has a blank expression. He is emotionless.

Is he mad at me now?

Why can't this day just be over? I need a restart. Well, not completely, just maybe a do-over with Hunter.

Ugh, I give up.

I drop my head to the ground in an uncomfortable thump and try to hide in the grass, praying the stars will take pity on me and let me join them as is.

The earth beneath me vibrates before Hunter stands over me. I try to ignore his presence and keep my eyes on the sky, but he lays down next to me in the grass.

My stomach clenches, not knowing what *this* Hunter will do next. I have to remember, he's not the little boy I once knew. He's familiar yet different at the same time.

A large calloused hand engulfs mine and a traitorous tear sneaks out.

My heart melts. This is the same boy I once knew, he's still in there. He's still my everything.

He never *stopped being* my everything.

We lie there, in his front yard, staring into the sky. My love for him isn't from a memory of when we were younger. He has the heart of that boy but hardened over time. I can't expect him to feel the same for me. To him, I'm his best friend.

To me, he's my other half.

Air rushes out of my chest in defeat. I've always known this and I can't help but fight it anyway.

"We can leave all this behind now. Just say the word." Hunter offers me an out.

Thinking back to the paths my grandmother showed me in my dreams, I sigh.

I know what I *want* to do, but it isn't what needs to be done.

Hunter squeezes my hand. "Tell me what you want."

"Stay," I whisper.

"What was that?"

I turn my head and gaze into the warm brown eyes of my soulmate. Pain tearing at my heart at my decision, knowing I don't only risk my life...but his too.

"Stay," I say a little louder, meaning not only in this fight, but for him to stay with me forever.

"Are you sure?"

I nod, staring at the glittering sky. "I'm sure."

"Okay. We'll stay."

A shiver passes over Hunter, and I can tell he is getting cold.

I send a soft blanket of warmth through my hand and into his body hoping it will work. At this point, my magic is all trial and error.

Hunter sucks in a steep breath. "Damn, no wonder you were lighting up like a Christmas tree. That's some serious heat you're packing." He gives my hand a little squeeze. "Thank you, Anya."

I hum out an acknowledgement and we stay there, like crystals recharging in the moonlight, we allow the moon's power to provide us the strength to continue this dangerous path we are on.

Yet, I can't step off it.

This is my destiny.

The moon shifts in the sky after a while.

"Are you ready—"

"You finally ready to go get some food?" Hunter says at the same time.

We snicker and my stomach growls out my answer.

"I think that's a great idea," I tell him.

Hunter stands, holding a hand out to help me up. "I think we better hurry before the Honey Bear comes out."

I roll my eyes and give him a playful shove. I'm still not sure how to act around him without flirting. Maybe I can figure out how to handle my feelings for him after a full stomach.

One problem at a time.

Chapter Twenty-Three

HAGALAZ

(SURRENDER)

We stop at the cafe, order some cheeseburgers, fries, and milkshakes, then head back to my place. Walking through the door, I leave it open for Hunter and bee-line it to my couch with the food bag in hand.

My body collapses into the soft cushion and I moan.

Has this couch always felt so magnificent?

Hunter closes the door, drops his weapons bag, and then sets our milkshakes down on the coffee table.

He sits next to me and the weight of the big lug has me jostling around, the water I drank on the way here sloshes, making me nauseated.

I need sustenance.

We don't talk while we scarf down our food and drinks. It's no surprise we were absolutely famished; we hadn't eaten since this morning.

Laying back against the cushion, I close my eyes. I'm pretty sure I can pass out right here.

Unfortunately, my brain thinks otherwise when the scene from Margaret's flashes through my mind. We still haven't discussed what happened.

With the slightest movement, I peek open one of my eyes to see if Hunter seems more approachable.

Hunter is sporting a cocked eyebrow and has one hand over the back of the couch, his body is aiming directly at me. The clenched jaw and thin lips tell me he isn't at all ready to talk about Margaret, but something else entirely.

I snap my eyes closed and pretend he didn't see me. I'm not ready to have *that* talk, yet.

He clears his throat.

Shit, he caught me.

Hunter gives a half-hearted chuckle and says, "Nice try, Anya, how about you act like an adult and finally talk to me about what's going on with you. Are you pissed at me for making us end the search?"

My heart drops to my stomach.

He's really upset, and he has every right to be with how I've been behaving.

An argument was not how I imagined this going, but the stubborn part of me doesn't like to be called out. My temperature rises with the fear of admitting the truth.

It's fight or flight right now, and I'm not proud of the one I choose.

"No, I'm not pissed at you. It has nothing to do with the decision to leave. I agree with you. We needed a moment to recoup."

"Then what is it?"

"Has it not occurred to you the shit I've had to go through since yesterday? The pressure I'm under?" My voice increases in volume.

Is it wrong for me to lose my temper? Yes. But if I admit...*things*, he will be the one running. And I can't lose him. I don't know how else to handle this.

I've never experienced loving someone who can't be with me, or worse, confessing said love when the feeling isn't mutual.

Gah, this is the time I need my girls here because I'm doing this all wrong.

He leans forward in his seat, resting his elbows on his knees with his hands clasped. His eyes are intense when he leans towards me.

I gulp down my heart that's sneaking into my throat and my leg bounces.

"In case you don't recall, let me refresh your memory. I've been by your side this whole time and been doing my *damndest* to make sure you are safe *and* supported." He runs a hand through his hair and releases a breath. "I get that you have been hit with one thing after another. I *get* it and I'm sorry. But what I *don't* get is how everything was fine between us. We were back to being our old selves, then suddenly, out of the blue, you're giving me the cold shoulder—avoiding touching me, let alone looking at me. I sure as shit don't want to lose you after this is all said and done."

Pain peeks behind his cold glare and nausea hits me. This time it isn't from the lack of food, but from the grief my insecurities are causing him.

Shit, I'm going to lose him after all. This is all my fault.

"Now tell me what the fuck is going on and don't you dare try to lie to me, Anya O'Clery." He leans in closer and whispers, "Don't forget, I have *always* been able to see right through you."

His eyes bore into my soul as he challenges me to bullshit him, and I shift uncomfortably in my seat. My chest is in a firm binding being tightened by the second. I place my head in my hands and rub my temples to prevent the incoming headache.

I don't want to do this, but he's right.

I *am* being immature and keeping my distance. But he's wrong when it comes to not losing what we have. There is no win-win for us. Only heartbreak and loss. And I'm scared shitless.

My short, quick breaths make me light-headed so I do the only thing I can think of to help gain control again. Laying my hand over my dagger in my boot, I draw energy from it. Like a sedative, it eases the anxiety.

I can do this.

I have *to do this.*

We needed to have this talk. I might as well end this shit show with a bang.

It's now or never.

With a calmer heart rate and the rope around my chest loosening enough to prevent me from passing out, I straighten and meet Hunter's eyes.

"Fine." Defeat washes over me. "You want to know what's wrong? I'll tell you." I shift to face him. "But first, I need you to promise to me that *whatever* I say next *cannot* affect our friendship. I can't imagine losing you again and that's my biggest fear right now."

"News flash, Anya. Pushing someone away is a sure-fire way to lose them."

His words hit me like a punch in the gut.

Did I already lose him?

No, he told me he didn't want to lose me. He wouldn't have said that if it'd already happened.

Damn it, this demon whispering in my ear filling me with doubt and fear is really doing a number on my psyche.

"I'm sorry, that's why I'm acting the way I am. I don't know how *to* act right now," I admit.

"How about you start with talking to me," his voice comes out a tad gentler.

I sigh. "Promise me that what I say next doesn't change a thing." My teeth bite into my bottom lip nervously, and I wring my hands.

The crease forms between Hunter's eyebrows and he runs a hand over his beard.

His lack of response has the knot in my stomach growing.

My posture slouches and moisture beads in the corner of my eyes, I bring my gaze to my hands in my lap.

"Anya..."

A warm hand wraps around one of mine, and I blink a couple of times before looking up. Hunter's eyes bounce back and forth between mine, searching for...something.

"There is nothing, absolutely *nothing* in this world or the next that would take me away from you again."

He says this, but he doesn't know what I'm about to say. My eyes drop to our hands and a calloused finger lifts my chin. "I don't know how I can make you believe that." He looks to the ceiling then back to me. "Fuck, Anya, I was miserable when my parents dragged me away from you. Half my soul was split from my body and I was empty. Nothing in my life truly made me happy. That's why I travel quite a bit with my job. I haven't had anything that made me *want* to stay in one place."

Hope niggles in the back of my brain.

His thumb rubs over my knuckles. "Please trust me in this. Whatever you say won't change our friendship. I told you before and I'll tell you again. You are stuck with me."

A rogue tear slips over the brim of my lid and drops onto our joined hands.

What if he has the same feelings for me? Could we handle a long-distance relationship?

If he doesn't, and all his flirting was me twisting his words, will he look at me differently? Will he pity me?

Fuck it, I can't take all these *what-ifs.*

Needing space and to prevent his withdrawal after my confession, I slip my hand out from his.

I suck in a large breath and jump right in.

"I'm so sorry for how I've been acting. You're right, I've been childish."

He smirks. "Say it again."

"I'm sorry?" I wrinkle my nose.

He shakes his head. "No, the part where I'm right." His dimple pops from his cocky smile.

This man is going to destroy me...piece by piece.

Yet his light joking helps me along.

"If you didn't hear me the first time you need hearing aids, old man."

He reaches for me, but I move out of his grasp. "Let me get this out first, please."

He sits back in his seat. "Continue."

"Okay..." I rub the back of my neck. "Before I met you, I was an outcast. I didn't fit in and felt like I was very different from everyone else. Other than my parents and grandmother, *no one* understood me. I wasn't living a normal life as a child." My hands fidget in my lap, fingers picking at my jeans.

Trying to lay it all out on the line sucks.

Hunter cocks an eyebrow and smirks. "It's no surprise you were a nerd."

"Well, that's about all I needed to say. There it is. Out in the open." Brushing my hands on my legs, I move to stand, but Hunter grasps me by the shoulder and brings me back to the couch.

"You've never been a good runner. Best not to start now." He holds up his hand when he notices my glare. "I'll be quiet, I promise."

"When I met you—"

"You were a cute nerd," he interrupts.

"I thought you promised to be quiet?"

"I never said *when* I would start. But okay, starting now. And...go!"

He's distracting me so my nervousness isn't *as* debilitating; he is giving me the strength to continue.

"When I met you..." I pause to see if he is going to chime in again, but he's holding up his end of the bargain. "I could see in your eyes that you were the missing piece in my life. I couldn't explain it, you were a complete stranger but we...*clicked*. As kids, we didn't need to talk, we knew what the other person was thinking or feeling. When you..." I clear the tightness from my throat. "When you left, I went into a state of depression. I couldn't sleep, I couldn't eat, I didn't want to leave my room. As we both know now, my mom used her power to heal my broken heart so I could finally sleep and function. All I remember was each day I woke, things got better but I still felt...off." I pause to study Hunter, making sure he's still with me. He's hanging on my every word. I continue, "I found a few good friends after a while, but they didn't last after high school. By the time I met Heather and Danielle, I started to feel I could cope with living half a life. They distracted me."

"I can see why. They *are* an entertaining lot."

With a half smirk, I say, "Shush and let me finish."

This time, both dimples come out from hiding and he zips up his lips with his fingers.

Each step I take closer to fully disclosing my feelings, the more nervous I become. With a flick of my fingers, I manifest a small marble of light and roll it around to soothe my nerves.

"This may sound crazy, but when I met you at the castle, when you were holding me 'hostage,' I felt an attraction to you. Your scent, your voice, your body felt calming and familiar to me. Even when my brain was telling me there was a high chance you were going to kill me." I shoot up my hand when I see his eyes light up. "And no, I don't have some weird kidnapping fetish."

"You certain about that? I'm sure we could role play," he growls out.

The heat in Hunter's eyes has the knot in my stomach evolving into a swarm of butterflies. Maybe he does feel the same. Or maybe he's just a flirt with everyone.

"Don't get your hopes up. I chalked it up to it being a very long time since I've had male company. Pathetic, I know, but at the time, it was the most logical reason."

"Okay, keep going, I'm all ears now."

I'm sure he is.

"After I was convinced you weren't going to kill me, I started to like you, even as cocky as you were. You were funny, smart, and you seemed to have another part I knew you were hiding from me. A softer side. I wanted to get to know you more."

Hunter holds his hands to his heart, "Aww... I knew you really liked me after all." Then the idiot winks.

The hold around my chest loosens and a laugh breaks free. "Maybe a little. Anyways, we got through the rest of the night. You didn't leave me as I thought you would, then we ended up here at my grandmother's house and I felt a strong pull to you. Yes, it was a physical attraction but it was also something much...deeper. There was something about you that felt familiar, and for the life of me, I couldn't place it. Not until you told me who you are, and the wall shielding my memories of you started to crumble. Hunter, you are *home* to me. You always have been."

"I—"

I hold up my finger to cut him off, I'm on a roll and I can't have him distracting me. "Please keep in mind, I'm not trying to go all creepy stalkerish on you, but I need the absolute truth from you after what I'm about to say. Don't you *dare* blow smoke up my ass to make me feel better or keep from embarrassing me. I'm already embarrassed so it can't get any worse. Remember, you said I won't lose you as my friend. It's too late to back out now. Can you promise to not sugar coat anything?"

With a raised eyebrow, I wait for his response.

"Oh, I can talk now?"

His surprised façade has me rolling my eyes.

"Anya, I have *never* sugar coated anything with you because I know you're tough and can take anything thrown your way. You aren't some sensitive little girl. I guarantee, you will only receive the truth from me. Now *please* put me out of my misery and tell me what's going on."

My teeth bite into my cheek and my focus goes to the orb between my fingers.

I can do this. I just have to rip off the band-aid.

Not raising my head, I word vomit, *"I'mfallinginlovewithyou."*

My breathing goes heavy and the orb glows brighter as it transforms into a stress ball in my palm—which may not be the best idea. Who knows what the ball of energy will do under the pressure of my tension.

Not willing to risk it, I absorb the light but feel like the lonely girl at a club with no drink in my hand not knowing what to do.

Do I put them in my pockets? Do I cross my arms over my chest? And where do I look?

Sitting on my hands and staring intently at the wood flooring seems to be the best option in this situation.

Should I be concerned he hasn't said anything?

The truth shall set you free. Well, in this case, a lie wouldn't seem so bad. I want this moment to be over.

The silence is an answer in itself, right?

I shove to my feet. "Alright, now that's out of the way, have a good night." I force out a chipper tone as I make my escape.

"Eek!"

Hunter pulls me into his lap, my legs to the side of him and his arms wrapped securely around me to prevent further escape.

Like the moment in the castle, I'm not afraid. I'm comforted. What this means, I don't know, but I have a feeling I'll be finding out real soon.

Chapter Twenty-Four

Tiwaz

(Twin Flame)

A groan escapes from the back of my throat. *Why does being in Hunter's arms feel like I've come home?*

It's as though the world is safe again and no evil can consume me with this large security blanket wrapped snugly around my body.

My safe haven.

In his embrace, he still can't protect me from myself. My brain wants me to run away from humiliation, yet my heart whispers *it's safe here...stay.*

Why is it always a war between what I know is right versus what I feel is right?

But...this isn't some fairy tale that has us frolicking away into the magical woods to our happily ever after.

Everything in me tenses. This is the real, hard, messed up life where there's a monster from Hell trying to fill this land with death and darkness.

Hunter's arms loosen and drop to my waist when I sit up. My soul cries out in protest but I ignore it and square off my shoulders. It takes everything in me to raise my chin and force myself to look at him.

His strong jawline under his short, dark beard has me wanting to reach up to caress the prickly scruff while rubbing my thumb over his soft lips. When my gaze reaches his eyes, I gasp. His milk-chocolate irises are dark and deep, with intensity burning behind them.

My chest heaves as I try to take in the air that has left my lungs. I clear my throat, saying the only thing I can think of to avoid plummeting into the depths of...Hunter. "Now, that's off my chest, I think it's time we head to bed. We need to get up early and discuss our plans for tomorrow."

A low growl rumbles from his chest. "I think that's a *great* idea."

Does he mean...a spark of hope flares in my chest, but then I shake myself and swallow down the hurt. He's just as ready to end this night and escape the awkwardness as I am.

His lack of response is answer enough that things are one-sided, despite what my fatigued brain thinks I'm reading in his eyes.

This is what I wanted, right? With the feelings not being mutual, I can end this fantasy now and prevent further heartbreak.

Oh crap.

I realize I'm still sitting on Hunter's lap staring at him when he's agreed it's time to call it a night. I shift to stand but as soon as I push off him, I'm being lifted off the couch like a ragdoll and set back on his lap.

Hip. To. Freaking. Hip.

I'm straddling Hunter McAllister in a not-so-friendly manner.

It's impossible to remain calm when I'm a deer caught in head-lights.

What's happening here?

I bite my lip. Part of me hopes this is what I think this is, but that irritating voice inside is telling me I've lost my mind and we need to forget this night ever happened.

"I umm... I thought it was time to go to bed. You..." I clear the tension from my throat. "You are welcome to take the bed. You'll fit better than trying to curl up on this couch." A nervous giggle escapes me. "No offense, Big Guy." I pat him on his chest.

Hunter captures my hand and holds it over his heart.

My body freezes, along with my breath.

"No." The one word comes out of his mouth with such finality.

No.

No, what? No, taking the bed or no, he doesn't return my feel-ings? Why isn't there a user manual for men? I would have read that thing, memorizing it front to back, before I even graduated high school.

Forget this, I'm too tired for games. I push against his chest once again to get up.

Hunter grasps my hips with his giant hands and pulls me closer.

Oh, fuck. I pant out a breath.

That is *not* his gun.

I try to resituate myself when Hunter groans and his fingers bite into my ass, holding me still.

His eyes burn into me with such heat. His sharp-eyed stare scorches my retinas and creates a flush over my entire body. I drop my gaze. I'm not sure that was a good idea when my eyes drop to his lips. I can't stop from unconsciously licking mine and my inner thermostat cranks up more.

"Fuck."

That's the last thing I hear before Hunter's lips crash into mine.

Our souls soar through the night sky, detonations going off around us. Two stars colliding into a cosmic explosion. Sparks course through my veins and light me up from the head-on collision.

Blue and purple wisps of our energy swirl around, caressing each other like long lost lovers. He is my next breath, an extension of me that has been lost for centuries only to come back at this very moment.

When I come back to earth, my hands are cupping Hunter's jaw and our mouths are hungry. His beard is a mix of softness and roughness as it rubs over my skin. My mouth craves his velvety smooth lips against mine, never to separate. They are a tender contrast to his thick, rough hands that pull my hips over his, over and over, hitting me in the exact spot I need. My core sparks with pleasure and I whimper.

I'm finally home.

Wrapping my arms around his neck, I slip a hand into his hair. With it short at the sides and longer on the top, I still have something to hold onto. The silky thickness between my fingers feels amazing as I pull his head closer. Hunter's tongue strokes mine. The cool minty taste of him does nothing to level the heat bubbling through my veins—increasing the arousal between my thighs.

I have never in my life been turned on by only a kiss.

I need more. So much more.

Hunter moans when I swivel my hips, grinding down on his length, faster. Our kisses become more urgent. *Desperate.*

His lips move from mine, licking and kissing his way across my jaw to my neck. He sucks on the spot directly below my ear and I can't hold back the mewl that sneaks out.

"I need you, Hunter," I say in between gasps.

He growls and stands, wrapping my legs around his hips. I hold onto his neck and we make our way down the hall towards my bedroom.

Laying me on my cherry oak bed, he tries to stand but I'm wound tight around him.

Hunter gives a throaty laugh. "Sweetheart, you have to let me go for a minute so I can get our clothes off."

I drop my legs and sit up but he pushes me back down. My brows furrow.

This man is awfully pushy.

"I've waited this long to see you. I need to unwrap you myself."

His words send tingles rushing over my skin, and I lay back down, staring up at him. I love this man so much, I can't believe this is really happening.

Hunter leans down to my boot, pulls out my dagger and places it on my nightstand. In a torturous tease, he slowly drags the zipper down my boot and pulls it off along with my sock, setting it on the floor, repeating the same unhurried motions for the other.

I squirm.

He is too damn slow. I unbutton my jeans, trying to help speed this up a bit.

Before I get to my zipper, Hunter's hand is pushing mine aside.

"Uh-uh. I don't think so. You are mine tonight. For once in your life, Anya, give me the gift of patience."

"Ugh, patience is overrated. Now stop going at a snail's pace and get on with it." I whimper.

He chuckles and unzips my jeans, sliding them down my legs along with my underwear. The cool air on my damp center has me sucking in a breath and goosebumps pepper my flesh.

Warm lips connect with my calf and his large hands run up the sides of my legs while he works his way up to my knee and to the inside of my thigh. The light scrapes of his beard along the way makes my nerve endings go haywire.

I cry out.

Hunter drives me crazy with his rough, callused fingers gliding up the soft flesh of my hips.

"Hunter," I plead, needing him more than I need my next breath.

His tongue licks the sensitive divot on the inside of my hip bone, sending stimulating sensations from my center to my hardened nipples.

It shouldn't have surprised me when his hot mouth lands on my core. My back arches when his tongue explores me, lapping me up until I'm trembling and moaning underneath him.

I can't help but move against his licks and kisses while my body tightens.

He is playing me like a violinist plays a powerful serenade, with such passion and perfection.

There is no holding back the whine that sneaks past my lips when Hunter moves his kisses up my abdomen, his hands pushing up my shirt to make room for his mouth.

"*Patience*, Anya." Hunter teases which makes me growl in response.

Chuckling, he continues to taste every inch of me, blowing cool air after each kiss, causing chills to run down my body.

"*Thank God*," I mutter, grateful I wore a front clasp bra as he flips it open with two fingers.

Hunter's hands cup the mounds of my breasts—filling his palms—and massages them.

"Just as I imagined, a perfect fit." He gives me a wicked smile then captures a nipple with his mouth.

My back arches as the jolt of electricity flies through me and I moan. The zing shoots straight to my center and has me rubbing against the knee he placed between my legs. I should feel embarrassed now, but all I feel is the strong need to have him in me, over me, anything.

I can't take this pace anymore, or these clothes. The suffocating feeling has me tearing off my top and tossing it aside. With a push of my hips I wrap a leg around Hunter's jean clad hips and flip us until I'm on top.

"Hey now, this isn't fair."

"Fair? You call what *you* were doing fair?" I drop my jaw in exasperation.

One dimple then the next pops out from his beautiful face and I narrow my eyes.

"You had your chance and you were too slow. Let's get this show on the road before I die of old age."

"A show is what you want, huh?" His devilish smirk has me shutting him up with my mouth.

He quickly forgets his teasing when he laces his hand through my hair, pulling me closer, angling my head to where he wants it.

It's a fight to push through the fog he creates, but I stay conscious long enough to pull his gun out carefully from his holster and place it next to my dagger.

Next comes his belt which I fumble with.

This thing is equivalent to a freaking chastity belt.

Hunter's chest rumbles and a chuckle sneaks out between his lips.

Shoving off his chest, I sit up. "Care to help me with this stupid thing or do I need to get dressed?"

"Hold on, let's not get hasty now." With a flick of his fingers the belt unclasps and falls to the sides.

I don't hesitate and make quick work of his button and zipper. The mistake I make is looking up at him once I have my fingertips ready to pull down his jeans.

Hunter's arms are folded behind his head and his dark-chocolate eyes are on me—making my heart jump and heat flood my cheeks.

"Shirt off. Now," I demand.

"Bossy. I like it."

Not waiting for him to do as he's told, I pull off his jeans in a yank, taking his boots with them, and his eyes go wide. We don't have time for slow and seductive. There's one goal and that's to get him naked...fast.

This large, magnificent man is a perfect specimen. His shirt is off now, showing he has ridges in all the right places with thickness around his waist dipping into his black boxer briefs.

A real man, not one with that weird V on skinny, toned men. A man should never have a flatter stomach than me. Some think that's sexy, but I like my man with meat on him. Solid like a linebacker. My finger traces the beginning of the Celtic tribal tattoo on his bicep, and I follow it up his shoulder where it spreads out, covering his right pectoral muscle.

After I follow the path of the dark swirls, I drift my hand down and drag his underwear over his hips, stopping to stare at Hunter in all his glory.

But I'd never tell him that.

My eyes are drawn to his erection—thick and ready for me—with a droplet of pre-cum glistening at the tip of the crown.

I lick my lips.

"See something you like?" His cocky remark has me meeting the humor in his eyes.

I shrug. "Eh, I thought it would be better. You know, to match the size of your ego." I don't hide my smirk.

Hunter rubs a hand over his chest. "Damn girl, you don't need powers to burn a man."

A shimmer of a gold chain catches my attention.

Curiosity pulls me forward, crawling back up his body and straddling his waist. Whatever is attached to the chain is hiding under his neck.

He lays weirdly quiet as I pull the necklace around, and as soon as it's laying in the center of his chest, I freeze.

"*Oh my God.*" My hand shoots to my mouth, and I stifle a cry.

There, on his broad, tattooed chest, is a gold chain with the Sun charm I gave him when we were little.

My eyes tear up. Fingering the charm, I find the "A" engraved on the back. It's, without a doubt, the original.

How could he have kept it after all this time?

A single finger tilts my chin up. When Hunter's eyes show love behind them, tears spill over the dam, dripping on his stomach. My blurred eyes bounce back and forth between his, searching for an answer.

I swallow hard to get the ability to ask him, but every sound that comes out is a choking sob.

"The moment you gave me your charm, I protected it with my life. This was the only piece of you I had left. I was afraid to let it go. My parents saw how miserable I was, so they bought me a chain and told me that instead of being terrified I'd lose the charm like I lost you, I could always keep a piece of you near my heart where you belonged."

A hiccup sneaks out and Hunter cups my face, swiping a tear with his thumb.

"I never take it off. Even when I was in the Marines, it was right next to my dog tags, which never left my neck. You may have been out of my life, but I held out hope that one day I would find you again."

"But...but you didn't know me when you saw me." I sniffle.

Hunter huffs. "I felt you before I saw you. And when you told me your name, I thought it was another cruel joke being played on me, especially when you didn't know the answer to the question I asked." He rests his forehead on mine, closing his eyes and caressing my cheek.

"Baby, I can't tell you how many times I thought I saw you, but when the girl turned around it was a punch in the gut when it wasn't you. I..." His voice cracks. "I felt I was being punished for my gift. For the very thing that took me away from you and killed my parents."

Like a running faucet, tears stream down my face with no end in sight. This man, this beautiful man, has my whole heart.

He never forgot about me after all this time.

And he wants me. This complete, emotional mess of a woman who may not have a job once this is over and will be a wreck if he leaves again.

A woman who's straddling a very naked, very sexy man on a bed bawling her eyes out.

Can I get any more pathetic than this?

Hunter reaches up to gently wipe away my tears. "I love you so goddamn much." He then grasps my chin in his hand before capturing my mouth.

His lips ignite a blaze that burns away the tears and my heart fills to the brim with his words. Everything happens so fast. We become desperate to get closer. The connection so strong, it's almost unbearable.

Hunter's mouth pulls away from mine, his eyes bouncing back and forth between mine. "I've loved you since we were kids. When I saw you at the castle, all the air was sucked out of the room. You were stunning and that was the moment I started falling for you."

Based on his actions, he's shown me he loves me but to hear the words makes me melt.

Hunter brushes a wisp of hair from my face. "I've never felt for someone the way I feel for you. To any outsider, they may say it's too quick, but what we have is *rare*. We're made for each other. Once I realized who you really are, I was a goner."

His forehead rests on mine. "There was no going back from that point. I love you." He kisses my nose. "I will always love you."

My hand comes up to cup his cheek, the hairs softly bristle my palm. "I'll always love you, Hunter."

He kisses the corner of my lips before sucking in my bottom lip. "I need to be closer. I need inside you, now."

Oh God, yes!

"I'm clean and on birth control."

This is one thing I've always had a strict rule about. I won't have sex without one, but with Hunter? I crave the feel of him with no barriers.

He groans, his lips going to my neck, sending shivers over me.

"I need to feel you. All of you," he growls. "I haven't been with anyone in over a year and I'm clean." Hunter's wide hands spread across my shoulder blades and he pulls me closer.

I raise up, use one hand to position him and slide ever so slowly down, taking him in a little at a time. I'm more than ready but it still takes me a bit to get used to him. It doesn't take long until he is filling me completely. His hard, silky warmth has me rolling my eyes back and moaning.

Once I'm fully seated on him, a guttural gasp escapes us both.

An overwhelming feeling of possession and fullness hits me. He belongs to me and I'm forever his.

A bond that can't be broken.

I wrap my arms around him, still not feeling as if I can get close enough.

Hunter starts to move and I roll my hips to meet him with each thrust. His lips are back on mine as we rock together.

"You feel fucking perfect, Anya," Hunter grunts into my ear, dragging his hand down to my hip adding to the electricity pulsing through to my core.

His words heighten the sensations flowing through me to the extreme. I'm climbing a mountain of ecstasy where I'm getting higher and higher with each thrust.

He reaches between us, his fingers rubbing as he hits the spot that sends me over the edge, and I shatter. Hunter lets out a primal growl as we come together, holding each other tight. Behind my eyelids, two stars explode in the solar system; the brightness envelops us both and we fall.

With my heart rate out of control and my body turned into gelatin, I lay on top of Hunter with my head in his neck. We are both sweaty and yet, he still smells delicious. It's the same subtle scent he wore in the castle—citrus and spice with an undertone of lavender. It's one I'll never forget.

What am I doing?

I'm lying here sniffing him, that's what!

Embarrassed, I break the silence. "Holy... Shit! That was..." I have no words.

"Fucking amazing," Hunter finishes my thought.

"Yes." A grin spreads across my face. "Absolutely." After some deep breaths I say, "Not trying to give you an ego boost here, Big Guy, but I have *never* felt anything like that before."

"You and me both, sweetheart." He sounds just as winded.

"Ugh, I don't want to move," I grumble.

"So don't."

If only. But I need to go clean up, so I peel my arms off of him and sit up.

Hunter reluctantly releases me, and I look down at him with a smile. I know I probably have a goofy look on my face, but right now, I don't care. Hunter's eyes are still closed. He looks handsome and young. The worry lines that were there before are gone, and he looks at peace for the first time since we found each other again.

I shift to get up and when he opens his eyes, they widen. "Anya, you're glowing."

"Well, duh," I roll my eyes. "After what we just did? I would be surprised if I wasn't." I shake my head at him, chuckling.

"No." His hand grabs my legs and holds me in place. "You are actually *glowing*. Like before, when you were on my front lawn."

Shit, I look down and see I'm really covered in a blanket of light. Well, *that's* definitely new.

If it were anyone but him, this would be quite awkward. I close my eyes and absorb the light back inside.

"Sorry about that, I must have released some power when we got carried away." I wince and bite my lip.

"Hey, don't be sorry. You are radiant, *no pun intended*. There's nothing wrong with it. This is who you are, Anya." He grasps my hand and pulls me back to him. "As long as you don't roast my chestnuts, it doesn't bother me. I love seeing you feel so comfortable around me that you can let yourself go. Completely."

Everything he does and says makes me fall more and more in love with him. And there is zero doubt over what he feels for me.

The charm around his neck has me wondering what will happen to us now. We still never talked about his job taking him away. I'm determined to do whatever we can to make this work. If that means dealing with a long-distance relationship, I'll have to handle it. It'll still be better than not having him at all.

Don't borrow trouble.

I pat him on the chest, climb off the bed, then head to the bathroom.

As I am showering, I hear the door open then close and I can't stop the smile from spreading across my face.

"I'll be out in a minute!" I holler over the shower and exhaust fan.

A cold breeze hits my wet body when the door of the shower opens and a naked Hunter strolls in.

"No, you won't. You aren't going anywhere until I say so." He stalks over to me, running his gaze down my body then back up to meet my eyes.

He towers over me, and I don't think I'll ever get used to it.

A squeak comes out of me when Hunter grasps my ass and lifts me up easily as if I'm light as a feather. Like second nature, I wrap my legs around his waist and he doesn't hesitate, entering me in a swift move, his mouth instantly on my neck.

My eyes roll back in my head. He's driving me insane. When he bites down between my neck and collarbone, I tighten around him and he pumps faster. Usually climaxing once during sex is a struggle for me, but twice? In one night? Hunter really does have some magical powers.

As long as he only uses them on me.

"I'm close." My back hits the cold wall of the shower every time he slams into me.

He stops and sets me down.

"Wait, I didn't say I was done," I panic.

Before I can think further on what he's doing, I'm turned to face the wall and bent over. My ass in the air, he grabs it before entering me again.

Whoa.

I've never been in this position before. Hunter is so deep and the spot he's hitting makes my knees give out.

Laughing, Hunter holds me up and cups my breasts. Massaging them and pinching the nipples. That sets me off, and in the black haze of pleasure engulfing me, I barely hear him shout my name.

After an amazing round two. Hunter helped me wash up, his sudsy hands move sensually over my body, appreciating every inch of me and savoring our time together.

I, of course, returned the favor.

He doesn't believe me when I tell him that his body is perfect. He seems to be almost embarrassed. I'm not sure why. The many scars scattering his torso and a few on his arms, give him character. He is imperfectly perfect, and he's all mine.

He promised me one day he would share the stories of each marking, but tonight is a night to be here and present with each other. Not relive our pasts.

I step out of the shower and Hunter already has a towel wrapped around his hips, holding mine out for me. As I reach out for the cloth, he snatches it out of my reach.

I lay a hand on my hip. "That's not fair, Hunter. It's chilly and you have your towel. Let me have mine."

"Arms up."

I do as I'm told and lift my arms. Eying him in the mirror as he steps around me, he wraps the towel over me and holds it closed at the front, cupping my breasts. Holding me close to him, he leans down and licks a trail of water dripping from my hair to my shoulder. He is hard again, and his erection is between my ass cheeks.

"Again!? Did you put Viagra in your Wheaties this morning?" I turn my head back and capture his mouth.

"How could I resist? With your delicious ass," he squeezes me. "Your beautiful hazel eyes." His lips gently touch the corners of my lids. "Your smart-ass personality." The corner of his lips tilt up. "And your addictive kisses..."

I open my mouth to protest—he sucks my bottom lip between his. Turning my complaint into a moan.

"I can't help that you make me constantly want you. Now that I have you, I can't stop." He sighs. "But it's time for bed. We need to be fully charged for tomorrow." He leaves a lingering kiss on my lips then pulls away, his grip is tight when he opens the bathroom door.

"Mmhmm...okay. But if you keep poking me in the middle of the night, I can't be responsible for what happens."

Hunter chuckles, shaking his head as he walks back to the bed. With a toss, his damp towel drapes over a chair and he pulls on his boxer briefs.

Catching my reflection in the mirror, I press a hand against my warm cheek. My face and neck are red from his beard, and I smile. This is what being well loved looks like.

I pull my hair back into a French braid and walk into my bedroom to slip into a pair of sleeping shorts and tank top. Hunter watches me and when I crawl under the covers, he switches off the lamp then pulls me over to his side of the bed, wrapping his body around mine—holding me like he is afraid to let go.

Once the quiet settles over us, I have a moment to think. I'm beyond thankful that Hunter and I found each other again, and hearing him say 'I love you' has been life changing. I never thought I'd find a partner, let alone my soulmate, my twin flame.

But the wendigo is still out there, heading directly towards town. That thought alone crushes the air from my lungs. It's my fault the wendigo has my scent and that everyone I love is in danger. I can't put the lives of my friends and Hunter in jeopardy if there's a way I can stop it. I have to do *something*.

There's only one path left to take.

But that means tonight may be our last night together.

Pain squeezes my lungs, and I will away the pressure that's trying to break the waterworks free.

I turn from my back to nuzzle into him. His warmth envelops me while the soft hairs on his chest tickle my cheek. Through the moon's dull light shining in my window, I find his nipple is a couple inches from my face, and I give into the temptation to lick it.

Universe, let me love this man once more.

Because there are no guarantees there will be a next time, no promises of a tomorrow.

It scares me shitless that today may be my last. Either for my own life or for those I love. Either way, everything will change from here on out.

Hunter shifts, moving himself lower and I meet his dark, heated gaze. "You're playing with fire, Honey Bear." His stare falls to my lips before he groans. "And I was trying to be on my best behavior."

Despite the growing sadness and pain that begins to consume me, I force a smile. Because if this is going to be the last time, I want to make it count.

"Maybe I want to be burned."

He pushes me onto my back and straddles me, holding himself on his forearms to hover just above. Close enough to feel his exhales against my lips, but not close enough to make contact. Which I crave. I need him to take me.

To brand me.

To sear this last time into my soul so I carry him with me for this life and the next.

"Make love to me, Hunter." The soft demand falls from my lips.

"Anya, I'll spend the rest of my life making love to you." His lips come down and barely touch mine with a feather-like kiss.

We stare into each other's eyes before our mouths take control. I reach up, grabbing the back of his head and bringing him closer, deeper. The emotions that pour out of me can't be stopped, and I know he feels it too. He senses my desperation and matches it with his own.

One arm keeps his body suspended over mine while the other wraps around my torso and pulls me in. His thumb moves under my tank top, gradually running his hand up until he gets to the soft side of my breast. I arch into him only for him to make his way back down again.

Our lips caress, our tongues dance, and our bodies absorb the energy from one another. This love, this feeling, is a first for me, and if Fate decides to keep on being cruel, it will be my last.

I suck in a hard breath against the pain that cuts through the passion like a knife severing my lifeline.

Is this fair to him?

"What's wrong?" he whispers. His hand has shifted to my face, pushing a strand of hair out of the way.

"I hope you know how much I love you. How much I care for you. Please don't forget that." I wrap my legs around him and pull him into me, feeling his length against my pelvic bone.

He freezes. "You sound like this is a goodbye."

It is.

My hand runs through the thick strands of his hair. "Kiss me."

He hesitates, then sits back in the shadows, making it impossible to see his expression.

"Please," I beg, worried he's about to end things.

"Sit up," he grinds out through a clenched jaw.

I do his bidding and he pulls my top up and over my head, tossing it to the floor. Before I can drop my arms, his hands gently run over them, his thumbs barely touching the sensitive undersides. Chills of anticipation rush from where he touches and tiny molecules of electricity bounce over my skin and make their way to my core.

His calloused fingers move to my hips and he loops them in my waistband.

"Up."

I lean back on my arms and lift my hips, allowing him to pull my shorts down. Once those disappear, his boxers follow.

"Come here," he demands and drags me closer to him, throwing my legs over his, lining us up. His hand goes to the base of my head, under my braid, and pulls hard exposing my neck. The mix of pain and pleasure has my nerves singing.

Gasp!

Hunter thrusts into me at the same time his lips connect to that magical button behind my ear. His teeth scrape over the sensitive flesh, then he licks and kisses his way down my throat until he gets to my collarbone.

My legs lock behind his back, my arms wrapping under his and grasping his wide shoulders. I don't want anything to separate us. Ever.

"Move when you're ready," he coaxes.

I rise up then drop down.

"Fuck," he mutters into my neck and thrusts hard inside me.

Slowly I continue to ride him, holding onto him in a tight embrace.

In this moment, our bodies are attached more than in the physical sense. My aura and his move together, swaying in the winds of our love. No other person could take away this connection we have. We are joined, connected for eternity.

We are twin flames.

Hunter nibbles my jawline, then peppers it with kisses until he captures my mouth again. The current inside me becomes stronger as the gravitational pull intensifies. My soul writhes, determined to connect itself deeper within this man, all while he burns me from the inside out.

A burn that hurts so good.

Everything around us disappears. There's no tomorrow, just now and the merging of our bodies, loving each other like it's our last day on this planet.

Which it very well might be.

The thought makes me cry out in heart-breaking agony and Hunter pumps into me faster, the fire builds with each thrust while his lips capture mine in a kiss that shows just how much he loves me.

Even if this is all we'll have, it's enough.

Lightning cracks, radiating waves that crash over me in an explosion of ecstasy. My breath rushes from my body with the rest of me, leaving a shell to join Hunter's before our souls come crashing back down.

My vision begins to come back to me and when the ringing in my ears subsides, all I hear is panting.

Our panting.

Pulling out of me, Hunter silently lays us down, kissing me on my forehead.

His chest rumbles, "I love you, Anya. You are beautiful inside and out. I will *never* let go of you."

Another piece of my heart breaks on his words because he might have to. Neither of us can predict the future, but I'll do whatever it takes to stop the wendigo. Even if it means sacrificing myself to save others—especially him.

Chapter Twenty-Five

ALGIZ

(PROTECTIVE)

Hunter's soft snore and regulated breathing against my cheek tells me he's fast asleep. His arm is wrapped snuggly around my stomach while the rest of him fits perfectly against my back. We've had a long day, so it's no wonder he's out cold after saying goodnight.

My stomach churns and nausea has sweat trickling from my temples. I hate this sickening feeling from the thought of leaving him, but I don't have a choice.

From under his arm, I slowly roll onto my back to see if it'll wake him. He moves a little to compensate for my shift in position and settles again. His deep breathing continues. I let out a breath of relief. He's not a light sleeper. Or, at least not after tiring himself out with our lovemaking.

It's time to put my plan into action. I need to do everything I can to save the ones I love. The people I care about. And the only way of doing that is leaving him here and drawing the wendigo away from town.

Becoming the bait.

The risk of something happening to him has me gently pulling the blanket back to make my escape. I use the edge of the mattress to leverage myself out from under Hunter's thick arm to slip to the floor and onto my feet. I can't lie here while there's a chance that anyone else could get killed.

I've never been sneaky and proof of that has me stumbling over the wood floor. I freeze and look back at Hunter. Besides his rising and falling chest, he's not fazed one bit.

I release a breath, thankful I don't have squeaky drawers as I pull them open one by one to grab clothes. It's going to be cold, but I need to be ready to run if I need to. Finished dressing, I leave my phone behind and slip my dagger inside my boot. Reaching into my jacket pocket, I pull out the herbal pouch Hunter made to hide my scent and place it on the nightstand next to Hunter. I'm hopeful it will continue to hide my scent on Hunter and keep him safe.

Is it smart for me to do this?

Absolutely not.

But could I live with myself if something happened to him?

Never.

There's no better way to do this. Despite my grandmother's warnings of never separating, I know this is the right thing to do. Whatever the outcome. I will not sacrifice Hunter.

Taking one last glance around, I wonder if I'll make it out alive. Who would inherit the house if I don't survive? I'm sure my mom and dad would take it, but that would only mean they would be closer to danger.

No. I can't allow the wendigo to kill me. Unless I'm taking that disgusting monster with me to Hell, I refuse to give up and let it destroy me.

I step out the front door onto my porch and softly close it behind me. A tightness wraps around my heart at leaving Hunter, but he'll be safe.

He has to be.

I zip up my jacket, an added barrier from the autumn breeze. This is going to suck.

The confidence in me drops a decimal before I stand up straighter and march my way to the natural spring behind my house. The water empties into the only stream in Shandaken, which is the one Hunter said runs from the castle. The very one the wendigo is traveling in an attempt to find me and the rest of civilization. By following the water, I can track the creature down and capture it, or bait it and draw it farther away. Either option will allow us more time to figure out how to handle the situation.

My boots crunch over the dead leaves. So much for being silent, but I guess that's what I want, right?

I pull my dagger out and watch the moon's reflection bounce off the blade.

Tonight is not as bright as the last time I visited the spring. It still gets the job done because as much as I'd prefer my internal flashlight, I have no idea what to expect if I light up. Will it attract the animal, or will it become a repellant? Keeping the light to a minimum in this situation may be best.

The trickling of water in the distance tells me I've arrived. I push through the last of the bushes and find the beautiful spring before me. The magic of this place never ceases to amaze me. I walk to the edge and squat for a moment to take in its energy.

"Fairies," I chuckle at the ridiculousness of this. "If you exist, I'm asking you to please guide my way and help me on my journey."

There's a pretty good chance I'm talking to myself. Yet it's hard to ignore my grandmother's stories now that I'm sure they have some truth behind them. I need every bit of help I can get.

With one final wish on the twinkling creek, I stand and move through the untraveled path along the water. The vegetation is thick; I have to watch my footing. A few thorny branches reach up and try to grasp my legs to tangle me in their vines. Unearthed roots attempt to trip me as they hide under the weeds. Memories of my dream the grandmother sent with the two dangerous paths pops into my head. I'm still unsure if this is the right choice, but the least I can do is not break my leg and make myself easier prey. Seriously, though, couldn't I have the power to view the future and see where each decision would lead me? Sort of like how I traveled into the past with the journal. I grip the hilt of my dagger tighter in frustration.

Beggars can't be choosers.

After a while, the spring takes a sharp turn to the right then opens up to tall grass and the larger body of water ahead.

The stream.

My shoulders relax a bit. No more vines and roots trying to kill me.

What a relief.

Now that I have a flatter surface to travel on, I should be able to move quicker. But man, do I wish I had Hunter's magic to try to light up the wendigo's tracks. I don't even know if it made it this far. Glancing around, I do my best to look for the signs. Nothing shows the tracks like we saw in the woods earlier. Then again, with the low position of the moon, I could be missing them with how dark it is.

As much as I don't want to use any of my energy, I really don't think I have much of a choice, I need to make sure it hasn't come out at this crossroads of water.

Creating a small orb in my hand, I toss it up a few feet and have it hover over the stream. Shifting it back and forth, I look for any signs of disturbance of the water or the ground.

Nothing.

One thing we did notice when tracking it earlier, was that the stream was stirred up, the sediment from the bottom formed cloudy underwater plumes. We could tell that it stayed in the water.

But we haven't the slightest clue why it chose this path. It's not like we know how smart this thing is. Did it intentionally take that way to ensure it wouldn't be tracked? Was it an impulse? Or an easy way to travel?

After I absorb my light, I begin my trek back to the castle, hoping I don't have to walk the eight plus hours before I find the wendigo. Or it finds me. It's going to be a long night, but I need to stay alert at all times.

I can't risk being taken by surprise.

"What was that?" My stomach drops and I freeze, holding my breath. I've been walking for what feels like a couple of hours, and this is the first sign of life. Rustling in the leaves has me moving into a fighting stance. One hand is a second away from activating my powers while the other is ready with my dagger.

I listen and wait for whatever is stalking me to show itself. This would be the best moment for my skills to grow, and I develop night vision. But I don't because this isn't a book or a movie. There is no promise of the heroine winning in the end.

For the last half hour, I've felt eyes on me, and I'm not a hundred percent sure it's the wendigo.

That doesn't mean I'm safe.

It's useless to squint, the dark is on the side of the pursuer, not mine. At this point, it's a standoff.

Who will move first?

I wait, then wait some more. Nothing. Yet eyes are still focused on me. There's no doubt about it when a shiver racks my spine.

How long will this take? The longer I stand here frozen, the more sweat drips down my back, tickling my nerve endings and making it feel like a dozen spiders are crawling across my skin.

I can't do this anymore. I take two steps towards the sound, anticipating the impending attack. Something darts to my right.

"Holy Mother of—" I shoot out an orb at the fast-moving creature and aim too high.

Shit!

In the light before it burned out, I realized what I'm dealing with.

Peter Fucking Cottontail.

"You again? What the hell?" I whisper-shout. "You have *got* to stop sneaking up on me like this. You are just like Hunter. One of these times, I'll accidently make rabbit stew out of you."

I rub the back of my neck. I'm so on edge, I'm attacking innocent animals. Chuckling, I shake out my shoulders and allow my body to let out the tension it has been holding on to.

Grrr...

A deep rumble has me shifting around to face a real predator. One that won't hesitate to pounce without warning.

And *this* is why I didn't want to let my guard down.

Are you freaking kidding me? What the hell is a cougar doing in these parts?

I remain stock still and hold eye contact. The moon makes it difficult to focus as it flickers across the predator's glowing pupils.

Keep calm and steady.

I back away along the water's edge. The cougar watches my every move with its head down and tail moving back and forth.

Temptation has me lifting my hand, but I put it back down. I need to save as much energy as possible. If I can help it.

One foot behind the next, I ignore the crunching under my steps and focus on the cougar. At this pace, it will take me until morning to get away.

I suck in air when it takes a step towards me.

"Okay kitty, let's not play this game. You go your way, I'll go mine, and no one will get hurt." *Please walk away.*

The cougar slinks back into the darkness where it came from and my jaw drops.

Well, I'll be damned.

The urge to relax has my back stiffening more. It's not the right time to let loose.

Not until the wendigo is secured.

With a final glance in the direction the feline went, I turn around and pick up my pace to follow the stream. I'm determined to keep going until I track down the monster, or it finds me first.

The only perk of hunting in the dark is the way my hearing becomes more heightened and acute. The wind blows through the tree branches, making a sound similar to rainfall. It allows the remaining dead leaves to float to the ground and start the cycle of life all over again when I break them with every step.

No one seems to care about the importance of life until their own life or the lives of others they care about are threatened. They don't pay attention to the little things like the sounds of creaking trees communicating to one another or a bat using its voice to find the last bits of food before the snow falls.

There's so much I ignored before I was ready to challenge my fate and risk my own life for others.

Is this my life flashing before my eyes?

Ugh, I need to get out of my head and focus on my surroundings.

The wind shifts, and I catch a whiff of something rotting. That isn't unusual in the woods. There are dead animals, rotting trees, decaying plants, and miles of musty water.

All normal for a forest.

The moon reaches higher in the sky, telling me it's after midnight and providing a bit more light to my path. I keep chugging along, looking into the water and studying both sides of the shore. There has to be tracks somewhere if the wendigo made it down this far.

The stench is growing stronger which means I must be getting closer to the remains of an animal carcass. It reminds me of—

A cold chill runs down my spine, and I pick up my speed.

Wait, what's that?

Almost tripping over my feet, I stop in my tracks. Across the stream appears a line on the ground, like someone dragged a large stick from the water. I scan for the best route to the other side and find a few larger stones sticking out. I move to the edge closest to the rocks and enter the water, praying my boots are waterproof, then step up on the first rock.

"Whoa," I correct my balance to keep myself on the rock instead of doing a trust fall hoping the water will be kind when it catches me.

I scan the area, then I hop to the next stone. Then the next.

Splash!

"*Sss...*" Coldness hits the back of my jeans from the water.

I missed the last rock and jumped right in the chilling liquid, giving myself a good wakeup call. Thankfully it isn't as deep as some of the other parts.

But it still sucks.

Keeping my guard up, I step out and kneel next to the imprint. I bite the inside of my cheek. There is a large hoofprint in the mucky shore. I inhale a sharp breath.

No.

I should be happy since this is the first sign of the wendigo.

Reality hits me.

The stench, the tracks... It's close.

Could it be watching me right now?

Searching around as I stay crouched on the ground, I'm partially relieved when I don't find the red, devil eyes anywhere. I flip my blade in my palm.

Now the fun begins.

Chapter Twenty-Six

URUZ

(SURVIVAL)

The stench of rotting flesh tells me I'm getting closer as it grows stronger and stronger. What doesn't make sense is why the tracks are taking me in circles. Twice, I've been led into congested woods only to circle back around to the stream.

I'm tired, I'm thirsty, and I have no idea how long I've been at this. To keep going is my only choice. My adrenaline and desperation push me through.

"What the hell?"

I find myself at the exact part of the stream I'd just been at not too long ago. The woods aren't a labyrinth where I take the wrong path and end back at the beginning.

Yet here I am.

What wasn't here before is a fresh set of tracks. Keeping my eyes to the trees, I kneel and hesitantly touch the new imprints in the ground.

How smart is this thing? Is it hunting me while I'm simultaneously hunting it?

I'm not sure where I go from here. Do I pick up my pace and hope to sneak up on it or do I sit like a chained-up goat outside a lion's den, waiting for it to pounce?

My back straightens. I'm not chained up. I'm not going to sit here to become the next victim. I have a duty to fulfill.

Whatever the cost.

Standing straight, I ignore the marks making their way back into the tree line and with my dagger out and my powers ready, I march my way in the direction of the castle.

The wendigo has latched onto my scent and from the continuous circles I've made, it's clear I have its full attention.

Now the challenge is to make sure it follows me to the castle, so I can contain it within the dungeon. Without being killed.

It's nerve-wracking. At any moment, the wendigo can jump out from the dark like the chainsaw-wielding psycho in a haunted house. Except *this* house of horror will end in real blood and death.

With heavy concentration, I slow my heart rate because it's filling my ears with a constant pounding. Instead, I focus on every creak, crunch, and snap of branches nearby. Every one of my senses needs to be on high alert, to be aware of any change.

Trees whisper and the water trickles as if everything is right in the world, oblivious to the darkness lurking in the shadows.

A vibration carries over the ground as the beast moves closer.

It's closing in on my location.

I bite my lip and my hand twitches, ready to light up at any moment, but it's not time. There's quite a bit of distance between us, and I don't think I'm close enough to the castle yet either. My legs pick up the pace and zig-zag around the many roots jutting up from the ground. I need to get the wendigo closer, but how much farther?

My attention shifts to the position of the moon and—*Shit!*

My legs propel me forward, tripping over the very roots I've been intentionally maneuvering around. I catch myself before I break an ankle.

Shaking my now stinging palm, I'm back to my feet and searching my surroundings again.

Silence.

The wendigo had to have heard me.

Is it listening, or is it ready to attack?

I sniff the air and my shoulders drop. I'm safe.

For now.

Glancing back up, I locate the beacon in the sky to judge my direction and the hours I've been out here, which I was trying to do until I nearly ate dirt.

The spot where Hunter and I stopped earlier has to be close because I've been out here for hours.

Water behind me splashes. Flipping around, I light up my palm, ready for the attack.

There's nothing there.

That sounded louder than a fish jumping out of the stream. It was more like someone, or some*thing,* hopping into it. The hair on the back of my neck stands and the breeze carries the offensive stench. There are eyes on me, but I can't tell from which direction.

Did it cross to the other side, or is it trying to distract me with the noise to pull my attention away from the wooded area? I shift my light to create a lantern, shining it into the foliage.

Nothing.

My mind isn't going crazy, I know what I felt and what I heard. It's out there, waiting for the right time to pounce. It's playing with me.

And I refuse to be a sitting duck.

Absorbing my power, I cautiously turn then hustle down the shoreline, staying right at the edge before the ground turns to wet muck.

A moment later, I blink multiple times to make sure I'm seeing straight. A soft glow up ahead catches my attention.

Is that...

The closer I get, the more the image before me clears from a haze into small flickering green flames. They hover over the water and move off to a path on the right.

Flutters fill my stomach. I've finally reached Hunter's tracking which tells me exactly where I am. It's impressive and a blessing the illumination still lingers. There's a good distance to go but having breadcrumbs to show me my way back will make things a heck of a lot—

"FUCK!" Lighting up my hands, I create a barrier between myself and the snarling wendigo that knocks me on my back. Snapping jaws burn as it hits the light between us. The burning in my arm and missing dagger have me cursing at myself. I've lost my weapon and warm liquid runs down my arm.

It got me.

Not knowing how bad the wound is, I use both hands as much as I can to push the bear-like demon off of me, but it's too big and the blood rushing from my arm is weakening me.

I take a deep breath and tune into the frequencies of the ground around me. Tapping into the earth's energy, allowing it to course through my body into my hands, I give one final burst of light and throw the creature off of me.

What the hell!

I take a large puff of air into my lungs. It must have been hauling ass to attack. I didn't hear it coming and the smell hit me right before it sliced into me. I must have let my guard down yet again.

Seeing the beast up close and feeling its weight was way different than experiencing the red-eyed monster in the journal's memories. Searching the ground, I locate my blade a couple feet away. I don't hesitate when I snatch it up and prepare for the next strike.

The wendigo pulls itself up, reaching a freakishly tall height. Even without the buck antlers, it towers. The smell and grotesque sight has me almost gagging. Bones protrude in multiple places and tar-like ooze drips from the bones, matting with what flesh and fur exists.

The demon eyes bore into me, and I begin to back up slowly as I did with the cougar. I don't think if I ask this thing to leave, it'll obey. I lay my hand briefly over the long gouge in my arm, hissing when I make contact. The monster follows my movement, sniffing the air, and a lizard tongue flicks out like it's trying to taste the metallic aroma of my blood.

This isn't helping.

I conjure an orb and the animal shifts backwards. Good, it fears my power. I levitate the globe between us, buying myself just a minute or two so I can bandage my arm.

Passing out from loss of blood isn't an option.

I slice the blade across the bottom of my shirt and pull off a strip of fabric. Keeping my eyes on the wendigo, I wrap my arm the best I can, using my teeth to tighten it.

Now it's time to capture this creature and get it back to the castle.

I use the same energy between us to throw a force field around the beast.

At the last second, it jumps out of the way then leaps towards me. I fire a follow-up ball, hitting it in the chest and knocking it back. I try for another force field, miss again, and have to dive to the side before the wendigo latches its three long claws into me.

I throw up a wall, only to have it dash around it, swiping at me again and again while it snarls and snaps its razor-sharp teeth.

"Uggh!"

I royally screwed up. There's no mistaking the path I chose was the wrong one. Not only that, but I went against my grandmother's warning of never separating from Hunter.

The man I've loved since our childhood. And now I'll never see him again, never experience a future with him, never have the chance to protect him.

No, damn it. I WILL protect him, I will change my fate.

Can I find a new path by creating my own?

Fuck this, I can't keep sitting here dodging teeth and claws while I make up my mind.

I need to act, and I need to act now.

So, I do the only thing I can.

I run.

Turning around, I shoot balls of light at it, a mixture of hitting and missing, but I can't try another force field. It takes too much power.

I need the beast cornered.

I keep running, jumping over logs, and throwing light at it over and over. It's impossible to cross the water now without wiping out and being eaten, so my only hope is to find another way to the castle. The hope in my chest flickers away, just as Hunter's trail does as the tracks become blimps in my peripheral.

My heart is pounding so hard against my ribcage, I'm surprised it hasn't busted through. The longer I run, the harder it is for my lungs to take in a breath. My pace is slowing even when I'm pushing myself. It doesn't help that all the power I'm using is exhausting me more.

The landscape changes to a mountainside. It's high with the occasional ledge that there's no chance of me climbing, especially with only one fully functioning arm.

Sprinting as fast as I can, heavy thumping shakes the ground from the wendigo keeping up. The momentary delays from me wounding it didn't slow it down much. It's as determined to get to me as I'm determined to stay alive.

Every hit it takes doesn't keep it down long before it's continuing its chase. It stays behind me, to my right, making it impossible to turn that direction without being cut off. Now I'm the one cornered.

Please be an opening in the mountain soon.

I'm not sure anyone hears my prayers, though, because I am only met with the steep rock cliff. Finding a large boulder ahead, I decide to try something new.

Placing a field around the stone, I hurl it at the monster like a bowling ball. It tumbles across the ground until it crashes into its target, throwing the creature quite a few feet, and sparing me an extra minute to take the lead.

Up ahead, a part of the mountain is darker than the rest and when I get closer, I see why.

A cave.

This may work. Taking one glance behind me, seeing that the wendigo is slowly getting back on its hooved feet, I illuminate an orb, aiming it as a lantern and dart into the dark cavern.

The roar behind me has me doubting this was the best move. But I had no choice, I couldn't keep running. It was my only move.

Not knowing how deep the cave is, I keep moving until the illumination bounces off the rocks. Snarls echo off the walls, not giving me any clue how close it is.

My skin pebbles with goosebumps and a chill crashes over me in a forceful wave. The heat lamp in my palm does nothing to warm the dread I'm feeling.

With a flick of my wrists, I activate my dagger and replace the lamp with a blazing torch.

I'm as ready as I'll ever be.

Chapter Twenty-Seven

DAGAZ

(OVERCOMING DARKNESS)

The scraping sound of the wendigo's sharp claws dragging along the floor has me shivering. I flex my injured arm, remembering one of those claws slicing through flesh and muscle. Either shock or numbness has taken over because it's not as painful as it was.

Rancid fumes coat my nostrils before I lay eyes on the creature. The odor weaves its tentacles around my lungs, and my chest spasms while I choke down a cough. Once I see a limb come around the corner, I throw up a force field between us.

The wendigo scratches at the light field, trying to get to me, but I hold it steady. His red eyes burn into me, the intensity greater than I remember from the visions. The blood-red carnage in its eyes looks like it came straight from Hell. A cold chill flashes fast through my body from the terrifying beast before me. Despite the fact I've already seen this thing up close and personal, it's something straight out of a night terror. And it scares the shit out of me.

Fuck this. I flex my hands and roll my shoulders back.

I have to act fast to make sure it doesn't escape. Moving my hands from physically touching the force field, I wait to see if it stays.

My shoulders relax when it doesn't budge.

I should be able to box the beast off through the barrier if I'm careful not to affect the radiating light between us.

Concentration is key for me to keep the magic separate and working off of each other. I don't hesitate, building the energy from my core, allowing it to branch off into my arms. I release the light, sending it flowing through the force field and out the other side to capture the wendigo.

Argh!

Yet again, it moves out of the way as my magic hits the wall.

How the hell does it know where I'm aiming?

I hate the growing feeling of needing to take the wall down and trap it in closer proximity. It's reckless, but the thing evades my every move. I can't risk it getting bored and moving on.

On second thought, after the damage to my arm, I can't make that mistake again if I drop the field. That would guarantee an attack. A shield is a must.

Studying the wendigo and knowing how fast it is, makes my next step tricky. I need to switch places with it—have *it* trapped in the corner with *me* on the outside.

But how?

Think, damn it.

I flip my dagger around, playing with the blade and chew my lip.

Any shield I create needs to be moveable and big enough to protect me, all while keeping the beast inside the cave.

If it was any other predator, I could move the wall by rotating it while pushing it against the back wall.

It's worth a shot with the wendigo.

The key is to keep it from running out of the cave. If I can push one side open enough, I can create another field to cut it off from the exit once I get enough of an opening, trapping it against one of the walls.

Hopefully.

It is smart and fast.

With both feet apart to steady myself, I brace my left hand against the force field as well as my right fist, which has a tight grasp over my dagger. If the wendigo tries to sneak around before I can trap it, my blade will be ready.

Ever so slowly I shift the barrier a small increment in the direction of the cave opening. The wendigo doesn't budge. I shove a little more, sliding an additional field from the corner of the original to the wall, blocking the monster in.

I can't contain my smile. Doing this slowly and with precision was all I needed to—

"Fuck!" Excruciating pain spreads over my cheek and on instinct, I slice up with my weapon, cutting off the very claw that tore through my face.

The limb drops to the ground and the wendigo's screams echo off the walls. I don't give myself a chance to think about what just happened as tar sprays from the decapitated limb like blood.

This needs to end.

Shoving the barrier hard and fast, I yell, *"Ahh!"* giving myself more strength and slamming the wendigo into the back cavern wall. The creature cries out in more pain. I ignore the need to cover my ears from the screeching and pull back a couple of feet to secure the light field on all sides of the mountain, there is no possibility of it escaping.

Once I know that the wendigo isn't going anywhere, I step back and hesitantly touch my cheek.

"*Sss...*" I hiss from the sting. That bastard did a number on me.

I look at the trapped animal. It's scratching like crazy trying to escape. Ignoring my trembling limbs from the fatigue, I channel more energy and reinforce the field to make sure it's not going to budge. There's still no guarantee the wendigo won't try to dig through the stone. The claw I detached from its body is already regenerating. It heals fast. But would it heal if I melt it into a puddle?

There is only one way to find out.

Sucking in several deep breaths—hoping the oxygen can give me the added strength—I roll the tension off my shoulders and shoot light through the shield to create a box around the wendigo. This time it doesn't have room to escape. But it still has enough space to gain momentum and fight back, so I decrease the encasement until it begins to crush the wendigo.

When the bright encasement is snuggly up against the disgusting ball of fur, bone, and antlers, I summon all the reserves of power inside me and crank up the heat. It's impossible to ignore the screams of pain. Part of me feels remorse, considering the wendigo is trying to survive, like us. Sweat drips into the cut on my cheek, and the searing pain reminds me we can't coexist. This monster is evil, from the depths of Hell. It doesn't belong here with us.

There are too many innocents already murdered.

How many more will die if we don't stop it now?

The sizzling sound mixed with the melting fur and flesh filling the air makes my stomach roll.

I allow the energy to course through my veins and out my hands, into the box. The light continues to burn brighter, and even when I feel the heat radiating off of it, it doesn't burn me or hurt my eyes. The wendigo's hair is now completely melted off and the black, tar-like substance drips off it in large globs. The sound coming from it will haunt my dreams—if I make it out of here.

I crank up the intensity of the heat and compact the box, pushing through harder and harder, making it hotter and hotter until the screams stop. There's silence from the creature. Despite my heavy breathing, I can only hear the boiling of its body.

I don't let up. Like a compactor, I keep crushing and allow the blaze to burn as bright as the sun. The stones around us begin to crack and small rocks rain down. I shake my head and blink rapidly to get the sand and rocks off me and out of my eyes.

A little more...I shove harder and more debris falls on me.

In one final push I reduce the cage to the ground and release it.

My chest is rising and falling fast while I pant to catch my breath. The cave has settled from its recent earthquake. It definitely wasn't from any natural seismic activity, but the strength of the light I created within the mountainside.

Leaving the force field up between what remains of the wendigo and myself, I survey the pile of black ooze on the ground.

I did it. I actually did it. I saved everyone.

Relief floods over me like a tidal wave and for the first time in I don't know how many hours, I collapse to the ground, barely slipping my blade in my boot before the world goes black.

Chapter Twenty-Eight

BERKANO

(SAFETY)

"Anya. Baby, you gotta wake up," Hunter's desperate voice sounds far away in my dream.

Where is he?

"Please be alive. Don't fucking do this to me. *Fuck!* She can't fucking leave me like this."

Why is he upset? Who left him? Is he talking about his mom?

Oh no, he must be dreaming about his mom dying. My heart squeezes in my chest. I try to roll over in bed to calm him, but my body doesn't move. To be honest, I can't feel much at all, other than an ache in my arm and a stinging ache on the right side of my face. Everything else is so heavy, including the lids of my eyes.

Trying my hardest, I finally get a peek, pulling myself from the dark abyss that is attempting to keep me in dreamland.

"There you are." Through the blurry fog, he runs a hand through his hair. "Holy hell." His breathing is rapid like he ran a marathon. "Anya, open those gorgeous, hazel eyes of yours. Let me know you're alright."

I move my head side to side as I gradually regain feeling in my body.

"Whoa," I say as my equilibrium is shifts off balance, and I squint at him. My head now rests in his lap and he's turning my face. "Ow." My hand flies up to the stabbing pain on my cheek where he touched.

"Damn, you have a deep gash. Here, take a sip."

There's some sort of light to the side of Hunter, and I'm staring up at his disheveled hair and swollen eyes.

"Have you been...crying?" I ask and test the drink he hands me. It's cold herbal tea. The liquid takes a moment to coat my parched throat, then energy begins to seep into my cells, easing the fatigue.

"Crying? No, I haven't been crying. I've been worried sick. I thought the wendigo got—I thought I lost you."

Yeah, he's been tearing up. My heart plummets to the very ground I'm lying on. This wasn't a dream.

Wait. This wasn't a dream.

I jolt upright and dart my eyes to the light shield, thankfully finding it intact and the black puddle lying motionless on the other side.

"Oh, thank heavens." I relax and fall into Hunter's chest. The warmth cocoons me and peace washes over. In his arms, everything is right in the world.

"Want to tell me what the hell happened?" He angles my cheek to get a better view.

"It's okay, the wendigo caught me off guard. Twice. I barely feel the one in my arm anymore."

Hunter grasps my arm and rotates it. I cringe, anticipating the pain, but it doesn't come. Stealing a glance, Hunter unwraps my binding and moves the fabric of my jacket and shirt.

"Where's the cut?"

"What do you mean, 'where's the cut?' It's a little hard to miss. Follow the blood and ripped flesh."

"See for yourself, smart-ass. There's nothing there." He pushes my arm in front of me.

Sitting up, I slip off my leather jacket and pull up my sleeve. Then pull it up more.

"It was here." I rub my skin. "I swear I'm not lying."

"Based on the amount of blood soaked into your clothes and your make-shift bandage, I know you aren't. Huh." He sits back. "Do you know what this means?"

I cock an eyebrow. "That I cried over a little scratch?"

He looks at me like I'm dense. "Really? *That's* what you're thinking?" His fingers rub the tension in his forehead before digging through his bag. "I'm trying to tell you, you heal fast. And it most likely saved your crazy ass."

Hunter turns me around to face him, pulls out some weird, green paste and slathers it on the cut on my face.

"*Sss...*" I hiss.

After he inspects his work, his eyes dart back and forth between my eyes, then he yanks me to him, being mindful of my cheek. He squeezes me tight and the air from my lungs pushes out of me in a rush. I can't breathe, but right now, I don't care because I'm safe. Hunter's safe. And I'm back in his protective arms.

Suddenly, I'm jerked back and the concerned man who was here a moment ago is gone, replaced by an enraged one with a vein popping out of his forehead.

I knew he would be mad, but I wasn't expecting the appearance of Mr. Hyde.

"You *stubborn, beautiful, irritating woman*," he grinds out between clenched teeth.

At least he called me beautiful.

"Why the *fuck* would you do that?" His voice escalates. "Why the *fuck* would you sneak out on your own and try to get yourself *killed*? Are you crazy?!" The decibels his voice hits echo off the cave walls. He holds up his hand. "Wait, don't answer that. You *must* be crazy, because no one in their right mind would have pulled the stunt you did."

Pressing my lips together, I understand my mistake. Without him by my side, I ended up running for my life most of the night with two huge gashes that could have been fatal. He has a right to be pissed off. But, on the other hand, I accomplished what I set out to do. The wendigo won't be hurting him or anyone else. I can handle a few scratches. It was worth it, and I'd do it again.

For him.

"I'm sorry, I did something reckless-"

"Hell yeah, you did," he interrupts and raises his voice again.

"Excuse me?" Yes, I know I admitted my mistake, but my defenses go up when he agrees with me. Isn't this the part where he is supposed to hold me and tell me *'Oh babe, you didn't screw up, everything is okay. I forgive you,'* right?

He gets up and begins to pace. "I can't tell you how pissed and worried I've been for *hours*. You have no idea the scenarios that ran through my mind when I found you missing."

Avoiding eye contact, I pull my jacket back on and stare at my hands. "I know."

"You know? And you left me anyway?"

"I had to." I lift my gaze to meet his. "I had to keep you safe. I had to keep Heather, Danielle, and everyone in my town *safe*. I knew it was dangerous, but I had no other choice. I *had* to do this."

He runs a hand through his hair. "*Fuck*, Anya. I'm beyond grateful you're alive and okay, but I thought we were a team. Partners don't bail on each other, and they sure as shit don't go off on a suicide mission." Hurt replaces his anger and a piece of my heart chips off and falls to the ground.

I put this barrier between us. The lack of trust.

In careful motions, being that I'm weak and sore, I stand and approach Hunter. I'm not sure if I should touch him or keep my distance.

"You may not believe me but I *am* sorry. I wouldn't know what to do if something happened to you. I had to try. I needed to keep you safe."

With a hand on my shoulder, he brings me in closer. "At what cost? My life is *not* worth more than yours. How do you think I'd handle it if I found you dead? Because that certainly could have happened."

"Yet, it didn't. I'm here. The wendigo is captured. Everything worked out." Shifting on my feet I ask, "Can you forgive me?" I stare up at him with the biggest puppy dog eyes I can conjure up. I'm desperate.

Hunter releases an exhausted breath. "Promise you won't pull that stunt again?"

"Well, since time travel outside of a journal isn't possible—"

"Anya," he cuts me off with a growl.

In all seriousness, I tell him the truth. "I promise. We're partners and I'll never separate from you again."

He pulls me in for a hug and kisses the top of my head. Nothing can pull me away from him.

"You scared the shit out of me, babe." He stills. "Where's the wendigo?"

"What do you mean?" Did he not see it?

"There weren't any tracks leading out of the cave, but it isn't here." He looks around and peers through the shield.

I rub the back of my neck, ignoring the ache in my arm. "Do you remember the boulder I practiced on?"

His gaze lands back on me. "The one you turned into lava?"

"Yeah. Well, I didn't want to risk the wendigo escaping so I...umm... I melted it." I gesture to the black, liquid remains. Weirdly it looks a little larger than it was not too long ago.

"You killed it." He stands and walks closer to the barrier and stares at the blob, stunned.

I bite the inside of my cheek. "Uh, not quite."

His brows furrow. "What do you mean, 'not quite'?"

"Do you remember when I told you about how the men unearthed it to begin with?" I give him a minute to think back.

The moment it hits him, his eyes widen in shock. "*Fuuuccckk.*" With both hands, he grabs his hair and starts to pace. "We don't know for sure that it'll come back."

"We know it was in that condition when it came to life and tore into all those men hundreds of years ago."

"Yes, but we also don't know how it came to be in the ground to begin with."

I can almost see those gears moving as smoke billows from his ears. Okay, there isn't smoke but it sounds better than saying he looks constipated.

He stops. "We can bury it. It didn't come to be what it did until it was unearthed, right? I say, we bury it to trap it."

My pulse picks up. This isn't the answer.

"Only until the next innocent person digs it up and releases it, yet again."

"We don't know that," Hunter argues.

"If we leave it and assume it's dead, we take the chance of it coming back. It may not be as easy to stop. Shit," I wave my hand.

"This wasn't even an easy feat to stop it. If we bury it, years later we also risk a repeat of what happened at the castle when they originally built it. The only thing those people won't have next time is someone like me to stop it. We need confirmation it is gone for good."

Hunter stops his pacing and comes over, taking a deep breath before he says something I assume may not make me happy. "What are your thoughts about taking it back to the castle?"

Shaking my head, I say, "And how is that any different?"

"We can secure it better than here and lessen the risk of it getting out again." He stares at me, waiting.

I sigh. "I guess you're right. It's better than leaving it here. But how do you expect me to get this thing back to the castle?"

"On my four-wheeler."

I shrug, it makes sense he'd use something faster.

"Are you kidding me? How exactly do you expect me to get it in the bed of the quad in the first place, let alone unload it when we arrive at the castle? Did you bring a shovel?" I throw my hand towards the ooze. Which has bones and is bulking up. It's not growing nearly as quick as it did during its original unearthing hundreds of years ago, but, regardless, it's regenerating.

"Shit." I groan and run a hand over my face.

"Is that—"

"Growing? Yup." I pop the 'p.'

Hunter turns to me. "Can you melt it down again?"

"I can..."

"Why do I hear a but?" He raises an eyebrow.

"It drains me. I use a lot of energy to heat it as much as I need to melt it. You found me after I did it the first time." The darkness that pulled me under before was too strong to fight. Doing it now when I am still so exhausted will be impossible.

"If we leave now, do you have enough power to get it back to the castle?"

"I wish I did. I need to rest a little longer. I'd revitalize faster if the sun were out. Are you okay with us hanging here a bit until the sun rises? That should be enough to help. How much time do we have until sunrise?"

He checks his watch. "About an hour and a half. Will that be a problem with the wendigo regenerating?"

I shake my head. "I don't know. I can't see it being back to full size by then. Plus, we'll have the sun's rays on our side. It'll help weaken it."

Hunter takes my hand and leads me to a wall, he sits then pats his thigh. "Time for you to get some rest."

"I'm not sitting on you. I don't want your ass to look like hamburger meat when it comes time to get up. There are too many sharp rocks."

"I knew you only liked me for my looks." He smirks and spreads his legs. "Then at least use me as a backrest. It will keep my ass pretty for you but give you a place to be more comfortable."

"Ugh. Fine. But if you start to hurt, tell me." I sit, lean back against his chest, and sigh from the warm comfort of him.

"Deal." He rests my head right under his chin. "Now, it's time to sleep."

"We need to finish planning how we're going to get that thing back to the castle." Sleep won't be happening. If we can prepare while I let my body recharge, that will be the most productive use of time.

"What's the problem? You can move it like you did the boulder."

"That was dragging it. Not picking it up off the ground. And containing it is one thing. Moving it around like a piece of furniture is a whole other ball game. How do you expect us to all fit snugly in the back of a four-wheeler anyways?"

"Babe, this isn't some small machine. This has enough room to fit three people comfortably. Plus, it has a complete bed on the back, like a truck. We can fit, trust me."

I'm not sure why he would need a heavy-duty quad. On second thought, one glance at his truck and it makes perfect sense that he's a man who loves his toys.

The thought of sitting next to it on our way back doesn't calm my anxiety.

How the hell could I make this work?

Holding it in a small space isn't the problem, it's the moving *and* being near one of Hell's monsters that is. The long, sharp claws, the rotting, dripping flesh...sounds like such an appealing way to spend my day. I've felt those claws twice. I'm not chomping at the bit to make it a third time.

My hand goes to my temple to relieve the throbbing that is starting to build.

Aoife and Gudrun moved the wendigo before, but that was across the ground. Pushing it out of the cave will only get us so far.

I look up at Hunter. "It isn't a question of *if* I can hold it, that's not the problem. I need to see if I can lift it and move it."

"What do you need; how can I help?"

"You can toss the beast over your shoulder and haul it out of the cave like the big strapping lad you are." I turn my head and lift my face up. Batting my eyelashes and smiling, ensuring that he sees only adoration in my eyes.

He leans back, tilting his head to the side. "Are you serious?"

"No." Dropping my charade, I say with a shrug, "Just wishful thinking."

He relaxes with a smirk. "Well, that's a relief. I'm too pretty to have my face chewed off."

I straighten and shift my body to come face to face with him. "And I'm not?" Propping a hand on my hip, I glare at the man.

"Noo...that is *not* what I was saying." He slowly speaks. "You're pretty too. You just have powers that can prevent such a thing from happening to you. But me? Not so much."

"Mmhmm..."

We can't carry it out and pushing it will only get us so far. "Okay," My lungs exhale a defeated sigh, and I rub a hand over my face. "I can't have the wendigo fight me, and I know what it feels like when it struggles against the energy field. Who knows how much it will move, but I need to limit its movements."

"I've got rope; we could tie it up. Think that would hold?"

I cock an eyebrow. "Are you offering to do the binding?"

His mouth opens and shuts. Nothing comes out.

"Yeah, I didn't think so." I tap my hand on his forearm over my shoulder. "One of these times, we're going to have to get your hands dirty."

Hunter draws me back down and wraps his arms around my stomach from behind and lays his head on my shoulder. "You have no idea how much it kills me to not take charge and lead the way, to take care of the threat on my own. If I could, you wouldn't have felt the need to run away and risk your life." He turns his head against my neck, inhaling. "I hate that I can't protect you and that you're the one protecting *everyone*. And no, it's not jealousy talking."

I turn in his arms and lift his face with a palm on his cheek. "I'm sorry. Humor helps me get through stressful moments. I didn't think it would upset you."

"Oh no, you make it easier that way. I'm a leader. I organize and lead my team to keep them safe. I'm not used to following others or making them do the dangerous work."

My eyes bounce back and forth between his. His focus is on me, but I can almost see the pain and helplessness behind them. "You may not realize it, but you're already my hero, Hunter. You've saved me in ways that no one ever could, not even me. You keep to your superpowers, and I'll keep to mine. We make a great team—as leaders, together."

In that moment, our lips find the love, strength, and comfort we need from each other. Energy passes back and forth between our mouths, taking just as much as giving.

"Together, always," Hunter echoes.

Chapter Twenty-Nine

THURISAZ

(CHALLENGE)

"I can't sleep," I complain.

"Of course you can't. Your eyes haven't even been closed for a full minute."

His chest vibrates under my head. It's calming, but not enough to keep my mind off what lies ahead.

We're reclined on the luxurious rock bed in the cavern, romantically lit by my force field.

If it could *only* be so romantic.

The wendigo's body ever so slowly regenerates. In the last half hour, it began to move, pulsing up and down like the thing has a heartbeat. I'd rather have imagined it heartless for its constant need to feed on others, trying to replace what it lacks.

But no, it's just a homicidal asshole.

The fur and bones are covered in the same tar-like substance and it's forming into what looks like a calf. A calf straight out of a Stephen King book. I shiver.

Hunter begins to rub my arms. "Are you cold?"

I huff. "I'm literally an embodiment of light energy. I'm not sure I'll ever be cold again." I angle my chin toward the lump on the other side of the shield. "I was looking at the monster from Hell. It's disgusting and creepy."

"You got that right. How about I get your mind off of it?" He kisses my earlobe and sends a different kind of shiver down my spine.

I clear my throat. "I don't think this is the appropriate place for that."

"For what? Talking?" He feigns a gasp. "You pervert. Did you think we would—that I would be a man who would take advantage of you? Here?" I can feel him shake his head. "I'm disappointed in you."

I playfully slap his leg. "Oh, knock it off. What do you want to talk about?"

He snickers.

What's he up to now?

"Tell me about the teenage you. What were you like back in high school?"

Well, that's out of left field, but I respect his way of trying to distract me. I'll play his little game. For now.

"Trust me, there's nothing you're missing from those years." I bark out a laugh.

Hunter shifts me until I'm facing him, my legs overlapping his. "I'm serious, I want to know everything I missed in your life."

It's not like my life was anything but boring. I tap my fingers on my lips, thinking back to school. "I found Andrea and Rachel, who were awkward like me, in the school's book club."

"Good, I know you struggled to make friends before I came along." Hunter reaches up and fingers a tendril of my hair.

He's right, I did struggle.

What changed? Oh.

"Now that I think about it, my mom blocking my memories and pain of losing you didn't block the confidence you helped me find before you left."

"I was worried about you having a difficult time." A crease forms between his brows.

I pat him on the cheek. "Oh Hunter, ye have little faith in my charming personality."

"Ah, apologies Milady. Continue," he jokes.

"The friendship was great while it lasted. We split after graduation. Then I found Heather and Danielle. The End."

"I feel like you're leaving out some pretty exciting information."

"I told you school was uneventful," I deadpan.

"Well, at least it's great to hear there were no boys involved."

I purse my lips. "Well...I wouldn't go *that* far."

Groaning, Hunter's hand goes to his face rubbing his eyes then stops when it lands on his beard. "Fine, tell me," He grumbles.

"No way, that's something we do *not* need to discuss."

He sighs. "Yes, it is. As much as I'd rather not hear about it, I really want to know everything. Despite how tough it'll be to sit through. Each of our experiences helped build who we are and guided us down different paths."

"Now you sound like my grandmother."

"She was a wise woman. Now let's get this over with." Hunter covers his eyes like he refuses to look.

Weirdo.

"Fine. But don't say I didn't warn you."

That gets his attention. "How bad is it? Please don't tell me you slept with the whole football team."

Frowning, I shake my head. "No, only the hockey team. Have you ever seen the goalies warm up? Whew." I fan my face and watch as the horror flashes over Hunter's face.

I chuckle. "You should see yourself right now. Priceless." I give a chef's kiss.

"You little shit." He tickles my side. "Now tell me the truth. You're killing me."

We are having the *strangest* conversation while in a cave next to a creature that wouldn't hesitate to kill us. Oh, we are *so* normal.

Yet, his distraction is working, so I continue.

"I volunteered in the library most of my spare time when I wasn't hanging with my friends. That's when I met my first boyfriend sophomore year. Tim was a cute computer nerd, but I realized that he was more into technology than me. He liked the *idea* of a girlfriend rather than actually having one. *That* relationship didn't last long."

Hunter holds his chest and gasps, mocking me. "How could anyone not be absolutely charmed by you?"

"Laugh now Big Guy, just wait until you least expect it…" I love the uncertain look on his face he gets when I threaten him.

He rubs his hand on one of my thighs. "Alright, I'll be nice." He gives me a soft kiss on the lips. "So tell me, after the ever-so-exciting Tim, who else did you make fall for you?"

"I was single until my senior year. There were a few guys who I caught interest from, but they weren't for me. They didn't want to get to know me past my looks. And yes, believe it or not, I wasn't a skinny girl who wore baggy clothes anymore. I filled out a bit and discovered girl clothes with the help of Andrea and Rachel. I wasn't the dork you used to know."

He gives me a squeeze. "I don't doubt it for a minute. You were beautiful already back then, but I never could bring myself to tell you. And look at you now, you are drop dead sexy."

Heat creeps into my face and neck with my blush.

His sweet smile turns to a stern frown. "Who was the guy that finally caught your eye? Did he hurt you? Where can I find him?"

Sighing grandly, I stare across the cave as if I'm daydreaming. "Dean... He was the attractive bad boy who every girl wished she could tame. He was an absolute dream." Out of the corner of my vision, I see a scowl.

He asked for it, didn't he?

Toning back the dramatics, I carry on, "Dean was sexy, and even though he had that tough exterior, he was really a sweet and caring guy. He never showed that side to anyone but me. He was always kind to me, he would say hi and give me this half smile that he didn't seem to give anyone else. One night, when I was out to dinner with the girls, I saw him. He came up to me and asked me out on a date. Of course, I said yes. What sane girl wouldn't?"

Hunter tenses and it makes me feel bad for teasing him before. "Are you sure you want me to continue?" I raise an eyebrow.

"If it is as bad as I fear, I need to know."

"We went on our date, hit it off, and became official that night. He was technically my first boyfriend since I decided to consider Tim more of a short-term friend."

"Smart. But acquaintance may be more appropriate," he adds.

"True. Dean and I hung out a lot, yet it didn't take me away from my friends or parents. He knew they were just as important. He was funny, attentive, and really the perfect guy." I cup Hunter's face and make sure I have his full attention. "With Dean, there was something missing. I never felt like I was falling in love with him. I cared for him deeply but there was that missing link. That emptiness he couldn't fill. We still became close and there was sexual tension which we finally gave into." I notice Hunter's teeth grind. "Still...even though I didn't have you to compare to at the time, the feeling for him was nothing like what you and I have." Sadness washes over me when I think of how Dean and I ended.

The tension in his face softens and he leans into my hand. "What happened? Did he hurt you?"

I harrumph. "More like the other way around. He fell in love with me. The bad boy was finally tamed, and I was the horrible person who couldn't return his feelings."

"It's not your fault."

"I thought something was wrong with me, you know? Why would I turn away this amazing guy who was always there and would move mountains for me?"

Hunter rubs his hand up and down my thigh, as if trying to comfort me. "You have no idea how much I understand that feeling. How did it end?"

"I was happy being with him. We never fought, and any disagreements were always talked out. When he started bringing up the future, like wanting to go to the same college together, finding an apartment, and starting a family once we graduated. I, uh...couldn't handle it." I inhale a deep breath and let it out forcefully. "Yes, we could have been happy together, but it wouldn't have been fair to him. My heart was yelling at me *'No! Don't do it!'* so I knew I couldn't commit. I never thought I was leading him on. I thought over time, I could get through those feelings."

"Damn. How did he take it?"

"I told him how I felt. I didn't want to lose him from my life. It didn't matter though; he said the only way he could move on was to sever all ties with me. It hurt because I lost someone close to me. A best friend. We agreed that one day, we would somehow try to be friends again."

"Did you ever? You know, get back in contact with him?" He frowns at this.

I touch my lips to his. "You have nothing to worry about. We eventually did, strictly on social media, though. He was happily married, and I felt a huge relief knowing that."

Hunter drops his gaze to my torn up, dirty jeans and plays with a loose thread. "I know you said you didn't feel as strongly about him as you do me, but do you regret breaking it off?"

A flash of that little boy I once knew peeks out again. The vulnerability he rarely shows when he drops his guard kills me. It makes me melt inside at the same time causing me pain that he has his own insecurities when he shouldn't.

It was the same face I saw when I woke up. Before he pulled his tough guy mask back on.

"Even if someone asked me before you came along, my answer would be the same. No. I have no regrets."

Hunter pulls me to his chest and holds me tight. "I'd be lying if I said I'm sorry you guys didn't work out. I'm beyond grateful that you decided it wasn't fair to him, or you wouldn't be in my arms like you are now. I'm sorry, Anya, if me bringing all this up is making you hurt—"

"No!" I interrupt him and sit back—ignoring the rocks digging into my ass. "Stop right there. You didn't hurt me. I'm glad I'm telling you this. For us to have a future, you need to know about my past. This is definitely helping to keep my mind off our other issue." I gesture my head backwards. "Being with you, I am finally home."

"God, Anya, how did I get so lucky?" He holds me like he's afraid I'll disappear if he lets go.

I laugh and shake my head. "You find this..." I wave my hand around our *humble abode*—our new watchdog included. "Being lucky?"

He shrugs. "Being with you makes all of this worth it."

I lean in, hovering over his lips and say, "You have more screws loose in that head than I expected."

He closes the gap and kisses me hard before pulling away.

"Smart-ass," he whispers.

"What about your past? Any love interests?" I tense up, trying to keep the jealousy at bay.

"I had to beat them off with a stick. There were weekly mud wrestling matches where the winner would go out on a date with me." He doesn't hide the humor in his voice.

Nothing could have prevented me from snorting at the image he created.

"What?" He sounds incredulous. "You don't believe me?"

Chuckling I say, "The many interests for your attention, *maybe*. The wrestling matches to win a date with you? No way in hell."

"I'm starting to question your attraction to me. I'm not just a pretty face you know," he huffs.

"Mmhmm..."

"Okay, fine. You're right. No fights. I did have a few girlfriends over the years, but they never lived up to my memory of you. So here I am, fighting alongside the love of my life instead of dealing with all the boring women in the world. I have a feeling that life with you will never be dull."

"If only you were lying about that." I stare up into his warm, brown eyes. "Want to hear something funny?"

"Does it involve setting fire to my nether regions? If so, that's *not* funny."

"Ha, no. There actually have been a lot of memories popping up randomly since the memory wall fell. It was something I remember overhearing my mom say to my dad when we were younger. She said that you were my twin flame. I had no idea what it meant until I looked it up that night online. A twin flame is different from a soulmate, it's the other half of your soul. I know now that she was right. I'm finally whole, I have no doubt about that."

His forehead presses against mine. "They weren't wrong. You do feel like my other half. I love you so damn much, Anya."

I whisper back, "I love you, Hunter."

Our lips connect, needy and full of emotion. But it is over a little too soon when he pulls away.

"I want so badly to continue this, but you and I both know how we can get carried away."

He's right, soon we'll have a set of demon eyes watching our every move.

Grinning, he says, "Let's continue discussing this teenage dork you were."

"Okay, okay, but I'm not sure what was more exciting about my teenage years. All the normal things a kid goes through, hanging out with friends, school, trying to figure out my future, or dealing with idiots in school."

"Are we talking about all the idiot jocks or are you holding out some juicy stories on me?"

Laughing, I say, "Yeah, that's a story for another time. It involves a bully and a freak accident."

A bird's chirping bounces off the walls. It's coming from outside the cave.

Saved by the chirp.

I grab Hunter's arm and check his watch. "It's time."

His smile drops from his face. Fun Hunter is snugly tucked away and the serious marine has stepped up to bat. He turns my cheek towards him. "You're healing up nicely, just a little scratch now." His fingers drift down to my chin before dropping his hand. "You feel like you're ready?"

I nod. "It's time for me to test my limits."

He gets up and helps me to my feet.

With a lingering kiss on my forehead, he says, "Worst case, we drag the wendigo back to the castle behind us."

I groan. "Says the man who *won't* be doing the heavy lifting."

A deep chuckle rumbles his chest.

My stomach knots with all the things that could go wrong. "But we don't know what happens if the barrier hits something. Will it bounce up like rubber or shatter and break, releasing it?"

"Baby steps. We try this first and if it works, I know what we can use to help limit the movements."

"Okay, but you may want to back up a bit." Lacing my fingers, I twist my palms out and stretch my hands—popping a couple of knuckles. I wish the sun were higher in the sky so I could soak up its rays, but it's still too early.

Without waiting any longer, I shoot an orb of light through the barrier to surround the wendigo that is now four feet tall and growing. Forcing the light under it as well to ensure that it's fully enclosed. The creature flinches but doesn't move any more than that.

Maybe it won't put up a struggle. Could we be so lucky?

Using the same hand, I try to lift it up from the ground. I get it about six inches before it drops from the weight.

My breath hitches and everything in me tightens. I freeze, waiting to see what the wendigo does.

"Are you okay?" Hunter moves close and places his hand on my arm.

After another couple of seconds of holding my breath, when the beast doesn't stir, I release it and answer. "Yeah. It's too heavy. I'm going to try again."

"We can find another way."

Shaking my head. "No. I can do this."

I visualize the prison of light as though it's a small box in my hands. I raise them up together and watch as the wendigo lifts from the ground effortlessly. A gasp slips out of me from the shock of how easy this was.

"Damn, Anya. You have him." I don't let my eye contact with the wendigo drop, but Hunter's voice is laced with amazement. "Can you take down your field while holding it?"

With a nod I say, "Yeah, that shouldn't be a problem. Keep your distance."

"You're good."

One more deep breath through my lungs, and I'm ready to go.

As I pull the wendigo into the wall of illumination, the creature shifts. I hold tight. Once it's up against the field, I absorb the energy into the hovering box, and it glows brighter.

"Shit, hold up."

My stomach drops. "Please don't tell me I shouldn't have done that."

"No, just...make sure it's secured. Give me a second." For the first time, I let my eyes drift away from the wendigo and land on Hunter. He's working quickly, kneeling on the ground mixing different herbs in a bowl then pouring them in a cloth pouch.

"Okay, we're good."

The crease between my eyebrows deepens and Hunter picks up on my confusion.

"I wish I would have thought of it before. Based on the herbs the seeress used, we now have a few that will make the creature dormant for us. I'm going to follow behind. Once we get to the four-wheeler, wait a second before you put him in the bed. I want to place the herbs first. They'll help us have an easier time on the way back."

The image flashes through my mind of Gudrun helping Aoife in the pit to move and trap the darkness.

"And you said you were useless. Look at you, being a cute Viking witch." I bite the inside of my cheek to hold back my smirk.

"Hush you, now let's get out of here. I'll follow behind with my gun in case something happens. I parked to the right as you exit the cave. Are you comfortable backing out?"

Smart thinking.

We need to have the wendigo between us in case something happens to the barrier. We can't risk the beast escaping and killing anyone else.

"As long as you let me know if there are any rocks I'm about to trip over."

"I got you, babe."

Knowing he does and trusting him more than anyone, I begin walking backwards using Hunter as my eyes behind me.

Not long after, the sunlight warms my back, and the ball in my stomach loosens a tad.

Energy flows freely and revitalizes me.

Just a bit farther and I can properly soak up the morning rays.

I turn my body, keeping the wendigo in front of me and—

A deep growl turns into an angry roar behind me.

Oh fuck...

Chapter Thirty

ALGIZ

(AWAKENING)

"Anya, what the hell was that?" Hunter yells from the other side of the wendigo, still inside the cave while I'm staring up at a towering seven-foot bear, ready to tear me to shreds.

Another roar rips from its chest and rattles me to the bones; its breath blows my hair back and speckles of saliva hit my clothes. My body trembles in fear. I'm afraid to breathe, let alone move. I'm trapped between two creatures that won't hesitate to kill me. I don't know if it's a smart move to keep holding onto the more dangerous of the two predators, or completely stupid.

Was I never meant to succeed?

One roadblock after another pushes me to give up. And boy do I want to.

Is it fate to die here and let an animal be the reason death is unleashed onto the world?

What about Hunter?

Air sucks into my lungs with a hiss.

No. I refuse to let anything happen to him. I fought for our lives already, I'll do it over and over again until the last breath leaves my body.

I tighten my hold on the wendigo, making sure whatever happens next, it stays contained. I need to try to warn Hunter to stay back. "Hunt—"

My scream echoes through the trees and cave when I see jaws bigger than my head lunge towards me.

I can't react fast enough to protect myself while holding the wendigo, so I do the only thing I can think of; create a protective barrier around me and pray. In a blink of an eye, a blur of grey flies between the bear and me, knocking it to its side.

Cries mixed with snarls and snapping jaws fill the air. The wolf puts up a good fight with the large bear, saving my life but risking his own.

"Anya!" Hunter's voice startles me.

I drop the shield covering my body and move the creature out of the cave to allow Hunter to come out.

"My God, Anya. What the hell is going on?" He reaches for me but then eyes the wendigo and drops his arms.

"The wolf saved me. But we have to hurry; we need to secure this thing so I can help him." A tear drips from the corner of my eye.

"They're wild animals, you can't save them. The wolf made his choice, we need to get out of here."

"No. I can't do that. Please, help me," I beg.

He scoffs and places the herbs in the bed of the four-wheeler. "It's ready," he says, none-too-happy. "I hope we don't regret this."

With the animals in my peripheral, I hustle over to Hunter. A yelp from the wolf has me nearly tripping over a tree root, but I right myself.

Focus, Anya. Don't lose it now.

My shoulders tense when I realize the energy I have around the monster is too big for the bed of the quad. I bring my hands together, closing the space between to condense the box. The beast begins to shake, but since it's not fully recovered, it doesn't have the ability to fight—yet. I set it down and secure another barrier around it to make sure it won't break free. Then I step back and drop my hands, turning to find two bloody animals locked in a horrific struggle.

Hunter comes around to my side, placing a hand on my shoulder. "Come on, you can't help them. We need to go."

The wolf is still holding strong, but he's slowing. The bear makes another attempt at us. Hunter raises his gun, but the wolf blocks the large creature yet again.

The bear is intent on coming after us, most likely to destroy the wendigo. I would love to say, 'have at it' to defeat the devil's pet, but there's not a single thing the bear can do to it that would permanently kill it. Even in its current state, it'll come back over and over again. If the wendigo was fully recovered, the bear wouldn't stand a chance.

I step closer to the fight, cautious to make sure I'm out of their path.

"Anya," Hunter warns and tries to pull me back. I shake him off and send a beam of light between the two to separate them.

It's not strong enough to burn, but enough to create a dam between them. As soon as they are no longer touching, I box off the bear in its own energy field. Both animals are out of breath, fatigued, and injured. Yet for some reason, the bear doesn't give up. It's fighting hard against its new prison. My eyes water and my throat burns from emotions I struggle to contain. I can't help but hurt for both of them.

My priority is the wolf, who is now laying on his side, his breathing labored.

No!

I rush towards him and hear Hunter in the distance, calling my name. He doesn't understand that I can't allow anything to happen to this animal. He put his life on the line to save me; I can't let him suffer. When I'm at his side, blood is dripping out of the wounds all over him.

A sob escapes me. The need to break down is strong, but I have to hold it together and try my damndest to help him. Bowing my head, I give myself a second to regain my composure.

"Anya," Hunter gently wraps himself around me. "I'm sorry, he isn't going to make it. You need to move. I can end it fast to stop his suffering." My hand swipes away the tears, and I turn to Hunter.

"No!" I grasp Hunter's forearm, stopping him from moving farther.

His gun is in his hand, ready.

"Please give me a minute. I need to think."

His hand covers mine over his arm. "Babe, we don't have time. Let me do this."

"I can't...please."

I have to do something, anything. Death is not an option.

I close my eyes and whisper, "Grandmother, if you can hear me. Please guide me on what I should do. I have to save him. *Please.*"

Energy around us stills, and I tune into the sounds of the forest. The wolf pants and the bear's angry growls are muffled. Beyond them, the wind blows through the trees, rustling the leaves but what's missing are my grandmother's words offering me wisdom.

"Anya, look." My eyes raise and follow to where Hunter is pointing.

The shimmering image of my grandmother hovers on the other side of the wolf.

"Grandmother," my voice comes out breathy.

"My light, your powers have developed fast, they have evolved much further than our ancestors before. The difference is that you have found your twin flame. You are finally whole, while the rest of us spend many reincarnations locating ours."

Hunter grasps my hand, and I squeeze back, taking him as my comfort.

"With your soul now complete, your power is greater than all of ours combined. Don't underestimate what you can do. You can fix this. Just trust in your light, trust in *yourself*."

"But—"

She takes that moment to disappear.

"Argh! Why does she keep doing that?" I fume.

"She came at least," Hunter offers.

"Don't side with her," I growl.

"Okay, okay." He pecks me on my cheek. "I'm going to step back and give you space."

Stopping him by pulling him back, I say, "Thank you."

"I'm not sure what you're thankful for, but you're welcome. Now, see what you can do."

See what I can do.

Hmm... I repeat her words, 'you can fix this.'

If I tap into my power, I can allow it to guide me. Following an impulse, I rub my hands together and they warm as my body tingles. Friction increases and the white light turns green. I pull my hands apart and allow the light to grow between them. The green energy glows brighter as I rotate and mold it into an orb. I move my hands wider to fill them with more healing energy and keep manipulating.

I don't think. I just do.

When I feel I'm ready, I place the orb in the center of the wolf's chest, channeling the energy to flow into his body. My eyes close and the pictures form in my mind of the light entering each limb, every organ, filling it with a healing energy. Like little magical fingers, it branches off into the bloodstream, the nerves, expanding through every inch of the wolf's body.

Hunter, the trees, the bear's growling, everything around me is silent, and I can only hear the beautiful vibrations humming through my body and into the animal's.

The pain I was feeling for this creature subsides and hope fills my chest. He begins to move, and as I watch the light fuse the final cuts and punctures together, I know that he's beyond well. He's better than he was before.

I open my eyes and despite the blood remaining on his fur, he is completely healed. He knocks me on my back, nuzzling and licking my face.

"Haha...stop." The tears that pour out with my laughter are no longer filled with pain.

I must look like a complete mess right now, but I did it. I saved him.

"Thank you, boy. Thank you for saving my life."

Sitting up, my hands cradle his head, and I lay my forehead on his.

He knew the risk, and he took it anyway. I send him a final thanks for his sacrifice and release him.

He licks me again then begins to walk off. When he is near the bear, he stops and glances back at me.

I nod. "It's alright. I'll take care of it."

He understands and darts into the woods from where he came.

Sitting back on my butt, I rest my hands on my knees and take in what happened.

"How the hell did you know how to do that?" Hunter asks in disbelief.

That's exactly what I'm trying to wrap my head around.

"I...uh...I don't know. I listened to the energy and watched everything unfold before me."

He clears his throat. "And the green light?"

"Yup, that was a first. Soon I'll be shooting rainbows out of my ass. Just you wait." I try to joke and turn to the pissed off bear.

Hunter helps me to my feet and wraps an arm around my side, pulling me close.

"I'd rather you try that rainbow trick and leave the bear alone."

If it were only that easy.

My shoulders slouch. "You know as much as I do, I can't."

He chuckles into my hair, tickling me. "The rainbow or the bear?"

I snort. "Either." Leaning into him, his energy charges me like a battery giving me strength.

"I know you don't want to kill it; I don't either. But if you let it go, it's going to attack. If you hold it here, once it's out of the barrier, it's going to follow us to the castle." Hunter's not wrong. "What are you planning on doing?" He asks quietly in my ear, head resting against mine.

I bite my lip. "I need to connect with it like I did the wolf. I don't know if it will work, but I have to try."

Hunter's body stiffens. "Do you think that's smart? You got lucky with the wolf."

"If it understands what we're doing, it may leave us alone. I don't want it hurt or following us. If we can't keep it far away from the castle and someone thinks it's the animal that killed Grant, they won't try to capture it, they'll kill it immediately."

He sighs, turning me in his arms and leaning his forehead against mine. "I know you want to rescue it, but you may not be able to get through to it like you did the other one. It's too dangerous."

"I have to try."

"Babe, you've done enough. You've played Russian Roulette too many times to count. One of these times, it's not going to end well for you. And I refuse to let that happen. You can't save everyone. We can figure out another way, you can hold it here in the box. That'll give us a full day to figure out another way."

I shake my head, "I can't leave it. If we don't return before the force field drops in twenty-four hours then you're right, it'll come to the castle. We also can't keep coming back here to keep it trapped. I need to try, let me do that," I plead.

"Fine," he growls, "but if you let down that field and it comes after you, I'm shooting it. Between the two of you, I choose you and always will. Got it?"

"Got it." I give him a lingering kiss then reluctantly remove myself from his arms and move closer to the bear.

Placing my hand against the force field, I try not to jump back when the animal attempts to attack. Like I did the wolf, I send my emotional energy to it.

It stops and drops down to all fours.

It can feel me.

I try not to get my hopes up, and I send more comforting vibes in a continuous wave and listen for a response. After a few minutes, I'm overwhelmed with so much anger, fear, pain, and worry. Based on the behavior, I expected these, but I didn't expect the feminine energy.

The bear is a she. She's worried for her family. Her baby along with one of her mates were killed by the wendigo already, and she needs to stop it before it hurts the rest of her cubs. The bloody image of the small, once adorable ball of fur flashes in my mind. It's not something she sent me but a memory of the slaughter.

Tears fill my eyes and threaten to spill over.

"My sweet girl."

This poor momma bear is doing what she is built to do, defend her babies.

"I promise I'll do everything I can to make this right." I push my fingers into my tear ducts then pinch the bridge of my nose.

I *have* to make this right.

I communicate with her the only way I know how. Visualizing locking up the wendigo in the dungeon where everything will be safe again, I manifest that image into a ball of light and send it to her. It enters the center of her forehead and her eyes glaze over.

Her trust in our actions is the most important thing for me at this very moment. I need her to understand and allow us to make the wendigo go away. Saving not only her family, but every other living being.

I know if the wendigo wins, death and destruction will plague not only the forest, but it will spread like a virus, infecting everything it touches.

I *will* have justice, I will fix this. There is no other option.

She calms and her tense body relaxes, telling me she's ready.

"Hunter, you may want to back up. I'm letting her out." I don't let my eyes leave hers once. I need her to believe in me entirely. Breaking eye contact will lose the connection we have.

"Are you sure about this? One move in your direction and I'm aiming to kill," his voice trembles with concern.

"She's okay now. Everything will be alright, she'll leave us alone and go back to her babies." I hold my breath, unsure if he'll agree.

"Fine."

It wasn't a happy response, but I'll take it nonetheless. A few steps backwards is all I need, and I slowly absorb the light.

She looks hesitant, not sure if she can move. I wait, only telling her telepathically that she's free. Her eyes break contact with me and she turns to walk off.

Crap. There's a hard limp in her gait. I can't let her go injured.

"Stop!" I yell.

"Anya..." Hunter warns.

I ignore him.

She pauses and looks back at me. In a slow pace, I walk to her, both hands up, sending a message that I want to take the pain away.

To my surprise, she lays down on the ground before I get to her. A sign she is okay with what I need to do next. It's hard to hold back the giddiness of not only being up close and personal with a wild bear, but what I get to do next.

Heal.

I step behind her shoulder where I see the wolf's deepest marks. Creating the same green healing light, I place it on the wound, spreading it through her body to heal the other injuries she received in the fight. She purrs. The deep rumbling tells me she is better and now comfortable.

Once I am done, I stand and back up, allowing her to get up on her own. I wrap my arms around myself and watch as she walks away, turning back once like the wolf to give thanks then make her way back to her family.

"I don't fucking believe it!"

I grab my chest, startled from Hunter's outburst.

"You tamed a fucking bear. Then you healed it, right after you healed a wolf."

"Yeah, it feels kind of surreal."

"Anya, you have no clue how amazing you are. Both inside and out, you are absolutely beautiful. I agree with Greta, you really are a Light Angel." Hunter's eyes are turned up, his dimples are popping out.

I blush at his words. I don't know what to say to all of that. Or really, what to think of everything that just happened, but I follow the magnetic attraction to Hunter and let him wrap his arms around me to hold me snuggly against his chest.

Before all of this, I didn't believe that I *could* be considered a Light Angel like my ancestors. But I really am.

Pride fills me for a moment until I hear, "I am proud of you, Honey Bear."

Groaning, I glare up at him. "I was in an accepting and happy place. You were being sweet and charming. *Then* you brought out Honey Bear," I raise my eyebrow. "Really Hunter?" I push away from him, shaking my head. "Come on."

I start walking back to the four-wheeler. Of course, he follows, chuckling like he's such a funny guy. That's until we both stop in front of the disgusting beast on the back of our ride, reminding us that this isn't over yet.

We still have the biggest challenge ahead of us.

Chapter Thirty-One

Ehwaz

(TEAMWORK)

We finally break through the opening in the trees to see the castle up ahead. The ride back was an exhausting one. Sitting backwards and holding the barrier down so the wendigo wouldn't bounce out was a pain in the ass.

Literally.

My ass and thighs are sore from trying to avoid falling off. I have to count my blessings that the monster didn't fight back.

Hunter slows his speed and reaches around to pat my thigh. "Are you okay with me parking in the back and you carrying it in?" His voice carries over the low rumble of the engine.

I scoff then raise my voice, "Oh, so you can't be a gentleman and drop me off at the door before you park?"

"I'd do the work but as you can see..." He wiggles his fingers over my leg. "I don't have light coming out of my hands."

Yet the man knows how to light *me* up with those digits.

Memories of his fingers working up the sensitive inside of my leg, tickling all the while sending electricity up—

Another squeeze to my thigh snaps me out of my flashback.

"You should know by now that if I felt it'd be safe, I'd drop you off at the door. If something happens, I need to be there to back you up."

With a mutter loud enough he can hear, I say, "Yeah, except *I* do all of the heavy lifting, *again*."

"Let's be fair, I did my fair share of lifting last night," from the smugness in his voice, he doesn't sound like he's hiding his cocky smirk.

My face flushes. So much for keeping my head in the moment. "That's..." I clear my throat. "That's not the same, and you know it."

"It's not my fault you're stronger than me." He feigns innocence—very poorly.

"As long as you can openly admit it, I'm perfectly fine being the boss in this relationship." I don't try to hold back my smile.

He pulls us up to the back wall of the building and shuts off the engine, turning around to face me. "I wouldn't go *that* far. As much as you'd *love* to wear the pants, I prefer you wearing nothing at all. I'll make it easier on you and take the lead when it comes to *everything* else."

His half smirk and underlying meaning makes my core heat; my stomach clenches with anticipation. Taking a deep breath, I calm myself down. He knows just the words to drive me crazy.

I give him a quick peck on his cheek before saying, "We *will* be continuing this conversation later. Right now, I'm good with carrying the wendigo. Just make sure you keep those herbs near and help me make sure I don't hit anything." My palms begin to sweat thinking of our next task. "Maneuvering in the smaller area is going to be the biggest challenge for me. If you can do your job, I can do mine."

"Yes Milady, I can do my *miniscule* job." He stands and offers a hand then hesitates. "Umm, is there a way I can help you off?"

Trying to stand with only the power of my wobbling legs, I don't get far when my ass lands hard on the stiff seat. Pain vibrates from my tailbone up to my shoulders, adding to the discomfort I'm already in.

The throbbing ache forces me to admit defeat. The wendigo has grown quite a bit since the cave. At this point I can't risk letting the creature go and need to keep my power aimed at it constantly.

"It's safe to touch me. If you can hold my—*Eek!*"

Hunter grabs me by the waist and plucks me off the seat, setting me on the ground.

"A little warning next time?" I huff.

He hums in satisfaction. "Just doing my part with the heavy lifting."

I scoff at that. "I'm heavy now, huh? You really know how to sweet talk women, don't you?"

"If you were, I wouldn't have been able to pick you up like a feather. We need to work on getting some meat on your bones."

My eyes roll. "Yeah, yeah. You can feed me *after* we get this taken care of."

Lifting the wendigo is harder now with the additional weight, but using both hands, I don't struggle.

When it's out of the way, Hunter reaches into the bed and grabs the herbs, then leads the way to the front entrance.

"Watch your step." He turns to walk backwards up the stairs, watching my feet as I take my time going up each stair. "Last one," he warns, then opens the double doors.

I continue slow steps until the wendigo and I are fully inside and Hunter comes around us to close the doors. The force field acts as our flashlight.

It's eerie being back inside, yet something about the place is starting to feel familiar...almost homey.

We head down the east hallway to the stairs leading to the dungeon and Hunter leads the way down, walking backwards to help me navigate. My neck strains and my shoulders tense; a clear sign a headache will be forming shortly. What I hope is a bead of sweat—and not a spider—drips down between my shoulder blades, making me shift.

From a few feet below, Hunter says, "Careful, in two more steps, the clearing is low. You may need to make that box smaller. Are you okay with it?"

I nibble the inside of my cheek. "I think so? But be ready if it starts to move." The image of the wendigo shaking free of my grip, tumbling down and landing on Hunter floods my mind.

Now is *not* the time for my active imagination. I shake my head trying to clear it of the vision, but it plays on repeat.

Ugh, I can't risk it.

"Better yet, come on back up. I'd rather condense it up here instead of in the middle of the stairwell." I turn sideways, dragging the wendigo behind me while I go back up the few steps.

The wendigo is now in the hallway with me and when Hunter joins us, I shrink the box. The creature shifts and I fumble a bit until I get a better hold.

"That oughta work, you ready to head back down?" Hunter asks.

When I give him a nod, he begins down the steps backwards again. I'm not sure how he's so controlled. I'd be falling on my ass if I did what he— "*Shit!*"

Stumbling down a few steps, my ankle twists and my heart drops as I see the wendigo drop a foot before I catch it.

"*Damn it*, Anya. Are you okay?" Hunter's voice is panicked.

Trying to catch my breath, I answer, "Yeah, sorry about that. Are *you* okay? I didn't hit you, did I?"

And here I was, worried about decreasing the size of the box on the stairs. I can't even walk down on my own.

He huffs out a breath. "I'm good. I was more worried about you. I doubt I'd have been able to catch this thing, but I'd have let it drop anyways to catch you. What the hell happened? Did it move?"

"No." Ugh. Not the time to be distracted. "It was all me. I didn't get my foot all the way on the step and my heel slipped down before I could catch myself." Rotating my ankle, I check it for injuries. It's stiff but not damaged.

"Now's not the time to fall head over heels for me, Honey Bear." He laughs, but it's strained.

"Hardy Har-Har."

"Are you *really* okay, though?" I can't see his face around the wendigo, but his voice is serious again.

"I'm okay. I only had to pick my heart up off the floor. All good now." I roll my ankle around in a circle one more time to make sure it's sturdy enough to continue.

"Take. Your. Time," he speaks slowly like I'm a child who struggles with understanding.

If he could only see the glare I'm giving him right now.

"And stop aiming daggers, Anya, I can feel them through this barrier."

My eyes go wide.

Well then...

"I don't know what you're talking about," I scoff.

He snickers and we remain quiet the last few steps.

"Last one," Hunter warns.

My boot hits the floor of the dungeon and my body relaxes a fraction when I let go of the breath I was apparently holding.

I follow Hunter down the halls to the wendigo's former prison and notice everything's different from when we were here last. Grant's body is gone, and with it, his blood. The stench of death still lingers under the mask of bleach. I'm sure the smell has already seeped into the stone walls. Regardless, the cleaning crew did an amazing job.

Setting aside my distracted thoughts—again—I take the wendigo directly into the thick stoned-in room and place it on the ground. Leaving it in the force field. Closing the door, I lean my forehead against the cool iron for a moment.

Almost there.

"You okay?" Hunter's hand rests on my back and begins to move in soft circles.

I open my eyes, and I'm met with the glow of the runes on the door but everything else is back to darkness.

"Yeah, just needed a little breather." I stretch out my arms. They're sore from holding them in one position for so long. "Now's the fun part. Repeating the activation process." I ignite a small torch in my hand to use as a flashlight.

"Do you know what needs to be done?" Hunter's voice is tight.

Sounds like I'm not the only one nervous about these next steps.

I can't screw this up.

"I do." When I assure him, my confidence lights like a spark on dry kindling. Slow and weak at first but with each second that passes, it burns brighter. "I made sure I paid close attention when Aoife and Gudrun burned the symbols and activated them. They're already created. All I have to do is tap into my power and flip the switch—so to speak." Rain drizzles on my self-assurance for a moment. "What if someone comes and opens this door again before we can figure out our next steps?"

Getting it back into its prison is a huge achievement, but now that the castle's been discovered, there's nothing to stop someone from releasing it again. It'll bring us back to square one.

Hunter pulls me over to him, his hands span my biceps, rubbing my arms. "I've got something that may help with that. Shine that light near my bag."

He releases me and reaches down into his bag. I situate my light closer, so he can see without it blinding him. He pulls out a large, sturdy, steel padlock.

"Umm...that's great and all, I mean...it's a really good idea, and I hate to burst your bubble. Where do you plan on placing that?"

I love this man, but I'm not sure he's thought this through.

He sets the heavy lock in my hand. "Hold this." He reaches into the bottom of his bag, pulls out two iron plates, handing those to me, then a couple of heavy bolts.

Okay, scratch that, he *may* have planned ahead.

Next, coming out of his bag, is a compact drill along with a bit and an attachment for the bolts.

"Hahaha..." I bend over laughing, trying not to drop all the supplies in my hand. "Alright *Mary Poppins*, I guess you *do* come prepared."

He's been toting that around this whole time? Geesh!

A dimple pops in his left cheek and he closes his bag. "Get over here, smart-ass, so I can get to work."

Aiming the light in his direction, he drills into the stone, then the door. It doesn't take him long, and he seems to know exactly what to do. He attaches one plate to the wall, bolts it down, and repeats, attaching the other to the iron of the door. After they're secured, he puts the drill away then places the lock on it.

"Done." He wipes his hands together dramatically. "That should slow anyone down from trying to let it out again." He stands in front of me with a huge grin.

My chest heats from my melting heart.

With one hand, I pull him by his shirt to me and lower my voice, "Sexy *and* intelligent, I think I hit the jackpot." I bring my lips to his for a quick kiss. "Thank you!"

Without warning, he grabs me around the waist and pulls me closer. I lean my weight fully into him, and he kisses me until I lose myself. The dungeon fades, and I focus only on the feeling of his soft lips on mine with the occasional bristle of his beard. A blaze lights me up and shoots to my stomach, spreading to my center, and weakening my knees.

When he lets go, coolness hits my face, and I groan in protest. My eyes are still heavy, and I reach up and touch my lips with my finger—wishing he didn't end it so soon.

"You're up next." His gravelly voice sends jolts of electricity to my tingling core.

I drop my head to his chest and take in the last bit of warmth I can. It's much nicer to be snuggled into his broad chest and ignore the reality around us.

"Come on, babe. We're close to getting out of here." Hunter takes my chin between his finger and thumb, lifting it to meet his gaze. "You've been a badass handling wolves and bears and creatures from the fiery depths of hell. You got this."

I've got this.

I'm not sure how long this will take, but if I'm lucky, not as long as it took Aoife and the seeress. If I truly have more power, this may go quicker.

Backing away from Hunter, I cup the flame I've been holding in my hands, and mold it into an orb. After setting the night light on the stone floor, I free myself up for this next task.

I place my hands over one of the sideways hourglass symbols in a corner—the Dagaz rune. Pulling from deep inside me, I channel an orange light into the burned imprint until it glows bright—energizing and stimulating the power within the door. I repeat the same action until all four corners have a Dagaz rune illuminating.

The thorn symbol in the center is next. The Thurisaz provides an added layer of strength and protection. I envision a bluish-black light absorbing into the rune from my hands, spreading outwards over the surface of the iron.

Five down, only a few more to go.

When I move my hands, I try to keep contact on the door with some part of my body, refusing to disconnect from the connection. I drag one hand and lay it over the top left Spiral of Life symbol and my other one rests on the right. Something inside me tells me I need to do these together to speed the process along.

"Mmm…that's a position I wouldn't mind trying later," Hunter murmurs.

"What?" I turn only my head towards him. His gaze is on my ass and legs. The same legs that I didn't realize are spread in a wide stance, while my palms are resting on the door. Heat floods my body in a wave from my face to my feet. And it has nothing to do with the electrical current I'm creating with my hands.

It has *everything* to do with a horny man who clearly has fantasies of playing cops and robbers.

His eyes widen. "Shit, I'm sorry. I didn't mean to say that out loud." He runs a hand through his hair. "Did I mess you up?"

"No. But if you can hold those comments to yourself for now, that would be great." I can't contain the smirk from forming on my lips. As quick as it comes, I swipe it away to continue working.

I turn back and take a deep breath, allowing rays as bright as the sun to flow from deep inside my chest, caressing every part of me as they pass by. My palms warm as the power shoots into the tri-spirals. When I'm finished, I begin to kneel to reach the bottom two, but I pause to admire the swirling energy on the spirals. It pulls me in like the fascination of watching a flickering flame.

I could stay here all day and night just to watch.

Shaking my head, I continue to the floor until I'm kneeling—thankful it isn't a pool of blood anymore.

Ugh. Now I can't stop wondering what Hunter is thinking.

I glance over my shoulder and catch him licking his lips. "You know, maybe you should turn around for the rest of this."

He throws his hands up. "That's not fair, I didn't comment about you on your knees."

I cock my eyebrow. "Ha! I knew it." My finger points at him accusingly. "*You* are making me paranoid now."

He harrumphs. "Fine." He turns to face the hallway. "This is bullshit. I didn't even say a thing," he mumbles.

"You know everything echoes off these walls, *right*?"

He growls in response, and I turn towards the door, snickering. *Okay, almost there.*

I reproduce the same rays to energize the bottom Spirals of Life, allowing them to pour into the others and become in sync. I imagine it's like tuning an instrument. If we keep them all in a smooth melody with each other, they harmonize and work together.

Butterflies begin their takeoff in my stomach when I come to the final symbols, the Triskeles—or triple spirals. This is the last piece to make the door self-energizing. It works as a long acting, self-rechargeable battery that will power everything. Completing this process is both exciting and nerve-wracking. I hope I'm doing it right.

The Celtic symbols are in the directions like a compass. I hold the North and South ones first, and this time, instead of pulling the energy from my aura and body, I feel the need to pull it from the ground. I visualize soft green tendrils from under the stone at our feet, weaving themselves up like roots through the floor. The emerald vines vibrate as they climb up my legs and body until they stretch over my hands and melt into the metal door. It fills the Triskeles like paint would as it's poured into a mold.

I shift my hands to the east and west Triskeles while the energy continues to channel from the earth and into the door. The sensation is almost euphoric as it takes over, knowing exactly what is needed for the job.

For safe measure, I join my power with the green light and give one final burst of energy into the door. The combined powers burn bright white at the seams of the door before spreading like a ripple along the iron and the stone surrounding it.

I steeple my fingers over my mouth.

"Is it done?" Hunter stands shoulder to shoulder with me—or more like my shoulder to his biceps—surveying my work.

"Didn't I tell you not to look?"

"Pfft, and miss all that? It was better than a fireworks show." He reaches down and his large callused hand envelops my delicate one.

Regardless of me being the one who has the power of light, he has the power to make me feel protected any time he holds me. I sigh, dropping my head to his shoulder, and stare at the markings. They are a mixture of two ancient bloodlines who combined their knowledge for good.

It really is done.

"Yeah. And if it's not the same, it's stronger than when it was created the last time the wendigo was sealed off from the world."

Hunter wraps his arms around my shoulders and pulls me in, kissing me on the top of my head. "I can't tell you how proud I am of you. You're seriously one badass woman."

My head slides from his shoulder to his chest, and I breathe in his delicious citrus and lavender scent.

"Ready to get out of here?" He asks, his chest rumbling under my cheek.

A heavy weight lifts from my shoulders knowing the wendigo is locked away where no one can be hurt. It's not a permanent solution, but it sure as hell's one that will hold us over until we can figure out what to do with the castle. We deserve a long overdue break from it all.

"Mmhmm," I mumble and straighten. "Let me grab the light." I begin to walk over to the orb on the floor but stop.

I wonder.

I call to the energy and it recoils into my hand like a yo-yo.

Hmm...that nifty trick may come in handy someday.

Hunter doesn't hesitate when he grabs my hand and drags me up the stairs and out the front door.

He's a man on a mission.

Once we exit, I absorb my light. Hunter closes the doors and swiftly pulls another type of lock out of his carrier bag, latching the handles together. "This ought to deter people."

And *this* is why we make a great team. The thought never crossed my mind to bolt the place up afterwards. I side-eye him. "Well, aren't you resourceful? I may keep you around after all. Not a bad idea to have a boy scout as my backup."

"Not a boy scout, babe, a soldier. Always prepare for the unexpected."

"Oh, pardon me for the mix-up."

"Forgiven." He ignores the sarcasm in my voice and leans down for a quick kiss. "And I don't think you have a choice about keeping me around. You can't get rid of me."

I tilt my head and smirk. "Sounds kinda stalkerish."

"Whatever floats your boat. We already know about your kidnapping fetish."

"I told you, I do not—"

Hunter cuts me off with his lips on mine. This man is maddening in so many ways. His arm wraps around my back, drawing me in and leaning me back. Every second his wonderful mouth is on me, I lose myself in a haze.

He pulls away way too soon, with a smug look on his face. "Now, it's time to get you home."

What just happened?

He drags me around the back of the castle to the four-wheeler.

All while I'm still in a daze.

My lips tingle, my nipples are hard, and I'm struggling to bring my focus back around to the here and now. The brief passionate embrace we were just in plays on repeat.

Before I know it, Hunter reaches around to help me off the quad first. "Mind pulling the truck out so I can load this up?"

I blink a few times, thrown off by not only the amount of time I lost in my head, but the sight of his black four-by-four hidden in the trees.

And here I thought he drove straight through the woods on the small machine.

"Uh, sure. That I can do." Stopping myself from tripping on Hunter, I realize he just placed the keys to his big, beautiful truck in my hands. There's no point in asking him how he got here. It's clear enough, and I'm not willing to bring up the situation where I left him behind. Better to leave that in the past where it belongs and move on to bigger and better things.

A smile spreads across my face. Like getting to play with Hunter's toy.

Wait, that didn't sound right. Oh, never mind.

The purr of the engine has me wiggling in the seat with excitement. Things are going good for me right now, and I'm going to bask in every minute of it.

I could stay inside and wait for him but why miss the show? I hop down from the truck and saunter my way to the rear of the truck. Leaning up against the side of the tailgate, I supervise Hunter while he loads up the machine.

More like watching his muscles flex as he manhandles it into the bed of his truck.

I back up to let him close the tailgate and discreetly check the corners of my mouth for drool. Climbing in the truck, I lean over the back of the seat to grab a water bottle and chocolate granola bar. "Ahhh!"

Hunter's hand connects with my ass.

The sting in my rear doesn't dissipate when I sit back in my seat with the treats in my lap. My jaw drops in shock when I face him. He raises both his eyebrows and smiles like a kid caught stealing candy, but isn't remorseful.

"I was *going* to offer you some, but forget that. You are on your own." I take a deep swig of the cool liquid and let it coat my throat.

"When you offered your sweet ass to me like that, I thought it was an invitation. A man has only so much control, Anya."

"Uh, huh." I open the snack and take a big bite while I ignore his excuses and exhaustion hits me. It's uncontrollable when my eyes close and my head hits the headrest.

Hunter's throat clearing pulls me out of my contented state.

"What?" I open my eyes slightly.

A deep rumble escapes his chest. "I was only thinking, I gave you a drink in the cave and that one is the last one we have. And I behaved—outside of our recent miscommunication."

"Miscommunication of your hand connecting with my rear?"

"All out of love, babe. All out of love. Are you going to make me pass out from dehydration?" He aims puppy dog eyes in my direction which is adorable and makes me cave.

Where the hell did he learn how to do that?

"Alright, here." I hold the bottle out to him.

"How about something sweet?"

The other half of the granola bar sits in my hand. My mouth salivates from the thought of having more of the crunchy chocolate to ease my stress. I guess sharing wouldn't hurt. I bring it up to his lips but he turns away.

"I don't want that one; I want yours." He reaches across the seat, spans his hand over my cheek and pulls me to him, capturing my mouth. "Mmm..." He licks his lips. "That *is* really good."

This man is dangerous.

He pulls me in for another kiss, and I shove the other half of the bar in his mouth—with a huge grin on my face.

I'm glad he saw it coming, or he would've had a face full instead of a mouthful—wasting a perfectly good snack. But it was the risk I was willing to take.

If he kept kissing me like that, we would never get out of here.

Hunter's eyes burn holes into me, and I glance down to the solid rod straining against his zipper.

I don't think I've ever been more turned on from torturing someone before.

We need to get back to my house so I point to the path ahead. "Drive, Big Guy."

He just growls.

I'm staring out the window at the trees, my eyes getting heavy when Hunter speaks up.

"I was thinking, we need to come back to the castle tomorrow to check on the wendigo. No need to rush, but I'd rather keep a close eye on it until we can figure out what Margaret's next steps will be."

"Yeah, about that. You really think she is going to push for ownership of the place?"

His response is a side eye, silently saying 'are you kidding me?'

"Scratch that. Stupid question." Anyone who knows the Bordeauxes has an idea of how low they would go for greed.

Which makes him chuckle.

I love the sound of his laugh. That deep, rich vibration emanating from his chest. It sends amazing sensations rushing through me and causes me to clench my thighs tight.

It has never been like this with any other guy. But I really need to focus on bigger issues right now and not question the connection between us.

"Not that I know what was discussed between the two of you because you haven't felt the need to tell me."

He runs a hand over his face. "We've got a battle ahead of us when it comes to her. She won't give up, no matter what. But we'll find alternatives, since killing the wendigo is out of the question."

The little break of relief and happiness is gone. Now a stab of dread hits me hard in my chest.

I knew it wasn't the end when we sealed the wendigo up, but I hoped for a *little* reprieve before fighting again.

My hand rubs the knot forming in my shoulder. "What happens if we go back and Margaret's there? How's she going to believe we aren't trying to *steal* the castle?"

"Well, I plan on renting a flatbed trailer for your car so the reason why we are back is easy. How to keep her away? That I'm not sure of." Hunter runs a hand over his face and beard. "Greta may have ideas on some sort of repellant to buy us a little time."

"What would help is if we can find the true owners, or at least the history of the castle. It could maybe give us a fighting chance."

"The issue is accessing the right systems to find more about the area and prior residents."

An idea pops in my head. "Luckily, with my job, I've got access to see if we can file it as a Historic Designation. That place is *extremely* old. If we can, I think this can possibly help deny Bordeaux's abandonment claim, *or* at least slow down her ability to alter the castle, the dungeon included. I know it's a longshot, but it's something."

Hunter massages his forehead. "Damn, I didn't even think of that. It's a great place to start. Can you access your work from home? That can save us a lot of time without having to fill out paperwork or have people ask too many questions."

"Yup, I have my work laptop at home sitting on the table."

"Good. We have to be ready, because as soon as we take action, it's going to bring others to the property. It's going to get tricky and quite dangerous, but it may be our only option." He reaches for my hand and laces our fingers. "We have tomorrow to look into this stuff. We can go home and rest."

It's like I'm forgetting something. What am I forgetting?

"What day is it?"

"Monday, why?"

"Oh, shit. I have to get to work."

"I think that's the last thing you need to worry about right now."

"Says the man paying my electric bill? Oh wait, you don't. I need that job."

"I'll take care of you."

"As much as I appreciate the offer, I can't. I need to be able to support myself, and I know you want to argue with me over it, just please don't right now."

"This conversation isn't over."

"Wake me up when we get home. I should have some time for a shower, small nap and a snack before I have to report in at 11:00. It wouldn't be the first time I was late, but it's better than nothing."

Closing my front door behind us, I let out a relieved sigh.

"I know exactly how you feel." Hunter says.

We make our way to my bedroom, stripping off our weapons like we're secret agents. It definitely isn't a typical couple thing to do, but as Hunter said, we *aren't* a normal couple. The blinds are still shut and the bed is a mess from last night. Memories of me sneaking out on him creep in my gut and make me nauseous.

A gentle hand rests on my shoulder from behind. "What's the matter?"

Right on cue, he knew something was bothering me.

I turn around and face the man I hurt. The man I ran away from to save.

"I'm sorry about last night...er...this morning."

He takes my chin between his fingers, forcing me to look him in the eye. "No. You aren't going to do this. It's over. We got past it. It all turned out okay. Don't add this onto everything else you are holding onto."

I huff. "Easier said than done."

"Then how about we help you forget?"

"Shower?" I suggest, raising an eyebrow. I mean, we're all sweaty and dirty from a long night of work. It would only make sense.

He grabs me around the waist, pulling me against him. His hardness presses against my center. "A shower sounds perfect," he growls.

With a squeak escaping from my lips, I'm flipped around. Hunter's hands grab mine, moving them to rest high on the wall while his leg spreads mine apart.

Leaning down, his lips nibble their way down my neck. "It's time for your strip search."

Chapter Thirty-Two

ALGIZ

(RECOVERY)

The sun's rays shine through a crack in my drapes, and for once, I'm not extremely and utterly exhausted.

In a stretch, I throw my arms out to my sides.

"Oomph."

I gasp and yank my arms to my chest with fists ready to defend against an intruder, while moving away from the solid mass I made contact with.

"Ow!"

Maybe the large thud from my body hitting the floor scared the criminal away. Wishful thinking.

My heart races a million miles a minute as I creep up on all fours to the edge of the mattress and peek over the side.

All the memories of last night into this morning come rushing back to me. "Oh my gosh, Hunter, are you okay?" Since he's not writhing in pain, I lay back on the floor and stare at the ceiling, trying to calm my heart rate. No wonder why I forgot everything. Despite only having a couple hours of sleep, it was a hell of a power nap. Let's hope I don't crash later.

A groggy voice from the bed says, "Yeah, but it was a close call for me *not* to be okay. Please tell me you won't beat me up every morning."

"I...uh...can't promise anything."

A deep chuckle has me groaning out loud.

Hunter's handsome but smug face peers over the side, looking down at me. "Is assault before your graceful escape a typical thing for you?"

Narrowing my eyes, I huff. "Well, since this isn't a common occurrence, that answer would be a big fat *no*." I cross my arms over my chest.

"Ahh...I knew I had women falling for my perfect body, but none of them punched me before falling *from* my body. I guess I made an impression on you, huh?"

The bastard has the nerve to wiggle his eyebrows.

I pretend to sniff the air and feign concern. "Do you...do you smell that? It smells like someone's boxer briefs are on fire."

"Wha?!" Hunter leaps from the bed patting himself down—I assume looking for the fire—before bumping into the night stand.

The lamp clatters to the floor.

Meanwhile, I burst out laughing so hard muscle spasms ripple through my stomach.

"Annyyyaaa..." Hunter growls.

"Bahahaha..." Rolling around on the floor with my hands over my cramping belly, I snort then laugh some more until tears stream down my face.

He comes around the bed and straddles me—pinning my arms above my head. He must be frisky, but the devious look in his eyes sobers me up like I've jumped into a freezing lake.

"Oh, shit." My eyes go wide.

"Oh, shit, indeed." As a panther pounces on their prey, swift and calculated, Hunter attacks me.

With his hands at my most ticklish spots on my sides and behind the backs of my knees.

"Hunter, no!" I gasp for air between my laughs. "Stop! I'm serious, I'm going to pee my pants, *stop*."

"Fine," he says reluctantly and hoists me up off the floor with him.

Bending over at the waist with my hands on my sides, I catch my breath then walk towards the bathroom muttering, "Evil ass."

"What was that?" His ominous voice is close, sending me high-tailing it to the bathroom with a squeak, slamming the door closed.

I finish my business and take my time opening the door, making sure the coast is clear.

"You look nervous." Hunter lays naked on the bed, his hands behind his head, staring at me like I'm on the menu for breakfast.

"No, not nervous. Just...cautious. You planning on being a bum all day?" I raise an eyebrow at him.

"With you by my side, that would be a dream come true, but we have things to do. It's ten in the morning and we still have a little time before we need to start the day." His heated gaze runs from my face, down my body. "Now, get over here," his low demand sends chills down my spine.

"Are you going to play nice?"

He shifts, rubbing his hand over his scruffy beard and hums. "Well, that depends on what you consider *nice*. But in this case, I won't do anything you won't like."

I push the door open the rest of the way and make my way over to the bed, my eyes locked on the naked man sporting morning wood.

Maintain eye contact, do not ogle the man. Maintain...eye...con tact.

The bed creaks from my weight as I crawl up and sit a foot away from Hunter. Like a magnet, my vision can't resist the pull as it drifts down.

A scream escapes me as he pulls me under him with lightning speed, muffling my surprise with his mouth. "Mmm..." I relax into him.

His hard length rests between my thighs but not close enough so I wiggle down.

Almost...right there—

The shrill from my alarm has me growling, igniting a fire in my hand. I reach out to burn the damn thing when Hunter grabs it, and turns off the alarm. He holds the phone out of my reach.

"Calm down, Honey Bear. The phone never did anything to you." He coaxes me to relax and I cock my eyebrow at him.

But yes, yes it did.

"Okay, maybe it cock-blocked you." His eyes go to the blazing heat in my palm. "But not for long."

Rolling my eyes, I extinguish the flame. "You happy now?"

He sets my phone down. "Very." His mouth crushes down on mine.

Mmm... It's not fair that he has to taste amazing in the morning. Meanwhile, my breath probably tastes like chalk. Dry and blah. Give the man props for pushing through like a champ anyways.

My palms reach around and cup Hunter's ass, pulling him closer to me. His weight drops down on me, heavy but not crushing.

"You know, we need to get up and figure out what our plan's going to be today." He starts to kiss me again. This man is not helping the matter.

"Well, then stop kissing me so I can get ready for work. You're going to make me late. We can't do anything until I try to convince my manager I have a family emergency I have to take care of." A conversation I'm dreading.

Hunter doesn't release me though. He takes a finger and drags it across my cheek. It's a relief it no longer hurts. "Your cut is completely healed, it's as smooth and unmarked as it was before you got hurt. It's amazing the power you hold inside of you." He lowers his lips and gently kisses the area. "And the power you have over me," he whispers, then moves to my neck and starts to nibble.

It's the one button that drives me the most insane and he knows exactly how to press it. The tingling floods over me and leaves me wet. It's impossible to avoid, and I'm kicking myself for doing this, however, I can't lose my job over it either.

With a groan, I push against his chest and roll out of bed. "Make yourself productive and make me something to eat before we have to leave."

"I was being productive a minute ago, until you stopped me."

My eyes roll. "Ugh, you know what I mean. Now get up or I'm walking to work."

"Alright, alright." He throws back the blankets and gives me an eye-full before slipping into his boxer briefs and jeans.

I take the very little strength I have left and divert my attention to getting ready.

I stroll into the kitchen and find Hunter sauntering his way around. The big guy certainly has magical fingers like he claimed—as he demonstrated last night. Now, he puts those fingers to work on making our breakfast. He looks amazing in his dark jeans, boots, and fitted, black, v-neck t-shirt that shows off some of his chest tattoos and part of the chain holding my charm.

Wanting to help, I grab a flipper from my utensil drawer and slink over to the stove.

"I don't think so, baby. Back that beautiful ass up and out of this kitchen." His chest rumbles against my back and hands grip my hips, pulling me out of my kitchen and into a chair.

My jaw drops.

What is happening? Is he kicking me out of my own kitchen?

It's insane I'm even questioning a hot man cooking for me. Isn't this a dream come true? If he chooses to slave over a hot stove to feed me, who am I to complain?

Throwing up my hands in defeat, I give in. "Okay, okay. Over-protective of your cooking space, I get it." I point my finger at him. "Just remember, that's *my* kitchen, and I'm only allowing this because *you* are the cause of my starvation."

"And what if I just want to take care of you?"

I side-eye him. "Or you could secretly be a cooking snob."

"Or maybe I'd like to decrease the chances of you injuring me."

My mouth drops. "That was *one* time! And I'm fully awake now."

Will I never live that down?

A smirk pops out a dimple and he winks. "Sit and behave, for once."

Moments later, Hunter brings over two plates filled with omelets and bacon. Dropping them off, he heads back for two glasses of orange juice and my favorite mug. From the smell of it, it's not my favorite green tea with lemongrass. His large hands manage to juggle everything to the table with no issue.

"Tanx," I manage my appreciation through a mouthful of food. I didn't wait for him, but it's his fault for making me work up an appetite to begin with.

I peek in my mug and find herbs floating on the top, my shoulders drop. This is Hunter's energy concoction. It's something I need, but not something I want.

Might as well get this over with.

Picking it up, I take a sip and my eyes widen at the sweet nectar that coats my taste buds. I chug down the contents.

"Wow, that was delicious. What did you do differently?" I set down the empty mug.

"I added your favorite...honey." His voice is low and gravelly, like he thinks that word is my aphrodisiac.

I chuckle. "You won't get over that, will you?"

"Haha, nah. But what my Honey Bear wants, my Honey Bear gets. Ow."

He laughs and rubs his shoulder where I playfully punched him.

I bring another bite of food to my mouth.

"Eeek!" The fork full of eggs and cheese clatters to my plate as those same magical fingers turn into the devil's, tickling my side. I push my chair back and out of his grasp, panting.

"You said you'd play nice. Be good, we have to go soon."

"I am. Tickling *is* a nice gesture and it makes you smile. You wouldn't be smiling and laughing if it was bad." He doesn't hide the wide grin spreading across his face.

I move my chair farther away, "Lies, all lies. It's just a form of torture."

Laughing, he gets up and pulls my chair right back to my original spot next to him, kisses me on my temple and says, "Now stop playing around and eat up, we have a busy day ahead of us."

My mouth drops open.

But he started it.

Hunter closes my mouth with a finger. "Eat."

Chapter Thirty-Three

PERTHO

(UNCERTAINTY)

The knot in the pit of my stomach is unavoidable as Hunter pulls into Julie's parking space at work five minutes before eleven. I'm not sure what I'd have done if we had a normal start time.

"What are you doing?" I gape at him holding his door open, getting ready to step out at the same time as me.

"I'm coming with, what does it look like I'm doing?" He cocks an eyebrow.

My heart skips a beat. "Oh no, you aren't."

"Why? Are you ashamed of me?" He smirks.

This only earns him an incredulous stare.

He huffs. "What's wrong with me coming in? It's not like I haven't before."

"Have you looked in the mirror lately, pretty boy? One look at you, and she'll think I'll be spending all week in bed, not dealing with a *family* emergency. You go do what you need to do; I'll let you know when I'm done."

He closes the door and shifts in his seat. "I'll wait."

My shoulders drop and I sigh. "You know you don't have to wait, there's no telling how long I'll be. I can walk home."

His eyes turn dark and his left eye twitches. "No. You will *not*," he growls. "I'll be right here."

"Okay, okay." I hold up my hands in defense.

I'm sure after my disappearing act, he may never let me leave his sight. At least until the wendigo is officially taken care of. And I don't blame him.

"Don't worry about me, I can keep myself occupied. I have to make a call to one of my PI buddies, Duncan, anyways. He's been looking for work and I can't handle any cases right now."

Right now.

I push away the devil's whispers trying to inch their way into my mind.

Hunter pushes my door open. "Now go. The sooner you get this over with, the sooner you'll be back with me."

"Stay out of trouble."

I jump down from the truck and close the door behind me. The temptation to climb right back in gives me a slight hesitation.

Against my will, I force one foot in front of the other and pull open the office door.

"Morning, Ms. Anya." James' fatherly smile reminds me of my own dad.

Once I shove the regrets about Hunter back into the box they came out of, I return James' greeting and turn down the hall towards my desk. Danielle is the first one I see. She's absorbed in her work and doesn't hear me approach.

Using the cubicle wall to lean against, I say, "Hey, you. I'm sorry again for not being a good friend."

Danielle pops up with a big smile. "Anya! Oh, don't be apologizing. You have nothing to be sorry for. We all have our lives and things come up." She tilts her head. "Wow, you have a glow to you."

"What?" I choke back. My attention drops to my hands, expecting them to be illuminated but they're normal. In a rush, I yank open my desk drawer and search for my compact mirror.

I open it as fast as I can, while trying to hide my face from anyone else.

My face looks...like my face. Normal and even toned. Relief washes over me, and I drop into my chair.

No glow and, thank the heavens, no nasty scar from my battle with Hell's guard dog.

Danielle leans over the wall, laughing. "Are you okay? I didn't mean there was something wrong with your face. You look a little different, almost like you're glowing. Outside of your current state of panic, you seemed happier. Is that dark-haired Thor the reason?"

A snort sneaks out. If only Hunter were here to hear someone else referring to him as a superhero.

"That must be it." I'm unsure of how to answer her.

"I brought *cuuppcaakkes*!" Heather yells in a sing-song tone.

Saved by bakery wizardry.

The stale air in the office overpowers their sweet aroma and prevents me from telling if she brought my favorite—cookies and cream. She knows they're my weakness. She even adds crushed cookies on top. They're the best you will *ever* have, and, strangely enough, they're almost...*magical*.

I've always joked about it, but what if they are?

Despite my second guessing, I allow the excitement to take over, knowing the weight on my shoulders will soon let up after one mouthwatering bite. If I wasn't glowing before, there's a good chance I may be now. Closing my eyes, I tap into my energy to make sure it's buried deep inside.

Why was I nervous to come in today?

I hustle over to Heather, giving her a kiss on the cheek before plucking the dessert tray out of her hands and barricading myself inside my cubicle.

Licking my lips, I lower my head and gently pull the lid up—tendrils of chocolate and cream tell me exactly which piece of heaven she brought.

After the couple days I've had, especially last night, I *need* these.

Danielle's lavender nails come into view, and I growl, holding the container away.

"Mine. Heather loves me more, and I'm in dire need. This is a matter of *life* and *death*."

Heather props her head on her hand against the barrier and laughs. "Don't worry, Danielle. I figured that would happen." She flashes a pearly white smile and opens up her large purse to pull out a smaller container, handing it to Danielle. "Have no fear, I came prepared!"

Like Christmas morning, Danielle's eyes light up when she sees her favorite peanut butter cupcakes. Chocolate cupcakes with peanut butter frosting inside as well as on top. And it wouldn't be Heather's signature cupcakes without a finishing touch. These have peanut butter cup crumbles sprinkling the icing.

"What would we do without you?" Danielle sighs.

"You wouldn't have a mouth-gasm, that's for sure," Heather announces proudly.

With a mouthful of cupcake, I moan. "She's right."

Danielle hushes us, "Shh...someone's going to hear you. We better get to work before the dragon lady comes in."

I pop the other half of my sweet treat into my mouth and skim through my emails. I know I'm not here to technically work, but I may as well be productive until Julie gets in. A report is back from accounting, I print it out and reach in the container for another dessert—

"James, I told you once, I'll tell you again," Julie's voice grates like nails on a chalkboard as her tone carries from the front. "If someone parks in my parking spot again, I'll have your ass fired and ruined from working anywhere ever again. Do you understand me?"

Oh shit. Hunter.

I should have told him to move. I'd thought he'd drop me off and leave. Sorry, James.

"Ma'am, but it's city owned. We have no control over—"

"I said. Do. You. Understand. Me?"

"Yes, Ma'am."

It's bad enough James has to put up with her crap. Now I'm up next on her shit-list. But weirdly enough, Heather's mini-cakes give me the courage I need to get this over with.

As though the girls know what's about to happen next, they both give me encouraging smiles.

In any other job, taking time off for a family emergency wouldn't be an issue. Here? With my manager? You better be dying if you can't come to work. I stand, turning around to head to her office—

Oh, crap!

I come face to face with Julie and I jump back. "Oh, I'm sorry, I was coming to see you."

Her eyes are red-rimmed with unshed tears. I've never seen her show any emotion except pure hate and disgust. What I'm seeing now proves there *is actually* a human being inside her.

"Alright, you idiots, pack up your stuff. We are closing for the week," she addresses us all.

Scratch that.

On second thought, she is one-hundred percent an evil demon incarnate. Maybe the watery eyes are from allergies.

Or a reaction from being out of Hell too long.

Wait...did she say we're closed for a week?

My heart races with a rush of hope running through my veins, and I bite down to suppress my smile. Clearing my throat I say, "Umm... Is everything okay?"

She snaps, "No!"

My head rears back like she slapped me from her outburst.

"Everything's NOT okay!" Her chest heaves and her usual put together face is now turning a strange shade of red. "Our sweet and brilliant boss, the owner of this *successful* corporation, is *dead*!"

I let out a sigh of relief.

Oh, that.

Julie wipes away an invisible tear. "Grant's body was found this weekend doing what he loved, acquiring property so *you* losers can continue to have a job. You should be worried, as we have no clue what *Margaret*—" Her lips curl in a sneer. "—will do with the company. All of our jobs are on the line." Her nostrils flair. "Now grab your stuff and *leave*. Don't come back until Monday for a meeting at nine AM sharp to discuss the future of this company. And don't be late!"

With that, she turns, stomps towards her office, and slams the door. The framed business license falls to the floor in a crash.

I stand there with my jaw to the floor.

"Holy. Shit." Heather comes up next to me and with a finger, she closes my mouth.

Danielle sidles up to my other side and we stare at the office door in silence.

When finding Grant's body, I never thought once about what would happen. I mean, I had way more important things to deal with.

Now I'm in a Catch-22. The announcement is an answered prayer, but it also opens up a new issue—the potential of becoming unemployed in the near future. This can end very badly for the employees. I'm not even sure where I could go for work to pay my bills. This town isn't hopping with job opportunities. I rub the back of my neck to ease the new tension that's formed.

Okay, one problem at a time.

And speaking of time, how long have I been here?

Shaking my head, I say, "Sorry girls, I have to take care of that family issue. I'll text when I can. Looks like we have a week off, have a great time." With the cupcake lid secured, I pick them up to leave.

"Whoa!" I stumble back from the two women in front of me with their arms crossed over their chests. I chuckle nervously. "That was close, we almost had casualties." I shift the container in my arms and gulp when the women narrow their eyes on me.

"What?"

Heather speaks first, "What? She asks us, Danielle. Did you hear that?"

"Oh, I didn't miss it."

Heather taps one of her French manicured fingers on her pursed lips. "Tell us. Why don't you seem surprised about the death? Did you *know* about him already?"

I flinch from her tone.

Danielle taps her foot. "Yeah, things aren't adding up." She softens, "Come on, Anya. We tell each other *everything*."

"Spill!" demands Heather.

Shit, good cop, bad cop.

I'm fucked.

"Okay," My eyes dart around the office to make sure no one is around to hear. "This has to be quick, and I can't answer a lot of questions."

Their eyebrows crease but nod to continue.

"We're still trying to figure things out…" I tell them about the 'animal' attack, explaining how Hunter and I got together only to find out he was my childhood best friend. We reconnected over the incident. I'm careful, though, when I let them know my family has ties to the castle, which is why I'm involved.

"Are your parents coming to help?" Heather inquires.

"No, they're too far away and they don't need the added stress right now. Hunter and I have it covered."

Danielle's lips thin. "We've talked a few times since then, why didn't you tell us?"

"I'm sorry. Everything was up in the air. The journal I had you both hang on to was from the castle. I didn't want the police to take it away or I'd never see it again."

"Why is that old thing important?" Heather's eyes twinkle. "Is it worth a lot?"

I shift my weight. "Don't get too excited. It's from an ancestor of mine and may give us details about the castle. Just like Grant, Margaret's trying to take ownership of the property." I check the time on my phone—forty-five minutes have passed. "I'll tell you more once we finish dealing with our issue."

I bite the inside of my cheek and turn on the puppy dog eyes—silently pleading with them to forgive me and let it go.

Heather is the first to move, shifting her body like she's a door opening for me to pass. "Okay, but we're expecting *every* detail." Her eyes narrow again. "I know you're keeping a lot out of your story. Whatever this *'issue'* is, be careful."

"As careful as I can be."

"Are you sure we can trust Hunter? He may not be the same person he was when you were younger." Heather's mother hen steps in. She has a gleam in her eyes; the gleam I know all too well. If I give her the signal, she would go ape-shit on Hunter, and make sure he'll stay away from me, for good.

Danielle hums out an "Mmhmm..."

They have every right to be worried, but I'm not some naive woman being led blindly to my death by a man.

More like a monster from Native American folklore.

"I appreciate you guys watching out for me, and, Heather, thank you for always being my bodyguard. But Hunter is actually one of the good guys out there. He's been nothing but perfect towards me, even with *my* grumpy ass."

That causes them to laugh.

I continue, "You have nothing to worry about. And if I have even an *inkling* that he may hurt me, I'll give you the go ahead to bring out Mama Bear. Deal?"

Heather's mischievous smile creeps me out. "Deal." In the next second, her mouth switches to one of an angel. "That is all I can ask for. Be safe, we love you, and try to have a little fun while you are at it."

Forget a devil on her left, angel on her right. They came to an agreement, and both took up residency inside her.

It's a dangerous and scary thing to imagine what goes on in her mind.

"Yes, be safe but try to take time for *you* as well. Keep in mind, though, we won't forget about your promise." Danielle adds, finally moving to allow me access to escape.

With my holy grail of cupcakes in one arm, I give half hugs to both of them and we say our goodbyes.

Once I step outside of the building, I snicker when I see Hunter's truck sitting in Julie's parking spot.

Oh, poor James had to deal with the witch because of Hunter. Sorry, buddy.

Hunter glances up from his phone when I climb up and place my cupcakes in the back before buckling in.

"That didn't take too long, how did it go?" He cringes as though he's nervous.

"Well, good news... I didn't have to ask for time off." I force a smile.

His face turns red and a vein pops out of his forehead. "She fired you? What the fuck, Anya!" Heat radiates from the man. "I'm going to have a talk with her."

He opens the door, but I grab his arm in time to pull him back in.

"Hold your horses, Big Guy, she didn't fire me. The whole office is closed for the week due to Grant's death."

The color in his face returns to normal.

"Now, as for if I have a job *after* this week? I'm not sure. None of us know what Margaret's next move will be with the place."

Hunter runs a hand over his hair and he relaxes back into his seat. "I'm sorry, babe."

I shrug. "I can't think of that now. Did you get everything taken care of on your end?"

Please don't say you have to leave soon.

"All good, everything's wrapped up, and I'm routing any new clients to Duncan for now. I'm all yours."

He said 'for now,' that doesn't mean after. I need to remind myself that we can make a long-distance relationship work. Other couples have gotten through worse.

Technically, if we can get through something as crazy as fighting an evil entity by using mystical powers, we should be able to make what we have work no problem.

Right?

I take his hand in mine. "Good. I know I should feel sorry for making you put your life on hold for me, but I'm really not." With a playful wink, I say, "I'd rather keep you with me as long as I can." A lump forms in my throat.

Does that make me a horrible person?

Making sure I add, "But I'm sure you can't wait for life to go back to normal."

Hunter leans over and gives me a lingering kiss. Along with the rest of my body, the lump dissolves into a pile of mush.

I hum my response.

He gives my bottom lip a nibble before pulling away. "I don't want to go back to normal. There's a lot that will change in my life after this, and I won't regret it one bit." He looks hungrily at my lips. "By the way, why do you taste sweet?" He smirks. "Did you sneak some honey?"

"Ha. Ha. Ha. You are *so* hilarious," I say deadpanned. "No, I had a cupcake that Heather made me. There's more in the container." Nodding to the back seat, I add, "If you're a good boy, I *may* share one with you." I wiggle my eyebrows.

"Mmm...why do I need my own when I have you to taste?" He kisses and licks my lips, savoring the flavor.

I don't know what I'm going to do without him when he leaves again.

Chapter Thirty-Four

BERKANO

(GROWTH)

"Oomph," the air rushes out of me as I collapse on my couch and close my eyes. It was the first thing I've wanted to do since I got to work. Come home, kick back, and relax. When we walked through the door, I dropped the delicious cupcakes on the coffee table in front of my favorite spot—within arm's reach if needed. Now it's time to run through what we need to do next on our list.

Wendigo captured. Check.

Leave of absence at work. Check.

Not die. Check.

Keep Margaret away from the castle? Fuck.

Kill the wendigo? Double fuck.

"Do you want to go take a nap? You have to be exhausted," Hunter's baritone voice has me opening my eyes.

"Nope." I shake my head. "Surprisingly, I'm not tired. Mentally exhausted and drained, sure. But I don't need to sleep. I'm pretty rested."

He plops down and turns to me. "We'll be okay."

He reads me like an open book with highlighted pages—knowing exactly what's going through my mind.

"But how can you be so sure?" My voice squeaks and I clear it.

He brushes a strand of hair behind my ear. "Because, no-matter-what, we have each other."

The warmth of his words shoots like whiskey to my stomach.

A split second after the warmth overcomes me, a sourness replaces it when my mind jumps back to Margaret.

What's better to ruin the mood than bringing up another woman?

Not in a jealous sort of way, more as the wicked witch of the West coming in with her flying monkeys—murdering the whole town to get what she wants.

"What about Margaret?" My eyebrows furrow when I cringe.

He leans forward, resting his elbows on his knees and placing his head in his hands.

This isn't going to be good.

A minute, maybe two go by and he straightens, looking at the wall across from him.

"She's going to be a problem, a *big* problem. She won't give up the castle."

"Shit. I was worried that's what I heard when she was yelling at you." I rub a hand over my face. "How bad is it?"

He pulls his eyes from the blank wall then to me. "She wants to finish filing the Abandoned Property Claim Form to take over ownership of it. This means we now have to worry about her, and whoever else she invites there to check the place out. This isn't good for us."

"How are we going to handle the wendigo if there are other people at the castle? Not only that, but if the claim gets approved, we'll have more roadblocks with no detour in sight." The walls of my lungs close in and my breathing becomes labored. "Hunter, it'll get out again and we won't have any control. So many more people will be killed." My chest heaves.

I can't go through what I did last night again.

Hunter grabs my hand, rubbing his thumb over my knuckles. "We have some time. I looked up how long the Abandoned Property Claim process takes, it'll be at least sixty days before it's even considered. The government office that processes them has to do full research to ensure there are no rightful owners."

Sixty days. Two months. Can we wrap this up in that timeframe?

"Can she file a restraining order to keep us from the property?" I ask in a hushed tone.

He shrugs. "The good news is, she doesn't know *you're* involved. But if she has just cause, she can put a restraining order against us to keep away from *her*. It doesn't stop us from going to the property unless she's there."

The tension in my neck wraps its tight fists around me until pain forms in my temples. I rub my head to ease it until Hunter picks me up and lays me across his lap.

"Wha...what are you doing?" I stutter out.

"We can't deal with what lies ahead of us right now. We'll figure this out, whatever direction it goes." He kisses me on top of my head.

His arms enclose around me and the pressure around my neck and lungs eases.

After a few minutes in his comforting embrace, he tips me.

"What are you doing?" I squeak out, wrapping my arms around his neck to prevent my fall, regardless of his arm wrapped snugly around me.

I catch a strong whiff of my latest sweet addiction. That's weird, it's not like we opened the box. I snap my head to the box in front of the sofa and see the lid is off and one is missing. Slowly, I turn towards the culprit with narrowed eyes.

His eye are wide, pupils dilated, and evidence of his crime is at the corner of his mouth and in his hand.

"Hey, who said you could have one?" My mouth drops open.

A mischievous grin spreads across his face. "Me."

"And you're the boss now?"

"Always. Now if you're a good girl, I'll share," he chuckles deep in his throat and takes another bite, leaving only a small piece between his fingers.

My head snaps back. "Wait, what? *You* will share *my* cupcakes with *me*?"

He cocks his head. "Are you going to be a good girl?"

"Why would I do that? It's way more fun to be bad." I snatch his fingers, wrapping my mouth around them and the last piece of cake. My tongue laps around his fingers, licking and sucking off every last morsel of chocolate and cream from them. When I'm satisfied, I pull them out of my mouth with a pop.

"Fuck," he growls. Hunter reaches up and laces his fingers through my hair and crashes his mouth down on mine.

Heat pools to my core in a rush, the ecstasy of the sugar rush along with his urgency and every inch of his body up against mine is almost too much to handle.

The sugar always de-stressed me from my day, but does it also work as an aphrodisiac?

He pulls away.

Staring at his luscious lips has me licking mine. Needing more of this high like I need my next breath. A break away from the chaos around us. I grasp the back of his hair and pull him back down.

"Wait," he breathes out.

Now I pause, waiting for what he needs to say, playing with the tendrils of his thick hair between my fingers. "Hmm?"

"Let me take you—"

"If you shut up, I won't have any problem letting you take me," I interrupt.

He draws back and his eyes turn serious. "No. Hear me out. Before we get carried away, I have something important to ask you." He clears his throat. "You've worked hard today and deserve some time to blow off steam and let loose."

"Isn't that what we're doing now?"

Where's he going with this?

"As much as I want that, it's not the kind I'm talking about. I'm talking about going out."

He has my attention and I sit up straighter on his thighs. The thought of letting our problems go until tomorrow doesn't sit well with me. I know what we're doing now is a moment of de-stressing and just being together, appreciating each other and the little time we have before the next bombshell lands in our lap. Hunter must see my struggle when he reaches down and squeezes my hand.

"No arguing. I'm taking you out for our first date."

And my worry begins to dissolve with tingling from his words, '*first date.*'

He brings my hand to his lips and kisses my knuckles. "I know, it's a little backwards, due to our circumstances." A crease forms between his brows. "Although, I don't think any part of our relationship will ever *be* normal. What do you say? Go on a date with me?"

Hunter shows a side of him he rarely lets out—vulnerability. He tries to hide the bouncing of his left leg and biting of his cheek, but I see through him.

Why do I feel like a teenager again?

I want to scream, *YES!* But I can't stop myself from torturing him. It's a knee-jerk reaction to tease him every chance I get.

If only for a little bit.

"Well... I was really wanting to do my nails tonight. I mean, I think I chipped my polish back in the dungeon." I study my hand, fingering my nails.

His face drops for a split second before he narrows his eyes. "You don't wear nail polish."

He caught me.

"Damn, you're good."

"Care to answer my question?"

"Depends on where you're taking me."

His grin mimics a Cheshire cat. "I'll take that as a yes."

Hunter then ignores my twenty questions. I'm half tempted to say I changed my mind since I'm not big on surprises, but he knows exactly how to pique my interest.

Chapter Thirty-Five

SOWILO

(OVERWHELMED)

It was nice to kick our feet up and relax a bit, chilling on the couch eating cupcakes, and researching Historic Designation requirements and file processes. After a couple hours, we fell asleep. Hunter's arms were wrapped around me tightly as we spooned. He told me he refused to go to sleep with a chance of waking and me not being by his side. It kills me that I put that fear in him, that I dragged him through the heartache and worry. Even with the outcome we had with capturing the wendigo, I'll never do that to him again.

Now I'm up, I'm showered, and I'm fully refreshed.

Okay, maybe it's being thoroughly ravished that gives me this refreshing feeling.

I'm not ashamed of having a second shower in a day. It's becoming my new favorite thing with Hunter. Plus, I still felt the need to get any lingering wendigo scent off me. I swear it has embedded itself into my sinuses.

And who am I to argue when the man suggests a nice relaxing massage under the shower's hot sprays, claiming it would make me feel like a new woman.

And boy, was he right.

My body heats at the memory of one of Hunter's rough hands spread across my stomach and the other grasping my breast while he took me from behind.

I glance down at my blouse to make sure my taut nipples aren't showing, then smooth out my top.

Hunter asked me out on our first date, so I decided to put in a little effort tonight. Paired with my wine-colored blouse, are my black skinny jeans and boots. My makeup is applied lightly, and I leave my hair down after blow drying it. He's pretty much seen me at my worst, it's only fair to give him a break from *that* horror.

I stand up from slipping my dagger in my boot and my jaw drops. I not-so-discreetly swallow hard to prevent from drooling. Hunter stands in my bathroom door.

Drop. Dead. Gorgeous.

From the ground up, he's in his usual dark boots and jeans. But tucked into those jeans is a crisp black button-down dress shirt with the sleeves rolled up, showing off his muscular forearms.

I clench my thighs at the sight. Who knew one simple body part would make a girl weak in the knees.

My gaze travels up his thick shoulders to a freshly trimmed beard and perfectly gelled hair. He's the most handsome man I've *ever* laid eyes on.

"You look stunning, Anya," his voice is low and his eyes burn into me with intensity.

Heat floods my face and neck.

Would I look weird if I fanned myself?

"Back atcha, Big Guy," my words come out breathy, and I shift on my feet.

We can't stay here or it won't end well. Actually...it would end amazingly, but we desperately need this night out. Grabbing his forearm, I drag him outside. "We need to leave, *now.*"

Before I drag him to the bedroom like a cavewoman.

I'm quite proud of my self-control, even as the itch inside me builds up. An itch that only Hunter's body can relieve. Here's hoping our date will help me ignore the heated tension.

Hunter drives us to The Staggering Coyote, a local dive bar. It's known to have great music, lots of dancing, and the most delicious food. The last time I was there was a few months ago. The girls and I went out for a night on the town—well, the *only* kind of night out in Shandaken.

Walking hand-in-hand into the bar feels natural. Hunter's firm grasp sends flutters to my stomach as he directs us to a small table in the corner.

He pulls out my bar stool before he sits down across from me. His full smile, dimples and all, shining like a beacon—for me.

We stay silent, basking in each other while the world around us carries on.

"What can I get for *you,* sugar?" A fake southern accent interrupts our moment.

A waitress is leaning her elbows on the table, pushing her cleavage in Hunter's direction. She only has eyes for him. "I'm off at midnight, if there's something you want that *isn't* on the menu."

I roll my eyes.

Oh please! Can she be more lame and desperate? I doubt that line ever works.

On second thought, I take that back. I'm sure there are plenty of horny men who don't hesitate to take her home for a quick romp—probably leaving her unsatisfied.

Trying to hide my smirk, I turn to Hunter to see his reaction. He must have been staring at me this whole time since he doesn't seem phased by the woman.

He reaches his hand over to mine and laces our fingers together. "I'll take whatever you have on tap, and my girlfriend here will have a glass of red wine, *please.*"

Her gaze lands on me, and her eyes briefly widen before she hides her surprise. She acts like she didn't even see me sitting here.

She stands there for another moment, her mouth agape, looking between us before she huffs and walks away.

Wow, she's something else.

I watch her storm off in what looks to be an adult temper tantrum.

Yup, too many unsatisfying romps.

"You here to see me or the annoying waitress?" Hunter's amused tone has me pulling my attention back to him.

"I don't think I've ever seen an adult act that way. Kids, for sure, when they don't get their way, but a grown woman? I didn't think that stuff happened in real life."

He chuckles.

My mind jumps back to him calling me his girlfriend. "Were you serious?"

His brows furrow. "Serious about what?"

"We never really discussed what *we* are. Were you serious when you called me your girlfriend? Is that what you want?" I chew on my bottom lip.

He shrugs and gives me a mischievous smile. "What do *you* want?"

He's not making things easy for me. What an ass.

I roll my eyes, "Oh, just stop. Tell me what you want between us. I know we love each other." Pulling my hand out of his grasp, I rub my sweaty palms on my pants. "But... I also know you travel a lot, so I understand if you think we're better off as a fling; or friends with benefits. I'll be honest, I don't want it to be short term, but I'll take whatever I can get." I lean forward. "Tell me straight, what is *this*"—I gesture between us with my finger— "to you, and what do you want out of it?" There's no stopping my leg from bouncing, but I hope he doesn't notice.

Hunter stands up and my heart sinks.

Is he going to leave? Did I push him too far?

He grabs his stool, slides it next to mine, and sits.

Okay, he's definitely not leaving.

He braces his legs on either side of me, before he pulls me close and growls. "When I told you that you're stuck with me, I meant it. You can't get rid of me, *unless* you tell me right now that you don't want me in your life." He rubs a hand over his beard then drops it to my thigh. "Although... I pray that isn't the case, 'cause, Anya? I'm in this for the long haul." His face moves closer to mine, his hot breath teasing my lips with every word he says. "I want to spend the rest of my life with you. If we weren't separated as kids, I would've pursued dating you when we were old enough. Which I'm sure wouldn't have taken too much longer."

Tears fill my eyes, and I chuckle to mask my emotions. "Ha, you sure about that? I don't think you would've had the guts to share those types of feelings with me back then."

He sits back a bit on his stool. "Hey, give me a *little* credit, I would have...in time." His hand rubs my thigh, creeping slowly up towards my hip. "I never want to be separated from you again. I hope that one day we'll be married and later, have kids. If I recall, you wanted two? If you don't, I'll be fine without. I just can't lose you."

I choke down the lump in my throat.

His body drifts closer to mine, and I can't stop the overwhelming feelings of shock and unconditional love.

This is something I've never felt before. The palpitations in my chest play like a drum solo at a rock concert. All the attention is on the pounding as my erratic heartbeat is craving a standing ovation.

If the wendigo doesn't kill me first, Hunter's words will surely give me a heart attack.

When he leans in as if to kiss my cheek, his lips graze my skin and make their way to my ear where he whispers deeply, "Right now, I see you as my girlfriend and, one day, I hope to call you my wife."

Goosebumps pepper my flesh at his words.

"Your grandmother called us soulmates. Your parents describe us as being twin flames. But you, Anya, are *my everything*." He sucks on my earlobe, sending a strong current down my neck, electrifying every inch of my skin and creating sparks in my core. "Now tell me...what do *you* want?"

"I want...I want..." I stutter but struggle to find the words. The levee in my eyes threatens to break and my throat tightens, risking a hysterical sob from escaping.

I'm far from an emotional person, but Hunter brings out a whole other side of me.

Instead of talking, I use my actions to answer him. Moving back slightly, I cradle his face in my hands and kiss him with every last breath in me. I pour my love and energy into the kiss so there is no mistake about what I want.

Remembering we are in public, I gently pull away and rest my forehead on his. "I want you. I want it all." My words come out broken, the flood breaks through and the rivers stream down my face.

I take a deep breath to calm myself a bit before I begin again. "I want you to be mine. My boyfriend, my best friend, my partner, and hopefully one day, my husband and the father of our children." I sniffle. "I love you so *damn* much."

Hunter kisses where the tears navigate down my face. We go in for one more lip lock—

"Ehem," a clearing of a throat interrupts us.

I drop my hands to swipe the remaining wetness from my eyes.

Our waitress has returned and when she sets down our drinks roughly, she spills a good amount of Hunter's beer. "Anything else?" she asks in a snippy tone.

Hunter looks annoyed by her behavior. "I'll take a replacement beer to start." He narrows his eyes and nods to the half empty glass. "Then we'll have the appetizer sampler, medium hot wings, and barbeque pulled pork."

I was about to tease him for ordering for me, but the look in his eyes stops me.

They leave no room for any misconceptions of what he wants from this girl. He lowers his voice. "And you better straighten out your attitude when you return, or you're better off sending someone else to our table next time."

I did *not* see that coming. It's fascinating to watch him quickly go from the uncertain, sweet man back to the confident and slightly *scary* man I met a few days ago.

Her eyes widen in fear and she nods. "Yes sir, I'm sorry," she says with a lack of accent, before rushing off.

I hope she doesn't spit in our food.

The burst of laughter breaks from my chest when she's far enough away. "Oh my gosh, Hunter, you scared the southern drawl from her." I hold my stomach and howl which has Hunter losing his stern composure.

"It wasn't hard. I've been around plenty of true southerners, I know they'd only see her as an insult." He chuckles.

"That's for sure." Wiping away the new tears from amusement, I take a few deep breaths to relax.

Hunter places a hand on my waist. "So...how about a dance?"

Shocked, I say, "Wait, you had two left feet as a kid. You're saying you can dance now? I'm starting to wonder if you're an imposter."

My heart goes heavy thinking about who his dance partners have been.

"By all means, I'm *not* a professional, but my mom taught me back in high school. She said if I ever want to keep a girlfriend, I need to learn how to dance without stomping on them with my big feet. I was determined to be good at it." He stands and shoves his stool away. "Now, come on, let me teach you a few moves."

"Hahaha...you assume that I can't dance." I cock an eyebrow.

"As *graceful* as you are? I'm not sure you can." He leans down and whispers, "But for the safety of our fellow dancers here, I'll give you a hand. I would hate for you to cause undue harm to anyone."

I scoff and lean my head away from his warm and inviting lips. "You're just asking for it, aren't you? You're lucky there are others around, or I may carry out my threat of burning off your clothes." I narrow my eyes at him.

"I highly doubt you could accomplish that without burning me as well."

"Practice makes perfect, right?" I flash an evil smirk.

His Adam's apple moves when he swallows hard. "Uhh...well..." he stutters. He has no comeback.

Point one for Anya.

I take a sip of my wine before hopping off my seat and dragging Hunter to the dance floor. My jaw drops as I see him move perfectly—smooth and in cadence with the beat. He sees my reaction and laughs, pulling me close.

"You might want to close your mouth or you'll catch some flies."

I stiffen. "Oh hush. I'm still debating if you're a body snatcher. You stole my Hunter and replaced him with…" I lean back and look up at him.

His eyes are crinkled. "With who, babe? An intelligent, strikingly handsome, and talented man?" He gives me a cheesy smile that reminds me of Flynn Rider.

"I was going to say an alien," I deadpan. "Whoever told you that you were those other things, I'm sorry. They lied to you." I suck in my lips to hold back my smile.

"What if I said my mother told me. A mother would never lie to her child."

I pat him on the cheek. "You have so much to learn, Hunter. So much to learn."

"Shut up and dance." He pulls me in, then spins me out as we dance and laugh.

After two songs, we head back to the table where our appetizers are waiting for us—no waitress in sight. With a thorough investigation of our food, I deem it's safe for consumption with Hunter's agreement. We eat without saying much because we're both famished after the day we had.

Right before we finish our last bites, another waitress brings our meals.

"Hi, my name is Nicole. I will be your server for the rest of the evening. Can I get either one of you anything else?" she asks kindly.

"I'm okay, thanks. Anya?" Hunter checks with me.

"Hi Nicole, I'll take another wine, please."

"Great, coming right up!" She smiles, taking the now empty tray of appetizers and strolls away.

"Thanks!" I call after her, relieved we no longer have to deal with the southern fake anymore.

Hunter and I small-talk between bites, enjoying this new point in our relationship. It's as though we've been going on dates for years.

Pushing my plate to the side, I lean my elbows on the table. "Man, I think I'm going to pop a button on my pants. I'm stuffed!"

Hunter chuckles. "You and me both, sweetheart, that was definitely filling."

I watch as he takes a swig of his beer. A droplet lingers on his lip, and I'm tempted to lick it off. Right when I lean over a bit, the music changes to a slow song and Hunter stands. Without asking, he pulls me back to the dance floor.

Where he gets this energy, I have no clue, but I'll take any chance I can to get close to him. I'm thankful this isn't a fast melody, or I'd be ready to explode from our meal.

Hunter holds me close with my cheek laying on his chest, and we slow dance to a song about finding love in unexpected places.

As Hunter sways me back and forth, I get lost in him.

When the song ends, his phone rings. He pulls it out of his pocket and says, "It's Duncan. You okay if I take this real quick?"

"Of course. I'm going to run to the restroom. You may have better reception outside. I'll meet you at the table when you get back."

He gives me a quick kiss and walks towards the front door. "Hey Dunc, what's going on?"

After I not-so-creepily watch him depart, I turn to head to the bathroom and—"Oomph." I hit a squishy wall. "Oh, I'm sorry, I need to pay better attention to my surroundings."

Before I look up, the man's hands go around my biceps. I'm a little surprised about the physical contact and try to step back, but I'm held in place—firmly. I wasn't about to fall, so at this point, the man isn't holding onto me for my safety.

"Hey there beautiful, where you going?"

The oily voice sends a chill down my spine and I freeze—my heart dropping to the floor.

I know that voice.

Chapter Thirty-Six

ANSUZ

(HEALING)

It shouldn't come as a surprise that I'd run into him one day. It was bound to happen in our small town, especially with this being the only bar. To be honest, it's a little surprising I went this long without seeing the asshat.

Kyle.

My possessive and controlling ex-boyfriend.

I look into his piercing, blue eyes and swallow down my fear.

"Oh, hi. Hope you're doing well...if you'll excuse me." I attempt to break free from his grasp, but his grip tightens. His fingers bite into my skin, and I try my best not to flinch.

He likes it when I show weakness and pain.

"Ah, you here alone? Where's your usual guard dog?" His lips curl in a sneer. "I don't see your friends here. That must mean you came to see me. Took you long enough to come to your senses," he snarls in my face

His breath smells of stale beer mixed with tequila. I can't help but wrinkle my nose. Most would say that when they run into an ex, they still have an inkling of feelings for them deep down.

With Kyle? The naive veil dropped a couple weeks into the relationship and revealed the ugly monster hiding underneath.

But by the time I opened my eyes, it was too late.

"I'm not alone, my boyfriend is here with me. If you can please let me go, I'll leave you alone. I'm sorry for bumping into you." I twist my arm to break free, but all it does is create an abrasive burning along my skin.

I try to replace my panic with anger. "Kyle, I am going to ask you one more time to *let me go*. Now!" My only source of self-defense at this point is my power. I have to be smart about it, though, with so many people around.

He uses his free hand to clench my hip, pulling me closer. I turn my head away in disgust.

"You always did love playing hard to get. That's what I enjoyed the most. The chase." He sniffs my hair. "Now that your bitch isn't here, there's no reason to make an excuse that you don't want to see me."

I clench my fists, trying to keep my cool over his hatred for Heather.

He pulls me closer to him; I struggle to get away. "You know what your fighting back does to me."

My skin crawls and every muscle in my body freezes, I clench my jaw. "Kyle, let GO!"

"She said let her the fuck go!" Hunter's growl from behind me fills the air.

Part of me is relieved, but the other part is worried about how bad this is about to escalate. I don't need them to make a scene.

"Who the fuck do you think you are? Go get your own *whore*, I already have dibs on this one." Spittle flies out of Kyle's mouth in his rage.

Curious gazes turn our direction.

There goes any hope of not causing a scene. It exited right out the front door, leaving me in the eye of the storm.

"Anya's mine," Hunter growls as he moves to my side. "Call her a whore again and I'll fucking tear your spine out with my bare hands and shove it so far up your ass, it'll impale your skull." His eyes blaze and his voice is dangerously calm.

Oh shit.

And Hunter thought *Heather* was evil.

Before they can beat the crap out of each other, or Hunter makes good on his promise, I take this moment to jump into action.

"Go fuck yourself—Son-of-a-bitch!" Kyle releases my scorching hot arm right as Hunter's fist connects with his nose—creating a sickening crunch on contact.

Blood begins to pour from his nose which has Kyle cursing more. He almost drops to his knees in pain when he tries to hold it with the hand that's red and blistering.

I had released just enough heat to get him off me, but not enough to draw unwanted attention to my powers. I didn't know I burned him *that* bad.

Kyle stumbles a few feet then high-tails it out the door, plowing through people along his way.

"Babe, are you okay? Did he hurt you?" Hunter spins me around and studies my body, stopping when his eyes land on my arm. There's a dark, reddish-purple handprint where Kyle had me. "What the fuck! I'm gonna kill the bastard."

Hunter turns towards the front door, but I pull him back before he can take another step.

"Hey, it's over, and I'm okay."

"Like hell you are."

"Excuse me, sir." The manager, a man in his mid-fifties stops in front of us.

"Yes?" Hunter asks, not at all happy.

"I'm not sure who started it, but we don't want any kind of trouble here. I'm going to have to ask you to leave."

Hunter stiffens. "Let me get this straight. You'd rather have an asshole like that in here, abusing women"—He angles my arm into the manager's line of sight—"than someone who has no issue in keeping scum like that out of here? You know what, I don't think this is the type of establishment I want to frequent."

I bury my face into Hunter's shoulder to hide from the large number of onlookers we've drawn in.

The manager's face goes red and he stares at the angry marks on my arm. "I'm so sorry, I wasn't aware. Do you want me to call someone to file a report?"

Hunter pulls my face out from hiding and raises an eyebrow in question.

I shake my head. I just want this to be over with. I'm more upset that our night has come to an end because of Kyle than having my arm bruised.

Hunter meets the manager's slightly panicked look and says, "No, if we can get the check, we'll be out of your hair."

The older man holds his hand up. "Please. Let us comp your meal for the inconvenience. We pride ourselves on being a safe environment. Stay. Enjoy the rest of your night."

Hunter looks to me to make the call.

"I'd rather not leave just yet," I say softly.

"We'll stay, but no need to take care of our bill. Thank you though."

The poor man's shoulders drop, and he lets out a relieved breath. "If you change your mind, *please*, let me know. We'd be happy to do whatever we can to make your night enjoyable."

"Will do. Thanks." Hunter responds with a nod.

The manager gives me a tight, awkward smile and walks away. The crowd's attention also turns from us when they realize that the show is over.

Thank goodness.

"Are you sure you want to stay?" Hunter's brows furrow.

Does he have to act like I'm some damsel in distress?

"Yup." I narrow my eyes and place a hand on my hip.

"Are you sure? Because I am getting a whole different vibe from you."

"I'm not some weak, pathetic woman who needs you to avenge me, you know. I appreciate you standing up for me, but I was handling it fine until you punched him."

He raises his hand. "Hey, I never said you were weak or pathetic—"

"You're bleeding." I cut him off and survey his knuckles.

He shakes me off. "The sooner you realize your battles are my battles, the sooner we can get past this."

"Mmhmm..." I mumble, half agreeing with him. My gaze drifts to his swelling hand.

"I'm fine, Anya." He flexes his fist. "See? Nothing broken, only a little scratch. I've had worse. Who was that guy?"

I groan. "Come on, Big Guy, stop trying to be tough and let me fix you up." Grabbing his uninjured hand, I pull him in the direction of the bathrooms.

"Honey Bear," he drags out. "I told you, I'm alright."

He thinks using that name will make me listen? Pfft. He thought wrong.

In silence, I drag his giant ass down the hallway until we're behind the closed door of the women's restroom.

"I—"

"Hang on," I interrupt, and put my hand up to shush him.

The room muffles the music and loud talking from the bar, but I walk by the stalls, checking for feet to make sure we are alone and without listening ears. I lock the door and turn around.

Hunter runs a hand over his beard and flashes a dimple with his sexy smirk. "Well, this isn't the *ideal* place, Anya. But if you're really worked up for a quickie, you won't hear any complaints from me."

"Nice attempt at deflecting, but I'm fixing your hand. Now hold still and be quiet."

He opens his mouth, and my eyes shoot daggers at him. He stands straighter and promptly closes it.

I place his injured hand between both of mine and close my eyes. Tapping into my green healing energy, I channel part of it from the ground and the other from inside me. It travels through my body until it flows into my arms and out of my palms, soaking into Hunter's.

He inhales in a hiss, and I continue my work. Watching the light—behind my closed lids—travel into his cuts, they sew together and suck the fluid from the swelling back into his body.

Once I see in my mind that the healing is complete, I open my eyes to check out my work.

"Perfect." My fingers brush over the once red and torn up skin. I look up at Hunter as I give the now-healed skin a soft kiss. His eyes search mine and his lips are parted.

"Damn Anya, that was... I can't even describe the feeling. It was..." He runs a hand through his hair. "Something else," he stutters out. Clearly stunned, he flips his hand around to study it. "Huh. Well, at least we know you heal scars too."

My smile drops, and my brows narrow.

"What do you mean, I heal scars?" Confusion overwhelms me. I only healed what I wanted to heal, his injury.

"I had a scar over the knuckle of my thumb from where the slide of a gun took a chunk out of it." He points to the perfect skin with his finger then flips his hand, tracing an invisible line in his palm. "And here, I had a knife go straight through to the other side." He turns his hand over again. "Do you see anything?"

I feel around and, other than the roughness of his fingers, there is not a scar in sight.

Interesting...

"Well, I hope you won't miss those. Sorry your hands are now unscathed." I bring it up to my cheek, nuzzling it. "They're like baby hands now. What will the guys say when you tell them about your *tough* war wounds, but have no proof to show?" I fake a sad pout. "Too bad you no longer look like a badass, Hunter. I'm sure it was good while it lasted, huh?" My acting skills are poor when I attempt sympathy and hide my laughter.

"Well thanks for *that*. Maybe I should have you do the other one, so it matches. Can't go around with only one perfect hand, now can I?" He studies it and huffs. "The girls will *never* fall for my charm now. They love the bad-boy image. I'm forever ruined for all future women."

I roll my eyes at his melodramatic statement, while he enjoys my moment of jealousy.

"You know? In that case...let me see your other hand."

He quickly snatches it away, and before I know it, I'm pushed up against the wall with a thump. His lips come crashing into mine with such heat. I give in for only a split second before I take control of my emotions and pull away.

For once, I need to be the sane one. I grumble, "Now's *not* the time, Hunter. And it's definitely not a turn-on to have sex in a dirty, bar restroom—at least not *this* one." I survey the grime on the floor and sink. "Save it for home." I give him a kiss then shove him away.

"Alright, but you owe me after taking away my manly scars. My pride is pretty damaged right now, so you'll need to kiss it and make it better," he says, as a grin slowly stretches across his face, suggesting exactly where his pride is located.

"Uh huh, whatever you say, Big Guy." I shake my head and give him a pat on the chest then walk to the door.

He grabs me around my torso to pull me back to him, flush against his hard chest this time. With one finger, he tilts my head to the side and brushes the hair from my neck. His lips touch my shoulder, kissing and moving their way up to the sensitive spot below my ear. The sensation makes my knees weak and I'm thankful he's holding me up.

"Mmm..."

"I thought you said the restroom wasn't a turn-on for you, babe. I'm not sure I quite believe you," he drops his voice into that deep vibration he knows I love.

"You play dirty, Hunter." And I need to get us out of here to avoid caving to Hunter. Turning out of his arms, I unlock the bathroom door.

A woman stumbles right into me, almost knocking me over if it wasn't for Hunter steadying me. She giggles as she rights herself then looks me and Hunter over. "Well, looks like at least *someone* is getting some action tonight. Lucky bitch." She continues to laugh as she enters a stall. The door slamming closed.

I take a quick glance at Hunter and his awkward expression is mirroring mine. We start to crack up and walk back to our table.

By the time we sit down, my cheeks ache from laughing so hard.

Nicole, our server, meets us with my wine in her hand. Perfect timing since I need a drink.

"You are *amazing*, thank you," I tell her and she smiles and nods before moving to the next table.

Once we're situated, with Hunter back to sitting by my side, he asks, "You going to tell me who that guy was?"

Ugh, it's the dreaded question I've tried to avoid since the first time he asked.

"A mistake."

"Yeah, I figured that part out already. I hate to guess, but was that an ex?" He doesn't act upset or jealous which I guess is a bit of a surprise to me. Even with how everything went down, most guys still act jealous when it's someone from your past.

I take a big gulp of my wine, letting the sweet yet peppery liquid hit my taste buds before sliding down my throat, relaxing my muscles.

I might as well get this over with. Like he said before, our pasts are what makes us who we are today.

Clearing my throat, I say, "That was Kyle. As you can tell from how he was treating me, that relationship didn't last long. He didn't take it well. I can almost guarantee Heather is the reason he finally backed off after I left him."

He chuckles. "Why am I not surprised? I could tell the first time I met her that she isn't someone I want to piss off." His hand rubs the back of his neck. "I've been through a lot of scary shit, but there's something about that little pixie that scares the hell out of me."

"Haha...you aren't the first to say that."

"I'm sure she would go straight for the jugular with a smile on her face." Hunter cringes like he is imagining it in vivid detail.

"You know her so well, already. I'm a lucky girl to have her on my team. She can come up with some *pretty* graphic and gruesome threats."

He eyes me cautiously which may be because I'm sitting there with a huge grin on my face.

"Is there a dark side of you that I need to know about?"

I place my hand on his leg and lean into his ear with a whisper, "Where there's light, there's darkness." I draw back to see his terrified reaction. The laughter in me comes out in a guffaw at his huge eyes. "I'm messing with you. I leave that dark shit to Heather."

"One of these times, that mouth is going to get you into trouble." He pokes me in the side.

"Then I'll keep it only on you." I say with sass. But the moment the words leave my mouth, I realize how it sounds.

Without missing a beat, Hunter leans in. "That better be a promise, because I have plans for that mouth, and those plans don't involve anyone else."

I expected some sort of smug comment, just not something that would set my body on fire like the heat wave he threw at me.

Time to cool off. With a couple of big gulps, I finish the rest of my wine and look around to find our waitress.

"Do you need another beer?" I ask, trying not to look at the one he's been nursing for a while.

"Enough avoidance. Did he hit you?" Hunter narrows his eyes at the door, as if anticipating Kyle coming back in.

"No, he just grabbed my arm."

"I meant when you were together. He seems like the type to enjoy hitting women for control."

I really don't have any other escape here. We can talk about my monster of an ex, or we can make ourselves uncomfortable from the mixture of all this chemistry and heat between us. I am not a fan of either one at this moment, but I need to put Kyle behind us. It's not fair to Hunter for not know about this part of my past. Even with how brief it was.

"He didn't hit me out of anger..." *How do I say this?* "He was charming at first, and we got along in the beginning. But then he started getting rough with me."

"Rough, *how?*" Hunter's attention is no longer on the entrance, but solely on me.

No pressure.

I lower my voice for the next part, "He began to manhandle me. Grabbing my arm like he did tonight and yanking me wherever he wanted. Most of the time, it was on his lap. At first, I flinched in pain and told him to stop. He acted sorry but the way his eyes would darken, something didn't sit right with me."

"How bad did it get?" he growls.

"I never felt a huge connection with anyone before—outside of you—so, I chalked it up to me not being able to commit. But things progressed. He became rougher in bed, and I would tell him to knock it off, it hurt. He would apologize, buy me flowers. But a few days later, he would turn it up a notch. He would get...*hard* each time he inflicted pain on me."

Hunter ran a hand over his face, looking distraught.

"I don't need to continue. That's the gist of everything."

"No, I need to hear this. All of it. *Please,*" his voice is low and controlled.

Too controlled, which has me on edge. This is the side of him that is deadly and dangerous. A side I've not seen before tonight.

I blink rapidly and take a few breaths. An uneasy sensation settles over me, fearing how he might react.

Will he blow up and storm out the door in search of Kyle? Or will he pull away from me, thinking I'm a damaged woman?

He deserves to know. "It finally came down to one night when he was being a jealous asshole over me walking out of the office with James."

"Wait, James, your security guard? The older guy?"

"The one and the same. Kyle didn't like me talking to other guys. He became possessive. When I told him James was a friend and a dad-like figure in my life…" My heart rate picks up and my palms are sweaty from the memory. "That's when he held me by the neck and kept tightening his grasp. Saying he needed to 'break me in' to make sure I knew who exactly I belonged to. The more he squeezed, the more turned on he got and the less I could breathe. He was rubbing against me telling me the pain makes everything feel so much better. I tried to fight, but my body was weak and everything was fading around me. I think my passing out was more of a turn-off because I woke up and he was gone."

At this point, the vein on the right side of Hunter's forehead is throbbing, and his face is beet red. I hadn't noticed that his hand was no longer on my leg but on the table, balled up in a fist. There's no doubt if he were holding a bottle, it'd shatter in his grip.

Gah, I hate putting him through this, but he begged to know it all. It kills me to see him this upset. Especially with it all being in the past.

I place both of my hands over his and close my eyes, focusing on the energy coming off Hunter. His aura is running hot with murky, red energy intertwined with black tendrils. I tap into my own aura, the rainbow of colors surrounding me, and I envelop Hunter with them. Mixing them with his until his blue begins to peek out from underneath.

Ah, there you are.

I take a small bit of my power, and I send a calming current into him before I let go.

My eyes open and Hunter's labored breathing is now smooth and relaxed. His hands are unclenched and he stares at them.

"You know, I'd rather be mad. You didn't have to do that." Disappointment laces his voice.

"I did, it's not good for you. The past with Kyle, it's over. After Heather helped me out of that situation…somehow, I was able to put it behind me and move on. I need *you* to put it behind you. I didn't agree to tell you this, for you to lose it. I also don't want you looking at me differently." With my finger, I tilt his chin up like he's done to me. "Like you said, our past shapes us, it makes us who we are. That history brought me to this very moment where I was able to give him second-degree burns. Maybe he won't touch another woman the same again." I smirk and shrug.

"Babe, you don't know how bad I want to fucking tear his balls off and shove them down his throat right now."

"Now you sound like Heather."

"I'm having a very difficult time letting this go. I know you can take care of yourself a hell of a lot easier now than you could before, but please don't expect me to just brush these feelings off. I love you too damn much. I can't promise if I see him again that I won't hurt him." He cups my cheek, staring intently into my eyes. "I will do *anything* to protect you." His head moves closer and his lips gently caress mine.

They are soft, with so much love behind them. His lips linger over mine for a moment before he takes a deep breath and sits back.

"Anything," he promises with a whisper.

A saccharine smile spreads across my lips. "If he tries anything ever again, would it make you feel better if I set his dick and balls on fire? I know it would make *me* feel better."

He chokes before he clears his throat. After taking a sip of his beer, he says, "Shit. And here I was afraid of Heather. I'm not sure if she's a bad influence on you or if it's the other way around. Remind me not to piss you off. I would have settled for the balls, but fuck, you're vicious. I may even feel bad for the guy."

I shrug. "Well...if I'm burning it, it would only be fair to give him a matching set. You should know by now, when I do something, I go all in. I don't half-ass shit."

"Damn, woman, I love you."

"And I love you. Now, I gave you what you wanted. You need to give me what I want." I cock an eyebrow.

"I like where you are going with this."

"How about I whoop your ass at darts? What do you say, Big Guy? You up to having your manly pride crushed farther?" I stand up, give him a smirk before walking towards the back of the bar where the dart boards are. I don't look back to see if he is following.

I know he is.

After three *very* close games of darts, I was able to beat Hunter. Since he's a competitive man—and one who apparently can't handle losing—he insisted on playing a game of pool next. He claimed it was unfair to stick with one game that I had more practice at.

I had no complaints. He didn't need to know that what consisted of a girl's night wasn't just food and drinks. It was playing competitive bar games with Heather and Danielle.

I like to humor him.

But to say the game was close would be a huge understatement. Hunter handed my ass to me on a silver platter. And he didn't win fairly, either.

That man plays dirty.

When it was his turn, I was nice and let him play. When it was *my* turn, he would walk by and run his fingers softly over my ass, or he'd turn on his stealth mode and right when I'd shoot, he'd lean over and kiss my neck—making me weak in the knees. He also thought handing over the pool stick should be a *hands-on* event. Which meant he'd pull me flush against him and kiss me thoroughly, or graze my stomach with his fingers, touching right at my beltline—driving me up a wall.

The man kept me dazed and aroused the entire length of the game.

I don't even need to try to recall the way he balanced himself on the side of the table, crossing his arms. His chest and forearms never looked so good as they did in the black buttoned dress shirt. The image is burned into my mind.

That wasn't an accident either. He knew exactly what he was doing. The proof was the cocky grin on his face, flashing those two mischievous dimples.

He was killing me.

Outside of the cheating, Hunter was the perfect date. Attentive and charming the whole night. Any stranger would think he was only trying to impress me, but his manners haven't changed since we were kids.

This is Hunter.

My Hunter.

His reminder of how we were together, and how we could be, gave me hope for the future.

And it was a refreshing break from the darkness waiting for us.

Hunter pushes the front door of my house shut and slams me up against it. His eyes study my face for a moment before his mouth crashes into mine with a determination to claim me. To make me his.

It's passionate, yet loving.

Even with how fast and rough he's being, this is different from the cruel possessiveness I'd experienced with Kyle.

Everything is different with Hunter.

My hand moves to run my fingers through his hair, pulling him closer to me. Our tongues massaging each other between nibbles. It could be the lack of oxygen during our make out session, but I'm pretty sure my head is swimming from the mixture of Hunter and alcohol.

"Mmm..." I moan when he pulls my leg over his hip, causing me to grind against him.

"Fuck, babe. I can feel your heat through your clothes."

I rest against the door and ride him while unbuttoning his shirt, my hands splaying across his skin as I slide it over his shoulders. Gliding my hands through the hair on his chest then over the smooth skin covering his hard muscles. I could run my hands over him all night.

He releases my leg to drop his shirt. The cords in his neck and biceps flex briefly before he brings his hands back, pulling my leg higher up, opening me farther to him.

Running my hands down his stomach, goosebumps spread across his body, and I smile.

It's hard to imagine I'm the reason for his reaction.

"What's that look about?" Hunter brings me in closer and stares at my lips.

"Just admiring my next tasty treat."

"Your treat? What—Ow!"

I lick his pectoral muscle where I couldn't help but bite, then kiss it.

Mmm...he tastes salty, like a salty, caramel cupcake.

My mouth trails kisses across his shoulders and up his neck where I leave my own mark. I highly doubt he realizes what I'm doing.

He'll end up finding it in the morning, and I'm sure he'll give me crap for it.

I'm looking forward to it.

A mix between a growl and chuckle rumbles from his chest. "Maybe I should be worried about the Honey Bear after all."

The vibration rattles down my body and lands where I crave more friction.

I need him, now.

My hands fumble with his belt and jeans while his work on mine. I begin to drop to my knees, but Hunter's hands go under my arms and lifts me back up.

"No, you had your fun. Now it's my turn."

"That's not fair, that really wasn't anything—" He drops to his knees, and his mouth lands above my pubic bone, pulling the air from my lungs. My skin tingles, and I throw my head back.

Before I know it, cool air hits my lower half as my undies and pants rest over my boots. His lips pepper a trail down the inside of my hip.

"Ungh..."

Right when he's about to meet my center, he stops. My eyes fly open as he stands back up.

"I wasn't complaining, why did you stop?" I try my best not to whine out my disappointment.

"You're burning up, we need to take care of that. He slides a finger over my chest, stopping at my collarbone where he drags ever so softly across my skin. His other finger moves up to my other shoulder, then a loud rip fills the air.

"Ahh...I loved that top!"

"You'll get over it."

What an asshole.

His signature sexy smirk has my nipples responding to him and not to the sudden death of one of my favorite blouses. He doesn't miss the reaction through my black, lace bra.

As much as I want to argue and demand he buy me new clothes, I need this man so much more.

Who knew there'd come a day when I wanted a guy more than new clothes?

I reach for the waist of his jeans, but he moves away.

"What the hell, Hunter?"

"I'm not done with you."

"Will you hurry already? I'm about to combust where I stand, and I'm sure I'll take the house down with me."

"Patience, love." He drops to his knees again, this time slipping one boot off and moving to the other. One hand pulls out my dagger while the other one slides off the boot and tosses it to the side.

"It will be fine on the table there." I point to the side table next to us.

He doesn't move to discard it, but raises to his feet with the blade firmly in his hand.

A hiss escapes me and my stomach tightens as the cold metal touches right above my belly button.

I'm not scared, but I'm curious what he's planning.

He drags it up, sending chills and electricity down to my toes. He stops when he gets to the bottom of my bra.

Lord, have mercy. I'll never think of my dagger the same after this.

I watch him and, with a quick flip of his wrist, he slices my bra in two with the edge of my dagger.

I gasp. "You...owe...me..." I struggle to make out the words because he's now circling my nipple with the tip.

A slight sting of the cold blade is driving me insane. I shift slightly to relieve the ache between my legs. "Hunter, please."

He replaces the dagger with his lips, kissing and sucking one nipple then the other.

The sound of metal on the wooden table has me wiggling out of the remainder of my jeans.

"I wasn't done." He demands.

"Too bad. You're slow, old man." The destroyed bra is in my way, so I slide it off my shoulders and get to work on Hunter's pants.

Pulling them off, along with his boxer briefs and boots, I am face to face with a bobbing erection.

"Anya..." he warns.

I stare up into his dark brown eyes and lick my lips.

"Don't do it, I won't last." His legs tremble.

Is that excitement?

There is no stopping the evil grin that cracks my lips.

With both hands, I grasp his hips and pull him to me. I run my tongue along the vein on his length, swirling around the tip before I take him all the way into my mouth.

"*Fuck.*" He slaps a hand on the wall to steady himself.

His hips flex and move with my motions until he roars, pulling out of my mouth.

I'm being lifted into the air and directly onto his wet cock. I sink down hard and fast, crying out in pleasure.

He wraps my legs around his hips, and when I secure them behind his back, he grabs my ass tightly. "Damn, I knew you'd be perfect for me, but never once imagined together we'd be *this* perfect. It's like your body was made for me and only me."

He's right, no one else would be a better fit. The fullness of him fills me both physically and emotionally. Two flames merging into one blaze, joining as though we were never apart.

We are whole.

Our mouths meet again in a heated passion, fighting to take everything we can. One of his hands laces around the back of my head, fisting my hair and tilting me for a better angle.

Hunter pushes me back against the door as he rocks against me with each pump. He's stoking me like he would a fire, causing the flames to grow until it consumes everything.

While trying to get closer to each other, I match him in speed as we continue to chase our high. My nails bite into his back and the hum of his growl sends me over the edge.

"Hunter!" I scream out and sparks fire behind my eyelids.

He rides out my orgasm by driving into me hard and fast a few more times and then stills, groaning out his pleasure.

I'm beyond thankful that he's got a good hold on me. I'm limp with absolutely no energy left. Whether it was our love making, or the day finally catching up to me, I'm dead weight in Hunter's arms.

I could fall asleep right here.

Wrapped around my twin flame. My love.

My head rests on his shoulder and we are both trying to catch our breath.

Hunter's arms tighten around my waist. "I can't wait for a life-time of this, sweetheart. Let's get you to bed."

"Mmm..."

He carries me down the hallway to the bedroom where he lays me down.

I open my eyes and find Hunter standing at the edge of the bed, hovering over me. I could never tire of seeing the look of adoration in his eyes.

His glistening body twinkles like a million stars. Then my eyes narrow. I don't remember him turning on any lights.

"Oh man..." I groan and cover my eyes with my forearm. "Not again."

Hunter chuckles. "Hey, no need to be embarrassed." He pulls my arm from my face and holds it over my head, so I replace it with the other one. He pries that one away too and leans down. Both my hands are pinned down.

The deep abyss of his eyes pull me in, and I get lost. He brings his lips to the corner of my mouth, then trails kisses to my jawline, until he gets to the very spot that has me wriggling against him.

"I don't think I'll ever get tired of your after-sex glow, Anya. You're beautiful. And you're *all* mine."

Chapter Thirty-Seven

RAIDO

(DISCOVERY)

"What are your thoughts about me taking you out to breakfast?" Hunter asks as we lie in bed, enjoying a lazy morning.

Hunter's milk-chocolate eyes sparkle from the morning sunlight peeking through the shades. He's resting on his elbow, leaning over me with adorable, disheveled hair.

My stomach growls. "Mmm...if it means I don't have to cook, I'm in." I throw the blanket off me and over Hunter's head and dart around the room grabbing my clothes out of drawers and tossing them on. Turning back toward the bed, the blanket outlines Hunter's body.

"Hunter?"

"Yeah?" His muffled voice replies.

I walk over to his side of the bed and pull the covers back. "What are you doing?"

"Well, you buried me alive. I figured you'd rather go alone. I chose not to argue with the Honey Bear." He smirks. "You're scary when you're hungry."

"Not my fault you were in my way. And why waste time when there are perfectly soft biscuits and mouthwatering gravy with crispy bacon waiting for me down the road?" I kick my hip out and lay my hand on it. "Hustle, McAllister. I'm hungry."

"Yes, Milady." He sits up and his muscles flex with the movement.

Act casual.

My belly grumbles.

Ugh, that's not casual.

"See? How do I know you won't eat me? You're drooling and your stomach is saying I'm on the menu for breakfast."

My gaze moves from his abs to his face, and, in a panic, I use my index finger and thumb to check the corners of my lips.

His dimples pop out.

Oh, I could kill the man.

"Get some clothes on or I'm leaving without you." I storm out of the room and stop when I see clothes and shoes littered on my entryway floor. My decimated bra and torn blouse lay as a reminder of the heat that built into an inferno that consumed us last night.

Unlike most flames that extinguish after the blaze, we are still burning white-hot.

I put on my jacket right when Hunter comes out. In a quick motion, I grab his boots and shove them into his flannel covered chest before I walk out the front door hiding the smirk on my face.

"Babe, hold up!" he calls out.

Of course I don't wait, he is a big boy with long legs. He'll catch up.

The cool autumn air hits me and has me rubbing my hands over my sleeves to warm the sudden chill.

It's not cold enough to need a heavy jacket, but it certainly takes a bit to get used to.

Hunter catches up to me as I start my walk into town. He grasps my hand, lacing our fingers together.

I look down at our joined hands and raise an eyebrow. "You sure you want to risk your hand right now by touching me?"

He snickers. "I'll take my chances. Plus, if you bite me, you can heal it and make it look better than before."

We're quiet the rest of the way. The only sound during our walk is from the wind blowing through the trees. I nuzzle into Hunter's side a bit, and the image of us cuddling under a thick blanket near a warm fire fills my mind. My heart feels so full, but there's a niggling doubt trying to compromise my happiness. I try to shove it off knowing nothing is perfect. But it's hard not to believe it's only a matter of time before the other shoe drops, and I'm the insect being smashed underneath.

"Wow, how often do you walk to town? The sight is breathtaking." Hunter snaps me out of my self-sabotaging thoughts.

My eyes focus on the multi-colored leaves raining down on us, swirling around like we are in a beautiful, fall globe. It is peaceful—when I'm not lost in my own head.

I shrug. "As often as I can; weather permitting, of course."

"With scenery like this, even in the bitter cold, I'd be tempted to walk."

"Have at it. I'd like to see how long you'd last when we have a few feet of snow."

He chuckles. "You underestimate my endurance."

"More like, I overestimate your sanity," I mutter.

"Smart-ass." Hunter gives me a light smack to my ass then wraps an arm around me, removing any uncertainty and replacing it with heat spreading from my head to my toes.

All too soon, we arrive at Bitsy's Diner, and I allow Hunter's chivalry to take over when he opens the door, ushering me inside with a gentle hand to my back.

"Annyyaa..." Hunter drawls out like I'm in trouble.

Turning around I find him using the glass door as a mirror while he inspects his neck where I left a love bite.

Oops.

My hand goes to my mouth to contain my giggle.

"You little brat," he chuckles and follows me the rest of the way in.

We stand to the side and I go up on my toes to whisper in his ear, "It's to make sure others know you belong to me."

His brown eyes darken, promising me payback later.

"I can heal you if you'd like."

He grabs my hand and pulls me forward without a word.

It's a 'seat yourself' kind of establishment which makes it easy. I search for a good table, but then my eyes light up.

Heather and her fiancé Greyson are sitting at a four-person table drinking their coffee. The lack of plates—either full or empty—tells me they haven't been here long.

How perfect is this?

I look up to Hunter, hopeful. "Do you want to have breakfast by ourselves, or do you want to join Heather and her fiancé?"

He dips down, kisses me on the cheek and whispers in my ear, "We'll have plenty of time to ourselves, and you haven't spent time with her since before all of this." He nuzzles my neck and murmurs, "On the plus side, if we join them, she may not come after me."

"And *why* exactly would she come after you?"

"For keeping you away from her. We know I'd never do that, but I'm not sure what she thinks. I say we take this time to clear the air of any misunderstandings."

He's serious. And he's definitely not wrong. One look at her and you'll think she's this innocent, ditsy blonde, but if she releases her mama bear side? You will have to sleep with one eye open.

If you make it that long.

I squeal, taking his hand and pulling him towards their table, stopping just a few feet away.

Heather and Greyson are lost in conversation. It's the perfect moment to screw with her. I press my finger to my lips for Hunter to keep quiet.

Imitating a high-pitched girly voice I ask, "Can I take your order?"

Heather, so predictable, doesn't even look up as she studies her menu. "What's the special today?"

"Well, for a senior citizen like yourself, our special today is grits. You know...like, to help with digestion and all that. You don't even need your dentures to eat it."

Her ears are the first to go red before it spreads to her cheeks. She ever so slowly rotates her head without moving any other part of her body. Almost like the exorcist, which sends a creepy chill down my spine.

She is about to lay into me until her eyes reflect recognition and she shoots out of her seat.

"Oh, shit," I say under my breath; I have a pixie barreling into me full force. A wall of thick muscle behind me stops us from tumbling onto the floor.

"*Anya*, hi! What are you doing here? Are you okay? Is your family issue all sorted out?" She looks at Hunter. "Hi, Hunter." She brings her attention back to me. "Is he treating you right? Do you need me to kick his ass?" She rambles then her eyes narrow.

"And *senior citizen*? *Really,* Anya? You know how these teenage girls get under my skin, the little twerps acting like we're older than dirt. I could—"

"I couldn't resist." Laughing, I cut her off before she finishes her threat. "You really are too easy to mess with."

"Uh huh, aren't *you* nice. It's too early to get me riled up. Next time, at least wait until I have my coffee first."

I glance at her steaming mug. "Looks like you already have it."

"I have to drink it, *woman*. I mean, you need to let the drug course through my veins first before you play chicken with death."

"Eh," I wave her off. "I checked to make sure there were no potential weapons in your vicinity first. I knew I had a high chance of survival."

"Tsk, tsk. Oh, young grasshopper, you have much more to learn. You underestimated the sharpness of these menus." She picks up her menu and shakes it at me.

"Damn it, you're right. I'm sorry." I hang my head in exaggerated defeat.

She taps a finger on her pursed lips and hums like she is contemplating my apology. "I forgive you—this time. Soo...what brings you here?" She lowers her voice, "What's going on with your family *thing*?"

"Our little *problem* is at a standstill right now, but we're taking a breakfast break before getting back to it. Mind if we join you two?" I glance from Heather to Greyson who sits there quietly. He's an observer, quiet, but I refuse to underestimate him. He uses his brains to take you down, where Heather uses her strong, tiny body. They're a perfect match.

Heather's answer is to push me into a seat next to her then go around the table to shove Hunter into the one next to Greyson.

I suck in my lips and bite down to keep from laughing at her way of maneuvering us where she wants.

She sits, her head ping ponging back and forth between Hunter and me. A crease forms between her brows and she wiggles her finger. "This thing here...is this serious?"

"Yes, it's definitely serious," Hunter answers before I can. "Don't worry, I will do *everything* in my power to make Anya happy and protect her." He says it like he's trying to convince my dad that he's the man for me and not to shoot him with a 12-gauge shotgun. "I also need to tell you that your cupcakes are the best I have *ever* had. Magnificent work." With a chef's kiss, he gives her a charming smile, clearly trying to make sure he stays in her good graces.

What a suck up.

"Hunter, you got something a little *brown* right here." I point to the tip of my nose.

Heather shoves my shoulder and beams at Hunter. "Give him a break, he's trying more than *others* have."

Should I even tell her about last night with Kyle?

I shake my head and decide against it, there'd be too many questions. Ones we won't be able to explain right now.

Someday.

"Hey, I'm Greyson, you can call me Grey," his baritone voice is low but it carries. The man is a tall, caramel embodiment of perfection with eyes like a hawk.

The boys hit it off, talking about what they do for a living and their military backgrounds. My shoulders relax. I didn't know it would mean this much to have them get along, but Heather is a big part of my life. Having Hunter fit in with her and Greyson really is a relief.

I turn to Heather only to see she has a crazed look on her face. My stomach hardens into a knot.

"What?" I ask her slowly, a little scared of what she'll say.

"You. You *shared* a cupcake?"

"Uh, yeah?" Unsure where she's going with this, and I try not to blush when remembering the moment when Hunter tried the dessert.

On the couch.

"In all the years I've known you, I have *never* seen you look the way you do now, and finding out that you shared one of *my* cupcakes with him is *monumental!* You don't even allow *me* to have one, and I made the damn things!" She throws her hands up.

"I may like him *just* a little bit." Holding up my thumb and index finger about an inch apart.

She snorts. "You are *so* full of it. Yesterday, you had this radiant glow, but I didn't ask you about it. I was trying to keep you from chewing off my hands to get to the cupcakes. But *now*? Seeing you with *Hunter*?" Sitting back, she crosses her arms over her chest. "I get it. You're in love, aren't you?" She grins like she won the lottery.

Heat spreads across my face, and I lean in. "Yes. I know it sounds crazy because we're moving fast, but I have my best friend back. We've known each other since childhood and, in these past few days, we are getting to know who we've become as adults." I sneak a peek at Hunter in deep conversation with Greyson then back to Heather, looking her straight in the eyes. "I like him even more now. I'm a little worried about how we'll make a long-distance relationship pan out when he goes back to work."

I know I'm a broken record on allowing my fear to take over, but it's hard not to.

Heather turns serious. "In the very few short-term relationships I've seen you in, I've *never* seen you like this. You've never cared if a relationship lasted or not. You'd rather be alone than with a guy. And as quick as you fell for him? It's real. I know you'll do what needs to be done to make the relationship work. From the looks of it"—She nods her head in Hunter's direction—"he'll do everything he can as well. I don't think you need to worry about it falling apart."

Do we have what it takes to stay together?

"What you guys have, is what Greyson and I've found. You found your other half, your soulmate. It'll work out. I have no doubt about it." She grabs my shoulders and pulls me into a huge hug.

Tears fill my eyes. She said exactly what I needed to hear.

Hunter and I will get through this, somehow.

"Thank you so much, Heather, I really needed this."

"Well, you should have come to me sooner. I fix shit. Even when everything falls apart in my own life, I still fix shit, or beat it into submission."

"You ever going to tell me what really happened in your past?"

Her eyes darken. "When the past finally stays in the past." She throws a veil over her demons and plasters on a smile. "Until then, let's bask in this happy moment."

I don't push her, and I never will. Even if it means I'll never know. It isn't my story to be told, but I want her to someday feel comfortable enough to tell me about the horrors of her past. And I know they have to be bad since she avoids discussing them.

Something tells me she wasn't always the badass Heather she is today. She wasn't born this way, she was made.

Maybe someday, I can be the one who can help *her.*

"Good morning, looks like you have some company. Can I get you two some coffee?" The waitress asks Hunter and me.

"I'll have a water, and, if you can, please bring her some green tea?" Hunter angles his head at me, knowing what I need.

I raise my eyebrow at Heather giving her a silent *'See? I told you the man's for me,'*

"Sure thing. Everyone ready to order?" The older woman pulls out an order pad from the front pocket of her uniform, pen ready.

She takes our orders and heads to the kitchen.

I glance between Heather and Greyson. "Are you both ready for the wedding?"

Greyson groans. "Don't get her started." He runs a hand over his short black hair. "I wouldn't consider her a *Bridezilla*, but she is driving me insane at home with all the stress baking."

This has me failing at holding back my grin. "Are you concerned you won't be able to fit into your tux?"

Heather snorts and giggles. "As if, the man's body is a weird genetic mutation. He can't get fat. Trust me, I've tried."

Greyson raises his eyebrows. Clearly, this is the first of him hearing about this. "You want me fat?"

"Pfft." She waves a hand at him. "It was just a *little* experiment which you *passed*. Lucky you. Why are you upset? Your co-workers *love* my baking."

"More like my co-workers are complaining about not being able to fit into their *own* clothes. And they blame *me* for it. All I'm trying to do is get some of our counter space back." He turns to me. "What it really does is free up room for her to fill it with even more. It. Is. Never. Ending. She needs to get back to work, and soon."

I hold my hand over my mouth, trying not to laugh.

Hunter sits back in his chair enjoying the entertainment.

Heather huffs. "What would you rather me do, drink and do drugs to control my anxiety? At least my relief helps others feel better too. Don't you remember the grumpy ass you were before you stepped into the coffee shop I worked at and tried one of my tasty treats?" She rests her chin on her fist, batting her lashes. "And I *know* you heard Hunter, my cupcakes are *magnificent*." She sits up and tilts her head to Hunter. "Wasn't that what you said Hunter?" Heather stares expectantly at him.

He looks back and forth between Heather and Greyson. "Uhh ...yes?" He cringes. "I'm really not comfortable... Umm... I'm not sure if I should get involved," he stutters.

The built-up laughter explodes out of me in a roar, turning heads towards our table. "I'm sorry. I just can't." I hold up one hand while the other holds my stomach as I crack up at the expense of Hunter.

The food comes and gives us a break from teasing the boys. We exchange small talk between bites, but all become somber when the check comes.

The time has come for us to part.

Between last night and this morning, the reprieve was needed to clear my head and energy. The burden isn't hanging fully on my shoulders and the laughter and lightness has really raised my vibrations.

I'm ready to take on our next challenge.

Heather and I wait by the door for the guys to pay—at their insistence.

"How did we get so lucky?" Heather asks me as she lays her head on my shoulder, staring at Greyson.

"The hell if I know. But I think it's wise we don't question this."

"That's smart. Oh, here they come." She lifts her head and sure enough, our handsome men are sauntering over to us.

They are surely a sight to drool over, and they aren't just affecting us. Heather bumps my shoulder and with a smile, she nods her head to the table of women gawking at the guys.

I whisper in her ear, "They aren't used to men like this around these parts."

She turns to me. "As long as they keep their claws to themselves. I don't like sharing," she growls out.

I snicker.

Me either.

Hunter grasps my hand, lacing our fingers, while Greyson throws his arm around Heather's shoulders and pulls her close. The four of us walk out of the diner together and stop a few feet outside to say our goodbyes.

Heather pulls me into a hug, and I tell her, "This was fun, thanks for letting us join you. We'll do this again, right?"

"Without a doubt. Call me when everything is all good. We need a girl's night to chat without all the masculine energy around." She pulls away and winks.

I turn to Greyson. "Bye Greyson! Be good to my girl."

"You know I will, we all know what she'll do if I don't." He laughs with no fear.

He's either very confident, or very stupid.

I'm going with the former.

Hunter shakes Greyson's hand, slaps him on the shoulder and says quietly, "You're a brave man. See ya around."

Hunter turns to me. "Ready to head out?"

"Onto our next adventure." I twine my elbow with his and start singing, "*We're off to see—*"

He stops me from my mid-skip and lets go of my arm. "Yeah, I'm not skipping with you. Not happening." He glances around to see if anyone is watching.

"Ugh, you are so boring. Don't worry about your man card being tainted. Remember, your manliness has already been destroyed with your girly hand." I lay a palm on his bristly cheek. "Now you can be free of your macho reputation."

He turns and bites at my hand, distracting me, then tips me over into a lingering kiss. He comes up for air. "You're crazy, you know that?"

I blink away the haze. "Yeah, but you love me anyways." With a quick peck, I pull out of his grasp, wink, and turn to walk ahead of him.

In a few strides, Hunter comes up by my side, picking up my hand. "You know I do, but sometimes I question my sanity."

"Oh, I question your sanity too. But it's better to admit you're not right in the head now than have me argue the fact with you for the next fifty years." With my hand on his forearm, I turn us down the next street in the direction of Greta and Harold's store.

Walking into the shop, I shouldn't be surprised by the wall of sage but somehow, I forgot about it in our excitement. The bell must have alerted Greta because she charges towards us, and before I expect it, she embraces me in a strong hug.

"My darlings!" Hands on my biceps, she holds me out for inspection. "How did it all go? Wait"—She holds up her hand—"don't say a thing. Follow me."

I swear, Greta and Heather may be long lost relatives the way they act.

We follow her behind the check-out desk and through a door that leads into a kitchen. Her kitchen, to be exact. I'm a little surprised there is a living space back here. It's not big, but it's perfect for the two of them.

We pass an entryway that leads to a living room that has an impressive bookshelf. I curiously peek around the corner and find some old, wooden art on the walls.

Squinting, I take a step closer to make out the familiar design and a chair moves across the floor behind me. When I walk to the table, Hunter is standing behind a chair, waiting patiently for me.

I take my seat and he pushes me in with a kiss on the top of my head. Butterflies try to flutter around my stomach, but I tamp them down.

It's going to take a bit to get used to his sweet gestures like this. I'm not complaining; he's just a rare jewel in this ugly world.

"Is Harold joining us?" I ask Greta when she walks in with a tea kettle. I have yet to meet the man and a part of me is curious if he has gifts like her.

She waves her hand at me, dismissing my comment. "Oh no, he will cover the store for us, and I'll fill him in later. This stuff sometimes gives him indigestion so he is better off out there anyways."

She sets two teacups in front of us and fills them. Based on the energy coming off the liquid, she's added something more than just loose tea leaves.

I smile. I guess this will be another occurrence with her sneaking potions into my drinks.

Hunter and I both sip our tea and wait until Greta finally sits. "Spill!" Her eyes are wide, and she rubs her hands together in excitement.

Hunter takes the lead and provides a recap of everything that occurred with the wendigo, including the animals fighting *and* my healings—which was a new development.

He, of course, didn't leave out how I was stubborn and did most of it alone.

With my back against my seat, drinking my invigorating tea, I watch Hunter as he tells our story. When he gets animated, it reminds me of the boy I used to know. I study his features, comparing what has remained the same from years ago versus now. There are many expressions that have me flashing back to the times he would tell me what he did that day, then other looks are new to me.

His brown eyes light up during his retelling of my healing. There is no mistaking the excitement being the same as when he'd pull out the candy stash from his pockets—the very same sweet treats his mom always tried to hide from him. When his cute dimples popped and an adorable smile spread across his face, the happiness in his eyes always followed. But where the enthusiasm had once brightened his round cheeks, now shines through his bearded yet defined jawline; a trait I can tell he got from his dad, yet still his own.

Greta silently takes in Hunter's words while sipping her tea. I can almost see the wheels in her head moving at full speed. When Hunter ends his tale of battling monsters—aka having a heart attack over me taking risks with wild animals, and slipping down the stairs—she doesn't speak for what feels like forever, and I begin to get nervous.

What if she says we did something wrong?

I had no idea my hands were shaking until Greta placed hers over mine, steadying them.

She finally speaks up, "Light Angel, do you even realize what you did?"

Oh shit, what did I do?

Nothing in my mind points to mistakes I made. There must be something I'm missing. My chest becomes heavy; my lungs feel like it's getting harder to take a breath. I look at Hunter, worried.

Why is he acting calm?

Does he not catch on that I may have royally fucked up?

"I'm sorry, I don't know what I did wrong." My leg bounces. "Please tell me, I want to fix it. I thought everything worked out." I chew nervously on my lip and sweat beads down my spine.

What if I can't fix it?

Greta chuckles and tightens her hold on me. "Wrong? You did everything right!"

Wait, what?

"I was referring to your communication and healing of animals. I don't think you understand how important this is." She shifts in her seat, moving closer to me. "Your ancestors have *never* had that power, they could never do what you did. And to hear that you didn't need help to secure the wendigo in its cage? Your powers *surpass* all of your ancestors and many others with gifts. You have fully come into your Light Angel power and have *ascended.*"

She grabs my face, looks me in the eyes and says, "You, my dear, are a blessing to us all. I am so proud of you." She releases my face, and I sit back, stunned.

I've come into my power and ascended?

I heard what she said, but my mind is trying to wrap around it all. Is that why my power keeps growing?

"How..." My voice squeaks. I clear my throat and try again. "How do you know that no one in my bloodline has been able to do what I've done? *I* don't even know how far it goes back. Aoife's journal stopped abruptly, and it seems to be missing pages."

She stands and walks out of the room.

As soon as I get ready to open my mouth to ask Hunter what that was all about, she comes back in with a wooden box that has a Triskele carved on the top. She opens it and takes out two very old books, one that looks similar to the one we found at the castle.

Greta settles back down. "This journal is from my ancestor, Gudrun. She was the Viking seeress who came over with your family. She explains her version of the events, but they match what your ancestor stated. Now this one"—She taps her finger on the second book—"this journal was Aoife's. I knew last time you were here, you weren't ready for this, so I held off. You are ready now. It is yours; take it. I only request that you look at it now, though."

I grit my teeth. She didn't feel I was ready for this before, but she does now?

Who put her in charge?

I close my eyes and take a few breaths, allowing my body to release the anger. I shouldn't react before I know what the journal actually contains.

Placing my hand over the journal, I tap into its energy and recognize it from the one we found in the castle. Opening Aoife's second journal, my heart races as I look down at the text.

"Oh my gosh, yes!" I flip a couple of pages to make sure my eyes aren't playing tricks on me.

"What?" Hunter rests a hand on my thigh.

"I don't get how Aoife could write in Ancient Gaelic before, then switch to English now but she did. Look! It's all here."

Hunter pulls the book over to see it better.

Both of my legs bounce and my body vibrates from excitement.

"Babe." He flips a couple of pages with creases between his brows. "This isn't in English."

I frown and fumble the book when I take it back from him. "What do you mean?" I tilt the book at an angle for Hunter to see. "Aoife says here, 'I spent my days helping the workers move heavy tools across the ground while I provided health to plants to grow and thrive. Our people had everything they needed with my help and soon, a daughter of my daughter will come into the world to carry on our bloodline.' See? It's all here."

He rubs his beard. "Anya, I can't see it because it's in Gaelic. I can't read Gaelic, and neither can you. Well, you couldn't...until now."

My jaw drops and my heart joins it on the floor.

"But..."

Hunter wouldn't lie to me. But how can this happen?

"You have ascended, Light Angel, and now you can read the ancient language," Greta chimes in, giddy.

I raise my head from the journal and find her eyes sparkling with unshed tears.

"See? You are ready now to receive this journal."

I'm embarrassed by my initial anger over her keeping this from me.

"I... I don't know what to say."

"Well, dear, I would recommend seeing what it says," Greta suggests.

Turning to Hunter, I ask, "How much time do we have?"

"Enough. Do what you need."

Despite having time as Hunter states, I still need to be quick.

This journal is much smaller than the first. I skim the pages from where I read out loud to Hunter and move on. This section is dedicated to talking about the extent of the Ó Bradáin clan's power and life after they imprisoned the wendigo. I already know about all the powers Aoife used with the wendigo up to this point. But it goes into further detail on how she helped the crops thrive and used the light energy to heal illnesses, infections, and sped up the curative process in people.

She spoke of long days and nights she and her daughter spent helping their people, which exhausted them. Her daughter had a small amount of the power that Aoife had, but on her daughter's eighteenth rotation around the sun, she would perform a ritual to pass on the majority of her power. This would happen in two more full moon cycles.

I skip ahead through what seems unimportant and slow down when the text discusses Aoife relying on Gudrun's herbal drink to keep her going, but the constant work was wearing on her. The Chieftains tried to give her breaks but she was too stubborn.

Well, now I know where I get that from.

The clan was growing and, with it, came less food to fill bellies, and more women were at risk of child-birthing complications. Gudrun was a godsend but was limited with her own gifts. Everyone sought out the Light Angel for her help.

When the elders passed away, the fear of unearthing another wendigo led to the refusal to bury their dead, so Aoife would burn the bodies to ash.

She says that anytime she used her power to burn, the bodies turned to ash, but the solid rock they were cremated on remained the same. She didn't have the ability to melt it into lava like I can. Maybe she never pushed her limit?

I speed through the words but slow when Aoife describes our bloodline originating a thousand years prior from a... My chest clamps down like it's in the jaws of a bear trap, the air leaving my lungs.

No... I pull in a greedy breath. That can't be right.

Chapter Thirty-Eight

OTHALA

(BLOODLINE)

Leaning back in my chair, I rub my forehead. The sound of liquid being poured drowns out the faint musical chimes I've been tuning into from the shop. It's the only thing I can focus on; everything else is surreal.

"Hey, you okay? What's going on?" Hunter drags my chair closer to him and wraps his arm around me, rubbing my back.

"I'm…" I don't even know if I can admit what I just read in the journal out loud.

"You're what? Talk to me, babe."

My mouth opens and closes.

"Hey!" Hunter takes my chin between his fingers and turns it to face him.

I blink a few times before he comes into focus, but the rest of the room is hidden behind a thick cloud I can't see through.

"Here, give this to her. It will help," Greta's voice is muffled.

"Babe, can you drink this?"

Everything feels numb, and I can't think so I do as I'm told and drink.

"Holy crap—" My chest heaves as I cough to clear out my lungs from the shocking concoction. "What the hell is that?" The colors and outlines of the kitchen start to sharpen, along with Hunter and Greta whose eyes are on me. "That tastes like dirt."

Greta chuckles. "That's ashwagandha, dear. It's very earthy and bitter, but gets the job done."

"I'll say. Please tell me I don't need to drink anymore." It's impossible to prevent my cringe.

"Well, you are back with us, aren't you?"

"Yeah… I guess so." I hesitate, hoping that means that's the end of the disgusting drink.

"Then it did its job." She seems a little too happy with the success of her poison.

Hunter rubs my arm. "What happened? Did you get pulled in again?"

I shake my head. My mind goes back to the words on repeat.

"Fallen Warrior."

"What does that mean?" he asks.

My gaze clouds over when I zone out again.

Hunter snaps his fingers in front of me. "Hey, don't make me force more of this stuff down you. Stay with me."

"Hunter, dear, you would know of it as a Nephilim. That's what Anya's bloodline is from. She isn't named Light Angel only for her power, but for who she is. She is part angel." Greta's chipper tone tells me this is great news.

And this is a good thing…how?

"Is that true?" Hunter asks in disbelief.

My chest tightens, and I lower my head. I'm not sure how Hunter feels about this. I don't even know how *I* feel about this.

The person who started my magical bloodline isn't even human.

I take a few deep breaths and gain the courage to talk. "An angel of light—a fallen warrior—took the form of a human and fell in love with an Ó Bradáin woman in the early days of Ireland. She gave birth to the first woman of many to pass down the angel's power. It got watered down, but the women would complete a ritual at each female child's eighteenth birthday, passing over a large amount of their power to strengthen her." Raising my head, I meet Hunter's gaze.

He's rubbing the back of his neck. "Well, I can't say that I ever would have expected it. That's...out of this world."

"No pun intended?" I smirk in an attempt to lighten the mood.

"I can see why you're overwhelmed." He removes his hand from his neck and grasps my hands between his. "But I don't see this being a bad thing."

The crease between my eyebrows furrow. "You don't?"

"It doesn't change who you are to me. And it doesn't change who you are"—he taps the center of my chest—"in here."

"You don't care that I'm not completely human?" I ask.

He cocks a grin. "I mean, it wasn't long ago you'd accused me of being an alien."

"Oh, har har."

"It's definitely not something you hear every day, but things between us won't ever change. Are you okay with it?" He lifts his hand and rubs his thumb over my cheek.

The warm caress calms my racing heart and loosens the constriction around my chest.

"I guess so. Not that I have a choice in the matter, but the longer I think about it, the more it makes sense. What I don't get is that none of the descendants had the power that I possess. Even the direct daughter of the Light Angel himself. Why am I different?"

Greta clears her throat, catching our attention. Compassion fills her eyes. "I hate to interrupt, but, like I said before, your soul is complete with Hunter in your life. Not a single woman in your family had that. Hunter brought the other half of your soul back to you."

"Why would that matter though?"

"Child, think of it like this. If someone had half a brain, they can only do certain functions, but not everything. You add the other half of the brain, making it whole, and you have full function. The women before you only had half their souls, so they only had half the power. You are the first of your kind."

First of my kind.

Hunter pipes up, "The power she has now may be only a fraction of what her true potential is?"

"Maybe. This has never happened in history, we don't know what is possible, but I say nothing is *impossible* at this point."

He catches my gaze again. "Babe, I know it's overwhelming, but we'll get through this. Can you see if there's anything else about the wendigo?"

Will *we get through this?*

I shake my head. "Sorry, yeah, let me see what it says."

I look back into the journal and find the clan chose to keep the place a secret to prevent anyone from taking over the castle by force. They still needed traders and outside workers for certain necessities, but they increased the risks. It was only a matter of time before someone became greedy and they couldn't chance it. Gradually, the people started moving away when more English settlers came to the land, but my family agreed to stay.

One of the final loyal traders who came to help was a Scottish lad who sold herbs and remedies for ailments and unique issues.

The name isn't listed, but this lad had the perfect herbal concoction, including a gift of his own, to help hide the castle.

Holy crap.

It didn't make it invisible, but it repelled anyone from coming near the area. Knowing it wouldn't last forever, they requested the assistance from the Ó Bradáin guardians to keep it safe.

One woman from our bloodline remained near the castle until the next came and took her place.

I *took my grandmother's place.*

Hiding the castle worked for hundreds of years until hikers discovered it and told Grant. It happened to be on *my* watch without me even knowing my connection. Yet, I was still pulled into being involved just as my ancestors were. There is no doubt fate has full control over our situation. Well, and a meddling grandmother, which I'm beyond thankful for.

And most likely our destiny too.

I clear my throat. "Hunter, umm... I'm about ninety-nine percent positive your ancestor had a hand in keeping the castle hidden for so long. He worked with my ancestors to protect these people."

"What are you talking about?" He flips the pages and growls, "I can't fucking read this." Pushing it back in front of me, he turns to Greta for confirmation.

She simply nods.

Hunter runs a hand through his hair. "My parents told me our Scottish ancestors immigrated to this area. That's why I chose this place to settle down. There hadn't been any talk of a castle. When it came up, I never put two and two together. Why would I?"

A feeling like indigestion causes my stomach to roll while a nauseating pain takes over. "Has this all...us"—I point to Hunter then back to myself—"been orchestrated against our free will to bring us here? Are we pawns in some master plan or game?"

Is any of what we have real?

Hunter's eyes grow wide, and he sits forward in his chair. He grabs both of my hands and brings them to his mouth in a kiss. "Our situation with being separated, then brought back together, may have been premeditated. But you and I? Our connection is *not* fake. It is *very* real."

My nose tingles and begins to run. I sniffle. "How do you know that? What if we just made-up all of this in our heads because some*thing* or some*one* is controlling us?"

"If we were forced together, part of our souls would still know it's missing something. We'd be like two negative magnets pushing apart as hard as they can. Together we're complete, we're finally whole. I feel it, and I know *without a doubt* that you feel it too."

"He's right, Anya." Greta brings my attention to her. "Your connection to each other is something that *cannot* be manipulated. Don't doubt that for even one moment, or it will tear you both apart, like the darkness."

Hunter uses his finger to wipe a runaway tear from under my eyelid.

I take a moment to see past my fear, past our situation, and look into his eyes. My feelings for him haven't changed. I've known the emptiness that existed without him. Even when I was happy with my high school sweetheart, Dean, I wasn't complete. And as much as I tried to push myself to be with him, I couldn't.

But with Hunter, I'm drawn to him because he's part of me. The missing part that I've spent life after life searching for until I found him in this one.

My twin flame.

I sigh. "You're both right. I'm sorry." I swipe a hand over my face. "This is all overwhelming, and with how everything has turned out, it's making me pretty suspicious."

Hunter pulls me onto his lap. "Don't be sorry. You have every right to question every single part of *your* life and mine. But like

Greta said, don't doubt what we have, or who we are to each other."

I nod and lay my head on his shoulder. "Thank you."

"Good, now see what more you can find out." Hunter slides the journal in front of us.

Sitting straighter I say, "I can go back to my own seat."

I move but he holds me to him, splaying his hand over my stomach. The heat coming off of him calms and cleanses like a steam room eliminating the toxins plaguing me.

He nudges the book closer. "Not a chance. Now read."

I run my fingers over the indents from the inking tool used on the parchment paper before I get absorbed back into my ancestor's story.

Pages upon pages document the life of worry and teaching daughter after daughter about their responsibilities to the town and their people.

Why did my mom have to question the truth behind the legends?

But if I'm being honest, would I have really believed the stories myself?

Yeah, I think I would have. I believed my grandmother's stories growing up, as much as my mom hated it. That's most likely why Grandmother skipped my parents and left everything to me.

When I make it to the back of the journal, I'm disappointed there's absolutely nothing helpful in here.

"Grr..."

"No luck?"

"Not even a hint of anything that can help. It's a dead-end." I look around the kitchen and notice Greta is missing. "Where'd she go?"

"She went to check on Harold. He's not very talkative and she worries it scares away customers sometimes." He rubs his hand over my stomach, sending tingles through me. "I think she wanted to give us some time alone."

I sit up straight, pushing his arm away when I turn sideways. "You kicked her out of her own kitchen?"

"I did no such thing. She'll be back soon." His hand grasps my thigh to shift me more comfortably on his lap.

My back bumps into the journal and knocks it onto the floor.

"Oh, shit." I drop to my knees and pick up the leather binding, smoothing out the pages to make sure they don't bend.

"What's that?" Hunter points under the table.

A few loose pages had slipped out.

"Hold this." I hand the book to Hunter and pick up the paper. A sinking feeling hits me in my gut. I hate that I damaged this only connection I have to my ancestors. "That's weird."

"What?" Hunter asks.

"I didn't see these pages when I was reading. These were intentionally folded and placed inside."

"A key to destroying the wendigo, perhaps?" Hunter runs his hand over his beard.

He's as nervous as I am, but it's probably going to be another disappointment.

I pull myself up into the chair next to him and slowly open the crinkling pages. Out of four, each piece of paper is newer, fresher. Like over time, they've been added.

"Whoa." This can't be right. I flip the pages, scanning the lists of names on each one, along with the brief statements.

"You found something." Hunter stands abruptly, he places one arm on the back of my chair and the other on the table—hovering over me. His heat, mixed with the citrus lavender scent of him, envelops me and pulls me off track for a moment.

I clear my throat.

"This lists the original owners of the castle." The words come out breathy.

"You're shitting me."

I shake my head. "The oldest parchment has the original contract where the Donnchadh clan ensured the descendants of the Ó Bradáin's had full rights to the castle, and three hundred acres of woods surrounding it." I try to calculate how much that is and fail. "I suck at math, how much is that?"

He hesitates a split second before answering. "That's about a half a mile radius around the castle."

"They've signed away their rights and added the next owner's name to the list."

Hunter meets my eyes. "This means if we can find the current owner, we can keep the castle away from Margaret."

"But then we have someone else to try and convince to stay away."

He kisses me on my temple. "One worry at a time, babe. Who's Eba?"

"Who?" The crease between my brows furrows.

"This name. Does it look familiar to you?" Hunter points to the most recent page.

I suck in a sharp breath.

Éabha Ó Ceallaigh.

"It's pronounced Ava, and it's my grandmother."

"Oh goodie! I returned at the perfect time." Greta stands in the doorway bouncing on her toes.

I hold up the papers. "Did you know about this?" My eyes widen.

She walks over to the tea pot. "Maybe a little more tea first?"

I slap my hand over my cup to stop her. My fingers dig into the porcelain as the anger builds up like the hot water in the kettle.

I'm ready to scream from the pressure.

"Anya, if she's the last owner, that means..." Hunter hesitates.

"Mmhmm..." I know exactly what that means.

That means we have been stressing out for nothing. Yes, we still have the wendigo issue, but Margaret won't even be in the picture.

If I'd had known when I moved here, maybe I could have prevented these fucking events from even playing out. No one would have died if I had known.

Hunter places a hand over mine, gently pulling my claws off of the cup. "Babe, this is good news. Nothing to be upset over."

"Nothing, huh?" I turn to him and his chocolate eyes coax me to relax. "She knew this whole damn time. She could have prevented this. My *own grandmother* could have prevented this. How the hell *should* I be feeling right now? Because happiness isn't it."

"I understand how you may be feeling."

"*Do you?*" I snap. My labored breathing has my heart racing. All while my blood boils through my veins. I hold the seat of my chair to prevent myself from lighting something on fire.

Hunter pulls my chair towards him. His hands grab the sides of my face and he drops his forehead to mine. His dark eyes reach out to me, trying to push past the walls I've erected.

"Listen to me. As much as you hate how this all came to be, it brought us together. Without every single event that happened, we may not be sitting together right now. We could still be on our own...and miserable."

My body stills and then eases into him.

"I'm so sorry," Greta's shaky voice chisels at my wall of anger.

Hunter releases me, and I make eye contact with her.

"Do you mind if I try to explain? I don't expect forgiveness, I only want you to understand why I kept this from you and maybe...just maybe it will make sense."

I nod. "Go on."

Greta wrings her hands like she did when she was worried about my reaction to the spiked water when we first met.

"If you knew what the women in your family were limited to doing, you may not have pushed yourself. You would have had it in your mind that it could not be done. As horrible as stress and worry are for us, sometimes it is exactly what we need to push out of our comfort zone to grow and become who we are truly meant to be. *You* pushed yourself beyond all limits."

The anger diffuses, and I drop my shoulders, slouching in my chair. "How could you have been so sure? What if it didn't? What if it *killed* me?"

"That was a concern, but your grandmother was adamant that you needed to do this on your own."

I tilt my head and narrow my eyes. "You both *knew* this would happen and you planned it? Was this when she was finalizing her will to drag me out here?"

"Oh heavens, no! We never guessed this would happen. She and I were close friends. After her passing, she still visited me from time to time. She only came to me recently to talk to me about you and the wendigo." She hums. "That is when we decided on this journal. She led you to the first one that was hidden in the castle. We needed the right moment to give you the second one." She steeples her hands as if praying. "Please know that we didn't mean to cause you harm. We only wanted to help you." Her voice is genuine.

My eyes close, and I read her aura. Light blue swirls around her. The color of the throat chakra—of truth. Leaning my elbow on the table, I hold my head.

I can't fault Greta for doing what she felt was right, and for following a dead woman's wishes.

There's no more fight in me. Only disappointment.

But who exactly is that disappointment directed towards?

"I don't understand why my mom or grandmother kept me in the dark, but I need to let it go and move on. I'm sorry for losing it on you."

Greta reaches across the table and pats my hand. "Don't you worry yourself over it."

"I hate to interrupt, but we really should be going. I think we need to stop at the County Clerk's office before we head back to the castle with the trailer. That's if they'll accept this." He lifts up the papers.

We stand and Greta looks down into her hands, like she's unsure what to do next.

I walk over and wrap my arms around her. "Thank you. I'm sorry again but I appreciate you for giving us this missing piece to the puzzle. It really does help."

Her arms wrap around my waist and she squeezes me tight. "We only want you to succeed, Light Angel."

She releases me. "Remember, your journey is one you were destined to embark on. As much as it can hurt, or not turn out the way you plan, it is the path you were set to take. There are great things, *wonderful* things ahead. It may not be easy, but it will be rewarding."

"Thank you."

Hunter and I follow her out to the front of the store where Harold is waving goodbye to a customer.

I crack a smile. He's about my height with a full head of grey hair and oblong glasses perched on the end of his nose. He resembles a wise grandfather.

"Ah...so this is the infamous Harold I've been hearing all about."

He grasps his chest. "And you must be our Angel from above." He bows. "It is a pleasure to finally meet you. Is my wife behaving herself?"

A smirk sneaks out. "As long as she stops drugging me."

His belly jiggles with his chuckle. "Yes, she has that tendency. All for good though."

"Of course. I wish we could stay and chat, but we have some things to tend to."

"Be brave, strong warrior. We will see you soon. Hunter." Harold nods in greeting and they give each other a short embrace.

Greta waves. "Wishing you both many blessings on your journey. Do not separate and watch out for one another. Goodbye my dears."

The trip to the County Clerk's office was quite a success. They advised us that my document alone is proof enough to anyone trying to contest the ownership of the castle. The best part is that we don't have to wait for the court to finalize the papers to lay our claim. I'm the rightful owner, and I have the right to remove anyone from my property.

With this document, I can also claim it as a historical site which will help us protect it and allow us to use tax exemptions. Lord knows I'm going to need financial help with it. A trip to New York's Historic Preservation Office will need to be placed on the back burner for now. Securing the castle is our priority.

Overall, this new revolution couldn't have worked out any better.

To cover all our bases, we filed a copy of the paperwork and deed with City Hall. It's inevitable that Margaret is going to fight over the property ownership. I'd rather be over prepared than have her find a loophole.

Hunter made a call to a connection he has in criminal law to make sure I can't be held accountable for the death of Grant, since it was on my property. As long as we can prove I was not aware of the ownership before or at the time of death, Margaret can't press charges.

Well, she can, but the judge will throw them out.

"We should stop at the hardware store to pick up a few 'No Trespassing' signs before picking up the trailer and heading to the castle," Hunter suggests.

"Why can't you just hide it like your ancestor did?"

"Well, for one, I'd need a shit-ton of herbs. Two, it won't work on anyone who already knows the castle is here. A missing building would be hard to explain."

"But you think that little sign will stop anyone from coming onto the property?"

"No, but it's a start. I have a buddy who owns a major military security company. He owes me a favor. All I have to do is give him a call, and I'm sure I can get him out here quickly to have everything set up."

I shake my head. "Oh yeah, I forgot that anyone would drop everything for *you*, princess. How could I forget?"

"And you better not forget it. I expect you to kneel before your royalty."

A snort escapes me, and Hunter wraps his arm around my shoulder. My head drops to his chest and he kisses the top of my head as we continue to walk back to the truck.

"Alright, smart guy, what's your idea on how we hold down the fort before your loyal minion comes out? The place is *huge* and it's going to take days to get hooked up. I don't even want to think about how much this is going to cost me." This will easily deplete all of my savings, if not more. There's no guarantee that I still have a job. It's not like there's a variety to pick from around here.

Hunter stops abruptly, and I stumble forward. "What was that for?"

"I just want to make sure I have your attention so I don't have to repeat myself later."

"Ooh-kay." I say slowly.

"We'll figure out how to keep people away from the..." He glances around then lowers his voice, his hand rests on my hip. "Issue. As for the rest, it won't take long. Johnny has a large and quite efficient crew. By cashing in my favor, we can get him out to the castle within a couple days."

"Oh, that's not too bad."

"Nah, we can make it work. The fencing will be our only expense. The security set-up won't cost us a dime. It's part of what he owes me."

How huge is this favor?

"Do I want to know what you did to earn this said favor? Because with the size of the castle, that's thousands of dollars' worth of work and equipment." My gaze bounces back and forth between his eyes—searching for answers.

"That's a story for another day." His eyes turn dark, letting me know it isn't going to be an easy story to tell, let alone relive.

If it's going to cause him pain, it's better if I don't know.

I rest my hand on Hunter's cheek, my fingers touching the smooth skin above his beard. "You don't have to tell me, but thank you. I really appreciate you cashing this in to help me."

His grip on my hip tightens as he pulls me closer. We are in the middle of the sidewalk, in the center of town. People stare as they walk by. People I see every day.

I'm sure they're creating their own gossip, especially since public displays of affection aren't common in Shandaken.

His face draws closer, inch by inch, until his forehead rests on mine, the tips of our noses rubbing together. The darkness in his eyes pulls me into their depths and the whispering passersby fade away.

"I will cash in *every* favor I have *ever* earned if it'll ensure your safety and happiness."

Shifting on my feet, I try my best not to cave to the weakness trying to take over.

Is he seriously making me swoon right now?

I open my mouth to try to say...something, but my hero swoops in and saves me from my struggle. He sucks on my bottom lip. The sweetness from breakfast lingers on his lips, and I lap it up like it's the nectar of life. Revitalizing me and saving me from drowning in the darkness pulling me under.

"Mmm... You taste delicious," he says as he pulls away. "But we should go."

"Do we have to?" I whine.

He laughs. "Well...unless you'd rather me take you up against this wall—which I think would be highly frowned upon—then yes we have to."

He wants to play dirty? I can play dirty.

"Since you offered..." I push him up against the brick, gliding my hands under his shirt, against his stomach.

His eyes widen in shock and he turns hard against me. The moment I catch a glimpse of the chocolate brown morphing into black, I give him a quick peck and turn to walk away. When I don't hear him, I look back and find him standing stock still, his mouth gaped open.

"Let's go!" I shout.

He shakes his head and pushes off the wall while adjusting himself.

I'm a little nervous about the repercussions, but it's his fault.

He started it, after all.

Hunter wraps his arm around my shoulder, and mumbles into the top of my head, "*You're gonna be the death of me.*"

Chapter Thirty-Nine

Eihwaz

(Intuition)

The reflection of the rented flatbed trailer sways in the side mirror of Hunter's truck. My stomach tenses at each sharp curve, nervous the hitch will break, sending the loader flying into another car.

That's to say if there were actually other cars on the road to the castle, which there aren't. It's not one frequently traveled.

Like how my life once was.

"So...with you being the owner of a large estate and a few hundred acres of land, does this mean you're my sugar momma now?" Hunter snickers.

"If that's true, then that means I'd have my pick of men, right? Do you think Jensen Ackles would be interested?"

"Oof." Hunter's fist rubs his chest. "Already trading me in for a better model, huh?"

"Pfft. Don't worry your pretty little head over it. I'm sure Jensen wouldn't be nearly as fun to tease as you are."

He rears back like he's been slapped and feigns injury. "Is that all I am to you? Entertainment?"

"And a great lay. You can't forget that." I bite the inside of my cheek to hold back a laugh.

"I feel used," he harrumphs.

"Well, Heather *did* call you my new toy."

He runs his hand across my jeaned thigh. The air in the truck heats up. "Care to elaborate on how you plan to *use* me?"

"Mmm...well, to start..." I purr and lean closer, lowering my voice. "I plan to use your *services*." Batting my eyes, I say, "To haul my car."

"That wasn't what I had in mind...*brat*." He gives my leg a squeeze. "But yes, if you couldn't tell by the large trailer I'm pulling, that's already in the plans."

"Oh *really*? That's *fascinating*, I had no clue."

"Smart-ass." Hunter smirks and returns his hand to the wheel. "Once we have your car loaded, we can park it at my place until we decide what to do with it."

His words have me sitting up straighter. "Hold on, that's wasting money. You're paying daily for it, right?"

"I told you, money isn't an issue."

"Do you think we can find somewhere that will pay for the parts today instead?"

Hunter bursts out in laughter. "You're cute to think anything on that car is salvageable."

My hand covers my face, cringing. "Scrap yard it is." The whole finality of it is difficult to take in. All that hard work to save up enough money for that car, and it went down the drain in one night. I know I have more important things to worry about, but it doesn't make it easier to cope with, regardless of whether or not the insurance covers it. It still hurts.

"Hmm..." Hunter hums out and rubs his neck.

My stomach drops. "What is it?"

He shakes his head. "I don't know. I just got this weird feeling. Can you do me a favor?"

"Sure, what's up?" I ask.

"Open the glove compartment."

I open it, and I'm met with a small pistol. Glancing over to him my eyebrows furrow in question.

Hunter cocks an eyebrow at me. "I'm not taking any chances. Humor me."

I grumble. "Fine. If I have to carry it, you should be okay with me burning some symbols in it."

He chuckles. "I was expecting you would. Feel free to decorate it with hearts and unicorns if you want. It's yours now."

This seems to be important to him. I take it along with one of the spare magazines he pulls out of his pocket. I remove the magazine and check the chamber to make sure it's empty before laying it in my lap. Taking a deep breath, I hover my hands over the pistol and envision the same protection symbols that are tattooed on me and engraved on my dagger. I allow the energy to flow down my arms and into the gun.

Removing my hands, the gun is exactly how I want. I charge the bullets and load it.

"You don't happen to have a—"

"Here you go," Hunter interrupts with a holster he pulled out of the pocket of his door.

Always the boy scout.

Narrowing my eyes, I slowly take the holster clip and attach it inside the waistband of my jeans then place my new gun in it. It fits comfortably, like it has always belonged there.

I wonder if Hunter's been honest about his gifts or if he is withholding some crucial information. You know, like mind reading.

What if he can?

I shake off that ridiculous thought and focus on the growing sense of impending danger. I'm not sure if it's Hunter's reaction that's making me on edge, or if it's something else.

Our slowing down has me glancing up. Hunter turns onto the grassy cobblestone path and we bounce in our seats. The trailer squeaks behind us as we slowly make our way through the clearing to the mangled remains of my car.

When the castle comes into view, my heart stops in my chest and the blood rushes from my head.

"*Fuck!*" We say at the same time.

A jet-black Aston Martin and a white utility truck with 'White Pine Contracting Co.' across the side are parked in front of the building.

There's no second-guessing who's here.

Margaret Bordeaux.

The double doors of the castle are no longer secured with the lock Hunter attached yesterday. They are now standing wide open.

"*Oh shit, oh shit, oh shit...* Do you think they made it downstairs?" My voice shakes.

He rubs the back of his neck with a hand while he maneuvers us to park in front of the front steps. "I sure as hell hope not."

Isn't it his job to lie to me to ease my fears?

"What if they did? What if this is like freaking Groundhog Day and we have to go through this shit again? When's it going to end?" My breathing comes in shallow pants and darkness tunnels my vision. A hand encloses mine.

"Breathe, baby. We will get through this."

"I... I can't. Something bad is going to happen." The familiar Chinese finger trap takes hold of my lungs and squeezes.

"We can't assume that. She may not have reached the dungeon yet."

"That's not it... I... I can't explain it."

Hunter brings my palm up.

"Do you feel that?"

A numbing tingle spreads through my limbs and a metallic taste coats my mouth. Everything spins so I close my eyes.

"All I feel is the tightness here." I claw my free hand over my throat to move the material away, struggling for air.

"No," he demands. "Focus on your hand." He moves it, and I try my hardest to ignore the panic, zeroing in on what my hand is up against. "Do you feel my heart beating?"

"No—wait." Through the wall against my palm, there's a faint thump. "Yes. Barely."

"Concentrate on the beat and *only* the beat."

A tear slips from the corner of my eye, and I squeeze them tight.

"Come on, baby. You can do it. Focus."

The pattering grows stronger. The cadence taps my hand and the constriction around me loosens.

"That's it." A strong warm hand cups my cheek at the same time his thumb caresses the back my hand.

My heart rate slows and becomes in sync with his. Air pushes into my lungs, expanding them with more ease, and I open my eyes.

Hunter's lips are thin and his jaw is clenched. "You okay?"

I nod. The impending doom is still digging its claws into my lungs, but a yellow light wraps around them to keep from being punctured. "Something is wrong."

"Maybe the only thing wrong is having to deal with Margaret's wrath."

He's probably right. Maybe I'm overreacting.

I lean down to my bag and grab a copy of the deed along with the temporary documentation to show proof of my ownership. With shaky, sweaty hands, I fold the papers up and place them in my back pocket.

He better be right.

His hand holds me back from climbing out of the truck. "Stay. I'll check it out. You're in no condition to go in there."

My trembling is quickly replaced with a burst of anger. "Hell. No." I grind out with narrow eyes.

He wants to sacrifice himself to be a hero because he doesn't think I can handle it?

A dimple pops through. "There's my Honey Bear."

"Did you—" He stops me with a quick kiss.

"Need you fully with me. Nothing gets you focused faster than pissing you off."

"You...argh." I turn and jump out of the truck.

Hunter rounds the front and hands me a flashlight. "Here."

"But—"

Hunter pushes my hand down. "Try to use *modern* technology this time and save your energy. Be ready for *anything*."

He means, prepare for the worst-case scenario—despite him previously trying to have me avoid thinking about it.

Even though my initial reaction is behind me, I'm still pushing away sharp nails trying to gain a hold of me.

Upon entering the castle, Hunter nods his head for us to go down the east wing to the dungeon.

It makes sense that we go to the source of the possible danger first.

Echoes of one set of boots fill the air. Mine. It's no surprise Hunter is in his weird stealth mode, silencing his steps. If he wasn't directly in front of me, I wouldn't know he was there.

Silence surrounds us and the floor lacks any sign of blood, so that's a plus.

Besides the vehicles outside and the front doors wide open, there's no sign anyone else is here. Hunter takes the lead down the stairs.

The gun Hunter gave me in the truck is secured in my waistband. The last thing I need today is to get arrested. But I'm also pretty sure my powers won't keep me out of trouble, it'll just be harder for someone to explain and be taken seriously.

Hunter's hand hovers over his side holster as we descend.

Halfway down the steps, metal clatters on the floor from afar.

BANG!

We rush down the remainder of the stairs and a woman's blood curdling scream echoes off the walls.

"Hunter!"

A distorted scream follows and my stomach churns. It sounds like a man is screaming while he's drowning in water. But there's no water...

"Fucking hell," Hunter says and draws his gun when we round the corner. A man, who I assume is the contractor, is on the ground with the wendigo tearing into his flesh with its sharp teeth. Blood pools out of the man's mouth as he gurgles out his cries; bolt cutters lie next to him along with the cut lock.

There's no way he'll survive this.

Another life taken.

My stomach rolls, and I try my damndest to push it down. Margaret stands in shock between the opening to the prison cell and the wendigo. She must have moved there after the contractor was attacked.

Damn it, woman, run!

We need to act, and fast. Indecision over what to do has me frozen in place.

Think, Anya, think. Do something.

Hunter's finger is on the trigger, aimed at the wendigo. His hesitation in shooting is most likely because there's a chance the bullets will go through the beast and right into Margaret.

One of the first rules in shooting, *know what's beyond your target.*

"Hunter, don't shoot," I hiss.

Margaret continues to stand, wide eyed, oblivious to anything but the horrific scene in front of her. The smell of blood mixed with the rotten stench of the monster almost makes me throw up. I swallow down the bile and push past Hunter.

"Anya, get back," he whisper-shouts at me.

He attempts to grab me to push me back behind him, but I side step his reach.

The wendigo ignores us and continues to feast, tearing into the man's chest.

"Screw this." At this point, there is no way to hide my powers. I shoot out an orb to create a barrier around the creature. *"Son-of-a-bitch."*

The wendigo leaps away from the orb and closer to Margaret. She cries out with a scream and the ball of light hits the wall.

I aim to shoot another—

What the fuck?!?

The giant creature from Hell melts into tar, attaching to Margaret's body and absorbing into her. The horns, the long claws, the mix of bones, and patches of fur all melt and soak into her like nothing I've ever seen before.

My mouth drops. Her body starts to convulse. She collapses to the ground, seizing and contorting into unnatural positions. She arches all the way backwards, her body folding over like something out of an exorcism movie.

"Anya, what the fuck is happening? Did it..." Hunter is as flabbergasted as I am.

"It...it possessed her."

I have no freaking clue what to do.

"Margaret..." I say cautiously, not knowing if she can hear me. There has to be *some* way to save her.

Her jerking ceases and she slowly unfolds then lays still on the floor.

Did it kill her?

A chill runs down my spine when she sits up and then slowly stands.

Maybe she's okay? Oh, who the hell am I kidding?

This lady is *far* from okay.

Hunter creeps closer to her. "Mrs. Bordeaux, are you okay?"

"Hunter, I don't think that—*No!*"

She jumps on Hunter, knocking him to the ground and holding him there.

"Shit!" he yells out.

I race over, grabbing her shoulders to pull her off of him. She doesn't budge. She's stronger than both of us. Hunter grunts under her as he fights her off.

I gather up my power to pull her away when she hits me. The distance between us grows as I fly across the room. My head hits the farthest stone wall with a sickening crack. Pain shoots down my spine, and the nausea from earlier was nothing compared to what I'm feeling right now. I close my eyes to drown it all out.

Everything in my mind turns hazy, and I'm suddenly tired.

Am I dreaming? Am I in bed? What's happening?

Faint grunting and scuffling are far in the distance.

Did I leave the T.V. on? Why am I so drowsy?

There is something important I need to do.

What is it?

"Anya!" a desperate cry pulls me farther out of the fog and a piece of my soul chips away.

Damn it, Anya, get it together, this is a matter of life and death.

Death...suddenly it hits me. My memories come flooding back. Hunter needs my help.

Adrenaline pumps through me, and I force my eyes open. Two grey blurs are wrestling across the room. I blink multiple times to clear my vision and push past the sickening pain. The images begin to clear, and Hunter is on the floor with Margaret slashing at him, snarling.

As I try to get up, rapid gunfire echoes off the walls and my pounding head drops me to my knees. The ear-piercing explosions have my vision fading into black, and I turn to throw up. Inhuman screams begin to grow louder as the ringing in my ears subsides.

Hunter must have shot Margaret. The roar and cries of pain are a mix of her voice and the wendigo's inside her.

But why isn't he still shooting?

Squinting my eyes, I find multiple glowing bullet holes through Margaret. Hunter is still fighting which makes me blow out a relieved breath.

He's okay, for now.

The energized bullets should have stopped the wendigo, if not slowed him down, but the tissue is healing faster than before. Possessing Margaret has made the beast tenacious.

Pushing up, I try to stand, but I collapse again.

"Hunter," I call out.

I have to get to him.

Remembering my gun, I pull it from my waistband and aim for the parts of Margaret's body that aren't as close to Hunter. I have good aim but with a possible concussion, I can't risk hurting him.

I steady the gun between both of my hands and pull the trigger. And then pull it again and again, trying to ignore the amplified discharges that send sharp pain through me.

The fear is almost crippling when the gunfire stops, and I realize I've emptied my magazine. The wendigo has more holes, but it's not stopping. It's not slowing down.

My body fails to cooperate at bringing me to my feet. I suck in a deep breath and try to fill my body with green healing light. The pain eases some but it isn't strong enough to fully heal me, and I don't have the time to wait. I'll have to push through the rest.

I stand with a little more energy. The room spins, causing me to stumble into the wall. Steadying myself, I try to use my light to create a barrier around the possessed Margaret, but my energy is blocked. It has to be from the head injury because I haven't used enough power to drain myself.

Yet here I am, powerless.

Hunter is battling for his life against a souped up wendigo, and I'm over here acting like a drunkard. Stumbling and useless.

I should have acted faster when we came downstairs. I fucked up.

Without my power, without a gun, I have only one option left to try to save him.

I can't fail him, I can't fail *us*.

Pulling out my dagger, I don't think twice as I hustle as quickly as I can to them, tripping and occasionally losing my balance, but I keep pulling myself back up and continuing my trek.

A few feet away from them I finally get a clear look at Hunter's injuries. He has deep gashes across his face, arms, and chest and he's bleeding profusely.

The beast tries to bite him and continues to slash at him, creating new lacerations.

He howls in agony.

When I finally reach them, I raise my dagger, pulling energy from everything and anything I can.

"Please ancestors, help provide me with the power I need."

I visualize the sunlight pouring through the castle's front doors, soaking into me. A yellow light grows inside of me and channels down into my blade.

The dagger glows as bright as the sun right before I jam it into Margaret's back and through her heart as hard as I can.

A blinding flash of light fills the dungeon, then everything goes black.

Chapter Forty

HAGALAZ

(GRIEF)

Waking up in the pitch blackness, the floor is cold, hard, and...sticky?

What the heck?

The heaviness in my limbs prevents me from moving a lot. Little by little, I shift into a sitting position and fight my rebellious body. Each movement amplifies the pounding pain in my head.

"Shit, that hurts," I mutter under my breath. My elbows rest against my knees with my head in my hands. The rancid stench surrounding me is hard to ignore, it's weaving into my clothes and making its home in my nose.

Yuck.

My stomach balls up from the familiar odor.

Where do I know that smell from?

Thinking back to the last image I remember before waking, and the first thing that comes to me is my head hitting a wall.

In the dungeon.

Gasp!

"Hunter!"

A faint wheeze breaks the silence.

"Hunter? Where are you?"

His low moan tells me he is *not* okay. I force myself to create a light, but only a small dull orb illuminates in my palm. It's better than nothing. Finally on my feet, I take a couple steps before my equilibrium throws me off kilter and I stumble, dropping to my knees.

"Shit, why does this have to be hard?" I whimper.

Moving the orb across my skin to my forearm, I shine it in front of me and begin to crawl. Bile rises in my throat as I try to ignore what I'm sure is blood squishing through my fingers and saturating my jeans.

Hunter is about ten feet away. The energy explosion threw me back when I stabbed the wendigo—in Margaret's body.

Did I kill it? Did I kill her?

Margaret's body lays motionless a couple of feet from Hunter.

I scramble on all fours as fast as my head allows until I reach him.

"Oh, Hunter. What did she do to you?" I whisper.

He's lost a lot of blood, his face is ghostly white, and his eyes fight to stay open. His skin's temperature matches his pallor—cold.

I pull out my cell phone. "Ugh."

Why would I have thought I'd have a signal?

There's no way in hell I'm leaving his side to call an ambulance. It could be too late by then.

Please don't let it be too late.

The dread I felt in the truck comes rushing back to me. *This* was what I feared. Not the wendigo, not Margaret. This is what had me hyperventilating, scared about what's to come. I somehow sensed the danger to my twin flame.

Hunter's weak grasp wraps around my hand. "You...okay?" he asks breathlessly, barely managing to get the words out.

I nod my head. "Yeah, I'm okay, but we need to focus on you."

He forces a tight smile and his body relaxes, his hand dropping to the cold, stone floor.

This man is insane. He's in seriously bad shape and he's only worried about me. We need to have a talk about priorities later.

Hunter's eyes drift closed and his breathing slows.

Panic sets in. "Oh, no you don't. Don't you *dare* go to sleep. *Look at me!*"

My blood pumps hard enough, it fills my eardrums. "It's gonna be okay. I got you. It'll be alright." I'm not sure if I'm saying this more to myself or him. A tear slides down my cheek and my body trembles.

The fact that he looks like he's peacefully sleeping scares the shit out of me. This isn't how someone who's been viciously attacked acts. The pain alone should have him screaming.

My hand shakes when I place it over his heart, feeling the shallow rise and fall of his lungs.

"*Please* don't leave me Hunter, I *need*"—I hiccup and pull in a strangled breath—"I need you. Just stay with me."

His breathing continues to decline, and I can barely hear his wheezing now.

"Damn it, Hunter! I can't lose you," a sob escapes. "Fight this, you stubborn ass. Use your so-called *superhero* powers and hold the *fuck* on." The pain in my head is nothing compared to what wracks through every bit of my soul.

"*Help! Someone help!*"

I drop my head in defeat. It's pointless. We are out here alone.

I am alone.

My shoulders quake from the sobs pouring out of me.

He took my heart and made it whole, he took away the emptiness inside me. He completed every missing part of me.

And now he leaves me?

Can Fate be *that* cruel to give me a taste of what we *could* be, only to tear it away? If the path I picked led me to this, I don't want any part of it. *Nothing* is worth losing Hunter. It breaks me into a million pieces. This isn't a story where I'm put back together, better than before.

No. This is the story of how my life, and my love, crumble around me. Burying me deep under the avalanche of the broken pieces.

There is no surviving this.

I can't—

I suck in a breath from the sudden intrusion in my mind. An image of the wolf, standing at the border of the castle's property comes to me. But all I see is him. He's well. He's alive...

He's alive because of me.

I can do this.

I sniffle and wipe my runny nose with my forearm then lay both hands on Hunter's chest. Squeezing my eyes closed, I concentrate on pulling in as much power as I can. From the self-generating symbols on the door, from our cell phones, from the sun shining in the front of the castle. I suck in energy from everywhere. Everything that hasn't already been exhausted by my dagger.

Drawing in wisps of green energy from the earth, it moves up me from the stone floor and, like vines, it grasps Hunter's body in its safe hold.

I remove my hands from him to manifest a healing green orb. Moving my hands around to create energetic friction, I open them up to allow more power to expand the ball of light, then condense it to build up the strength. I repeat the process until it pushes against my hands, ready to unleash its power.

My hands containing the healing sphere hover over Hunter's chest. In one rapid movement, I shove it into him and allow it to explode throughout his body, filling every inch, every cell of it.

"*Please* don't leave me Hunter."

Holding my hands over him, I allow the energy from the earth to course through me and into him. His faint heartbeat thumps against the light between my hands and his body.

It's a small fraction of the strong cadence that helped me push past my fear in the truck.

Let go of the fear and doubt, Anya.

The only way I can help Hunter is to not allow the darkness to pull me under. I need to rid every part of me from negativity that may be holding me back.

I release all the darkness that has its hold on me. My fear of losing this fight, of losing Hunter, of losing my job.

I release the hatred and grudge I hold against Kyle. I forgive him. I forgive Grant and Margaret of their wrongdoings.

I bundle up all the black and grey energy that hides in different areas of my body and soul, then expel it out of me and back to the universe—allowing the healing energy to fill the gaps with pure light.

Bringing my focus back to Hunter's injuries, I use the earth's light to help his body sew itself back together and create blood faster than humanly possible. I continue to pulse the current through him until every part of his body is healed.

But it still isn't enough. His pulse is continuing to decline, his heart is weak.

"Nooo... Someone please help me!" I cry out. "Grandmother, please forgive me. I'm sorry for ever doubting you as a child. For brushing off your attempt to train me. I'm listening, I need your knowledge, your guidance, your powers...*anything*!"

I can't do this on my own.

I can accept failure in any other part of my life, but I cannot accept failure with *this*.

Turning my head, I wipe my face on my arm and the runes on my glowing dagger illuminate from where it sits in Margaret's back.

The runes.

The idea pops in my head, unsure if it'll work.

I need to at least try.

Opening the buttons of Hunter's shirt, I hold my right hand over his heart and, just as I did to the guns, I burn a rune into his skin. A tri-spiral, Spiral of Life, glows with the last of my power.

I bite the inside of my cheek and wait to see if it'll bring him back to me.

"Come on. You are supposed to be saving me! You can't be the damsel in distress," I choke out. "Nothing can take you down. You're stronger than this." I sniffle. "Come back to me," my whisper barely discernible through my cries.

He lies motionless.

Nothing I can do is changing his fate.

Our fate.

My body collapses on his and my head lands on his chest. His cold skin cools my hot cheeks, which tells me his heart isn't pumping the blood as it should throughout his body.

His faint pulse is harder and harder to hear.

I need to know what I can do to make this right.

To make Hunter whole again.

To bring him back to me.

Hunter exhales his last breath.

His heart beats its final beat.

I am met with silence...and emptiness.

He's gone.

Chapter Forty-One

DAGAZ

(ASCENSION)

You must choose a path. Neither will be easy, and you will find loss in both. Taking the right direction, though, will open up a destiny filled with blessings. Do not let fear sway you. Choose not with your mind, but your heart and soul.

I chose the wrong path.

My grandmother warned me. And I fucked up. I've sacrificed everything, and even though I'm sure the wendigo is dead, I still lost in the end.

My heart is completely shattered.

All I want to do now is lay here and die in Hunter's arms. I can't go on without him.

I know if anyone heard my thoughts, they would think I'm overreacting, but they haven't lost their twin flame. The other half of themselves.

I can't live a life without him again.

All of the events were coordinated by Fate; it used me as its puppet.

A puppet that's being punished for my sacrifices.

I pull myself up and give Hunter a kiss filled with all the love and light I have left in me, then lean my forehead on his. Despite him breathing his last breath, his blue aura still lingers inside him.

It's faint but there.

In desperation, I cry out, "Grandmother, Light Angel ancestors, how could you do this to me? How could you allow this to happen?" I choke on a sob. Piece by piece the whole of my being breaks away, dissolving into nothingness. "I did what you couldn't, and I'm still punished. What did I do wrong?" My anger builds. "You *owe* me. You need to help me make this right. I need you all more than I ever needed anything in my life. I'm asking anyone who hears me to lend me your power, your strength, your help. Please, *please*, help me!" I'm begging with everything I have.

It doesn't matter that I've tried and given it my all already.

Hunter would have never given up on me. I can't give up on him.

With one final attempt, I rotate my hands, pulling in energy, and even though nothing appears, I keep going. I know it takes time to regain my powers, to build them up without outside help to charge them.

But I won't give up until I take my last breath.

Closing my eyes, I suck in air and exhale deeply to clear my head the best I can. I use my third eye to unveil what is hidden from plain sight.

Focusing on my surroundings, I try to locate just a small bit of energy. Scanning the rooms, and I search every bit of space where some could be hiding.

The rays from the sun are distinct, and the yellow light pours down the stairs and into my body as though I've called to it. As it enters me, the warmth washes over me in waves.

My hands tingle as power flows into them creating a spark before forming into a ball. Through my third eye, I see energy stronger than if my eyes were open. The sun's radiance spirals around Hunter and me. Quickly following it, green, blue, and magenta swirls of energy creep out of the walls of the dungeon.

The colors form into images of people, some familiar, while others I've never seen before. They place their hands on my shoulders, head, and back.

My head clears, my pain lessens and the orb between my hands burns brighter. The tears are still falling down my face, but they aren't tears of sadness. They're from the surge of power and emotion that flows from these entities into me. My ancestors heard my cries and are here to help.

I am not alone.

My family surrounds me, lending me their strength.

A surge of heat at my front has me opening my eyes, and I stare wide eyed and slack jawed at the sight before me.

On the other side of Hunter, is a beautiful man. He's unlike the others here. He has the purest of white light surrounding him. An angelic aura filled with peace.

"Thank you," I say, breathily.

He looks at me with a strong sense of pride resonating off him, pride and love that a father would have for his daughter; or rather a grandfather would have for a granddaughter he cherishes.

"Please help me," I plead.

Without speaking, he lightly grasps my wrists and his white light travels through my body before it absorbs into the ball of energy.

The angel guides my hands over Hunter's chest—directly over the Spiral of Life I burned into him. Together, we push the orb through the symbol, into Hunter's heart, allowing it to spread and blossom throughout his body.

I focus on the energy and watch it work its magic.

After a few moments, the light fades and, with it, my final attempt at saving Hunter.

I lay back down on his chest and my disappointment sends more tears from my eyes to his bare chest.

There's no change.

Glancing around, I find myself alone once again. My ancestors are gone.

We've tried everything possible, and it still wasn't enough. I cover him back up but forgo buttoning his flannel.

I shift and lay in the crook of Hunter's arm, remembering this morning when he was holding me close.

But his arm doesn't come around me.

It won't, ever again.

My tears soak his shirt until it feels like an hour has passed, and I know I need to let go.

But I'll never fully be able to.

What I can do, though, is give him the proper arrangements for his friends to say their final goodbyes.

My heart crushes and my chest heaves.

Is this really it?

Is this the cost of defeating a monster from hell?

I push to get up—

A groan rumbles under my palms.

"Oh my God!"

Hunter actually groaned, as in breathing again and alive.

"Hunter, can you hear me?" My heart beats hard in my chest.

Please don't let it be me finally losing my mind.

He groans again and mutters something that sounds like 'off.'

That is not *a figment of my imagination.*

"Off? What do you mean '*off*?'"

He grinds out, "Chest... Off."

Chest? Is he hurt inside still?

I glance down. "Crap." I remove my hands and weight from him. I didn't realize I was pushing on his chest.

Tears of happiness stream down my cheeks. "I'm so sorry, are you hurting? How are you feeling? I need to call an ambulance for you, but we don't have working phones. Do you need any—"

"Hold up," he interrupts me and his hand covers mine, which is flailing around like a madwoman as I ramble. "I'm a little sore, but give me a minute to get my energy back so I can sit up."

He lays there a moment, and I anxiously tap my fingers on my leg.

He's back. He's really back!

When he begins to sit up slowly, I jump up to help him. He rolls out his neck and shoulders, then studies his arms. "Why am I not bleeding? I know she took quite a few gashes out of my arms and my chest for sure." His eyes go wide. "Is my face messed up? I think it's numb, I can't feel the pain."

Laughter bubbles up in my chest and spills over. More from hysteria than anything else at this point.

"Don't worry, your pretty face is still perfect." I catch my breath. "I...umm...healed you. I didn't have much energy, but I was able to take in a lot from around us." Biting my lip I cringe and say, "There's no point in checking the phones, I had to pull power from those too. When that didn't work the first time, I asked for some help."

"Hold up...the first time? How many times exactly *did* you try to heal me? And who helped you?" Hunter's brows are furrowed and he glances around.

"I didn't know what else to do. Everything I tried didn't work at first, but then my ancestors helped...uh...including my...multi

-great grandfather. I was so scared, Hunter, I was terrified to lose you. I actually *did* lose you!" And now I'm bawling my eyes out.

I went from crying to laughing to crying again. I am *not* handling this well.

Hunter's arm goes around me. "Hey now, it's okay. I'm here, I didn't go anywhere and I'm *not* going to. I told you that it would be hard to get rid of me. But what do you mean your ancestors helped, and do you mean the *original* Light Angel?"

"Yes, the original angel who started the long line of Light Angels. He shared his white light with me and helped guide me." I snuggle into his chest and melt into his warmth.

Gah, he's really here.

I give him a tight squeeze. "It was amazing. The love and power all my ancestors poured into me. Then seeing the beauty of the angel. That may have been my one and only chance to see them."

As elated as I am at Hunter being with me, safe and with his heart beating again, a part of me is sad that my ancestors left me without saying goodbye. I didn't get the chance to thank them for bringing back my Hunter.

"Well, they didn't leave you empty handed. They left you with a bit of a gift."

Huh?

Looking around I come up blank. They didn't take the two dead bodies with them. They could've at least cleaned up this mess before they left, but apparently that's *my* job.

"I'm not sure if you're seeing things from your prior injuries, or maybe you're a little changed from dying, but there's no gift. We should probably get out of here to figure out what story we need to tell about what went down." My headache is gone and the only ache that exists is the impending responsibility to clean up and deal with the authorities.

Hunter pulls me away from him, his hands resting on my biceps. "No, I meant your light. It's usually a golden yellow, but now you're glowing white. You're the only thing lighting up this place, Anya."

Moving my hand in front of me, my mouth falls open. I'm illuminating and it isn't my normal color. It's the same white as my angel grandfather.

"Wait a minute... I died!?" Hunter's eyes are about to bulge out of his head, and his jaw drops.

I want to tell him more, but the mixture of emotions hits me like a tsunami. The dam breaks and I lose it.

Hunter pulls me in. "Let it all out, babe. I've got you."

Everything that's happened to us leading up to this very moment goes on replay. The shock from the gift the angel gave me was what sent me over the edge. But since my emotions are free, guilt slips in and hits me hard. If we hadn't gone to the County Clerk's Office and City Hall, we may have been able to save Margaret and the contractor.

My family's secret killed three people. Their blood is now on my hands, and I have to live with it.

"I killed her, I stabbed her in the heart." Saying it out loud has me sobbing more.

What if Hunter looks at me differently now that he knows I'm a killer?

He rocks me back and forth. "Shh...everything's going to be okay. But I want you to listen to my words very carefully, Anya."

I sniffle and bring my gaze to meet his.

"Remember when I told you a few days ago about my past? About the evil people I had to kill?"

I nod.

"I told you about how I had to understand that the blood was on the hands of the people that murdered my parents. The lives that I had to take were on *their* hands, not mine." He rubs a hand over my back, still rocking us. "This here…" He points to the blood bath before us, "was all due to the actions of the wendigo, *not* you. There'd have been so many more who would've died if it wasn't for you. Not only did you protect people yesterday and today, but now you've saved lives for many generations to come. You destroyed the wendigo for good. You can't save everyone, just like I couldn't save everyone in my company. You have to understand that you did *not* take an innocent life."

"But—"

"But nothing. The wendigo killed the Bordeauxes and the contractor. You destroyed the wendigo. Margaret was already gone by then. I can vouch for that. There was nothing human about her once the wendigo possessed her."

My head drops. I want to blame the wendigo, but there are a lot of *what ifs* where I could've chosen differently and had an alternative outcome.

Hunter lifts my face with his finger. "Hey, you promised me that you wouldn't allow this to destroy your spirit. Please don't break that promise."

I listen to his words and play them back in my head.

He's right, I finally concede. I have to admit to myself there's nothing we could've done. We didn't know that they'd be here. Margaret's greed brought her here, and it was that same greed that allowed the wendigo to possess her. She was gone the moment it took over her body.

Taking a few deep breaths, I push out my guilt and pain the best I can. Although the heaviness lifts from my chest, this whole thing was a very traumatic experience. I still feel a sense of loss, knowing I won't be back to normal for a while.

I'm thankful that I have Hunter to help me get through it.

I look up into his milk-chocolate eyes. "Thank you, what would I ever do without you?"

He chuckles and clears his throat. "Well...you would live a long, boring life with boyfriends who don't know how to please you for one. Ouch." His hand rubs the spot on his shoulder I playfully slapped.

"I think we can call ourselves even now, can't we? Since I saved *your* life."

Hunter rubs the back of his neck. "Speaking of...you want to tell me about me dying? The last thing I remember was being so relieved that you were okay. After that, I knew it was okay to close my eyes for a bit." He cringes. "I'm hoping you're kidding."

Chapter Forty-Two

SOWILO

(SUCCESS)

It was wishful thinking for Hunter to leave it at me healing him, instead he's focusing on the dying part.

Why couldn't he put two and two together? He was dead, now he is alive after I healed him. Simple as that.

But I have to give him credit, he was dead just a little bit ago, his brain cells may need to catch up.

I purse my lips. "Well...you know how I said I healed you, but not enough the first time?"

"Yeeaahhh..." he draws out.

Gah, why does this have to feel awkward?

"Your wounds were healed, but your lungs and heart gave out." My chest tightens along with my throat. "Your body quit." I'm not sure there will come a day when this won't choke me up. The next words I struggle to get out. "I...umm...I still felt your spirit inside your body. A part of you was still holding on. I...I couldn't imagine life without you and I couldn't let you go. That's when I begged my ancestors for help. Really, I begged *anyone* who was listening to help me. I never thought anyone would actually come though. I mean, maybe grandmother, but everyone else? There were so many here."

He blinks. Then blinks some more.

Shit, does this guy have a DNR, Do Not Resuscitate, that I went against?

Hunter interrupts my thought, "You're telling me that I was dead."

"Uh, yeah."

"Like, not breathing, no pulse...dead. Not alive anymore. Completely gone. Gone, gone?"

"Umm...that *is* usually what dead means." I mean, I'm not sure how much more one would describe dying, but I'm pretty sure he covered it.

Hunter picks up his arms, studies them, then pokes his face with a finger. After his inspection, he opens his mouth and feels around his teeth with his tongue, spending extra time on his canines.

I narrow my eyes. "What are you doing?" The words come out slow and cautious. Maybe he *did* lose his mind after all. If I'm lucky, it's only temporary.

But if not, I'll take him as is.

Whoa, that sounded a little creepy.

"Everything I've watched in movies or read in books shows anyone reanimated usually has missing or rotting flesh. Sometimes they gain fangs. I'm trying to figure out which one it is for me," he says, completely serious.

I snort. "You're whole. Every part of you is the same as before." Glancing down at his lap I say, "I mean I didn't check *everything*, but I'm pretty sure you're completely whole. Minus the light scars from your wounds, and *maybe* some new ink?" Cringing, I wait again for his reaction, hoping he brushes off my last words.

"Ink?"

Nope, he definitely is focusing on that word.

He stares down with his brows pinched and spots the spirals on his bare chest. Tentatively, he touches it as if it'll hurt. When it seems to be healed as well, he rubs at it as if to wipe it off.

"I'm sorry. I was trying everything and anything to bring you back. I can try to heal it up if you don't want it. You won't hurt my feelings." I bite my lip nervously. I hope I can heal it. My hand goes to his chest, but Hunter grasps my wrist and places it on his thigh.

"No," he demands.

"No, you don't like it? Or no, you don't want it removed?" I cock an eyebrow.

"No, I don't want it removed. A small part of me is nervous what will happen if you remove it. But a bigger part of me wants it to stay. It's a gift of life you gave me. It's a part of you tattooed on me forever. I can't imagine ever taking it off." He releases my hand and cups my face with what I'm sure is a bloody hand, but I don't care.

Right before he brings his lips with mine, he says, "Thank you, Anya. Thank you for *everything* you did to save me. I know it couldn't have been easy. Shit, when I thought I lost you, my whole world came crashing down around me. You are the bravest, strongest, most amazing woman I've ever met. You are truly magnificent."

He kisses me and my world is finally whole again.

"How are we going to explain all this?" I point to the horrific scene surrounding us.

After about a half-hour, we regained the strength to get up and we're now standing in the center of the dungeon by the wendigo's prison.

"I haven't worked out those details yet, but give me a few and I'll think of something. But first, you may want to remove the evidence from the crime scene?" Hunter points to Margaret's body laying face down in a puddle of blood—my dagger still embedded in her back.

I make my way to her body and wrap my arms around myself. Even though Hunter has told me I didn't kill her, it's hard to ignore the proof before me.

Hunter comes up behind me and wraps an arm around me. "Let me do it."

"No. I put it in her, I need to be the one to take it out." Trying to not think more about it, I remove my blade. The wet suction sound has me gagging.

Weirdly enough, it comes out clean.

I inspect the metal and it's spotless, which is the weirdest thing, but it's pointless to question things that don't make sense anymore.

I look up to Hunter and ask, "Do you think they are going to see it's a knife wound, not an animal attack?"

"I don't know, babe. But whatever happens, we're in it together." He rubs circles around my back to comfort me. I wish I could say it's helping.

I guess we don't have a choice but to allow Fate to take over yet again. And if that means I am arrested for killing her, so be it.

Justice will need to be served and Karma may feel I deserve it.

We grab our dead flashlights, the pieces of Hunter's lock, his gun, and the shell casings. Looking around, there's not a single bullet in sight. The walls are absent of holes. It's as though they tore through the wendigo and disappeared.

Another thing we can't explain.

"Are you ready to get out of here?"

"Yes, more than ready."

Hunter waves me ahead, and I don't hesitate to lead us out the front doors in no time. As soon as we step into the sun, I'm hit with the recharging rays. I suck in a cool breath of fresh air before turning to scan Hunter's body for any more injuries.

I search his face for signs of pain. "How are you feeling?"

"A little sore still, but more just muscle aches which will go away in time. How are *you* feeling?"

"Fatigued...and shaky. I think my concussion is healed already, so that's a plus." I give him a small smile. "Lucky for you, I'll survive after all."

"Good, can't have you risk everything only for you to end up leaving me."

I choke down a lump in my throat. Those were my exact thoughts not too long ago.

Raising my hands to place them on Hunter, I freeze. The proof of my sin stares back at me. Blood covers my hands, arms, and... *what the hell?* The dark red is splattered everywhere.

My lips quiver at the same time my body begins to tremble.

"Hey. It's okay. You're in shock."

"Bbb...but the b...blood." I stutter, my body shakes harder.

"Come here." He pulls me in and my face hits the nape of his neck. His hand goes to my hair, running his fingers through it and making hushing sounds while he rocks us back and forth.

We stay that way until the constricting vibrations lessen.

With a small voice I say, "We need to charge our phones to try to call the police. What are we going to tell them?"

"I don't think we have much of an option. We tell them the partial truth of it being an animal attack. Margaret and the contractor left the door open and it found them downstairs. It must have felt trapped again and attacked."

"That's true, but what's to stop them from going hunting for any potential predators?"

The wolf and momma bear flash through my mind as the first that would be hunted, without question. I can't let that happen.

"We can reassure the police we'll be installing secure locks, fencing, and a security system to prevent others from getting in," he adds.

"That's all well and dandy, but it still won't stop them. Three people were murdered. They won't care if we lock this place up like Fort Knox, they're gonna search for the animal they think now has a taste for human flesh," my voice becomes desperate. "I need to warn the wolf and mama bear."

Hunter rubs a hand over his beard. "If you see them again you can warn them, but they may have already left the area. There's no guarantee they are nearby and we can't waste time searching for them."

"That's fair." *I hope for their sakes they are far away from this mess.*

"Hear me out. I have an idea, but...I'm not sure you're going like it."

I groan. "Do I even want to ask? Just give it to me straight. Is it something I'm involved in?"

"Uh, a bit, yes."

"Ugh, of course. I'm going to have to go to church quite a bit to repent for my sins, anyways. That's until they lock me out, or have me committed. Give it to me."

I'm beyond exhausted from all the emotions and loss of energy, I want this nightmare to be over.

"The male bear. We can say we shot it and end the search party before it begins. Then we tell the detective that I chased the bear out to the woods where I hunted it down, eliminating any further risk."

"How the hell are you going to conceal the gashes all over its body? And how about the lack of a bullet?"

"Well, the injuries are where you come in. I'll handle the gunshot."

"Are you suggesting what I think you're suggesting?"

"That you heal up the bear to look as if it was never attacked? Yeah, I am. But don't bring it back to life. It might have worked for me, but we don't know how that will work on a bear. I'd rather not tempt fate by bringing a zombie animal into this world."

How amazing would it be to bring back the bear and cub?

But damn it, he's right. I've already tampered with the laws of nature enough.

"Fine, let's have the phones start charging before we go."

"You betcha, but I have to ask. Are you okay with the story?"

"I really don't have much of a choice. The truth isn't possible. But I must say, I'm glad you're on my team. You're good at this..." I wave my hand. "Storytelling. I hope you use your skills only for good."

Hunter leans down to my level. "I won't ever lie to you." His eyes dart back and forth between mine. "Do you believe me?" he pleads.

There's no question about it.

"You don't have to worry. I can tell when you're lying. I'm glad that the cops can't."

"Making others believe me is my other super power." He wiggles his eyebrows. "You're the only one immune to my charms." He flashes a cocky grin.

I chuckle. "Oh, I'm sure."

It didn't take long to find the bear and his cub. With our exhaustion, the forty-five-minute trip on the four-wheeler felt much longer. My stomach knots like a double twisted pretzel at seeing them again.

"What are we going to do with the baby?" I stare at the ground, avoiding the gutted animals.

"It can stay, they may think the dad attacked it."

"Wouldn't that be a concern that if there's one baby, there may be others still on the loose?"

Hunter runs a hand over his beard. "Yeah, you're right. I hate for you to have to keep doing the majority of the work but..."

"What now?" My stomach twists tighter.

"How do you feel about cremation?"

I shift on my feet. "For myself, I'm all for it. For this little thing? I have to admit, I'm not a fan."

"Do you have any other suggestions?"

"Ugh, no. Fine. I'll do it."

This'll prevent others from thinking the rest of the family is still roaming the woods. I try to remind myself that the fur ball is no longer alive and that this will help keep the other animals safe.

Instead of using my low reserves, I take advantage of the sun's power as it courses through my veins.

"Rest in peace, sweet baby," I whisper.

In no time, the cub is surrounded by my force field. There's no taking my time and prolonging it. I bring it above the ground to prevent any scorch marks, and I burn it to ash with a quick pulse of energy.

With a heavy heart, I release the barrier and allow the October wind to take the bear home to its mom.

Hunter comes from behind and wraps his arms around me. "You okay?"

"I will be." His hands splay around my blood covered stomach. "How does the blood not bother you? I feel absolutely disgusting." I turn up my nose.

"My need for you overpowers the blood."

I give in and melt into him.

Not too long ago, I lost this man.

And now he's holding me in my nasty state, after I cremated a baby bear, and before I heal a dead bear for him to shoot.

How fucked up are we?

Oh well, we're together. Nothing else should matter. Except cleaning up our mess.

I tilt my head back to look up at Hunter.

Will I ever get sick of him? I doubt it.

"We should get this over with."

Hunter leans down to press a soft kiss to my lips before releasing me. "I'm here if you need."

Kneeling at the bear's side, I lay my hands over the unscathed fur. The essence of this animal is absent—which is for the best. If there were a hint of a soul left, I'd be more than tempted to try to bring it back. But now? There's nothing more I can do.

With the power from the earth's energy field, I call upon the wisps of green energy to weave itself through the bear's flesh, stitching together the wounds and growing back the clumps of missing hair—making the bear *almost* whole again. I heat the bear's insides to hopefully throw off the coroner—in case they check the time of death—then sit back on my heels.

Yes, I've read too many crime novels, but that may have helped us.

Not that I know how warm to raise the temp, but it's better than the coldness from before.

"I'm gonna take you back to the castle." Hunter grasps my elbow and helps me to my feet.

"But you need to shoot him."

"And I will, but without you here. This has been hard enough—"

"I—"

Hunter holds his palm up to stop me.

"I *get* you are strong and don't need protecting. But let me do this *one thing* for you. Let me take you away for this part."

He's right. I'm close to breaking, again. Despite how tough I'm trying to appear on the outside, I'm a fragile crystal on the inside right now. "As much as I'm willing to agree with you—*this time.* It'll take you too long to drive me to the castle then come back. How about I start walking back, and you pick me up on the way? Give me a five-minute head start before you shoot, but then we can get this nightmare over with."

"Are you sure?" He seems uncertain.

"You're a human lie detector. You tell me." I challenge.

He sighs and his shoulders drop. "Alright. Go now, but please place a force field around you.

"Wha—"

"Hear me out," he interrupts. "It'll make me feel better knowing you're safe, and it'll muffle the sound."

I can't complain. This is better than him taking an extra two hours just because he wanted to take me back. There's no sense in arguing with him further.

"Okay. Be careful, though."

"I know how to shoot without hitting myself, babe."

"You better, or I'll kill you, then bring you back to life. Don't test me." My arms cross over my chest and I huff.

Hunter swats me on my ass. "Get going."

"Fine, fine, I'm going." I begin walking back the direction we came.

"Eh-hem?" Hunter clears his throat and I turn back to him. His finger is making a circle around what I'm sure is the outline of my body.

Oh, yeah.

I draw in the sun's rays and form a thick barrier around me then hold out my hands in a *are you happy now* gesture. Once Hunter gives a satisfied smile, I continue on my walk.

Shortly after, I hear a small pop, followed by a faint rumbling.

It's difficult not to visualize what Hunter had to do. I focus on my shallow breathing, and slow my pace to relax the tension in my body.

The pretzel in my stomach begins to unwind.

It doesn't take long for the rumbling to grow louder. Hunter comes into a clearing and my heart skips a beat.

Will I ever get over the relief of seeing him alive and well after he's been out of my sight?

How the hell am I going to deal when he leaves for his next job?

I drop my shield and wait for him to pull up next to me.

"Hey, little girl, wanna ride?"

I scrunch up my nose. "Could you *not* say that like a guy in a white utility van offering a puppy?"

"What if I offered you *books*?" He says it like it's my kryptonite.

Which it is.

My eyes light up. "*Now* we're talking. I'll be your Belle, if you're my Beast. Just give me the library, and we will live happily ever after."

"Beast? I'm not that hairy." He runs a hand over his beard.

"And *that's* what you get hung up on?" I climb up behind him and wrap my arms around his waist. "You might as well be. You did die, and I brought you back. Now, where's that library you owe me?"

He groans. "I'm working on it."

"Yeah, yeah, just drive."

We arrive back to the truck and Hunter checks his phone. Lucky for us, it has three bars of signal. Which is beyond strange, but I'm not about to question it now.

He looks up Detective Shane's number and hits the call button.

I only hear Hunter's side of the conversation.

"Yeah, the tow truck didn't have the right equipment, so I had to get a flatbed for Anya's car. That's when we found..." He provides his side of the story and answers what I assume are a number of questions.

"Thanks Detective, we'll see you soon." Hunter turns to me. "They're leaving the station now. We have about an hour to an hour and half before they arrive."

This is about to feel like déjà vu with the detective, police, ambulance, and coroner coming out again.

"What about this mess?" I wave a hand over my body. "It's going to be hard to explain my rolling around in someone's blood."

"Ah, I got you covered."

"Of course you do, my handsome boy scout." I blink adoringly up at him.

"Soldier, not boy scout," he grumbles.

"Toe-may-toe, toe-mah—oomph!"

Hunter shoves a pile of clothes and a couple water bottles into my chest with a cocked eyebrow.

"Damn, you're sensitive."

He ignores me and pulls off his bloody clothes, rinsing off his hair, face, and beard before scrubbing his arms.

I really should be doing the same, but I'm struggling to tear my eyes from his body. I'm transfixed as water slides down his toned chest and thick abs.

He's simply gorgeous.

"You need help, or are you planning on using your drool to wash off the stains?"

I discreetly suck the corner of my lip in, checking for saliva. "I am *not* drooling."

"Whatever you say, sweetheart. Come here."

"I can do it my—Hey!" He yanks my jacket off, then strips me of my shirt. "I'm not a child." I set my dagger on the floorboard of the truck and kick off my boots. When my hand begins to unbutton my jeans, Hunter pushes them aside to do it himself.

There's no point in fighting the man. I know I'd ultimately win, but I'll let him have his way. I guess it's nice to be taken care of for once.

Plus, what woman doesn't have a fantasy of being pampered by their man?

"This is going to be cold," Hunter warns.

Okay, maybe not this type of pampering.

"*Sss...*" I hiss out, then remember I have an internal heater. With only a thought, I crank up my internal thermostat, and purr as steam comes off my skin.

"That's not fair. I had to deal with the cold water."

"I can heat you up if you want." I hold my palm out.

He raises his hands. "Oh no. I'm good. Now, flip your hair over so I can get the rest of this out, then you can get dressed."

I turn upside down, and let Hunter scrub out the dried blood.

"Okay, you're done. Can you dry your hair too?"

"Hmm... I can try." Rubbing my hands together, I create a small amount of energetic friction then run my hands over my hair, heating it without burning. It takes a couple minutes of combing my heated hands through it, but soon it's dry.

Ooh...this will come in handy.

While I dress, Hunter loads up his four-wheeler, and hoists me onto the bed of the truck, where we sit and wait for everyone to arrive.

About a half hour later, a caravan of first responders emerge from the narrow drive of the property, followed by...animal control?

My eyes widen. "What's up with animal control? I heard you tell the detective the situation was handled."

Hunter places a hand over mine. "It's okay, they need to take the bear's body away. Test it for diseases that could have caused it to be aggressive. We need to let them take it."

I'm not thrilled about it, but if it'll keep the rest of the animals safe, we don't have an choice.

Hunter helps me off the tailgate as Detective Shane heads in our direction.

"Wish I could be seeing you both under better circumstances. You really need to stay away from this place." The detective's displeasure in our involvement is clear in his tone.

"If only we could. We just found out that Anya here, believe it or not, owns the place."

"You're shitting me." The detective's face drops. "How long have you known about this?"

"This morning. Right before we came out, we took the information we found and filed the papers. But I assure you, we have a plan to put up enough security and fencing to keep others out, as well as any wildlife. Not that we'll have any problems now since the bear's no longer an issue."

"Well, I wish you both the best. If you want my advice, I'd recommend selling or tearing it down. This place creeps me out." He clears his throat. "Now, let me get your statement Ms. O'Clery, then I'll leave you two alone."

I provide my statement and show an unstained copy of my deed. Everything else happens in a blur while we watch everyone work around us. My thoughts go to my new concern.

Will they identify a dagger wound in Margaret's injuries?

Shit, shit, shit. I should have tried to heal it.

If they find it, there won't be any doubt I'll soon become a suspect for murder. But then again, they would've said something about finding a stab wound in her back.

I release a sigh of temporary relief.

Now I await my Fate.

Chapter Forty-Three

URUZ

(PROSPERITY)

While the first responders finish up, Hunter gets in his truck and backs the trailer up to my car. As soon as the trailer's lined up, he hooks the car up with the winch and starts the crank. Metal flexes and creates dreadful creaks and squeals that have me cringing. It's a painful sight to watch my mangled car be pulled onto the trailer while pieces of it fall to the ground.

Instead of focusing on the destruction that was once called my car, I move my attention to Hunter.

A perfect distraction.

Whether he's working the winch, or picking up large pieces of scrap from my car, his flexing muscles are a piece of art that makes the nightmares sit in the back seat.

"Anya...Earth to Anya!"

I shake out of the trance. "Huh?" I answer without looking up. His thick thighs strain against his jeans when he shifts into a squat to pick up the side mirror from the ground.

"Eyes up here." A deep chuckle rumbles from Hunter's chest.

I glance up to find him with that signature cocky grin on his face.

Only hours ago, I'd thought I'd never see that grin—those dimples—ever again.

A vice-like grip wraps around my heart.

But here the man stands, appearing unharmed and full of life.

Is it possible that my heart can feel this full of love, while at the same time, still hang onto the pain of losing him?

"I was asking if you could grab those last few pieces on the ground, and throw them in the back of my truck." The car is loaded and Hunter secures it with a tarp. He tilts his head. "You okay?"

"Yeah, just tired."

Wood scraping against metal brings my attention to the last squad car making its way down the grassy drive and back to the main road. They must be finished. One less thing to worry about.

Picking up the pieces of my car has me realizing that my pain over Hunter's death supersedes the sadness over my car. I wouldn't say it's numbness; it's more about realizing what's important in life. A material thing, such as a car, means nothing compared to what I almost lost today.

It takes me a few trips, but after a final check for any remaining pieces on the ground, I holler at Hunter, "Alright, that's the last of it. All good?"

"Yeah, we're good. Hop on in, sweetheart. Let's go home."

Dragging our feet, we make our way inside my house. We've already dropped off the trailer, with my car, at Hunter's place. A call to the insurance company is my first step before any decisions can be made. But that's for another day.

"Hunter, how about you hop in the shower first. I'm going to order some food." I don't think I can relax enough to really enjoy a shower. My priority is to make sure Hunter is recovered and taken care of.

I know he's back to his healthy, normal self, but it still doesn't stop me from worrying and wanting to take care of him.

Maybe one day I'll feel less paranoid.

"Sounds good, I'm starving. I'll be quick." He gives me a peck and heads down the hall with his duffle bag.

Willing myself not to drool, I watch his tight ass and thick thighs flex as he strides down the hallway.

Once he is out of view, I settle on the couch and pick up my phone to order us a couple of pizzas. It's not the healthiest, but it's time for comfort food after the day we've had. I steal a moment to myself to go over everything that happened, and what I could've done to prevent all the losses.

Demons hiding in the shadows of my mind whisper in my ear, making sure I don't forget.

The guilt isn't debilitating but it still weighs on me.

Images of their bodies flash behind my eyes. I can't stop myself from overthinking what they could've felt in the moments before their death.

How can I get past feeling solely responsible?

Fresh citrus and lavender wafts into the room. The familiar and comforting fragrance centers me.

It starts to bring me out of the darkness trying to pull me under.

Without a word, Hunter appears, hovering over me before he takes my face between his hands and kisses me.

A kiss full of love and...*is that appreciation?*

Do I deserve it?

As I'm pulled deeper into Hunter's love, little by little, the doubt leaves me.

The emotions behind his lips caressing me are filled with promises of a long future together.

A future we almost lost before it even began.

"Mmm... I'm not complaining, but what's that for?" I ask when he pulls away.

"Thank you for not giving up on me. I love you, Anya."

Enter the butterflies in my stomach fluttering around in a harmonized pattern. The wind between their wings pushes away the remaining darkness.

"I love you, too. But there's nothing to be thankful for. I'm simply a selfish woman. I wanted you, so I fought to keep you." I smirk. "Keep that in mind, if another woman tries to take what's mine. I'm selfish *and* territorial." Standing up on my tip-toes, I suck in Hunter's bottom lip then say, "My turn to get cleaned up." I step back and turn to walk towards the bathroom.

Smack!

I suck in a breath and hold back my reaction to Hunter's hand colliding with my backside. It's so hard not to turn around to meet that mischievous smile he's probably sporting. He's waiting to see how I respond.

I refuse to give him the pleasure. Instead, I go get cleaned up, so I can wash the remnants of death off me.

Every bit of me wants to collapse to the tile floor in my shower and cry. Cry and scream and yell at the world for everything I've had to endure. For everything I've lost, despite getting some of it back. I need to remind myself that Hunter and I are getting a fresh start.

A do-over of sorts. And I won't let my emotions take over and ruin this. I let the water take my pain, take the fear, take the memories that bind me, and roll them off my skin in waves. The droplets cascade down my skin, collecting and carrying my troubles away, down the drain. Leaving me refreshed and renewed.

When I open the door to the bathroom, the heavenly aroma of marinara, gooey mozzarella cheese, freshly made dough, and spicy pepperoni fills my nose and tickles my taste buds. My stomach growls on my way to the kitchen where there's a bottle of beer and a large glass of wine sitting next to the pizza boxes.

What I see next steals my heart and sends heat to my core.

Hunter is on my couch reading a book.

Could the man get any hotter?

I move closer and my jaw drops to the floor. It's one of my favorite books, *Stolen Hearts* by Gail Haris.

OMG, have I died and gone to Heaven?

I blink a few times. I've never seen this happen.

Is *this happening?*

I mean he's not flipping the pages, skimming through, or holding back laughter from making fun of it.

No. He is full-on engrossed in the book.

"Holy shit. Hunter, do you know how freaking hot you are right now?"

A man reading a book is a turn on; a man reading one of *my favorite* books is so damn irresistible.

He looks up from reading with wide eyes. "Are you shitting me? This girl was kidnapped at birth and never knew about it?"

"I think I'll keep you after all." I say with a sigh. If heart eyes were real, I'd have them right about now.

"Wait, was there ever a doubt you wouldn't?" He uses a tissue to mark his page and closes the book.

Swoon.

"Well..." I hesitate.

He gets up and his demeanor turns predatory when he begins to stalk towards me.

Oh, shit.

I back up slowly. Thankful I know my house like the back of my hand and don't have to look behind me to see where I'm going.

"Well, what, Anya?" he growls out.

"I...uhh...eek!"

He leaps for me, and I dart around the kitchen to avoid him, but, because of the hunter he is, I don't stand a chance. He wraps a leg around both of mine and holds me tight in one arm while the other tickles me.

"Okay, *stop*! I give up! There was never a chance." I squeal.

He laughs, delighted in torturing me.

"That's better." He kisses me on my cheek and releases me. "Now, you grab the food, and I'll get the drinks. I don't trust you to not spill them all over the place."

"Hey now! What about the pizza? You apparently trust me enough for that."

"Easy, even if you stumble, the food may still be salvaged since they're in boxes, the drinks...are not."

Okay, he has a point.

I stack two plates on top of the pizza boxes to bring them to the couch while Hunter grabs our drinks. We plop down and start dishing out our food.

The warm stretchy cheese hits the spot for me.

"Mmm..." I moan. This is the good stuff.

"Knock that off."

I frown. "Knock what off?"

"You know what I'm talking about. If you keep moaning like that, your dinner's going to be over, fast."

I stare down at my delicious pizza pie and back to him. Weighing my odds.

I shrug and take another bite, this time quietly, and smile.

Once we're done eating, Hunter takes care of our dishes, and sits on the couch next to me, pulling me into him.

I momentarily freeze at the memory of the last time I was in the crook of his arm. He was dead, and I had wanted to die with him.

But he's here.

With me.

He's alive.

So I snuggle into his warmth, and we just sit there, in the silence, drinks in our hands, deep in our own thoughts.

The connection between us is so strong we understand what is needed without words.

We need each other.

Hunter is the one steady thing in my life with everything else up in the air, like the unknown future of my job that I will have to face next week. Not to mention the fact I don't have a vehicle to get around in.

Who knows how much time passes as we sip our drinks, but when I take the last gulp of my wine, Hunter takes my glass and his empty bottle to the kitchen.

I wait for him by the hallway, watching as he washes out the wineglass and sets it on the drying rack. The way he moves about my kitchen is natural.

Like he belongs here.

He notices me when he turns.

"Ready for bed?"

I hold out my hand to him and we make our way to my room.

When we're near my bed, Hunter gently removes my shirt and bottoms. It wasn't meant to be sexual. Yet, it's almost as though the sweet and caring motions turn me on just as much as the seductive ones.

But tonight isn't a night where we need to make love. It's a night where we need to just hold each other.

I was so close to losing him.

Hunter tucks me into my side of the bed before going around to his, slipping under the covers, and turning off the lamp.

His arm wraps around my stomach, and he pulls my back up against him. His heat warms me from top to bottom, and I snuggle in deeper, grasping his forearms and holding him close.

As if he can read my mind, Hunter says, "It'll be okay, Anya. Remember, you promised me you wouldn't blame yourself." He whispers into the top of my head.

"I know. I remember. I'm going to try my best, but I can't say it'll be easy. I hope you can be patient with me."

"Being patient with you is easy. I just want you to be okay. Now go to bed, Honey Bear." He kisses the top of my head and tightens his hold on me. "I love you."

"I love you too. Thank you for being you."

Chapter Forty-Four

WUNJO

(KINDRED HARMONY)

alking in the thick woods, I follow the now familiar path from my previous dreams. Against the boulder, between the two impossible paths, leans my grandmother with a smile on her face. Well, that's not the greeting I'd expected, but I'll take it. Especially with the struggle these past couple days.

"My light, you have done well. More than well, actually." She places her hand over her heart and moisture beads at the corners of her eyes. "I'm so proud of you."

Those words hit me harder than I expected. A balance scale tips in the favor of pride over disappointment. "Even when I took the wrong path?"

A knowing smirk spreads across her face. "Did you, though?"

"But, Hunter died. How could that be the right path."

"Everything that happens to us, good or *bad, transforms us and leads us in the direction we are meant to go.* Who *we are destined to become."* Her smile disappears and she picks up my hand. Her *small fingers are soft and warm*—a contrast to the iciness from the castle. *"I'm sorry you had to suffer. It was not expected, but you handled it better than I could ever imagine. You rose above your fear. You pushed forward. You refused to give up, and, in doing so, you defeated the wendigo* and *brought Hunter back."*

"Why does it feel like I screwed up?"

"You need to understand that any way you handled this would have been hard. Do not doubt your decisions because you followed your instincts and succeeded." She sighs. *"This is only the beginning of so much more."*

"Wait, what?" My jaw drops and with it, my stomach.

She chuckles. *"Deary, don't worry. Your light is beyond powerful. Your mother and I only made incremental differences, but you are meant to help so many more. You were destined to make a difference on a much larger scale; to save those who are helpless to save themselves."*

Her words bring me a mixture of hope and dread. *"So there's no happily ever after for me?"*

"Your happily ever after is your future. You would never stand for a dull life. I'm surprised you lasted this long. The road ahead will continue to be a challenge, but you will have contentment and happiness."

It makes me nervous for what's to come, but now that I have this new power, the possibilities of helping others are endless. I finally have a purpose in life.

The seed of hope she planted is beginning to grow roots, winding themselves around the dread and taking over.

"Thank you, Grandmother. Thank you for guiding me and helping Hunter and me. Will I see you again or is this your goodbye?"

"You never know." She winks. "Be good to yourself."

The woods begin to shimmer along with my grandmother and light fills the back of my eyelids.

"Good afternoon, Honey Bear. You ready to feed the beast?"

"Beast?" I shoot up from the bed and ignite my hands, holding my palms out and ready for our impending attack. "Where? Hunter, stay back!" I frantically place myself in front of Hunter, searching for the creature.

"Whoa, Anya. Put those away. You're safe. *We're* safe." Hunter's hands rub up and down my arms.

My heart pounds hard in my chest, and I pant like I've just run a marathon. I take in the room around me and calm my heart rate when I find there's nothing here that'll harm us. The afternoon sun shines through the blinds, the comforter is bunched up at the bottom of the bed, and the bedroom door is open, as we left it last night. Nothing ominous is standing in the room or hallway, ready to pounce.

We're alone.

With narrowed eyes, I turn on the source of my panic.

"You jerk! You scared the *crap* out of me." I push his chest. "Why would you say something like that?" I shove him again, but he snatches my hand and pulls me down with him. He's laughing the whole time, while I'm still trying to catch my breath.

Hunter hovers over me. "I meant your *stomach*, babe. I was trying to sleep, but your stomach was growling. Rather loudly, I might add. I was afraid you'd take a bite out of my shoulder there for a minute." He bites his lip, holding back a laugh but failing. "It was a close one. You were already foaming at the mouth, and my shoulder has the wetness to prove it." He glances to his right shoulder and my eyes follow, finding the glistening skin. "You should really come with a warning label."

Oh, he's a dead man.

With a strong twist of my hips, I catch him off guard and flip us over, me landing on top of him.

"First of all...you had *enough* warning the night we ran into each other at the castle."

The corners of his eyes crinkle. "In my defense, between your beauty and my need for self-preservation from being eaten by the wendigo, I was blind to your vicious cravings at the time. You need to be carrying a bigger warning. Make it red, maybe?"

"That's your own damn fault for not paying attention. And secondly, I do *not* foam at the mouth. I drool in my sleep. Deal with it." I harrumph.

"More like, *drown* in it," he mumbles.

I sputter and slide off Hunter, reaching my hand under the sheets to cup his length. He grows larger, and I emit a *little* warmth as a warning.

He backs up quickly. "Shit, I'm sorry! Forgive me, forgive me."

I smirk at the wide-eyed man in front of me. Not that I'd have hurt him but sometimes, it's the woman's job to knock the man down a peg or two.

"I'll forgive you..." I release him and a mischievous smile spreads across my lips. "If you make me breakfast." Laying back down, I stretch my arms and legs out. Surprisingly, I feel very refreshed and energized.

"Are you sure you can wait that long?"

Why does he say it like that? Like it'll be hours.

My lamp is the only thing on my nightstand, my phone is absent from its usual spot, so I ask Hunter. "What time is it?"

"A little after noon."

Shit. No wonder why I feel refreshed. We've slept all day.

He places a strand of hair behind my ear. "How are you feeling?"

"Physically, I'm great. Mentally? I'll get there." I shrug.

"This isn't going to be easy, but I can guarantee you will win *this* battle in the end."

I roll to my side and prop up on my elbow, staring at my gorgeous-as-sin boyfriend. Two of my fingers walk their way from Hunter's thick waist to the new tattoo burned into his chest. With the faintest touch, I glide my fingers over a nipple and watch the goosebumps pepper his flesh. "How are *you* feeling?"

"Eh, I can't complain. I mean, I *was* dead yesterday, and I did get to sleep all night and day next to a beautiful angel."

Splaying my hand on his chest, I bury my head into his side. "Can you please not call me that?"

"What, beautiful? Would you rather I call you hideous?"

Taken aback, I pop my head up, but my irritation slightly dims when I'm caught up in his dimples. "Argh. You're really asking for your clothes to be burned off, aren't you?"

Under the covers, he wiggles out of his boxer briefs. "Ha, can't burn them off if I don't have any on." His face is smug.

I tap a finger to my lips. "I say we should test this theory of yours."

The humor leaves him and panic sets in.

"Uh...how's sandwiches sound? And tea? We don't want my angel getting more hangry."

Heat floods my face. "*You—*"

Hunter jumps out of bed, naked, and high-tails it to the kitchen like his ass is on fire.

I pick up his underwear from under the covers and dangle them from my fingertips. "Hey, Hunter? Did you forget something?" I say with a saccharine smile.

He peeks around the corner, studies the boxer briefs then my face. "I'm umm... I'm good." He clears his throat. "Thanks, though."

I toss them at his head. "For heaven's sake, just put them on."

"Your wish is my command, Milady." He bows and slowly backs away.

I should've burned holes in them after all. But I can't fault him completely; in his smart-ass way, he's still a charmer.

And he's still my kryptonite.

With one last stretch, I get out of bed and change into a pair of jeans and a tank top. The view when I walk into my kitchen has me forgiving Hunter for calling me an angel this morning. He's bent over in the fridge, grabbing the ingredients for our sandwiches.

What I wouldn't give to run up and slap *him* on the ass for once.

But…I'm starving so I'll hold that impulse back for now.

Instead, I open the cabinet and pull down two plates.

"What do you think you're doing?" The deep growl makes me jump and the plates clatter to the counter.

I turn around and Hunter's hands cage me to the counter.

Temptation pulls me closer. I fight and lean backwards. *"I'm helping.* Why in hell do you need to keep sneaking up on me?"

And why does he always have the ability to make butterflies in my stomach go haywire? I should be mad at him right now.

Not turned on.

My eyes trail down his face to the gold charm around his neck, then travel over the contours of his stomach to the black fabric barely covering him.

"I never said *you* were going to make our food." He grabs my hip and pulls me close, making my resolve crumble. Bit by bit.

I bite my bottom lip and reach up to trace the Spiral of Life tattoo over Hunter's heart. It begins to glow.

"Huh. Well, that's new."

Hunter lowers his head, his breath heavy against my ear. "You need to stop that, or you won't be getting food after all. And I'm willing to risk my life over it, Honey Bear." He sends chills down my spine.

A moan rises from my throat. "Mmm...what exactly does that do to you?"

He presses his hips into mine. His hardness grows against my stomach.

"What do you think?" he says through clenched teeth.

Interesting... I wonder...

I trace his tattoo again and think about how hungry I am.

His stomach growls and he clenches it. "Good lord, what the hell are you doing to me, woman?" He stands back and stares at my fingers tracing the symbol on his chest.

I snort and giggle.

This is so freaking cool.

I've created a link to Hunter that allows me to transfer my emotions into him.

"Experimenting, and I have to say, you may be the luckiest man alive." My eyes light up.

"At this moment, I'm beginning to doubt that. From my point of view, you just found another way to control me."

"Oh, come on. You have the ability to feel exactly what I'm feeling now."

"I'm pretty sure I had that figured out *before* you burned this into me." He cocks an eyebrow, but a hint of a smile peeks through from under his beard.

My fingertip barely touches the edge of the spiral. "I can try to heal it, or you can trust me to not abuse this new power."

"Babe, as long as you promise me you won't share your menstrual cramps with me, I'm good with this."

I suck in an excited breath. "Ooh... I never would've thought of that before. You are brilliant!"

Hunter shifts on his feet. "Whoa, I said to *not* do it, I wasn't giving you ideas."

Leaning back on the counter with a sigh I say, "Okay, I promise. No sharing my monthly visits." I straighten. "Are you okay with this?"

I'm excited about this latest connection, but I'm not sure he's thrilled over it. It's one more thing that he has no control over.

Because of me.

"Well, since we're in agreement." Hunter reaches out, his hand grazes my skin as he moves his touch across my forearm to my hand. He places my palm over the tattoo. "How do you feel when I say, I want to spend the rest of my life with you?"

Hunter and I gasp.

An intense warmth flows over me, settling itself in my chest. I'm close to bursting from the love pouring through my hand into my heart.

These aren't just my emotions.

They're Hunter's too.

"Do you feel this? It's...unbelievable," Hunter says breathlessly, his heart races under my touch.

"Mmhmm..." It's all I can do to respond.

The energy from the symbol pulses under my hand, pouring out Hunter's truest feelings back at me.

Pure, untainted love.

If there were any doubts about his feelings for me, this moment has taken them all away.

Every. Last. One.

Hunter lets go of my palm, and I slide it up to his bristly jaw. I raise to the tips of my toes and press my lips to his. His kisses match mine perfectly. They aren't greedy. He's patient and gentle because that's what we need right now.

I separate us with only a few inches between our faces. "My heart and soul will always belong to you, Hunter."

He leans his forehead on mine. "My *everything* belongs to you, Anya." He pauses, staring those big brown eyes into mine. "My heart, my soul." A smirk slides over his lips. "My dick, and my irresistible ass..."

There's no stopping the snicker that escapes me. It shifts our deep conversation to light and easy. Hunter's skill to draw out uncontrollable reactions from me is a gift in itself.

The floodgates can no longer hold steady and burst open. My laughter drowns the silence around us.

"There's never a dull moment with you," I say while holding my aching sides.

With both dimples on full display, he quirks an eyebrow. "You say that like it's a bad thing."

"No. It's a very good thing. *We* are a good thing."

"Mmm...that we are. We'll be even better when we get sustenance in our bellies." He nibbles my earlobe. "Maybe I'm the one to fear when hungry."

"Hmm... I think I need to help prep our food then."

"Wait a min—"

I silence him with my finger. "We're partners, right?"

His shoulders relax. "Always, sweetheart. Now stop looking at my amazing bod, and let's get some food." He shakes his head and turns back to the opposite counter where the meat and cheese sit. "Geez, a man can't even walk around shirtless without you making him feel like a piece of meat." He huffs.

"Just shirtless, huh? Not the fact that you're practically naked? News flash, you're leaving very little to the imagination."

Hunter turns his head back and winks. "Just a little appetizer before the main meal." His back flexes as he wiggles his ass.

I walk to him chuckling, and snatch the bread out of his hands. "A meal that won't make itself. Unless you've developed other powers I don't know about."

"Not yet, but I'm sure you can find the right rune to make that happen."

"Until then...pass the ham."

For the first time, we have no plans. No obligations, and no lives to save.

Everything we've done to date has revolved around the wendigo and the danger it involved. Without it, things feel slightly off.

Like we're meant to do more.

Chapter Forty-Five

KAUNAZ

(FORGIVENESS)

Hunter finishes placing our plates in the dishwasher. "Think about what you want to do today while I get some clothes on."

I push my bottom lip out. "Do you have to?"

"Unless you plan on leveling the playing field, then yes, I need to get something on. These hardwood floors are freezing."

"Fine. If you have—*Hey!*" I jump out of my chair, removing Hunter's foot from under my pant leg. "*Damn*, those are cold. Go. Go now."

"Ah babe, you're just warming me."

I form a globe in my palm and smirk, "You sure you want that?"

Hunter scurries away, laughing as he high-tails it out of here. Guess he didn't want me to warm his feet.

If we're going to get anything done today, I need to find my cell phone.

Hmm...where did I put it in my state of exhaustion last night?

"Ah ha. Found ya." The small black device peeks out from under the book Hunter left on the coffee table. Picking it up, the phone illuminates.

Oh good.

Thirty percent power, more than enough for a call to my mom.

I plop down on the couch and scroll to my mom's name on my recent call log.

"Anya?" She answers on the first ring.

"Hey Mom, I'm checking in."

"Oh baby, how are you? Are you hurt? Is everything okay?" Her voice turns frantic.

"I'm okay. The problem is taken care of—for good."

"What do you mean 'for good?' And you didn't answer my other question." She turns serious. "Are. You. Hurt? Where are you? Is Hunter still with you?" Her voice gets louder during her rant.

"Mom, take a deep breath."

I move my ear away from the speaker when she releases her breath into the microphone. Loudly.

We always practiced relaxation methods when I was growing up. A coping mechanism for stress, worry, or pain. Who knew today I'd be reminding her to do them.

"Alright," she lets out. "I think I'm ready. Tell me everything and *don't* leave out anything."

I've caught my mom up with everything that's occurred since we last texted. Well, maybe not *everything,* but the important—*censored*—parts. My mom and I have always had a close relationship, one where I felt I could tell her anything without her judgment. Except my sex life. It's not that she doesn't want to hear it, it's that it gives her this impression she can return the favor. I made that mistake once, and still wear the scars.

Never again.

On the plus side, my mom wasn't surprised when I told her about Hunter and my speedy relationship. You'd think becoming as serious as we are in such a short time would be weird and rushed, but she understood this was *my* Hunter. My twin flame. It's safe to say, she was excited and already planning for me to bring him home to visit.

And now onto one of the hardest parts of our conversation. Admitting I took a life. I take a deep breath against the band that constricts my chest whenever I think about what I did to Margaret, then spit it out as fast as possible.

"Oh Anya... Do you know how many more people would have been killed if you hadn't made the sacrifice you did?" She lets out a sigh. "Maybe not while you guarded the castle in *your* lifetime, but inevitably it would've escaped again. Yes, an innocent life was taken—"

My snort interrupts her.

"Okay, maybe not *so* innocent. She was a *wretched* woman. So was that husband of hers. But, we don't talk ill of the deceased. This could have been God's way of removing their toxins from this world...or Karma coming back for the kill."

I choke back a chuckle. "Mom!" I shouldn't be shocked, her filter isn't always a hundred percent intact. She claims it's due to a brain-to-mouth malfunction. Always claiming her mouth works faster than her brain. Which makes things quite entertaining when being around her.

"Sorry, honey. I'll pray for forgiveness tonight. Don't you worry about me. But, I'm *sure* the Devil is regretting having them in Hell with him. They'll give him a run for his money. I can see God sitting on his throne laughing his ass off, saying 'Payback's a bitch.'"

"Oh my God, *Mom*. Just stop before you doom your soul for eternity. You said we shouldn't talk ill of the deceased." There's no holding back my laughter at this point.

I miss this woman, but I also know I need to bring up the elephant in the room.

She sighs dramatically. "I'm sorry, better yet, you should say a prayer for my forgiveness too. You may have more pull than me. Anyways... I'm happy you and Hunter are safe. I've been driving your dad nuts with worry."

My heart skips a beat in my chest. "You didn't tell him, did you?"

"Of course not. He wouldn't have hesitated to come out there which probably would've gotten him killed." She drops her voice, "Are you sure you're alright?"

"I am, I promise. There's umm...one thing I need to get off my chest though." My palms begin to sweat.

Mom is quiet and I have to check my phone to make sure she didn't hang up.

She clears her throat. "I have a feeling it's about our bloodline, right?"

She seems to be as excited over this conversation as I am. *Not.*

"Yeah..." I start softly, it's hard to hide the pain in my voice. The feeling of betrayal is hard to ignore.

Here goes nothing.

"Why didn't you let Grandmother share our family history with me? I could've been better prepared and not so...so blindsided. I didn't even *know* I had powers, Mom. My 18th birthday ritual was so secretive and in Gaelic. You told me it was a silly family tradition, and not to worry about it. Naive *me*, went with it, and I never did get any answers." I wipe the tear falling down my cheek. "I really feel that I was set-up for failure because *everything* was kept from me. This really has taken a toll, both physically and emotionally. A lot of it could have been avoided if I'd just known."

My mom sniffles and guilt rushes over me.

But I need answers; I need to stay strong.

"I'm sorry I didn't let your grandmother tell you about everything. I admit, I forbade her to discuss that part of our family, and the so-called responsibility. She wanted to tell you, but outside of our light power, it was hard to believe the stories about the castle and creature it was imprisoning. A part of me felt like it was made up to scare me as a child. I didn't want you having to go through that, or stop you from doing what you want because of a fairy tale." She chuckles dryly to herself. "Look where that got you. She *still* tied you to that place anyways. Maybe her leaving the castle to you was her way of keeping hope that you'd one day discover the secret, and accept it as your own. But yes, I take full responsibility for you not being prepared. I am *so* sorry, Anya. With my reluctance to accept that part of our family, I risked your life, baby girl."

Unsure how far the secrets went, I ask, "Did you know grandmother was the last owner of the castle?"

"Not a clue. She didn't even tell me she was leaving her home to you."

The tone in her voice tells me she's being truthful.

"Why didn't you say something after her lawyer announced I'd inherited everything?"

"I wanted you to make choices as an adult, not be brainwashed and forced to take on a responsibility. An obligation that may, *or may not*, have been real. Living a life of paranoia is not something I wished for you. Our family's fairy tale, which I chose to ignore and protect you from, almost *killed* you. And you almost lost Hunter, if it wasn't for the way you shined through and brought him back." She blows her nose and her voice becomes quiet, "I don't blame you if you never forgive me. *I've* been struggling with trying to forgive myself for it."

Tears roll down my face. I don't know what to say. She's unloaded a lot, and I need a minute to process it all.

A couple of minutes pass with her sniffling. On the couch, I slouch over my knees, rubbing my forehead as I stare at the floor.

"Anya? Are you there, honey? I understand if you can't forgive me, but please don't push me out of your life."

"Mo-m," My voice crackles. I clear it and try again. "Mom, I'd never push you out of my life. I needed to know why. I needed answers because all I felt was the pain and confusion. I'm trying to put myself in your shoes. If I had a daughter, would I do the same? Maybe. I can't fault you for trying to protect me. And I *do* forgive you."

My mom sobs on the other end of the phone and it tears my heart out.

"Can you promise me something?"

"I..." She sniffles again. "I can try."

"I'm going to cut the ties to this whole thing and let it go. I need you to do the same. Cut the strings of your guilt and release it. Can you do that?"

True healing is only found when we can let go of the darkness we hold inside. Release all the grudges, the hatred, the pain, the judgements, and let the light take hold and consume. This was how I was able to reach my full potential and heal Hunter.

She hiccups. "I never realized there'd come a day I'd hear my words used against me."

"Only for good though, Mom. You with me?"

"Yes, I'm with you. I got my machete out."

"Damn, woman, how many ties do you need to cut?"

Thank goodness we are talking imagery and not real sharp objects here.

"More than you need to know about, but I'm ready."

We are quiet as we work on chopping our emotional ties.

Closing my eyes, I visualize two black toxic strings linked from my mother to me, and from my grandmother to me. This cord holds onto all the secrets, the betrayal, *everything* they've done—or haven't done—that's hurt me.

With imaginary scissors, I sever the dark rope and watch it fall into an abyss. The emotional ties that held me back finally let loose.

"It's done," I take a deep breath, feeling the lightness from the weight coming off my chest.

"Hmm..."

"You okay over there?" I'm a little worried about my mom. She's a strong woman, but I'm not sure where her breaking point is.

"Just a minute... Okay. I got them all. Wow, that feels so much better."

I smirk. "Right? Such a relief. I'm glad we have that behind us."

"You have no idea. Now..."

My stomach tenses, not knowing what she's going to say next.

"When's the wedding?" Her voice perks up.

I run a hand over my face and groan. "Mom..."

She giggles. "Okay, Okay. I'll wait a week before I ask you again."

"Try a year, or two."

"You two won't last six months without a ring around that finger of yours. But I'll refrain, for now. Is everything else going okay?"

"I'm peachy. Other than having to figure out the car situation. Oh, and the slight chance I may not have a job soon."

"Yuck, I don't envy you there. The job situation will work itself out. Filing the claim for the car? Good luck with that." She says it as though it's better me than her. "Your father does all that paperwork stuff for us. Heaven knows I would be lost without that man. Do you need help with your bills?"

"No, I have some money saved up if needed. Can you fill dad in with the details for me? I'm not quite sure how to bring up these past few days with him yet. This is all new territory for me."

Now it's her time to groan. "Why do *I* have to do it? You kno w...you would be my favorite daughter if you told him..."

"Mom, I'm your only daughter." I deadpan.

She huffs. "Well... I guess I owe you this. But keep me posted on how things are going with the castle. I want to come see you soon. And tell me how your job works out. I'll send prayers and positive vibes your way. I love you, Anya."

"I'll definitely keep you updated. Bye mom, I love you too."

I hit the end button and stand, shaking off the conversation. Hunter must be working since he's nowhere in sight, so I might-as-well keep adulting. I walk to my kitchen table to open up my laptop. Getting lost in finding the right website to register an account takes all my focus.

Why didn't I think to do this when I got the car to begin with?

In a drawer to the left of the table is where I keep my spare chargers and cords. I reach over and rustle through until I find a USB cord to upload the photos of my car.

A dark shadow hovers over me when I sit back.

"Holy crap!" I jump out of my chair in attack mode, a flame flickering in my palm, ready to fly.

Hunter stands in front of me, one hand up in defense, the other holding my favorite mug.

I extinguish my power and grasp my chest. My heart pounds hard against my ribcage, I swear it's trying to break free.

"Sorry, I wanted to come see how you were feeling after your phone call."

I study Hunter intently. He sounds genuine, but if not for the dimples popping out, I'd have believed his spooking me was innocent. I think he gets a sick pleasure from scaring the crap out of me.

"Damn it, Hunter. You have *got* to stop with the stealth mode around me. One of these times I won't hesitate. It would be a shame too. I *really* like your handsome face, and would rather not see it half melted."

His face turns alarmed, like he didn't realize the possibility.

He sets down the steaming mug, the herbal aroma dances around me and calms my nerves.

"Sorry, babe. I'll make sure I start announcing my presence." He rubs his hand over his beard. "I can't afford to lose my beauty. You may not admit it, but I know for sure you only love me for my looks."

I let my head fall to my palm. "Yes, Hunter, you discovered my secret. I'm only using you for your looks, and as soon as those go, I'm trading you in for a newer model." I raise my head to meet his gaze and snort. Failing yet again to hold back my smile.

He holds a hand over his heart. "Hey now, that's harsh." He drops the act, and his sweet dimples fade away. "But in all seriousness, how'd it go with your mom? I only heard a bit. I was caught up in a work email. Are you okay?" He pulls up a chair next to me and positions me between his knees.

My hand drops to his thigh. "I'm feeling better about it. She thought she was protecting me the best she could. She didn't want me growing up believing in fables, only to end up having it ruin my life. The stories were a little too far-fetched, even with our powers, but I forgive her."

Hunter rubs a hand over mine. "I'm glad you called her. I know a large part of you was hurting. You didn't need to be holding onto this, having it eat at you."

It's amazing how well he reads me, and he didn't need to use the Spiral of Life tattoo to do it either.

Hunter shifts, and looks to see what I'm up to. "What's next on your list?"

"Auto insurance. You want to help?" I plaster on a charming smile and flutter my eyelashes.

I know I'm laying it on thick, but desperate times call for desperate measures.

"Look at the time... I think I have a few more emails that have urgent requests." He pats my hand and scootches his chair away to stand.

"Chicken shit," I mutter.

"I know how much you were looking forward to this. What kind of boyfriend would I be if I took all the fun away from *you*? Enjoy." He leans down, places a chaste kiss on my lips then walks to the couch.

Why will no one do this for me?

It's one more *fuck you* from the wendigo to me.

A half hour later, I realize why everyone refused to help. But, I'm grateful my claim is *finally* complete along with the twenty some-odd pictures I uploaded. Well...it's more like five, which was the maximum the site would allow without the website crashing.

Which it did.

Quite a few times.

After the third time, I learned to type out my claim documentation in another application and saved it.

Good old 'copy and paste' to the rescue.

My poor car was totaled from every camera angle. It wasn't hard to find ones that worked. What *did* take long was trying to locate all the details it required. No one warned me about that part.

Hitting submit, I receive a notification not to take further action with my vehicle until I receive an email confirmation with instructions.

Now the fun part...the wait.

I'm praying it doesn't take long, or I'm going to need to rent a car soon. It's going to be more of a burden if I keep having to use Hunter to get around. Not that I don't like his company, but I know he may not always be around. He has responsibilities of his own.

Leaning back in my chair, I sip my tea while I check on Hunter to see what he's up to. The last time I checked, he was on his phone scrolling through what I'm sure were messages.

I choke on my drink and start coughing.

"You okay over there?" Hunter asks without glancing up.

Trying to clear out the liquid from my lungs, I cough a few more times before I can take in air without drowning.

What I *was* expecting was Hunter to be on his phone. What I *didn't* expect was to find him reading the same book from earlier. He's so engrossed in the story he doesn't even look up to make sure that I'm really okay.

"And what if I wasn't okay?" My voice comes out scratchy.

"Then you would have to wait until this chapter was over before I could come rescue you."

Ugh, how rude.

"I'll make sure I pause my dying until you're ready."

"Shh... This keeps getting better and better. You're interrupting me. Now go back to doing whatever you're doing, minus the choking part." The hand not holding the book waves me off, dismissing me.

That definitely was not what I was expecting.

After watching him for a couple minutes, I realize he's serious, and there's not much that could pull him away right now.

Who would have thought my Big Guy was a bookworm? It's not like he cared much for them as a kid.

Hunter's phone starts to ring and he growls—which has me giggling over his frustration.

He stops, placing a bookmark in the book.

Wait, is that my *bookmark? The one that's been missing for a while? Where did he—never mind. How could I have forgotten he's really good at finding lost things?*

"Yeah." He answers grumpily.

Oh man, I now know not to interrupt him reading...like ever.

He straightens up. "Hey detective, what can I do for you?"

The blood from my head drains and my chest squeezes in a vice.

Did they do the autopsy? Is he asking Hunter to bring me in, or keep me here for them to pick me up?

The room begins to close in on me and heat floods my body. I get up from my chair and start to pace the living room. Sweat begins to bead up under my arms and between my shoulder blades.

All Hunter says are a bunch of 'uh huhs' and 'yeahs' before he says, "Thanks sir, I appreciate the call," and disconnects.

I'm on Hunter in a heartbeat. Wanting, no, *needing* to know my fate.

"What did he say? Are they coming for me?" I ask anxiously, wringing my hands.

Hunter places his hands on my shoulders to stabilize me. "No babe, they aren't coming for you. It was all good news."

I hold my breath.

"Yes, they performed the autopsies. Both the contractor's and Margaret's cause of death were determined to be an animal attack."

I cry out in relief, and my knees give out on me. Hunter catches me before I make it to the floor.

"Whoa, there. Let's go sit down."

"There's more?" I take in Hunter's facial expressions to try to figure out if there is a 'but' to all of this.

We sit down side by side and he brushes the hair out of my face.

"Not much more. Tests came back from the bear and there's nothing of concern in the results. There's no need to issue a public alert to the surrounding areas. That means less attention on the castle and the animals around it. We still don't need a bunch of curious idiots nosing around the place. But that's it. That was all he had to say."

The relief has tears streaming down my face.

"Hey, what's going on? You should be happy." He grabs my hips and pulls me across his lap. My head lands on his neck and he rubs his hand up and down my arms. "Shh...babe, it's alright."

Once I stop crying, I am finally able to talk. I sit up and look him in the eyes while I wipe off my tears with the backs of my hands.

"I'm sorry, I seem to be a nervous wreck all the time around you. I question *your* sanity sometimes and why you're still hanging around."

"Maybe because I'm madly in love with you. Now, what has you upset?"

"I'm happy, and *so* relieved that I won't be going to prison for murdering Margaret. And the animals, they're safe now. These are happy tears, tears of joy, which I promise I rarely ever do. These past few days have just been a lot."

"You scared me, I thought there was something wrong." Without hesitation, he places my hand over his heart, and we both are flooded with each other's emotions.

His are filled with concern, while mine are an alleviation of fear.

"Alright, I have to say, I'm really digging this new ability. I can usually read you, but you gave me a gift that'll never have us questioning our feelings. Thank you, Anya." His large hands hold my face and he leans in for a kiss.

He's right. This will only bring us closer.

I kiss him back then wrap my arms around his neck and bury myself in his warm citrusy scent.

"What else do you have planned for today?" Hunter's chest rumbles against mine with his words. "I'm all caught up on my work."

I shift to face him and snicker. "Oh, I could tell, when you transformed from an innocent bookworm into a fire breathing, book dragon."

"Pfft, don't be so dramatic."

"What? Me, dramatic? You were the one willing to let me choke on my tea and die because of your precious book."

"See? Dramatic. Coughing is a sign you're still breathing. If you stopped, I would've set the book down to check on you."

"Mmhmm..." I mumble, not believing him.

"Anyways, since I had to stop reading to take the detective's call, I'm all yours now. What's next?"

"Between the security at the castle, a new car, and my job up in the air, I've got a lot to deal with. I'm not sure what to focus on next, but I'll figure it out."

"We. *We* have to deal with it, as in together. You aren't in this alone. We agreed we're partners in this crazy life together. I share every burden with you. This is what I signed up for and I will never regret it. Remember, you're stuck with me." He gives me a wink and his signature cocky smile.

I *am* stuck with him, and he's equally stuck with me.

The poor bastard...

Chapter Forty-Six

Fehu

(Abundance)

"It's not going to change if you look away." Hunter stands over my shoulder at the kitchen table, looking at the computer screen with me.

Specifically, the screen that's showing my checking account.

I'm not sure how long it usually takes to receive an insurance payout for a totaled car, but three days doesn't seem realistic.

"I think they made a mistake. Maybe they paid me someone else's, and they're gonna take it away when they figure out their screw up."

"But didn't you receive an email confirmation of the deposit from them?"

The very same notification is pulled up on my phone. It has my name, the claim number, and the amount, matching the deposit I'm monitoring in my account right now.

"Uh, yeah, but this isn't right. I swear when I submitted it, it said thirty days to process. Not three. I can't use this yet. Maybe that's what they meant, don't use it for thirty days."

Hunter picks up my phone. "No, it doesn't work that way. I've had a buddy get his in two weeks. Babe, take this as a sign that Karma finally has your back for once and is taking care of you instead of screwing you over."

Or maybe it's Karma's way of being sneaky and thinking it has me fooled.

I eye the amount on the screen suspiciously. "No offense, but Karma's a bitch, not some guardian angel looking to make my life easier."

Not only did I receive the payment quickly, but the insurance also advised I have a *no fault clause*, so my premiums won't increase.

Hunter leans down and kisses me on the cheek, sliding a hand over mine and—

The screen jumps to my desktop. "Wait, what did you do?" Hunter distracted me and closed out of the browser. I frantically log back into my account to see the amount still sitting there.

"See? It's still there. And it will continue to be there until you spend it. You have documentation that the money is owed to you. Now relax and let's focus on something else. Like maybe what you want to do today." Hunter takes my shoulders into his highly skilled hands and kneads away the tension.

My head falls to the side, and I give into the magic of Hunter's fingertips.

An annoying ring snaps me out of my paradise. Glancing down at my phone laying in front of me, I groan.

It's Julie.

Why would she be calling on a Saturday?

I answer it. "Hello?"

"Report to the office immediately!"

The line goes dead.

There's no point in checking the screen for confirmation. Julie makes a habit of making her demands then disconnecting.

"I hope you didn't have anything urgent you needed to do." I look up at Hunter.

His brow furrows. "What's going on?"

"That was my manager, Julie." I cringe. "Do you mind dropping me off at work? I'm not sure how long it'll take. You don't have to wait for me."

I really hate having to ask for help; I'm sure Hunter has better things to do.

"You aren't walking." He clenches his jaw.

"We aren't in danger anymore. I won't be eaten on my way home."

"And I don't give two shits. You. Aren't. Walking. Understood?" A protective rage flashes in his eyes.

As tempting as it is to to argue, I won't. It's nice to have someone who cares so much that they become demanding to ensure your safety.

But it doesn't mean I need to show him I cave easily.

"Fine, be bored. If it's a whole eight-hour work day, you'll regret it," I sing-song the last part.

"I highly doubt that. Now get your stuff, we're leaving."

Needing to put my boots on, I stand and brush past him. "So bossy," I mutter.

"You like it when I'm bossy."

"I also liked it when your hearing wasn't so keen."

"What?"

Selective hearing it is.

"I'll text you when I have a better idea on a timeframe."

"Don't worry about it. I'll be here." Hunter is still determined to wait on me.

"But—"

"Shut it," he rudely cuts me off. "I'm waiting. Now go inside and deal with *whatever* it is you need to deal with."

"Yes, sir." I salute him.

He growls seductively. "I think I can get used to that. Hurry up. The faster you get this over with, the faster we can go home."

"So demanding." With a smirk, I shut the car door and walk through the front doors of my office building.

On auto pilot, I raise my hand to wave at James.

Huh, that's strange. He's always here. Why isn't anyone manning the security desk?

A prickle skips across the back of my neck.

My hand heats as my new defense mechanism is preparing for danger. Stepping past the security desk, I find the wreckage that was once our office. I walk through the papers strewn about the floor past what's left of our cubicles.

What the hell happened?

Most of the cubicles are broken down, dissected like someone believed a hidden treasure was inside. Some are laying haphazardly on the ground, while others are up against walls, ready to collapse. File cabinets are open as if someone was searching through them in a hurry.

Muffled voices become louder the farther into the office I go.

The conference room comes into view and my stomach unclenches. The majority of my co-workers, including the home office staff, sit and chat.

Opening the door, I walk in and take my usual seat between Danielle and Heather.

"Hey. What the hell is going on?"

Danielle releases a breath. "Oh good, you're here. I was worried you wouldn't be able to make it."

"Hey, Anya." Heather leans on the table closer to Danielle and me. "Does anyone else have a bad feeling about this? Did the place get robbed?" Her eyes go wide and she gasps. "Do they suspect *us*?"

"I haven't the slightest clue, but it looks like we're about to find out." We grab each other's hands, waiting nervously.

Not even a minute later, Julie storms in without a hello or welcome.

No surprise there.

"I'm sure you have heard from the gawd-awful gossip in this pathetic town that both Grant *and* Margaret Bordeaux were killed in weird animal attacks. Where does this leave us? Well, that is what Monday's meeting would've been about, but our Chief Financial Officer, Derek Metch, who will be in at any moment, has some disturbing news for us all."

Julie's whole composure shifts the moment Derek enters the conference room. She smiles sweetly and bats her eyes at him. "Derek?"

It figures the dragon is horrible to us, then on a drop the a dime becomes sweet as candy when someone who is financially influential walks into the room.

We're a satellite facility for our home office where Derek works. He's the only one in management who isn't a dick.

Derek steps up to the head of the table, Julie right at his heels. "Thank you all for coming on such short notice. The news of losing Mr. and Mrs. Bordeaux was shocking and quite disturbing." He turns beet red and rubs the back of his neck. "What is also upsetting and impacts every one of us is that we have to close our doors for good."

My stomach drops, and I squeeze the girls' hands.

"Upon our owner and his wife's deaths, evidence was found in their home of their involvement in illegal activities."

The room erupts with gasps and chatter.

"Please everyone..." With a loud whistle, the room goes quiet. "Please understand, I had no idea what they were doing. As the police advised me, they were befriending families who were close to foreclosure. They had somehow falsified documents through our mortgage assistance program."

Heather's grip tightens. When I discreetly turn towards her, she has an *I told you so* look on her face.

"...families lost everything," Derek continues. "And the Bordeauxes bought it all from the bank at a low cost. They were setting up struggling families for failure, destroying lives. I don't know the full details of how they organized all this..."

But we *do.*

"All I know is the FBI has been involved, and all the assets of the Bordeaux's and this company have been frozen." The room turns to chaos. My co-workers shout 'But that's our money' and 'We have bills to pay.'

"Team, please. Let me finish, and then I will try to answer as many questions as I can." Derek clears his throat, "As I was trying to say, once the law enforcement agencies sort through all the financial records, we'll see if we are able to fund your final paycheck along with the vacation time you've accrued. I am working with the local police and the FBI to help you all, as well as the victims that were involved. I am beyond sorry about this. If you need a letter of recommendation, please send me an email, and I'll get one to you as soon as I can. You will find my business card in front of you on the table. Again, please know that I had no clue this was going on, and even though I am *also* jobless, I will still continue to fight for you every step of the way. Okay, now I'll take your questions."

Everyone talks at once causing arguments to break out.

"Please everyone, one at a time," Derek announces and hands shoot up.

I feel bad for him. He doesn't have to stay, yet he's doing it anyway to help us. He deserved to be running the company, not Julie and the corrupted Bordeauxes.

Time flies by with question after question. The good news is, our health insurance was paid up to the end of the year, same for our life insurance. Which is weird. I know we receive monthly bills from the insurance companies because it's my responsibility to scan and email them over to our finance department.

Derek had to have some sort of inkling that something shady was going on and paid everything out. I get it that we only have a couple months left, but still.

It makes me wonder.

Too bad he couldn't have done that with our paychecks, but I'm sure that would've shot up red flags immediately.

Derek says his goodbyes and my co-workers begin to file out. Some are crying, others are pissed off. I don't blame them. The two people who should be in front of the firing squad aren't alive to deal with the repercussions of their crimes.

I'm not quite sure what to think.

I turn to Danielle and Heather with a forced smile. "Well, that was fun. Anyone have anything lined up?" I try to joke, but it falls dead.

"Actually," Danielle stares at her shoes as she says, "I applied for a job on Monday, after we left here. It's a personal assistant position for the CEO at Johnson's Steel Mill. I got the call yesterday and they want me." She looks up to meet our eyes. "It has full benefits with more pay than I make here, and the employee turnover rate is pretty much non-existent. They treat their staff *really* well." Her eyes tilt down, as if she's worried and waiting for our approval.

I wrap my arms around her. "That is great Danielle! I am so happy for you." Part of me is relieved she'll be okay, the other part is crushed because this means we're splitting up. I turn to Heather, hoping she has a back-up plan too.

Heather chuckles. "Yeah... I've got nothing. *However..* . Greyson's aunt has been bugging me for months to join her in her bakery about twenty minutes from here. I might take her up on the offer. Just until something better comes along."

"Seriously? That is the perfect job for you. This sounds like you found your true calling. There's no doubt the customers will become addicted to your mind-altering sweet treats."

"Yeah, we'll see how it goes. It'll at least be a paying job." She shrugs.

The idea of splitting up isn't as scary now that I know they will both be taken care of.

And close.

The girls turn to me with waiting expressions.

"How about you? Got anything on the back burner you can go for? Any local libraries hiring?" Heather wiggles her eyebrows, and I laugh.

"No, but I'll find something. My savings account will hold me over until then. Honestly, this is the perfect time to figure out what I *really* want to do with my life." The more I think about it, the more I warm up to the idea.

What's in store for me and my future now?

Danielle claps her hands together. "I think that's a *perfect* plan. I'll keep an ear out if the factory has any other openings. Just in case."

"Oooohh...a sabbatical sounds amazing!" Heather bounces up and down. "You should go to Fiji, or wait, Hawaii. When your family thing is done, that is..."

"That sounds more like a vacation rather than time to re-evaluate my career path. I need to be *saving* money, not splurging on an expensive trip."

She holds her hands out like a balance. "Eh, sabbatical, planning your future, it's all the same thing."

"But on a positive note..." I add. "My family dilemma is now over and done with. And, I have a surprise for you both." I was going to wait a few days before I showed the place, but what better way to distract us all from our recent unemployment than a trip to an old castle. Hunter did ask me earlier to think about what I wanted to do today.

"Are you both available around..." I check the time on my phone. "7:00pm?"

That should give us time to do a little prep work.

"What exactly are we doing?" Danielle questions.

Heather waves Danielle off. "I don't care what she has planned. I'm in!"

Danielle rolls her eyes. "It had better be to catch us up on what the hell happened with your issue like you promised, but count me in too."

"Awesome, okay." I send them both the coordinates that are now burned into my head. "I'll meet you both here."

"Well, that's not cryptic or anything, but I'll be there." Danielle agrees.

Heather stares at her phone and huffs. "How the heck do I put this in my GPS? Why can't you be normal, and give a regular address?"

"I'm sure Greyson can plug it in for you since he's a tech wizard."

She rolls her eyes, knowing I'm right. "Oh fine, but this better be good. I'll be giving up an evening of therapeutic baking for it."

"It'll be worth it." A smile spreads across my lips. For a moment, they both eye me strangely before shrugging off my obvious weird behavior.

Danielle puts her phone away. "You girls ready to pack up whatever's left of our stuff, and high-tail it out of here?"

"Let's do this!" Heather pumps a fist in the air, then hustles to her desk.

Walking over to my office space—or what's left of it—I move papers around to see if any of my stuff is strewn on the floor.

"Anya." Julie barks.

I snap up to stand and face her. "Yes?"

"You need to go through the office to find anything salvageable and put it in this box for me." She shoves a cardboard box into my chest.

What the fuck?

"Wait, what?" She totally blindsides me. "We all lost our jobs, and with it, our paychecks. I'm not doing this. I'm taking my own stuff and leaving."

She cocks her hip and narrows her eyes at me. "No, you do as I say and collect all the valuables."

Oh, hell no. I'm done with this bitch.

In a perfect world, I'd be the adult and walk away. But not today. I've been to hell and back. I refuse to allow her to get away with verbally abusing me.

"You know what, Julie?" I smirk.

"Hmm?" She purses her botox-injected plump lips at me.

"You can take this box," I start off soft. "And shove it up your tight, fake ass." My voice escalates. "I don't answer to you anymore, which means losing my job is truly a *blessing* in disguise. I'm finally free of your judgmental, vindictive, jealous, gold-digging ass."

"*Excuse me?*" Her face turns red and a vein pulses in the middle of her forehead.

"Did I stutter? Do you need me to repeat it? You know, they say the hearing goes first with old age."

She gasps. "How dare you! I'll have you...I'll..."

Did I just make Julie speechless?

"You'll do what? Fire me? *Oh right*, that sucks, the only power you had is *gone*. Good luck to you. Maybe your next job will be in a warmer environment. You know, give you a better chance of warming that chunk of ice you call a heart."

"You...you..."

Ignoring her, I grab what remains of my stuff. When I stand, Heather pops up at my side and waves. "Buh-bye Felicia!" She loops her arm into mine and raises her middle finger over her head to Julie, who's still stumbling over her words. "You are my freaking hero." Heather whispers in my ear.

Danielle was smart and left when she could. No one needs to stay behind with the dragon lady.

The door closes behind us, and I suck in the cool, fall air. My job was toxic, my manager was horrid, but I'm finally free.

Heather stops me right outside the building and squeezes me tight. "I'm so proud of you. I wanted to get in a lick or two, but that? That was *awesome*. It made it all worth letting her go without my wrath." She pulls back and releases me. "I'll see you tonight; I can't wait."

"Thanks, Heather. See you soon."

Hunter takes that moment to pull his monster truck to the curb. My stomach flutters knowing he didn't leave, but was watching for me. I knew he was too stubborn and would stay, but knowing how much he fought to ensure he was here for me still melts my heart.

Without hesitation, I climb in and pull him in for a lingering kiss.

"Mmm... What was that for?"

His cologne calms my nerves, and I smile. "It was a thank you, for being you."

"Well, okay... I can definitely get used to your thank-yous."

"Guess you need to work up those points to earn more, huh?"

"Wait, I have to work for them?" He grabs the back of my neck and pulls me in. "Maybe I'll just give *you* thank-yous instead." He nibbles on my bottom lip then releases me. "So, how'd it go?"

How'd what go?

I lean back, getting out of the *Hunter zone* so I can think clearly.

"Umm, I now have an indefinite time frame of being unemployed," I say with a half smirk.

His body goes rigid. "What happened?"

I fill him in on what happened at the office. Everything Derek said confirmed what I'd expected of Grant and Margaret.

Their secret is now out, and hopefully the victims can be repaid and get their lives back. I would be more than happy to skip my last paycheck if it means that money goes to them.

Hunter's smirk has me wary.

"What's that look for?" I tilt my head to the side, studying him.

"Oh, nothing."

"Hunter?" I demand, like a mother asking a child to tell the truth.

"Okay, okay. I *may have* put in an anonymous tip about The Bordeauxes. The Feds already had interest, this just helped show them where to look and what exactly to look for."

I grab his face between my hands and kiss him. "You're a genius."

"Remember that," he growls out.

I roll my eyes and sit back.

"Anything else happen?" he asks.

My recap ends with my confrontation with Julie and my, maybe not so professional, outburst with her.

Hunter pulls me into a tight hug. "I'm so damn proud of you for standing up for yourself."

"You don't think it was wrong of me?" I squirm in my seat.

"Oh, hell no. The way it sounded, she deserved every bit of it. Maybe she'll think twice before beating down others. And maybe not, but it's a possibility."

Wishful thinking, but she's not my problem anymore.

"Now I have to figure out what I'll do for a job." The palms of my hands perspire from the thought of starting over.

Acting like it's not an issue, he reassures me with his hands rubbing my arms. "Let's take things one day at a time. We'll figure things out, I promise."

A few hours later, Hunter and I stand at the bottom of the castle's front steps. My jaw is on the ground as I take in the changes.

After I caught Hunter up on my employment situation—or lack thereof—I mentioned my plans for the girls to tell them my secret and show them the castle. It's risky, but I've thrown caution to the wind at this point.

What could go wrong? Wait, scratch that.

Last time I spoke those words, the Devil's pet came out to play.

Hunter was on board with my decision. He then surprised me with some of his own plans he'd arranged a couple days ago when he was going through his work emails.

He called his friend who owned the security business and asked for a last-minute favor. This so-called favor has to have been huge, because the building is now wired to the max.

The speed and amount of work they did on such short notice amazes me.

What also amazes me is Hunter's attention to detail. I never thought of how a security system would work without power, but he took that into consideration and made sure it wasn't an issue. There's no telling how long it'll take to have electricity up and running. There aren't any other buildings or street lights pulling power into this area.

Maybe I'll keep it as is.

There are solar panels and mini wind-turbines on the roof. The solar panels are placed where the sun hits them between the trees during the day. When the sun's away, the wind turbines are the back-up.

Up in the mountains, we always have a breeze.

The power keeps the cameras and a few motion detector lights going. It's not set up to illuminate the inside of the castle yet, but with time, we'll get the rest of the place up and running. Hunter and I discussed our next trip out here, along with his suggestion to get a generator, but there's no rush.

So much to do, but, like he said, we need to take things one day at a time.

We make our way inside, and I conjure a lantern with my powers to brighten the place up. He's been excited to help me plan this evening. Even on such short notice.

Hunter places the boxes of pizza on one of the wooden tables, then sets out to light candles. He pulls out the ones we used the first night and creates a cute walkway into the dining hall from the front doors.

When the main area is flickering with the small flames, I run out to the truck to grab the wine, cups, plates, and napkins.

Before I have the chance to take the supplies out of their bags, a rumble of a car's engine has me dropping everything and running to the front entrance.

Hunter follows me out and must have noticed my impatience when he holds my hand, rubbing his thumb over the fleshy part between my knuckles.

Usually that action calms me but this time, it doesn't help. I bounce on my heels watching as the girls pull up next to Hunter's truck and park. The shock on their faces is clear through the windshield. It's probably the same look I had when I first arrived at the castle.

"Holy. Shit!" Heather exclaims when she steps out of Danielle's car.

"*Surprise!*" I yell, pulling out of Hunter's grasp and running to meet them.

Danielle's mouth is wide in awe. "Wow. This place is beautiful! Almost impossible to find, but *beautiful*."

"Ha, imagine trying to find it in the dark when there was no visible path. *That* was a lot of fun when I came here the first time." A chill runs over my skin at the memory, and I pull my jacket on tighter.

"No shit. We had to turn around twice because we kept passing it. Heather told me to off-road it through the trees." She side-eyes the blonde in question. "I wasn't about to be stranded or destroy my car. But we found it. I still wasn't sure if my car would make it through." She takes in the castle, from the bottom to the top. "Is this where you were invited to your supposed meeting that never happened?"

I nod. Now's not the time to catch her up on the details of that yet.

Heather's face lights up. "It's also the place where our boss and his wife were attacked, right?"

Always one to go for the morbid facts. With a smile on her face.

"Yes, the one and the same."

Danielle's eyes widen in horror, while Heather has a look of glee.

She's also one who enjoys watching serial killer documentaries. There's nothing wrong with it, but she has an interesting fascination with them I can't describe.

"Don't worry, we're safe. I promise you. Come on in, we'll give you the candle-lit tour, and I'll explain *everything*."

I take their hands and guide them up the stairs.

Danielle pulls back. "Whoa, wait a minute. Do you even know who owns the place? What do they say about everything that's happened? We aren't breaking and entering, are we?"

Always the person who thinks about the important details. She makes sure I get out of my head and think logically instead of with my emotions. I love that about her, and I'm going to miss working side by side with her.

Heather rubs her hands together. "Oooohh... I *knew* it was going to be a fun night. But, Anya, you could have prepared us." She looks me up and down. "Breaking in is best done in dark clothing." She shakes her head. "There's so much you need to learn."

"Heather, you worry me sometimes." I turn to Danielle. "It's okay, I own the place."

"You what!?" She blinks a few times and holds up a hand. "Okay, I think I heard you wrong, because I thought you said you *own* the place."

"Yes, you heard right. If you come in, I'll tell you the details." I try to coax her forward.

She resists and narrows her eyes, still hesitant and obviously suspicious.

"Why do I feel like Gretel walking into the witch's house of candy?"

With a sigh, I say, "I promise you both, it's safe. And look..." I point to Hunter who's awkwardly waving from the entrance when he sees all eyes on him. "Hunter is here with us and is *great* at protecting people. Now, can we go in?" With a light tug to her hand, she gives in but takes her time, studying every bit of the way.

Then there's Heather who has a pep in her step as though she's going on an exciting adventure to Candyland, not entering an old, abandoned castle where three people were recently killed.

Chapter Forty-Seven

GEBO

(BESTOW)

"I think I've fallen in love," Heather exclaims. "When can I move in?" Her eyes twinkle from a mix of excitement and the flickering candles.

My brow creases. "It needs some work."

Danielle adds, "It needs *everything*. Electricity, plumbing, a thorough cleaning, an exorcism..."

I snort. "An exorcism? Really, Danielle?"

"Well, you can't be too sure Grant and Margaret won't haunt this place. Better to be on top of it now, instead of waiting for them to come back from the dead."

I cough to cover the wheeze in my chest and Hunter rubs my back.

I have to remind myself that she doesn't know what happened with Hunter. That's something I *won't* be sharing.

After our tour of the castle, Danielle, Heather, and I return to the dining hall to join Hunter. He stayed behind saying he wanted to set up the table.

And boy, did he.

Hunter shifted a wooden table into the center of the room, and it's now adorned with candles, a bottle of wine, and pizza. Each place setting has a plate, napkin, and plastic wine cup. It's clear he wanted to make this night special for me.

We all settle onto our bench seats, Danielle and Heather on one side, Hunter and I on the other. We girls don't hesitate to dive into the pizza pies, and Hunter stares at us like we are a herd of rare unicorns.

I guess he's not used to women who aren't afraid to eat.

Between bites, Danielle says, "I'm going to need the details on how you came about owning this place. Who owned it before you?" Her gaze darts around the room, absorbing every minute detail.

Food sticks in my throat mid-swallow. Picking up my cup, I gulp down half of the alcohol. Not only to help the blockage, but also to calm my nerves. "Well...with what I have to say next, it *may* make a little more sense."

Danielle wipes her mouth with a napkin and folds her hands under her chin. Heather shoves more food in, becoming more intrigued by the minute.

Now that I've grabbed their attention, my palms sweat, and I fidget with my plate.

What if they think I've lost my mind? What if they use the opportunity of us splitting from our jobs to cut me out of their lives?

I bounce my leg to keep my body from trembling.

Hunter's hand curls around mine, and his fingers caress my knuckles.

I meet his gaze and smile. At least, whatever happens, I won't be alone.

To help release some stress, I blow out air through my pursed lips—*Ugh*—which clearly doesn't relax me; it just moves a few tendrils of my hair and tickles my nose.

Why am I even questioning how they'll react?

These are my girls. We stick by each other through thick and thin.

Limiting the details to a need-to-know basis, I begin. "I need you both to keep an open mind."

I rub the tense muscle in the back of my neck. Danielle is side-eyeing me with her hands folded in front of her, the picture of uncertainty. *She doesn't quite believe me.* She makes me nervous.

But with one look from Heather, she gives me the strength to go on. Her elbow lean on the table with her hand holding her chin, hanging on my every word.

Do they think I'm making up this elaborate ghost story, like we're sitting around a campfire trying to spook each other?

Hunter lowers his mouth to my ear and whispers, "Are you ready to show them your new talent?"

No.

But this is the main reason I brought them here.

"I promised to tell you both everything, and I did. What I told you, plus what I'm going to show you next, I need you to promise me you won't tell anyone. Maybe one day you can tell your guys, but give me some time, this is still all new to me."

"You know we won't tell a soul," Heather replies.

"I'm confused, but yes, you can trust us." Danielle is still looking unsure.

Hunter gives me a reassuring nod.

Releasing his hold on my fingers, I stand up and move away from the table. With an outstretched hand, I ignite a small flame in the center of my palms.

"*Wicked*!" Heather yells, jumping to her feet to get closer.

"Holy Mother of Mary. Wha—How are you doing that? Is that some kind of parlor trick?" Danielle's a little weirded out, moving her head to study my hand and everything around it.

"It's okay, here, let me try this." I morph it into a glowing orb. I walk over to where she's sitting, and bring it closer to her. "Go ahead, touch it. It won't hurt you."

Heather doesn't hesitate, she moves around Danielle to where I'm standing and grasps the sphere in her palm. "Whoa..." Heather's eyes glaze over. "This is so cool. It's warm, it gives off a strong sense of...comfort. You have to try it, Danielle."

Danielle doesn't move, Heather huffs, taking the hand she is holding the light with and grabbing Danielle's to place it where hers was.

Danielle gasps, shifting back. Her mouth parts and her chest moves rapidly.

I send a little more calming energy to the orb, trying to help control her spiraling. Her shoulders slouch and she drops her hand. "That was..." Her mouth opens and closes. "I don't know what to say. What is it?"

Unsure how much to tell them, I settle for the truth. "The women of my family are descendants of an angel of light."

Heather backs up in a hurry. "Oh shit. Isn't the angel of light more of the devil's thing? It's how he shows himself to others to deceive them? Are you—" For the first time tonight, Heather's face isn't showing excitement, but behind her light eyes, there's something I've never seen from her before.

Fear.

"No. No, no, no," I say quickly. "This is a true angel of light. He was made to help bring light to the darkness, not the other way around.

"Like Uriel?" Danielle guesses.

My mind tries to remember the different angels that I learned about growing up.

"Wait, he's the angel of fire, right?" I ask.

"Yeah, and if you ask me, that's where you would have gotten this from. I mean, if what you say and what you are showing us is real." Danielle rubs her temple. "I can't believe we're having this discussion."

Maybe she's onto something. Maybe the angel is similar in power to him.

"Babe," Hunter's deep voice pulls me out of my thoughts. "Think about it. It makes sense. When you saw him, do you think it could have been Uriel?"

"Wait, you *saw* the angel?" Heather's eyes become saucers.

"I did. He helped me. But how would I know if he was an archangel or not? We weren't sitting there chitchatting." Heather is still scared, and I've no clue what brought this on. Except her thinking I was the spawn of Satan. "Heather, it's okay."

"Wouldn't a devil say it's okay?" She eyes me warily.

So much for keeping things from them. I need to try to get through to her because I can't lose her. She wasn't even the one I was worried about scaring away.

"Can you give me a chance? Can I try something?"

"What the hell are you planning?" Her leg bounces.

"Please? You know me. You felt the energy. You are tuned into someone's energy and can read a person from across the room. Was any part of what you felt *wrong*?"

"Umm, no. But it wouldn't be the first time my instincts failed me."

"Let me try something and after that, if you still aren't sure, I'll leave you alone and never bother you again."

Heather looks to Hunter then Danielle. Danielle shrugs as if saying *might as well try.*

"Okay, but if you try fucking me over, I'll give you hell to pay. You know I won't hold back."

This better fucking work.

"Oh, I know. Let's sit." We sit straddling the bench, facing each other on the next covered table over. I know I could transfer images to the wolf and bear, I need to see if I can do the same for Heather. To show her what I saw. "I'm going to place my hands on the sides of your head. Okay?"

Heather looks at both of my hands, checking for...a weapon maybe? Then she nods.

I place my palms on the sides of her head and close my eyes. Channeling my power and emotions into her, I play out the events in fast forward from the moment I came home from my walk and found the invitation to the castle. Heather gasps but doesn't retreat. She lays her hands over mine as though she wants to see it all, wants to *know* it all. I show her the wendigo, I even show her the possession of Margaret and me stabbing her in the heart.

I relive the memories and pushing them to the surface hurts. I believe the only way for Heather to understand is to see *everything*. Even what I'd rather keep from her.

Tears roll down my face. The final bits I share are the angel, my grandmother, and all the others I felt and saw surrounding me—paying special attention to my angel grandfather. Heather needs to know he isn't evil. He gave me the power to bring Hunter back.

When I finish, I open my eyes and release my hands, but Heather holds them tight as we bring them down in front of us. Her face is wet, her eyes rimmed with red.

"Are you okay?" I ask, sniffling to keep my snot from running down my face.

Her lips part. "Fuck, Anya. You are asking *me* if I'm okay, and you just went through hell and back?"

That's an understatement.

"Well, didn't you teach me well? Didn't you say you telepathically taught me how to fight and survive?"

"The fuck I did. Girl, that was all you. Now look at me, you made me ugly cry."

"Hahaha...your ugly cry versus mine are way different. I hope you forgive me. I don't feel evil, but I understand if you aren't comfortable around me anymore."

"Shut up and come here." She pulls me into a constricting embrace, whispering, "There's not a damn evil cell in your body. I'm the one who should ask for forgiveness. I doubted you."

I draw back. "You had a good reason."

She sucks in a breath and her body goes rigid. "Wait, did your little trick see what's in my mind too?"

What is she hiding?

"Nope. And that was the first time I tried that—with a human that is."

Heather relaxes. "We need to talk soon. *Alone.* There's a lot I need to tell you."

She's acting a little odd—and secretive.

"I don't know what the hell happened, but you aren't doing anything to me." Danielle is sitting at the other table holding her hands up. "I believe you saw your grandmother. I believe you have some weird power—as much as I'm trying to wrap my head around it. But you keep those hands away from me. I'm perfectly fine knowing what you've told me so far. I'm good. There's nothing more you need to show us. Right?"

She's made her choice. She wants to limit the supernatural things in her life, and I don't blame her. Now, Heather knows and it really feels good to get it off my chest to someone other than Hunter and my mom.

Giving Heather another glance, trying to figure out what she meant, I finally let it go.

For now.

We head to the table with Danielle and Hunter. "This is it. Everything I wanted to show you. You guys mean the world to me, so having you know and understand what's happened to me is important. What do you think?" I bite my cheek waiting.

"Does it hurt?" Danielle asks.

I shake my head. "Not at all."

"You had this power all your life, didn't you?" Heather chimes in, "Why didn't you tell us before?"

"The day I placed my hand on the journal was the first time I've ever experienced this."

"I don't believe that." Heather taps her fingers on the table.

My stomach drops. "Do you really think I'd lie to you after all of this? After I *showed* you?" There goes me hoping this would all be easy. The girls accepting me, believing me.

She dismisses me with her hand. "I mean maybe you don't remember having it before. But that time we had a girl's night, a sleepover, we reminisced about the past. When we were unstoppable badasses."

Where's she going with this?

"Yeah...and you apparently were the only one who was a teenage badass. We were nerds. What's that have to do with this?"

"Okay, your bully in high school, what was her name?"

"Oh, I know that one. Courtney!" Danielle answers.

Heather bounces in her seat. "Thank you!"

Hunter turns, moving his leg to the other side of the bench to face me fully. "Wait a minute, babe. Is this the bully story you promised me?" He seems to be excited about this. He leans a forearm on the table and his other hand on his thigh, his eyes sparkle with intrigue.

How was that event anything to be concerned about?

Heather chuckles. "Well, well, well. So our Anya mentioned her teenage years, huh? She must really like you. It took a full bottle of wine before she finally spilled the goods. Can I tell the story, Anya, please?" she begs.

"Why the hell not. I'm not sure where you're headed with this, but feel free to do the honors. You'll probably make it much more entertaining than it actually was anyways." With my fingers laced, I cup my knee and lean back, curious about how this'll pan out.

Heather rubs her hands together and her evil laugh puts my stomach in knots. She licks her thumb and pointer finger and smudges out the candle in front of us. In a dark and ominous voice she starts, "Once upon a time—"

"Heather..." I warn. With my power, I flick my finger at the candle wick and relight it.

Danielle gasps.

Oops.

I forgot this is new to them and can still be weird, something the brain isn't used to understanding.

Heather whines. "You're no fun." She clucks her tongue. "Okay. In high school, this girl Courtney was *super* jealous of anyone who received more attention than her. Anya *thankfully* got through her ugly duckling stage and started gaining the attention of a few jocks. The ones that bitch Courtney was crushing on. Of course, Anya became the number one target. She didn't do the usual things that most bullies did like name calling and spreading rumors. Oh, no. This sick chick would walk around with a lighter, either sneaking up behind other girls and burning parts of their hair, or cornering them in the bathroom. It was really messed up."

Hunter's posture gravitates towards Heather. It's hard not to, she has a knack for storytelling. "I didn't know you guys went to school together," he inquires.

"Oh no, we didn't meet until she moved here," she says as a matter of fact.

"You could've fooled me. From the way you're telling this story, it sounds like you were there."

"Ha!" The outburst came out before I could stop it. "Hunter, you have to realize, any story you tell Heather, she gets so caught up in it, it's like she experienced it first-hand."

"It's called *empathy* and a great imagination. Now, do you guys want to keep interrupting, or will you let me continue?" She gives us the stink eye.

I silently gesture for her to continue without hiding my amusement.

"One day, Anya was washing her hands in the bathroom when Courtney and her mob came in and shoved Anya into the corner."

"How the heck did you know I was washing my hands? I never told you that."

She taps her head. "I know things. Now hush." She turns back to Hunter. "There were about ten girls that held her against the wall—"

I clear my throat. "Eh-hem?"

"Alright, it was only two other girls. Anyways...as they were holding her, Anya was fighting the best she could. But the moment she saw Courtney bring out the infamous lighter, she froze." Heather has a suspenseful tone, and I have to stifle my laugh. "The flame was burning bright and getting hotter as it came closer to Anya's face. As soon as Courtney was about to go all pyro to her hair... Dun, dun, duuuunnnn..."

"Oh, just get on with it, Heather," complains Danielle.

As outrageous as she makes the story sound, she is definitely one who keeps things entertaining.

"Pfft." Heather scoffs. "I've had a better audience before, you know. But I'll get to the point since I'm clearly boring *some* people." She shoots dagger eyes at Danielle. "As the flame inches towards Anya's beautiful face, the craziest thing happens. In a blaze, the fire blew backwards into *Courtney*. Burning her eyebrows and the hairline around her face. The weirdest thing? It didn't burn any of her skin or injure her." She shakes her head like to this day she still can't believe it.

Hunter snickers. "I'm sure it wasn't as bad as you claim." He turns to me. "Right?"

I flinch. I would love to say it was an elaborate story, but Heather's spot on.

She beats me to a response. "Anya showed us her yearbook and this girl couldn't even *make* her hair look decent with a headband. She had to draw her eyebrows on, which I have to say, was *quite* interesting with all the photos showing her constant surprise." She giggles. "Oh man, to this day, I wish the yearbook showed a picture of her when it rained." Her finger taps her lips. "Never mind. That'd probably have caused me nightmares. Of course, Anya felt bad for her, but you know Karma finally got its revenge, and she never bullied anyone again."

She turns to me and rests her chin on her fist. "Now tell us, Anya, at that moment in your life when you were attacked, what was going through your head, what were you feeling?"

"Are we playing psychiatrist again, Heather?" I cock an eyebrow.

"Humor me," she deadpans.

After all this time, it's hard to think back to every detail of that moment. It was overwhelming and scary. "I'm not sure what you want to hear. I was feeling what anyone would feel. I was cornered. Trapped with nowhere to go. I knew I was going to be scorched." I just didn't know the extremes of how bad. The look on her face is still burned into memory. "I can't forget the evil gleam in her eyes. It creeped me out. All I wanted to do was push her and the fire away from me, but I couldn't get my arms free."

Hunter's blank stare and parted lips confuse me.

"What's that look for?"

"Do you have any idea what you did?" His eyes bounce back and forth between mine and his lips press together. "You really don't, do you?"

Danielle is confused, Heather has this crazed look on her face as if she is waiting for a light bulb to turn on, and Hunter is expecting something too.

What am I missing?

Thanks to Heather's recap, the memory is refreshed in my mind, and I play it over and over to find out what I'm missing.

The flame shifted, and it wasn't like a breeze came into the girl's bathroom. Everything was still and stuffy as usual.

It was a freak accident.

On repeat, the image of the fire shifting, it was if someone controlled—

No, I couldn't have. That didn't... My mouth drops open.

"*Ha, ha!*" Heather jumps out of her seat. "By golly, ladies and gentleman, she figured it out!" Her grin couldn't get any wider. She looks as though she won the jackpot before Danielle grabs her arm and pulls her back down to sit.

"I...I did that? That's not possible. I wasn't eighteen yet. I didn't have powers until the ceremony with my grandmother and mom."

Hunter rubs my leg. "How sure are you about that? I mean, nothing sticks out to me from when we were kids, but you can't think of anything else that may have been a sign?"

Memories flash like a slideshow of when I was younger, searching for any signs that I'd had *any* bit of power back then. I was a normal kid, I feared fire like everyone else. I got burned—*oh.*

I remember burning myself when I was about seven. I got too close to a bonfire and my shirt sleeve caught on fire. My dad was convinced I was burned. He'd been hysterical while my mom wasn't concerned at all. My skin was untouched.

On second thought, she was really calm about the situation. As if she already knew I wouldn't be harmed by it.

"How did I not see this? It's been in me all along and I'd never once noticed."

Hunter takes a stray hair and places it behind my ear. "You gotta admit, it was pretty badass what you did—without even knowing it. If no one told you, how could you've known? Look at your mom for example. She always seemed normal to me. But she was hiding the power too."

He's right. Other than those two incidents, nothing else stood out, nothing made me believe I was different, or that my mom was.

"Do you think she would've blocked my memories of any powers?"

"Wait," Heather interrupts. "Your mom can do that? She can block memories? How much does she charge?"

"Ha, I don't recommend it. She did it without my knowing and made me forget Hunter."

Both girls turn to Hunter and Danielle says, "How bad of a kid *were* you? Bad enough to have someone's mother have to wipe their kid's mind?"

Hunter holds up a hand. "Hey, it wasn't like that. I had to move away."

"And you hurt our Anya?" Heather cracks her knuckles.

He squirms in his seat, picking at a notch in the wood table top. "Can you help me here, Anya?"

"It's fun to watch you under fire. The tough marine is afraid of a couple women."

He leans over and whispers in my ear. "I'm afraid of the little one." Which has me giggling.

"Okay, I'll save you, yet again." Turning to the girls I say, "No, he didn't hurt me. Well, not in the sense you're thinking. His moving away destroyed me. His family had no choice but to leave and we lost all contact. It took a bit for me to push through the wall my mom built around everything that was Hunter. But thanks to him, I now remember it all."

Heather purses her lips. "Okay, good. I was starting to like him. I would've hated having to hide his giant-of-a-body."

Danielle huffs. "Heather, I swear, you need to stop watching serial killer shows. It's going to get you arrested one of these days."

Heather shrugs.

"I'm curious." Hunter leans forward. "How did you put it all together with her having powers as a teen?"

"Easy, the story always stuck out to me as weird, and it never made sense as to how it happened. When Anya showed us her power, it popped in my head. It was a missing puzzle piece that finally found its rightful place."

Danielle hummed. "It makes sense. When Anya told us the story, I chalked it up to the lighter malfunctioning. It didn't help that we all had quite a bit of alcohol *and sugar* that night. I really didn't give it a second thought."

Damn, I think I need to re-evaluate my whole childhood now. Or maybe a call to my mom someday soon to figure out how things really were when I was a kid.

"Well, thanks for taking me down memory lane, Heather."

"Anytime. I'm so excited for you. And just think of all the assholes' houses we could burn down, and it won't be tracked back to us for arson. Your magic will be untraceable."

"Oh hey now, only for good."

Heather gives me a pitiful glance. "Anya, ridding the earth of assholes *is* for the good of the world. Plus, you now have an *in* with good old Pops."

She refers to my angel grandfather as a golden ticket into the pearly gates.

Hunter stands, helping me to my feet. "I hate to break up your plans to eliminate lowlifes, but it's getting late and it's already dark."

Heather points to him. "See? He gets me. Eliminate them all," her voice deepens.

"Come on, Heather, let's get you home safe to Greyson." Danielle pulls her out of her seat.

This night turned out better than I planned.

"We can do this again," I offer.

Hunter wraps an arm around me. "And I wouldn't be opposed to having some more male presence next time." Then he adds, "Not that I don't enjoy all of your company."

"Grey would *love* this place. Since you two already have a bromance starting, it would be so much fun."

"A what?"

I pull on Hunter's arm and give him a silent, *'I'll explain later.'*

"I'm in. A couples' night out sounds entertaining." Danielle grabs her purse and we all head to the front doors.

The moon isn't as bright as it was a couple nights ago but it still illuminates the path from the castle steps to the vehicles.

We say our goodbyes, and when Danielle walks to her car, Heather pulls me in for a second hug.

"Thank you," she tells me.

"For what?"

"For everything. For being you. For sharing your secret. For helping me to be able to share mine soon."

I suck in a breath. She's really ready to tell me. In exchange for sharing my gift with her, she's comfortable enough to reciprocate with her story. A story she keeps hidden from the world.

She gives me one last smile. "We have much to discuss." Then turns and makes her way to Danielle's car.

My head rests on Hunter's chest. "That turned out good." I glance up into his dark eyes. "Thank you so much for helping me. I couldn't have done it without you."

His arms pull me in tighter. "Babe, I told you we're partners. It was fun. And I have to admit, it was pretty cool when Heather put the pieces together. That moment back in high school is proof you always had the light in you. You didn't need a ceremony or anyone else to give you this power. You had it all along."

I really did.

"It's crazy to think about. But it's nice to know I've had a built-in defensive system since I was a kid."

"If it wasn't for me moving, you may have never been in the situation with the bully to begin with."

Pulling back, I place my hand over his heart and gaze up into his chocolate eyes with all the love I have for him. "You had no control. If you were there, you still wouldn't have been able to stop it. It was the girl's bathroom."

He sighs. "I know, you're right. It's hard to not blame myself." With one hand, he holds my chin and lowers his face. "I know you can take care of yourself, but I want to take care of you. I'll do *everything* in my power to protect you from here on out."

This man, he's something else.

"I know you will, you've proven it to me already. And in true Hunter fashion, you went to the extreme and got yourself killed over it."

"Damn straight I did, and I would do it all over again if I had to." He rests his forehead on mine.

With every breath, I take him in. My other half, my twin flame.

Softly I say, "Let's not make it a habit, alright? I wouldn't trust you to be brought back a second time." I move my hand from his chest to his scruff covered jaw and kiss him.

Hunter's lips take over, caressing mine, using his tongue to open me up to him. Our tongues clash and make beautiful harmony that vibrates every string down my body.

He slows our kiss before releasing me. "I promise I won't test out how many lives I have." He sighs, wrapping an arm around me. "But I do know one thing, in each life, I'll only love you. Let's go home."

"I *am* home."

Epilogue

TRISKELE

(PAST, PRESENT, FUTURE)

Anya

The past couple days with Hunter have been great. He's been staying with me, and it's as if we've been living together for years. Last night was a date night. Our first one that didn't have any drama, which was a relief.

When I woke, the new morning sun provided me with a fresh start. I have the man of my dreams, my best friend, and now it's time to figure out what to do with my life. That means coming to terms with losing my job.

It isn't the end of the world. I'll find a new one, even if I have to waitress until something better comes along. The important thing is, I didn't scare away my two best friends with my secret.

I know I'll get through, and today—I'm determined—will be a good day.

The last load of our laundry is now in the dryer and when I hit the start button, Hunter's phone rings from the other room.

"Hunter McAllister here...*shit...* "his voice is muffled by the wall separating us.

I walk into the living room and he's pacing.

"When do you need me?"

Scratch that, it's turning into a shitty *day.*

My heart hits the floor like a block of cement has been chained to it. This call gave it the kick over the edge to sink me into the deep abyss, drowning me as the air squeezes out of my lungs. I knew this was coming eventually.

He runs a hand through his hair. "Tomorrow? Can I call you back on that? Okay, thanks. Bye." He hangs up.

There's no denying he received a job offer and the time we have together will be cut extremely short.

How long will he be gone? When will I see him again?

I hate that he needs to leave, but I can't hold him back from helping others either.

This blows.

The only thing I can do is ensure he doesn't feel guilty for leaving so soon. I plaster on a smile, trying to make it look as real as possible. Hoping and praying he doesn't see through it for once.

"You got another job? When do you need to leave?" Hoping I heard wrong and 'tomorrow' isn't his answer.

Hunter rubs the back of his neck. "Yeah, it's another case. This one's pretty urgent. If it wasn't, I'd turn it down." He pauses, his eyes darting back and forth between mine.

Is he reading me like a book again?

My face heats and the tightness around my chest constricts. I keep quiet.

"I wanted to discuss something with you." He sits down at the table and pulls out a chair for me to join him.

Fuck. This can't be good.

Bile rises in my throat, and I swallow it down.

He promised me that nothing would break us apart. I know he loves me unconditionally. I *felt* what he feels for me. I'm praying that this isn't one of those clichés *if you love them, then leave them* moments because I may have to slap him upside of the head.

After I cry.

He raises his hand, running his thumb over my lips. "Hey, what's with the sad face?"

"I'm not sure what you have to say is going to be good news." I shift in my seat.

He takes a deep breath. "I have an idea I've been tossing around, but it never seemed to be the right time to bring it up. I think *now* is the perfect moment." He releases my face and grasps my hand between both of his, leaning over in his chair. "Okay...now bear with me until I explain everything. No questions until the end, got it?" He waits for my agreement.

Bear with him until he explains everything? Isn't that what someone says when they cheat on someone else?

I know he doesn't have a secret family or a side piece.

The hand he's not holding clamps down on the chair, bracing myself.

"Okay."

"Alright. You're currently between jobs, and still trying to figure out what you'd like to do next. How do you feel about...about coming with me on my jobs—"

"*What?*" I blurt out.

He huffs. "Anya, you agreed no questions until the end." His lips press together in a tight line, obviously irritated.

Yes, I shouldn't have interrupted but 'come with him on his jobs?' Does he think he can be my sugar daddy and I'll no longer want to support myself?

That isn't fair to him, and I'll go stir crazy. I need to be able to help somehow. I can't hang around like a child needing a babysitter.

I close my eyes to calm myself and when I open them, I find a younger version of Hunter. One that flashes occasionally when he's feeling vulnerable.

"Go on," I encourage.

"If you join me, you can *finally* get away from here and we can be together all the time. Now, you won't be bored or feel like you're freeloading off me either..."

Read my mind much?

"...I know everything about you and know exactly what you'd be thinking."

A chill runs over my skin. His intuition when it comes to me is always spot on.

"My job entails a lot of research, sometimes that alone causes me to work longer hours than needed. I'm good at it, but having an extra set of eyes on a lot of these cases would really be a help. You could assist me with research and anything else that comes up along the way. You'll be paid for your work, of course, but it will be a partnership. If you find you want to do something else along the way, you can leave at any time to go do what *you* want to do." His thumbs rub over my hand. I'm not sure if it's to calm me or him. "You can't leave me, just the job. So...umm... What do you say? Do you want to travel around the country with this sexy"—he cocks an eyebrow—"superhero boyfriend of yours as your partner?" He pops out a dimple. "So that we can kick-ass together?"

I'm breathless... Stunned.

But I'm mostly in shock.

His words alone captured my heart, making it a no-brainer on what to choose.

The dimples cemented my decision.

I pinch my leg to make sure this is all real.

It's real.

His grin falters. "Anya? Are you going to say anything? Don't feel forced, it's just an idea. You may not think it's ideal, but I really would like you by my side, always. Can you please say something?"

"*Yes!*" I launch myself at him.

His chair tips back, but I create a force field to catch our fall. One of Hunter's arms is wrapped around me while the other is gripping the table with white knuckles. With a bit more power, I set us back on all four legs and feel his heat between my legs.

Forehead to forehead, I say, "But you have to promise me, if you're starting to get sick and tired of me, you tell me."

His laughter has his minty breath blowing into my face, making me lick my lips to try to taste him.

"Ha!" he barks out. "That will never happen."

I glare at him which causes him to grumble.

"Fine, it won't happen, but...if for the rare situation that it *does*, I will let you know." He wraps his arms tighter around my back. "Are you *sure* you want to do this with me? I knew it was a shot in the dark. We'll still keep this place as a home base, and I'll make sure we come back often enough for your family and friends."

The excitement in his tone builds on the embers that sparked when he told me his plan, making them grow with anticipation.

"That sounds perfect."

"Yeah?" he questions, disbelief hiding behind his eyes.

"Yeah."

His smile spreads across his face as he picks me up and swings me around. "I love you so fucking much, Light Angel. Thank you."

Ignoring the nickname, I giggle. "I love you too, thanks for the job... *Boss!*"

He stops spinning, setting me back on the floor, his milk-chocolate eyes go dark. "Boss, huh? Does that mean you have to do *every-*

thing I tell you to do?" The elated, sparkle in his eyes is replaced with a wicked gleam.

"Hmm...probably. What do you have in mind?"

Hunter

"Babe, this is *not* what I meant."

"But as my *boss*, you ordered me to have my way with you. This"—She points to my naked torso—"is my way."

"That doesn't include burning my clothes off." Standing in Anya's bedroom in just my boxers and jeans, I rub my chest. "I swear you singed some hair."

She crosses her arms over her chest. "There were no clauses in our employment contract."

"That's because there *was* no contract."

"Are you firing me now?"

The little sprite pouts. She's one manipulative woman, but she's *my* woman. My girl is so damn beautiful, but she has a crazy streak that loves to bust my balls.

I wouldn't wish for anything else.

She keeps me on my toes and there's a constant yearning to get to know everything about her, including every inch of her body. I love to make her body sing and light up like a radiant Christmas tree.

But I prefer not to be engulfed in flames.

"No. But I prefer if you'd not *fire* me either."

Anya rolls her eyes. "Ugh, stop being a baby. It was really hot seeing those pecs reveal themselves as your shirt melted off your muscles." She licks her lips, and despite my fear of her continuing this experiment, I grow harder.

Remembering the feeling of her warm mouth wrapped around me has me almost giving in to her.

Almost.

I'm not completely controlled by my dick.

"Yes, hot. As in burning. Fire. Flames. Not as *oh that's sexy.* You've turned into a freaking pyro."

She pops out a hip, and it takes so much strength not to eliminate the few feet between us, grab that hip, and pull her up until her legs are wrapped around me.

"The only way to perfect this skill is to practice," she suggests.

"This is a skill you should never need. Ever."

"I mean, if you'd rather me practice on someone else, I guess I can find a willing subject."

Hell no.

"Fuck no, you won't," I growl out. Never will she have the company of another man, specifically naked.

The little minx thinks I don't see the smirk she's hiding. I know the game she's playing, and, unfortunately, she may end up winning this one.

My balls curl up in fear.

Maybe it was my recent death that killed a few brain cells because I find myself agreeing with her. Wanting to let her truly have her way with me.

The intensity behind her hazel eyes breaks down the last walls I have as my defense.

Fuck.

"Get the fire extinguisher as back-up," I warn.

"You don't trust me?"

"Do you hear yourself right now, Anya? You are about to ignite the rest of my clothes in flames."

"Exactly. You have a lack of faith in me. You don't trust I'll protect you. It's not like you'd be the only one losing something if this goes wrong. I enjoy him very much." She waves to my crotch.

My stomach tightens, wondering if she won't give me a warning and just flick her wrist.

I move my hands to cover my manhood. "Don't do that."

"Do what?" she asks in exasperation.

"Point. Keep those hands down. No pointing, no gesturing. I don't want any accidental discharge."

She wiggles her fingers in the air. "These aren't guns, ready to go off at any minute."

I cock an eyebrow at her and gesture to my missing shirt.

"That wasn't an accident," her voice is low and seductive. "Now, relax." She closes the distance and pulls my hands away from my package.

"I'm trying to, but you're playing a dangerous game."

She lays her hand over the tattoo on my chest, and I suck in a breath.

That will never get old.

Anya's love courses through me. She brought me back to life, she fought for me. This isn't someone that would place me in harm's way.

"Let's get this over with." I sigh and close my eyes. Then I remember how turned on she was when she melted off my shirt. I'm not going to miss this.

She backs up and I fight the urge to cover myself again. Instead, I hold my breath and pray I am left with everything intact.

Anya lights up a transparent orb in her hand; her eyes brighten with the reflecting glow. With a quick toss, the energy flies through the air and covers my pants.

In no time, my pants are gone. Instead, I have the smell of burnt fabric and a heat like the rays of sunlight beating down on my legs.

She ended up taking both my pants and boxer briefs, which is a relief. Even from a few feet away, I can see her pupils dilate and her heart rate increase. My baby's turned on. The potential trauma that could've occurred was well worth the pleasure of seeing her aroused.

My body relaxes, and I stare her down, letting her take the lead. Until she lights a marble-sized ball of energy.

"Anya, as you can see, you took off all my clothes. And from the looks of it, we're going to have to do some cleaning later." I stare pointedly at the pile of ash at my feet. "You can put that away now." I gesture to the tip of her finger where the light sits.

With her other hand, she uses a force field to move the ash left behind from my clothes to the corner of the room.

Well, that's handy. But it doesn't solve the issue of the flickering glow she's still holding onto.

"Babe?"

Anya tilts her head to the side. "Do you trust me?"

"Uh, yeah. I think we've established that." I rub the back of my neck.

"Then let me try something."

Oh fuck, what now? She's calm. Why is she so calm?

She sends the ball towards me and it's headed lower.

What the fuck?

I want to run the hell away from it, but I have to prove to her that I trust her with everything in me. I hope I don't regret this.

I hiss when the warm energy runs up the front of my cock then down the backside, sending a vibration into my balls.

Holy fuck does that feel good.

She plays a little longer. The heat from her power swelling me more and more until I can't take it any longer. She runs it up and down over me and it's...amazing. Like an electric current pulsing through me in waves, it heightens my sensitivity by connecting with every nerve ending in the area.

"How does it feel?" she purrs out.

Like I'm about to blow. But I can't tell her that. I'm clenching my ass cheeks hard to not move with the rhythm and lose it.

"How 'bout you come over here and find out?" I need her so fucking bad right now.

She smirks. "I don't know, I'm having fun from here. I'm really enjoying the show."

Gritting my teeth, I grind out, "Anya, get your angel ass over here, *now*."

Without letting me go, she takes her sweet time closing the last couple of steps. She's still fully clothed, which is unfair if you ask me, but I can remedy that.

"That's it, babe." One more step and—

"Eek!" she cries out as I snatch her around the waist and bring her against me.

She's feeling the vibrating heat from the energy she created. It's lined up perfectly to her center.

She moans and rubs up against the light which applies more pressure around me.

My head drops to her forehead. "*Damn.*"

Anya raises her mouth to the corner of my ear, "So, this is what it feels like."

"Mmhmm...but you're way over dressed." My hands make contact with her smooth skin under the hem of her shirt. Goosebumps pepper her flesh as my thumbs travel up inch by delicious inch until I reach the undersides of her breasts.

"Wait." She pulls back and removes the energy from around my cock.

The hypnosis she put me under clears, and I study her eyes, searching to find what's wrong.

"What? Are you okay?" She looks well. I'm not picking up on any distress.

Nodding, she bites her lips and takes three steps back.

What the hell is she up to?

Not sure what her plan is, my legs move closer to her.

Anya giggles. "No. Just wait." She holds up a hand to stop me.

Umm...okay.

She's being secretive, and I'm not quite sure what she's up to.

A bright yellow light engulfs her from shoulders to floor, creating a barrier around her body.

Well, shit. This isn't fair.

"Hang on, we never talked about you making a magical chastity belt."

"You're so impatient. Just wait." Her eyes narrow as her smile spreads across her skin.

Her cryptic ass better hurry up. I'll figure out how to break through that barrier one way or another.

The next thing I know, her clothes are melting off and ashes float to the floor.

Okay, I agree, that *is* hot.

Her pale body illuminates with a gorgeous glow. Her bare skin is a masterpiece that even the most talented artist couldn't replicate.

There is nothing like my Anya.

There is *no one* like my Anya.

There's only one. And she's mine.

A growl bubbles out of my chest. "Come here." Like a predator, I don't wait for her to move before I stalk towards her and attack. Doing exactly what I wanted to do earlier, I hoist her up and wrap her legs around me, trying my damndest not to sink into her.

The last couple of steps to the bed feel so far away, but when we get there, I lay Anya down softly, treasuring the precious gift she's given me.

Her hair fans out around her head, and she stares up at me with those sparkling brown, green, and gold irises. She looks at me like I've hung the stars in the sky and I could do no wrong.

Damn, I hope I don't screw this up. Losing her, like I lost my parents, would be the end of me.

I drop my head to her chest, breathing in the lavender and peppermint scent. My shoulders relax. This isn't fair to her for me to ruin our moment.

"Hey, what's going on?" She lifts my head to meet her gaze. "Are you in pain?"

"No babe, just some demons trying to come out from the shadows. I'm good now."

She frowns. "Are you sure? We can stop."

"I think not." With the demons shoved back in their cage, I'm back to loving my girl.

Without giving her warning, I crash my lips to hers, hungry and begging for her to help me push past my fears and just *feel*.

She's my twin flame, the light to my dark, the good to my bad.

Our tongues tango in a sweet dance. An equal partnership, knowing when to lead and when to be led.

The power she caressed me with is nothing compared to having her, all of her, right here. Under me. Her softness, her love.

My everything.

Drifting my hand down, I run it to the very spot I'm craving to claim. My hand slides lower until I'm between her folds.

She's dripping wet.

"Fuck, Anya. You are so ready for me."

She takes that moment to move her mouth down my neck, to the scar from a bullet that entered below my collarbone and exited right above my shoulder blade in my trap muscle. She licks it before kissing and sucking it, sending a sensitive tingle down my spine.

Holy hell.

I plunge two fingers into her and make her gasp.

With my mouth, I take in one of her nipples and suck hard until she cries out and tightens around my fingers. It's music to my ears.

"I need you, I need you now!" she demands.

And when my woman needs something, she gets it.

I make sure of it.

Every fucking time.

I remove my fingers and guide my erection up and down her wet center. My eyes roll back at the velvet sensation at my tip.

"Yes, more," She mewls out, her body writhing under mine.

Lining myself up, I thrust into her and suck in a breath.

Every damn time, it feels like I'm coming home.

Being inside her, having her wrap around me, it's not only erotic, it's comforting.

"You better start moving or I'll..."

"You'll do what, Honey Bear?" Ever so slowly, I rock my hips against her, making sure I angle up to hit the right spot.

"I'll...oh hell, keep doing that."

Whispering in her ear I say, "Yes, Milady." And continue rolling my hips forward then backwards, gradually building up friction.

Sweat begins to bead off of our skin and Anya picks up the pace.

Thank God, because I've been dying since she started her energy tease.

"I need you deeper," she moans out.

I flip her over so she's lying on her stomach. Her plump ass has me almost drooling as I raise it up and sink right back to where I belong.

Thrust by thrust, she sets the speed. When she tightens around my shaft, I know she's close, so I reach around and press down on her clit, rubbing it fast. Her hands grip the sheets, and I pick up my pace, using my palm to press on her pelvis to intensify the pressure. She shifts up on her hands and knees.

"Right there, don't stop," she pants out.

Shit, I couldn't stop if I wanted to. I lean over her, my chest against her back and we both gasp.

"Hunter, it's…"

"I know, baby, I feel it too." A euphoric surge powers through us, and if not for the tingling in my left pec, I wouldn't have realized what was happening.

Her body is flush against mine. Her skin is igniting the symbol causing it to glow and the sensations coursing through our bodies combine into an electrified vortex.

It's impossible to hold back the groan. "Come for me now." I'm about to break but push through a few more thrusts until she squeezes me—spasming around my shaft. I let go with her.

Everything in me releases into Anya, my love, my energy, my seed.

Like a sexy succubus, she takes it all.

It's as though it activates the light inside of her.

The room fades to black and we collapse on the bed. Despite the tingling numbness in my limbs, I took what little bit of energy I had in my reserves to turn us mid-fall to ensure I didn't crush Anya—keeping myself still firmly planted inside her. I'm not ready to leave her warmth.

"*Fuck*, Anya." I kiss the back of her neck between the hairs plastered to her skin. The mixture of sweetness and saltiness of her glistening skin makes me want to lick her whole body. If I had the energy.

Never in my life have I had my vision black out during sex, and nothing has ever been as earth shattering as that was.

She hums her pleasure, and I'm on top of the world for being the man to make her feel this way.

Reluctantly, I pull out and lie next to her. She turns and lays her head on her arm with a satisfied grin. Her skin has its usual incandescent blaze.

"I love seeing that after glow on you."

She covers her face with her hand. "Ugh, seriously? I hate this." Her cheeks flush.

"Anya, there won't be a day that goes by that I won't stop working to make that light radiate from within you. I want every last drop of sunshine, every last bit of your love."

"Every last threat to your chestnuts?" She sneaks a peek through her fingers with a smirk.

I bark out a laugh. "You are welcome to hold *that* back, indefinitely." My hand splays across her back and I bring her close. "What will I do with you?"

"I have some suggestions."

"And we have plenty of time for you to put those to good use, but I hope you know when I mean I want every last drop, that means both inside and out." Peeling her hand off her face, I bring it up to my lips and kiss her knuckles. "I don't want you to ever feel like you have to hide. Let all of you shine through."

Anya hums. "I'll only shine for you."

M.K. Collings's Creations

Book 1 – Light Angel
Anya's Story
Book 1.5 – Light Angel: Heather's Recon Mission
Anya Bonus Novelette
Coming Soon...
Book 2 – (Hunter's Story)

Other upcoming books in the Celtic Bloodline World
(Heather's Story)

About the Author

M.K. Collings began her life escaping into magical realms with her childhood best friend when they were kids. These two adventurers would barely make it through the grasps of evil trolls and goblins to help their fairy friends survive in the forest; all while searching for magical stones that healed and opened portals to other worlds.

M.K.'s reading turned from childhood fairy-tales to suspense, horror, then eventually she loved nothing more than to lose herself in many shades of romance. From Historicals to Suspense, Mystery, Comedy and Paranormal Romance novels, all of which helped her escape from the stressors of life.

While working a full-time job, being married to her best friend, and wrangling two crazy kids, she became an avid reader, turned book reviewer.

Then one night, Fate opened the door of her imagination, and unleashed a whole new world. A world with characters who refused to allow her to sleep until their story was told.

A small ember instantly sparked into an uncontrollable wildfire.

This was the start of Light Angel, and the beginning of many more novels to come of Paranormal Romance designed by Destiny, Fate, and Karma.

Don't miss out on insider content, a free bonus story (Light Angel 1.5-Heather's Recon Mission), merchandise, upcoming releases, and all things M.K. Collings by visiting,
https://linktr.ee/AuthorMKCollings

ACKNOWLEDGEMENTS

First and foremost, I need to thank my mom. If it weren't for her, I'd not believe that things happen for a reason. To trust in God and if it is meant to be, it will happen. She reminds me to this day that the "adventures" I go on only lead me down the right path and to the next step in my life I'm meant to be at.

My husband's first words when I told him I was writing a book were, "It's about damn time you write your own book. You read all the time; I was wondering how long it would take you."

Yes, my jaw dropped to the floor because this was NOT something I expected to come out of his mouth. He's confirmed I am indeed crazy, but still supports me on this crazy train. He's never given me doubt that I couldn't do this, always telling me "Why can't you do this?"

That was until he realized how much time and energy it takes to write a book and he renamed this book "The Neverending Story." Sorry babe, that name is already taken. But regardless, he was the inspiration for Hunter. He was the first who challenged me, to keep me on my toes and who brings out the best part of me. I couldn't imagine life without him.

My best friend, my husband, my partner. Thank you, babe!

To my children, thank you for helping me brainstorm ideas, for checking on me to make sure I'm doing okay and still writing. Despite your wanting to give me the pen name of Dr Strange, you have put up with a lot, with me absorbed into my computer for days, weeks, years to make this happen. To my daughter, if I got anything out of this writing journey is that you've discovered writing yourself. At 13 years of age, you have impressed me and have been my writing buddy. Even when you tried to get me to hurry and finish my book so you can read it, then groan when I remind you not until you are 18 years old. You will always be my writing partner.

I can't forget my dad who taught me to research, research, research and not to forget to read user manuals before I take action. To prep and be prepared for anything. He is the reason why I took two and a half years to complete this book and get my business up and running. Making sure I have all my T's crossed and my I's dotted. So you can blame him for the delay, haha...

To my oldest brother, thank you for helping me plan on the business side of things, answering my endless questions. It's been a huge help.

To my second oldest brother, you spent hours helping take my dagger sketch and digitizing it to my preference with all the requested material. You gave me tips and tricks so I could begin creating my own graphics. Thank you for your patience and skills.

To my real-life Heather, you are my Soul Sister. You mean more to me than you ever could know. You have been my biggest fan from the first words I've written and despite your own obstacles and challenges, you still put everyone else first. You are a warrior with the most craziest karma I've ever known. You inspired Anya's best friend, Heather, and I can't wait to let the world see just how amazing and strong you are in Heather's story.

To my soundboard, cheerleader, designing partner, proofreader Jamie-Kay, we met in the book world, and we hit it off immediately. Who knew that you would be a crucial part in my writing career that even I didn't see coming. You've helped me fight the demons in my head that tried to get me to quit. You have helped provide raw/intense feedback every step of this journey and it's hard to imagine doing this again without you by my side.

To my Shades Sisters, thank you for welcoming me, taking a chance on me, and allowing me to always pick your brain. Anytime imposter syndrome sneaks its ugly head in, you all are my own army and you crush them. You girls are the best support group anyone can have.

To my Critique Partners Jada & Nicci, this book is just as much yours as it is mine. I can't thank you enough for all the endless nights we discussed and debated over what to keep and what to improve on. I've learned so much from you two. You both have pushed me to my limits and beyond, making me a stronger writer. Thank you.

To Gail Haris, you saw something in me that I didn't even see myself. An author. You were one of the first to read my raw and rough drafts and you said this could be epic. You had faith, you had patience, and you were the most amazing mentor through this journey. You have a pure heart of gold, it may be perverted but it is a beautiful heart nonetheless, LOL. I love you to pieces, I hope you know how much I feel blessed for having you in my life.

To my editor Stacy from Hand in Hand Editing Services, years ago, you started as my coach at my previous job and Fate brought us together in the book world at the most perfect time. You knew what my book needed, even when I didn't. This was meant to be and it is only the beginning of so much greatness... I hope you are ready because you can't get rid of me now. Your skills and magic are much too valuable.

To my secondary proofreader, Eila Cooper Overcash, thank you for taking the time to help with the final touches.

To my Shades of Romance Readers, MK's Magical Misfits & Street Team, I couldn't do this without your blind support and feedback. You've held on for so long with faith in me and I'm making my dreams come true because of you.

And to you, the reader. Thank you for picking up Light Angel. For giving it a shot. I know it's always risky reading a new author, let alone a debut one. I poured my heart and soul into this and I hope you enjoyed every minute of Anya & Hunter's story. Please consider leaving a review to tell me what you think.